GUILTY BYSTANDERS

Crane spotted Burt Hill and called him over. "Organize the aid teams to go down to what's left of the village," he ordered. "Pull it all together."

"Yes, sir."

Crane turned to see the edge of the cliff. Motiba was there, and he joined him. The sea was smooth as glass, unusually beautiful in deepest teal blues and greens. But where the village had stood was only empty beach, not even a boat or shack littering the pristine sand that gleamed in the deadly sunlight.

"I'm sorry," Crane said, low and hoarse.

Motiba looked up at him, tears working their way down his cheeks. "I know I should not blame you for this," he said, "but I do."

With that he turned and walked off, leaving Crane absolutely alone with his demons. No one came near. No one reached out a hand or asked if *he* were all right. To the people left on the plain he was as distant and as untouchable as the dead that surrounded him. But they were wrong. The dead, at least, knew peace.

RICHTER 10

Arthur C. Clarke

& Mike McQuay

BANTAM BOOKS

NEW YORK TORONTO LONDON SYDNEY AUCKLAND

PUBLISHING HISTORY
Bantam hardcover edition published March 1996
Bantam mass market edition / May 1997

ISBN 0-553-57333-0

Published simultaneously in the United States and Canada

PRINTED IN THE UNITED STATES OF AMERICA

OPM   10   9   8   7   6   5   4   3   2   1

To the memory of Mike McQuay,
who never lived to know
what a good job he had done

—A.C.C.

Genius in one grand particular is like life.
We know nothing of either but by their effects.
—CHARLES CALEB COLTON

The world is always ready to receive talent with open arms.
Very often it does not know what to do with genius.
—OLIVER WENDELL HOLMES

PROLOGUE

NORTHRIDGE, CALIFORNIA
17 JANUARY 1994, 4:31 A.M.

Fingertips tingling and toes numb, pajamas damp with sweat, Lewis Crane came wide awake. Every one of his worst night terrors was real! And at that horrible moment he knew he'd been right all along and the grown-ups had been wrong: The Wild Things *did* live in the back of his closet; a dragon *did* sneak in when the sun went down to curl up under his bed. The monsters were invisible in the dusty moonlight seeping through the slats of the blinds, but Lewis knew they were there. They roared hideously and stomped around the room, making his bed wiggle like a trampoline he was trying to climb onto. He screwed his eyes closed and clamped his hands over his ears. But the monsters didn't go away. They got wilder and made even louder noises.

Suddenly pitched out of bed, Lewis screamed for his parents.

His voice was so little and the noise was so big that his Mama and Daddy would never hear him. He had to get to them. Heart pounding, he tried to make himself stand up, but fear kept him rooted to the floor as it started to buck beneath him and the walls began to undulate like the enormous pythons he'd seen at the big zoo in San Diego. His bookcases were quivering, the chairs trembling, and the video games stacked on top of his computer came tumbling down. Something whirred over his shoulder—the picture that had hung above the little table next to his bed—and landed beside his knee, glass popping out of its frame and spraying his leg.

"Mama," he cried. "Mama, Daddy, help me!"

Everything shook. Everything. Books and Tonka trucks flew off the shelves; his Power Rangers and Ninja Turtle action figures danced as if alive on their way to the rug; Matchbox cars and crayons sailed through the air. The mirror over his dresser and the aquarium next to his desk smashed onto bare parts of the floor, glass and water showering him from clear across the room.

"Daddy," he wailed again just as his chest of drawers crashed to within an inch of where he sat. He jumped up then, but the floor heaved and he lost his balance, banging down hard on his knees.

And he plunged into the end of the world.

His body shook violently, his whole room shook violently, and he heard the most awful noise he'd ever heard in all his seven years. It sounded like the ground for miles around was cracking open and his house was splitting apart and maybe even the sky was getting torn into pieces. Tears ran down his face. He began to crawl to the doorway, cockeyed and funny-looking as if a giant had twisted it sideways. He thought he heard his mother call his name, but he couldn't be sure. He was sobbing now. He wanted her, wanted his father, too. He had to get to them.

The hallway was full of dangerous stuff, and he stopped for a second. There were chunks of plaster and metal rods all mixed up with jagged spikes of wood and ugly shards of glass from the furniture and pictures that used to be so neatly strung along the walls. The pile was higher than his knees and he was scared that he was going to hurt himself crawling through it, but the house was rolling around so much that he didn't dare try to get up and run. He took a deep breath and started to crawl as fast as he could, his arms and hands getting bashed and cut, his thighs and feet feeling stung and torn.

He reached the dining room, and a sob caught in his throat. He could hear his parents. Mama was calling his name—but Daddy was screaming in pain. There was a lot more light out here, but he didn't like it because it was bluish and kind of winking over everything in a spooky way. He shivered, then turned, put his hands flat on the wall, pushed his legs out, and climbed palm over palm until he was on his feet. The whole room was rolling around, making Lewis suddenly remember the deep-sea fishing boat he'd been on last summer. It had dipped way down and way up, swung side to side, and if he hadn't been on Daddy's lap, and if Daddy hadn't been strapped into the big chair bolted to the deck, they and the chair and everything else would have gone sliding from rail to rail. Could the house be riding a humongous wave? Silly. Their house couldn't get blown all the way from Northridge out to sea. But that other noise, that sort of rumbling . . . it sure sounded a lot like a big wind in a bad storm.

"Lewis!" he heard his mother shout, "Lewis, run. Get outside!"

She lurched into the room and started to shuffle toward him. Her nightgown was scrunched around her chest, hanging from the waist in rags that tangled around her knees. Joy and relief flooded him. He let go of the wall, stumbled forward, then froze. Mama was making a grab for the edge of the dining room table coasting toward her, but he could see behind her, see the huge breakfront Daddy had bought her for an anniversary gift slowly toppling away from the wall. . . .

Glass exploded, splinters of it striking him, shredding his pajamas. And he heard the crash and Mama's scream and saw the stars through the sudden hole in the dining room ceiling and everything seemed to stop for a second. Then he was scrambling over the wreckage, clawing his way to his mother whose face and right arm were exposed to the night.

"I'll get you out, Mama," he called, tears tracking through the dust coating his face.

"Run, darling," she whispered when he reached her. "Run to the street."

In vain he pushed on the side panel of the breakfront.

"Please, Lewis," she said, strangely calm. "Do what Mama says."

"But you . . . you're—"

"Don't d-disobey me. Do what I say right now."

Lewis' mind was spinning. He couldn't move that piece of furniture. Not alone. He needed help.

"I'm gonna go find someone to help me get you out from under there," he said, taking a step back as the rolling of the floor slowed somewhat. The rumbling was distant now and he realized he couldn't hear Daddy screaming from the bedroom anymore. "I'll be right back, Mama. Understand? I'll be right back for you and Daddy."

"Yes, sweetheart," she said, voice weak. "Hurry . . . hurry outside."

He limped around the rubble, got to the living room, and was just going through the opened front door, when another section of the roof fell in with a great crash. Out on the walk, he smelled gas and saw the beams of flashlights darting around front lawns up and down the block. The street was lumpy and broken, the houses across the way all crumpled in front. Panic shook him, but he didn't have time for it. He needed to get help fast.

He heard people, and he headed for the voices and flashlights, screaming as he ran.

"Help! Help me! Please . . . somebody!"

Then he tripped on a new hill on the lawn and fell hard, facedown. He hurt all over . . . and he cried. But he didn't stay there. Struggling to his feet, he was suddenly blinded by a beam of light.

"It's the Crane boy," a man looming over him yelled. "Come here quick!"

People were all around him forcing him onto his back

on the ground. He tried to shove them away. "Help, please. My Mama and Daddy are still inside. Mama's trapped. You've—"

"Easy, son," came the voice of the man holding him down. "It's me. . . . Mr. Haussman from across the street. Don't worry, we'll get your parents out."

"God, look at him," a woman said as people played their flashlight beams across his tattered pajamas. "He's bleeding pretty badly. I—Oh, my Lord! Look at his arm!"

Lewis rolled onto his side to see what she was pointing at. A piece of glass as big as a baseball card was sticking out of his upper left arm. He didn't even feel it. He didn't feel the arm at all.

"My Mama's trapped," he said, and a shadow reached down and jerked hard, pulling the shard from his flesh. "Please help her."

The woman choked and turned away as Lewis stared at the blood squirting furiously out of his arm where she'd removed the glass.

"Dammit," Mr. Haussman muttered. He ripped the rest of Lewis' pajama shirt off and tied it just above the squirting blood. "We've got to get him to a hospital."

"My pickup truck," said Mr. Cornell, the next-door neighbor. "We can put him in the back of that."

"Get it," Mr. Haussman said, and Mr. Cornell went charging off.

"My parents. . . ." Lewis said, trying to get up, only to have Mr. Haussman push him back down.

"We'll get them out," the man said, then turned to the others, specters behind the beams of their flashlights. "Can somebody get into the house and look for the Cranes?"

The ground shook again, everyone reacting loudly, one lady even moaning as if in pain.

Several men ran toward his house, Lewis noted with relief. "What's happening?" he asked, grabbing Mr. Haussman's shirtsleeve.

"Earthquake, son," the man said, tightening the knot on his makeshift tourniquet. "A big one."

"I-I smelled g-gas," Lewis said, trying to rise once again.

"Gas?" Haussman looked alarmed. "Oh, no."

He lowered Lewis to the ground and stood, directing his beam at Mr. Cornell in the pickup truck next door. "George!" he shouted, "don't start the—"

A monstrous explosion turned the pitch night into bright day. Lewis, propped up on his elbows, watched a giant fireball engulf his house, Mr. Cornell's house, and the pickup truck itself.

Agonized screams tore the air. Burning men ran from his house; Mr. Cornell was a fiery, writhing twig in the cab of his truck. Lewis lay stupefied as smoldering debris fell all around him, his mind frozen in pain and horror.

He was a child, but he understood that he had just lost everything . . . that the love and protection of home and family were gone forever. Fires crackled and raged barely fifty feet from him, causing sweat to spring out of every pore, and making the grass, already slick with his blood, become slippery as ice. Both elbows glided out from under him. Flat on his back, he stared up at a starfield that was startlingly brilliant and cold and very far away.

Lewis Crane was alone.

Book One

Thirty Years Later

Chapter 1

THE *NAMAZU*

**SADO ISLAND, JAPAN
14 JUNE 2024, DAWN**

Slivers of first light poked through the crack around the flap of the tent, and Dan Newcombe, stretched out on his cot and naked except for his shoes and his wrist pad, tried even harder to stop the numbers. They'd been scrolling through his brain for forty-eight hours, keeping him awake and growing edgier by the minute.

Close by, someone began to pound a vent into the ground. The numbers in Newcombe's head shattered with the harsh metallic clank of each blow, re-formed before the next strike of the mallet, shattered again . . . until he couldn't tolerate it for another second and jerked to a sitting position, plugging his ears with his index fingers. No good; he couldn't keep that sound out and the numbers were still running through his head. Worse, another person was starting on a vent, pounding out of rhythm with the first.

Newcombe got up, walked to his workstation, and turned on the lantern; it barely lit the two chart tables covered with electronic gear, and he glanced at the faceted, jewel-like knob on its top. Dull green. The damned lantern needed recharge. And he needed light, lots of it, now. In a world of lies, he was getting ready to bet his life on the truth. And truth demanded light. He hated lies, which meant he hated the way Lewis Crane did business. But even Crane had to appreciate the truth on some level, because he, too, was betting his life, along with the lives of at least a hundred others, maybe even thousands of others, on Newcombe's calculations. Crane always thought big.

Newcombe picked up the lantern, carried it to the tent flap, and stuck it out. Immediately pulling it back inside, he blinked at the blinding light it gave off. When he'd adjusted the brightness, he placed it back on the chart table and noted with satisfaction that every corner and fold of the tent was fully lighted, especially the herky-jerky little lines of the seismos. Those lines were a language to him, a language he could interpret like no other human being alive. He trusted seismos. Unlike people, they were dependable, always truthful. They treated every man, woman, and child the same, never changing their readings because of the skin color or gender or age of the reader.

He juiced the computers to a floating holo of seventeen seismograms hanging in the air before him in alternating bands of blue and red; their little white cursors registered the beating heart of the planet.

Heavy seismic activity was crying out on all seventeen graphs, which meant that everything ringing this section of the Pacific Plate was in turmoil. He could sense it right through the floating lines. He knew Crane, wherever he was, could sense it, too—only Crane didn't need any instruments, just his uncanny instincts . . . and that dangling left arm of his.

Today could be the day.

Newcombe activated Memory with the lightest touch on the key pad, and the graphs replayed the history of the last eighteen hours. His eyes widened at the sight of perfectly aligned seismic peaks in five places on all seventeen screens. Foreshocks.

He tapped Crane's icon on his wristpad and asked loudly, "Where the hell are you?"

"Good morning, Doctor," Crane said warmly, his voice coming through Newcombe's aural implant in dulcet tones. "Fine day for an earthquake. Perhaps you should join us for it. I'm down at the mines."

"I'll be there in a little while," Newcombe said, tapping off the pad, disgusted that Crane could sound so hearty, happy even, at such a moment.

He stared at the graphs, back now to current readings and still screaming turmoil.

"And I thought the Moon had set."

Astonished, Newcombe whirled toward the sound of the droll, sexy voice of the only woman who'd ever challenged his mind, heart, and body at the same time. "Lanie!" he exclaimed.

"In the flesh, lover," Elena King said, smiling broadly, her sunblock-coated lips gleaming.

Even wrapped head-to-toe to protect herself from the sunshine, she looked appealing and provocative. And despite the opaque goggles covering her eyes, he could tell she was eyeing his nakedness with a mixture of desire and humor. Newcombe felt almost giddy and rushed across the tent to her.

"Oh, Lanie," he said, dragging her against his body for a long, intense hug. He gently thrust her to arm's length for a quick inspection, removed her floppy hat and tossed it over his shoulder, then pushed her goggles up like a headband behind which her thick, wavy black hair cascaded down her back. Looking into the hazel eyes that had entranced him for years, he slowly pulled her close again and lowered his head for a lingering kiss.

Savoring her lips, Newcombe realized he'd like nothing better than to lose himself in this woman. But there were the seismos. There were the numbers. And this could be the day. Reluctantly, he broke off the kiss, murmuring, "How did I get so lucky? What brought you here?"

"You don't know?" Lanie asked incredulously, freeing

herself from his embrace and taking a couple of steps back. "Your buddy Crane didn't tell you he hired me last night?"

Now it was Newcombe's turn to be incredulous. "Hired you?"

"Yes! Hired me! And ordered me to get my butt down here right away."

His gut clenching with fear for Lanie and with rage at Crane for putting her in danger, he snapped, "Your transport still on the island?"

"How should I know?" She frowned. "More to the point, what the hell's wrong with you suddenly?"

He darted to the foot of his cot and snatched up his Chinese peasant pants. "What's wrong with me?" He stepped into the pants and yanked the drawstring tight around his waist, then located his work shirt. "What's wrong with me?" he repeated, louder, while thrusting his arm through a khaki sleeve. "Nothing's wrong with *me*." He pointed at the holos. "*That's* what's wrong. This island's about to crack up . . . fracture into little pieces!"

"Hardly a secret, friend. Everybody, everywhere is talking about it." She grinned. "You trying to tell me you don't want me?" She'd scarcely had time to blink, when she was in his arms again, being kissed hard and fast.

"That should answer your question. I want you anywhere I can get you, Lanie—except here." He pulled her goggles over her eyes and rested his hands lightly on her shoulders. "We're going to get you away from this damned island fast!" He turned back to the end of the camp table, rummaging in the clutter there for his goggles.

"I guess you didn't hear what I said." She caught the hat he'd found on the table and tossed to her. "As of last night I work at this godforsaken place, just like you do. I'm part of the team doing field work until it's time to go back to the Foundation where I will work right alongside you, lover boy." She shook her head. "I don't get it. Crane told me you recommended me for the imager's job."

"A couple of weeks ago he asked if I knew any good synnoetic imagers. Of course I mentioned you, but he

never said a word to me about hiring you, much less bringing you here. If I'd known that he—"

"Stop right there. I'm a professional and an adult. Dan,
in case you've forgotten. We're talking about my decisions,
my work, my life—"

He rounded on her. "You don't have the slightest idea
what you've got yourself into by coming to Sado. Crane
calls this operation Mobile One. Everyone else calls it
Deathville. Our leader's nutty as a fruitcake, if you didn't
guess, and he's surrounded himself with other nuts ...
crackpots, university rejects, oddballs and screwballs."

"Some would say they're creative, and eclectic, and brilliant. Misunderstood, maybe, but talented and smart—like
Crane himself."

He snorted, turning back to the camp table. "Yeah,
sure." He found his goggles and put them on, then
marched over to take her hat from her hands and jam it
on her head. He grabbed her by the hand and ducked with
her through the flap. They emerged into the still, wet air
of the tent city with its ubiquitous cold mud, or Crane's
Crud as it was termed by insiders.

Excitement jangled in the very air of the camp, packed
with disaster aid workers, grad students, newsies in steadicam helmets, visiting dignitaries, and local hires. All were
wrapped like mummies against the sunshine. Newcombe's
Africk heritage provided him with enough melanin to protect against the deadly UV rays of the sun, about the only
advantage a black man had in this world as far as he could
tell.

A cart carrying coffee and rice cakes wheeled by, splashing mud. Newcombe stopped the operator and took a cup,
adding a big spoonful of dorph. He drank greedily, the
hard edge of his anger at Crane blunting immediately. He
sighed, glad to have his spiking, dangerous emotions even
out. Now he could think, try to understand why Crane
had chosen to bring Lanie to Sado. Maybe, in his own
way, Crane was trying to improve Newcombe's attitudes
and morale, which had eroded seriously this past year
they'd worked together. It was the relentless carnival
atmosphere Crane created at his Foundation in the moun-

tains just beyond LA and in these field situations that most disturbed Newcombe, but he could hardly expect the Big Man to understand that. Leave it to Crane also not to understand human nature and believe he was doing a good thing for Newcombe by bringing his lover to the most dangerous spot on planet Earth.

"It's so . . . so colorful," Lanie said. "Vibrant really. The primary blues and the reds of the tents. . . ." She looked at the cerulean sky, adding, "And the colors of all those hot air balloons and helos up there."

"That how you got here, by helo?" he asked, pushing through a cadre of Red Cross volunteers to stare at the source of the clanking that had annoyed him earlier—grad students pounding interlocking titanium poles deep into the ground.

"A news helo," she amended, her voice as edgy now as Newcombe's. The camp dogs began to bay fearfully, and she raised her voice to be heard over them. "Crane has people coming from all over, because of the 'five signs.' What are they?"

He scarcely heard her question. His attention was fixed on the students who were starting to insert long brushlike antennae into the poles sunk into the ground. "This your stuff?"

"Yes. The brushes are electronic cilia to measure the most minute electromagnetic vibrations in the smallest of particles. Crane wants to understand how the decomposed matter of dirt feels and how water feels and how rocks feel."

"Yeah . . . I've heard it all before," Newcombe said, turning to face her, anonymous now beneath hat and goggles. "Look, Lanie, I told you Crane's a nutjob. He's got these crazy notions about becoming part of the planet's 'life experience,' whatever the hell that is." He swept his arm to take in the long line of poles leading up to the computer control shack mounted on fat, spring-loaded beams. "This is all just so much nonsense."

" 'Nonsense' like this is what makes up my career, *doctor*," she said, cold. "The Crane Foundation finances *your* dreams. It can finance mine, too."

"My dreams are realistic!"

"And you can go straight to hell." She turned and walked away.

"All right . . . all right," he said, sloshing through the mud to catch up with her. He spun her around by the arm. "I apologize. Can I start over?"

"Maybe," she said, with the barest hint of a smile playing on her lips. "You didn't answer my question. What are the five signs that have everyone so worked up?"

"I'll show you," he said, "and then I'm getting you out of here."

Lanie didn't bother to protest. She was staying, and that was that. Just then a small electric truck pulled silently into the confusion near the computer center, tires spraying mud. A cage full of chickens was on its flatbed. Burt Hill, one of Crane's staff, according to the badge he wore high on the shoulder of his garish shirt, stuck his heavily bearded face through the window space. "Hey, Doc Dan!" he called. "Get a load of this." He forked his thumb at the flatbed.

People immediately crowded around, cams rolling, the tension palpable. Newcombe pushed his way through to Burt, who'd climbed out of the truck, sunblock shining off his cheeks, the only part of him not covered by hair or clothing. The chickens were throwing themselves at the cage, trying desperately to escape. Wings flapped and feathers flew amidst fierce cackling.

"The animals know, don't they?" Lanie said, standing at Newcombe's side.

"Yeah, they know." He looked back at Burt. "I need your vehicle."

"It's yours. What else?"

"Let the chickens go," Newcombe said, climbing into the control seat. Lanie hurried around to get in the other side.

Hill moved to the cage and opened it to an explosion of feathers, as the birds flapped and squawked out of the truck and into the startled onlookers who scattered quickly.

"And Burt," Newcombe called through the window

space, "get things under control here. Don't let anyone wander outside of the designated safe zones. We lose a newsperson and the whole thing was for nothing."

"Gotcha, Doc," Hill said as Newcombe opened the engine's focus and turned the truck around. "Stay in the shade!"

"What does Burt Hill do around here?" Lanie asked, annoyed that Dan hadn't introduced her.

"He's Crane's ramrod, security chief, majordomo . . . whatever. Crane and the Foundation couldn't get along without him."

"And where did Crane find this gem?"

Newcombe laughed. "You're not going to believe this. Crane picked Burt out of a group of patients in a mental institution. Told the head shrink he needed a good paranoid schizophrenic in his organization. They're very detail oriented, you know, and extremely security conscious."

"You're making this up."

He smiled. "Ask Crane. That's the story he told me. Whatever's the truth, Crane is closer to Burt than anybody else on his staff."

Mud spewing around its wheels, the truck sped out of Mobile One, as Newcombe added programming to head it toward the mines. Despite the dorph, he was keyed up now—and hating himself for getting excited about the disaster to come. Dammit, he wasn't one bit better than Crane, jolly old Crane. The truck bumped onto a dirt road that cut through a vast field of goldenrod whose beauty made Newcombe feel even more disgusted with himself. If his calculations were right, and he was damned sure they were, then all of this—the throbbing green foliage and vibrant yellow flowers, the ancient swaying trees in the distance, the people on this island—would be so much primal matter within hours. He slumped in the seat, chin on chest, wishing he'd put a second heaping spoonful of dorph in his coffee.

"Am I supposed to keep my mouth shut," Lanie suddenly said, "or am I allowed to ask how you've been the last six months?"

He straightened, glancing sheepishly at her. "I'm sorry

I've been out of touch. Things have been . . . intense back in LA."

"I translate that to mean you've been trying to get me out of your system."

"I care too much," he blurted. "I don't like that kind of weakness in myself."

"Okay, and I guess I translate *that* to mean you've avoided me because you can't control me."

He grimaced. It was the truth. "You wouldn't move out to the mountain with me. And don't start giving me your 'career' routine."

"Fair enough," she said, settling back in her seat and taking in the countryside. "What's the line on this island? It seems uninhabited."

"Not by a long shot," Newcombe said slowly, "although there aren't a whole lot of people here." He pointed toward a far-off peak. "That's Mount Kimpoku, where the Buddhist priest Nichiren lived in a hut; he foresaw the *Kamikaze*, the 'divine wind,' which destroyed Kubla Khan's fleet. There's also an exile palace someplace, but I haven't seen it. Too busy. Most of the island's population lives in a fishing village east of our tent city. It's called Aikawa, and there's an adjacent tourist compound with a theater company, demon drummers, the usual. The Aikawans liked us at first, mainly because we brought jobs. Now they hate us."

"Hate you?"

The truck turned onto a dirt roadway leading down from the plain into a cypress and bamboo forest. An old-fashioned jeep passed them going the other way, the driver beeping and waving as his passengers, all camheads, gaped.

"You'd better start getting it through your head what you've bought into," Newcombe said. "Crane is the prophet of destruction, my love. For four weeks he's been telling the world that Sado Island is going to be destroyed by an earthquake. After a while, the people who live here began to get the notion that he was bad luck and was ruining what little tourist business they had. They've been asking us to leave for days. It's gotten nasty."

Lanie thought about that, shaking her head. "I don't understand. Why aren't they glad to be warned?"

"Can you really expect people to up and leave their homes, their jobs? And where are they supposed to go to wait it out—if there's anything left to wait for after it's over?" He directed the truck into a large clearing filled with helos and surface vehicles. "The damned government isn't convinced this disaster is going to happen, so it won't relocate them. These simple people can't do much . . . except hate the messenger. Since quake prediction isn't an exact science—"

"But Crane's trying to make it exact."

Newcombe touched the control pad again and the vehicle pulled up beside a Japanese news helo and shut down its focus. Above, choppers were crowding the sky, angling for better positions. "Crane's a maniac . . . a money-hungry, power—"

"Dan!" Lanie shouted, "what's gotten into you? You can't open your mouth without attacking Crane." She frowned, remembering the voice messages he'd left, the long e-mail dialogues they'd had when Dan had first joined Crane. He'd respected and admired the man then, cherished the total freedom Crane had given him to pursue his research. Perhaps familiarity had bred contempt? Or the two men had become so competitive—

"That's the mine where we can find Crane." Newcombe pointed toward a large cave some fifty feet away, its entrance almost obscured by the throng of people milling around.

Excited, Lanie quickly got out of the truck and began to walk fast. "I can't wait to see the tale this day tells," she said over her shoulder to Newcombe, who was staring darkly as he trotted after her. She stopped and faced him squarely. "I need to ask you one more question. Why, really, do you hate Crane so much?"

At any other time or place, Newcombe thought, he probably wouldn't be inclined to give Lanie an honest answer. But today, considering what he knew was to come, he couldn't be anything less than honest with her. "When

I've looked in the mirror lately," he said, "Crane's face has been staring back."

Lewis Crane was alone. He stood with his hands behind his back, studying the stone relief carvings on the walls of the played-out gold mine. The carvings, created a century back by convicts who'd been sentenced to work here, depicted the hardships of a life of punishment in the Aikawa mines—men toiling, struggling, suffering, with no choice but to continue or die. Not so different from his own life, he thought, except that his punishment was self-imposed.

"Sorry to interrupt," the low, strong voice of Sumi Chan came through Crane's aural, "but you really do have to drag yourself away from contemplation of things past."

"Oh, do I now?" Crane responded. "You've got the motley horde organized, have you?"

"Absolutely not, but I do have them rounded up, and more than ready to hear from you."

"Hear from me . . . or make a meal of me?"

"Crane, this is serious. It will happen today, won't it?" Sumi asked anxiously.

"This isn't the time to lose your nerve. Not now. A show, you said, a show to raise money for the Foundation, for the work." Sumi Chan was one of Crane's greatest allies. As an executive of the US branch of the World Geological Survey, the small young man had championed Crane's proposals and gotten funding for the Foundation, often with surprising speed and under the most difficult circumstances. "We've got a show that's going to bring down the house."

Sumi groaned. "But will the house come down today?"

"Have faith, and cheer up. We're on the verge of realizing a dream. Soon no one will be able to think about EQs without thinking about me."

"Not as history's joke, I hope."

"We're all history's joke," Crane muttered. "You going to watch from the ground?"

"I'll stay in my own helo," Sumi said, clearing his throat.

Crane laughed. "You love me. You think I'm a genius,

but you don't trust me." He turned and started walking along the narrow shaft of the mine toward daylight. "Someday you will have to commit completely to something."

"I've consulted with my ancestors, Dr. Crane, and they have advised me otherwise. I'll be watching from the air." Crane thought he heard Sumi chuckle. "Besides, I have a large insurance policy on you."

Reaching the mouth of the cave, Crane stopped in the concealing gloom and looked out at the sea of wrapped bodies. "You ready to become famous?"

"I shall be the first to take credit for your success." Sumi did laugh aloud then, letting the sound die only slightly before he padded off.

Crane settled into the posture he used with newsies, the benign dictator, then moved out into the morning light pulling down his goggles and pulling up his hood. He stuck his left hand into the pocket of his white jumpsuit; he had only thirty percent use of that arm and to have it dangling at his side might give him the appearance of weakness.

The press was out in force, perhaps forty different news agencies represented. Forty accesses to the world . . . and the world would be amazed and dazzled before the end of the day. He was about to step out when he spotted Newcombe with a woman he didn't recognize, probably the imager he'd hired; they were pushing through the crowd. The woman reached him first.

"Ms. King, isn't it?" Crane asked, reaching out to shake her gloved hand.

"Is it really going to happen today?" she asked, skipping conventional courtesies and revealing how excited she was.

He pushed up his goggles and winked. "If it doesn't, we're in a lot of trouble. Good to have you on board."

Newcombe moved between them, nose to nose with his boss. "Why did you bring her here?"

"To work for me," Crane said. "Now—"

"Put her in a news helo. I don't want her on the ground when the Plate goes."

Goggles back in place, Crane said, "She's part of the team, she shares the life of the team."

Lanie jerked Newcombe's arm. "Dan—"

"Then she quits. She's not a part of the team."

Crane smiled. "Don't trust your own calculations, Dan?" Without waiting for Newcombe's response, he asked, "Do you quit, Dr. King?"

"I most certainly do not."

"Bravo," Crane said. "End of discussion." He pointed at Newcombe. "You know there's no time to argue. Can you feel it?"

Newcombe nodded, jaw muscles clenched. "This is the worst place to be," he mumbled.

"Right." Crane said dismissively. He quickly stepped forward, facing the crowd. "The ancient Japanese," he said without preamble to the large group, "called earthquakes the *namazu. Namazu* . . . a giant catfish. The Kashima god kept it pinioned under a mighty rock with divine powers called the keystone. When the god relaxed a moment, or for any other reason loosened his grip, the *namazu* would thrash around wildly. An earthquake." He paused, his hushed audience rapt. "Of course there were plenty of people who weren't about to be passive in the face of disaster, so they'd start doing battle with the fish. Unfortunately, the *namazu* was not only powerful in his own right, but he had allies. Very good allies, as it turns out, who would rush to his defense. Does it surprise you to learn that the *namazu*'s allies were the local carpenters and artisans—all those who stood to profit from a quake?" Crane's expressive brows rose over his narrow goggles. "Which only goes to prove that nothing much has changed over the last few thousand years."

The laughter of the newsies mingled with the whir of dozens of CD cams. Crane merely smiled until his audience settled again into attentive silence. "Attempts to predict earthquakes have been made, I suspect, since man first felt the earth tremble beneath his feet. So long the province of the shaman and the Cassandra, earthquake prediction remained a low priority for the scientific minds of our age . . . until that fateful, that cataclysmic moment in our history."

Even before Crane could speak the name of that fearful event, the crowd let out the now ritual response to its mention: a long, low moan, a keening mantra, and the swallowed last syllable. Ahh-hh, men.

"Yes," Crane dared to continue, "the exercise of the Masada Option caused research on earthquake prediction, like so many other things, to become vitally important and desperately urgent. Yet, until now, precise prediction was not possible. I come before you to make official and firm the prediction I've been discussing these four long weeks here: Before this day is out, a quake of between seven and eight on the Richter Scale will destroy a significant portion of this island and all of the village of Aikawa."

The newsies gobbled like turkeys. Crane let them react for a few moments, then waved them to silence. "How can I make this precise prediction is a long and complex story, only a few highlights of which we have time to share with you now. My chief assistant and valued colleague, Dr. Daniel Newcombe, reminds me to tell you that we are not in a safe place—"

There was laughter again, but it was nervous laughter, edged with hysteria in some.

"We have a few minutes, however, before all of us must leave for the secure location identified by Dr. Newcombe. We'll use our time here to go over a few things." Crane could feel minute tremors, but knew he was unique in that. "First, let's look at the well from which the prisoners who worked this gold mine over a hundred years ago got their water. As we move to the well, Dr. Newcombe will begin giving you some explanation of what we're all about today."

"Science is research," Newcombe said, Crane noticing the authority that always crept into the man's speech when he had control of a crowd. "By studying the past, we learn the future. By knowing the geology of a given area and researching past temblors in similar terrain, I've developed a system I call seismic ecology, or EQ-eco, the earthquake's way of remapping any given ecosystem. I have mathematically calculated the effects of a Richter seven epicentered on the Kuril subduction trench twenty K from this island and have mapped an area on the plain above us that I believe will not be affected by the quake. When it happens, we should all be up there, not here in the valley."

"Some of our techniques may seem like magic," Crane said, simplifying, always simplifying, "but many are as old as civilization. There are five predictive signs of an earthquake that will show up in a well. Take turns peering in as I describe them to you."

People lined up, shoving, to check out the well, the sun now rising high enough that light spilled in. Newcombe moved close to Crane.

"We've got to get these people out of here right now," he said, his voice rasping. He grabbed Crane's good arm. "I think I just felt another foreshock."

"You did," Crane replied, smiling. "But it's still waiting, our big fish, still straining. Another few minutes here, then we'll lead them out."

"Sign one . . . increased cloudiness in the water," Crane said to murmuring all around. "Then turbulence . . . then bubbling. . . ."

"It's doing that!" a woman said, her voice harsh, loud with anxiety.

Good. He had them, Crane thought. Then he said, "Changes in the water level. And for what it's worth, the level is eighteen inches lower than when we measured yesterday.

"Finally," he said, drawing up the heavy string to which a cup was attached, "bitterness in the water."

He handed the cup to a man wearing a 3-D steadicam helmet, gesturing for him to drink. The man took a tentative sip, then gagged and spat out the water.

"Bitterness." Crane lowered his voice to add, "There is a saying that applies to life and earthquakes: The wheel grinds slowly, but exceedingly fine. The giant wheel of Mother Earth and its massive movements is going to grind up this island today. And there's nothing all the power of Man can do to stop it."

"Crane!" Newcombe said sharply. "The sky!"

Everyone looked up. The morning sky was turning a ruddy orange with the increased electrical activity on the ground. It was happening. Crane could feel it pulsating through him, playing him like an instrument. The whole world was changing for them.

"My friends," Crane said, "you must follow us quickly up to the base camp. It's the only place you'll be safe. Those of you in helos might want to view this from the air. It will be . . . spectacular. Let's go!"

He ran with Newcombe and King to the truck, Lanie jamming herself between them on the small bench seat.

"God, we're cutting this close," Newcombe said. He touched the control pad and the truck peeled out quickly, other vehicles scrambling in disorder behind, mud flying everywhere. He glared at Lanie. "We can still get you on a helo."

"Don't concern yourself, doctor," she said without looking at him. "I have complete faith in your calculations."

"It's good drama," Crane said. "People running for their lives, running to the only safety that exists for them, safety that we have provided. This is going to be great."

"What about the villagers?" Lanie asked. "Can't we warn them, too?"

"I've done nothing but warn them," Crane said, turning to face her, smiling when he saw she was flushed with excitement. "They threw me out of Aikawa three days ago and threatened to have me arrested if I came back. Their fate can't be helped."

"There must be something we can do."

Crane looked at his watch. "We've got about a hundred and twenty seconds," he said. "I'm wide open for suggestions. Hit me with an idea."

Her mind racing, but failing to churn out a single practical suggestion, Lanie put her hand on Newcombe's shoulder. "Dan?"

The truck was fishtailing up the hillside and demanded Newcombe's attention. Finally, though, he was able to respond. "We're here to watch people die," he said coldly, "so that the Crane Foundation can raise more money for research."

Lanie gasped as if struck and glanced quickly at Crane to see his reaction. He seemed perfectly composed, untouched by the comment.

"He's right," Crane said. But what Crane didn't say, although he'd realized it at that second, was the extent of the fatalism in his character revealed by Newcombe's lack of it. It was a quality, Crane suspected, that Newcombe would never develop. Still, he knew there were great similarities between them. While both felt the horror, they also felt the exultation of what was to come. And the latter was as ugly as it was paradoxical.

The truck sped through the camp in the direction of the Sea of Japan. Crane's left arm throbbed like a beating heart; images swirled through his mind of crashing buildings, trapped people, firestorms. The pain and turmoil threatened to overwhelm him and he summoned all his energies to fight his demons, bring them down to calm, and to swallow the sword of self-doubt.

Newcombe took them within twenty feet of the plain's sheer drop-off to the sea below, then directed the truck to halt. Crane could hear a distant rumble and knew they had barely a minute. He climbed out, his mind all centered, all controlled, as other vehicles skidded up near them. A jumble of people filled the plain.

He walked with Newcombe and King to the edge of the cliff and looked down. One hundred meters below, nestled between the rock face upon which they stood and the sea beyond, sat the village of Aikawa. Several hundred wooden buildings with colorful red roofs hugged the horseshoe-shaped coastline in picturesque tranquillity. The small fleet of fishing boats had already put out to sea, their sailors, no doubt, wondering about the orange sky. The villagers were approaching the last day of their lives as they had approached every day that had gone before. Children's laughter, real or imagined, drifted up to him.

"Crane-san."

Crane turned toward the source of the angry voice. Matsu Motiba, the mayor of Aikawa, impeccably dressed in a black suit and solid silver tie was flanked by men in uniform.

"Good morning, Mayor Motiba," Crane said, looking past him to the hundred or more people jammed up behind him. Pressing the voice enhancement icon on his wristpad, he said, "Ladies and gentlemen! As you see, yellow lines have been painted on the plain. For your protection, please stay within the lines. I cannot guarantee your safety otherwise."

"It is time for this charade to end," Motiba said.

"I quite agree, sir. It is time."

"What," the mayor said, uncharacteristically sarcastic, "no desperate pleas for evacuation, no horror stories to frighten us?"

"It's too late," Crane said solemnly. "There's nothing I can do for you now except help with the survivors."

The mayor sighed deeply and took a piece of paper from a lieutenant in a white parade uniform with a logo that read Liang Int on the shoulders. "This is an urgent official communiqué from the government on the mainland." He handed it to Crane. "You are to disband your campsite and leave this island immediately. Your credentials and your permits have been revoked."

Shaking his head, Crane looked up. Hot air balloons filled the skies; the helos zipping around the balloons dipped down like birds of prey to shoot footage of the village. He could certainly understand the mayor's feelings.

"Do you hear me, Crane-san? You must leave now."

The paper fluttered from Crane's nerveless fingers, his gaze going to the sea. The flying fishes, one of Sado's most famous sights, were jumping crazily, throwing themselves onto the beach.

He glanced at the mayor. "I'm so sorry, sir," he murmured. "*Gomen nasai.* Fate has decreed that today you will be a survivor. Believe me when I tell you that it is no blessing." Then he looked past the mayor and addressed the crowd. "You may be able to hear the rumble now. Gather as close as you're able, because you must stay within the lines."

Crane then turned back to Aikawa, his body growing

tense and still, a trance engulfing him. The noise and commotion around him receded into the void of bleak silence within. Time and again he'd walked to the edge of his own sanity, challenging his fears and his anger, wondering when the monster of the Earth would devour him. He hated what was happening, hated it with a passion that would tear most men to pieces.

The waterspouts began hundreds of meters from shore, the ocean heaving, throwing two dozen geysers fifty feet into the air. Motiba, who'd been grabbing at Crane's sleeve, had stopped and was staring transfixed. The spouts came closer to land, exploding out of the water as the inhabitants of Aikawa understood at last that Lewis Crane was no madman, no vicious hoaxster, but a seer, a modern-day Cassandra whose warnings they had foolishly, blindly, tragically refused to heed.

The ships in the harbor were tossing and tearing away from their moorings, capsizing, and being hurled into the village streets. Another hand was clutching at Crane. He quickly gazed to his left. Elena King was locked onto his bad arm, her face a study in shocked surprise. He couldn't feel her touch, though her fingers dug into his clothing and her knuckles were white with strain. The spouts reached land, the rumbling sound growing louder and louder until the roar turned into booming ground thunder. The sea was a maelstrom that spat sand high into the orange sky. And then the quake hit.

Seabed sucked into the subduction zone beneath the Eurasian Plate, then jerked the surface of the ground with it, feeding a chunk of the Pacific Plate back into the furnace of the planet's core. Bedrock, grinding to dust, collapsed in upon itself; great rents and tears in the skin of the earth widened into mouths that gulped the boulders, people, trees, buildings, and boats near its lips.

The plain danced violently beneath them, and Crane hoped against hope that he hadn't misplaced his trust in Newcombe to map the paths of destruction—and, thus, the small, safe place upon which they stood. Below, the villagers who had not been crushed and trapped within their houses had escaped to the streets, their screams rising to join those of the people watching in horror with Crane. The mayor was crying out. And behind, Mount Kimpoku was busily rising another twenty meters into the air while the ancient mines Crane had just visited fell in upon themselves, erasing forever the carved records of those who had suffered there. Sheets of volcanic rock slid into the sea, screaming against the morning. Sado Island was disintegrating all around them.

The motion of the earth changed to a wild swivel, hurling the people around Crane onto the hard-packed dirt plain as the village below disappeared in rubble and a fine mist of ocean spray. The rending of the island, Japan's sixth largest, was stentorian, the sound of a dying animal bellowing in rage and sorrow that brought tears to Crane's eyes. He remembered . . . he remembered. And he knew that even worse was to come.

Only Lanie still stood beside him, her deathgrip on his arm the sole sign of the ultimate fear that comes with understanding of the true powerlessness of mankind. "Courage," he whispered to her.

And then perdition stopped. Ninety seconds after it had begun, the Earth had finished realigning itself and deathly quiet reigned. Slowly people began to shake themselves off, to stand up, to look around in awe and shock. The island was half as large now as it had been a minute and a half before. Landmarks had disappeared or moved. Nothing was the same. Nothing would be the same.

Miraculously, there were survivors below. They, too, were shaking themselves off, picking themselves up. Emergency teams began to mobilize for the trip down to what had been Aikawa with fresh water, medical supplies. Motiba stared in stupefied horror at the remnants of his life; his glasses were askew on his face, his eyes distant, unfocused.

"I must . . . go," he said softly. "To my people . . . I must—"

"No," Crane said. "You cannot go down there yet."

The man ignored him and ran back through the crowd.

"Stop him!" Crane yelled. "Bring him back! All of you, hold your places. Look to the shoreline!"

They looked. The Sea of Japan had receded hundreds of meters from the island, leaving it high and dry, a seabed full of writhing fish and of boats drowned in mud.

Two Red Cross workers dragged the struggling Motiba back to Crane's side. "Let go," he shouted, hysterical now. "Why do you hold me?"

Gently, Crane patted the man's trembling shoulder, then pointed out to sea. "We hold you because if you go down, you will be killed. See!"

A mountain of water was racing toward the island from several kilometers out . . . rushing to fill the void caused when the heaving of the Earth had shoved it back.

"*Tsunami,* ladies and gentlemen," Crane said calmly, too aware of the cams and very careful not to betray the horror that gripped his soul. There was time now, a few minutes only, perhaps, to speak as if all were normal. "After it subsides, we will go down and look for survivors. I trust that you representatives of the news media will pitch in and lend a hand."

He turned to see Newcombe putting his arm around Elena King. Crane pulled her hand from his dead arm and gave her completely over to Newcombe. "You did a good job on the location, Dan. Let's just hope we're up high enough."

"How can you be so calm?" Newcombe's emotions were in shreds, his voice the growl of a hurt animal. "Those are people down there . . . and they're dying."

"Someone has to keep his head."

"What kind of goddamned Cassandras are we?"

"Get used to it, doctor," Crane said. "This is merely the beginning."

"But why?"

Crane ignored him and turned to Motiba, the man completely broken down, crying silently. He took the mayor in his arms, clutching him tightly. "You must be strong, Motiba-san," he whispered.

"Let me die with them," the mayor pleaded as the water charged them, roaring, grasping.

"No," Crane said simply. "Someone must live . . . to remember."

Eating the screams of the survivors on the plain, the *tsunami* assaulted them first . . . then the water, advancing like a juggernaut from all sides, slamming into Sado Island, reached higher, climbing. The wall of water smacked the land like a monstrous hand of God. The people on the plain turned as one and fled as a pack as far back as they could until the water crested and gushed over the top, reaching them and driving them down onto the ground. Waves carried pieces of broken buildings and bodies, crushed cars and uprooted trees. Churning thick with the debris of life, the water poured over Crane, boards banging against him. After the first deluge, the water proved to be shallow. Crane huddled on the muddy, pool-speckled ground, hands over his head, just as he'd done when he was seven years old.

He hunched there, shivering in fear until the water fully subsided, then climbed to his feet to look with horror at the dead spread over the plain. Many of his own party had been hurt by the tidal scum that had washed so high over the island. And he noticed that the Red Cross workers were tending to their own first.

While most people were dazed, many of the camheads were already up and rolling viddy. And it hit him then that he'd done it. Given the world the show. Everything Sumi Chan had advised him they needed to get the publicity, the funds, the aura of authority to attach to him so that he could do the work that was his life. And in that moment of great tragedy, he knew great triumph. Oh, yes, he thought cynically, horror made sensational copy. And what better than this?

He spotted Burt Hill and called him over. "Organize the aid teams to go down to what's left of the village," he ordered. "Pull it all together."

"Yes, sir."

He turned to see the edge of the cliff. Motiba was there, and he joined him. The sea was smooth as glass, unusually beautiful in deepest teal blues and greens. But where Aikawa had stood was only empty beach, not even a boat or shack littering the pristine sand that gleamed in the deadly sunlight.

"I'm sorry," Crane said, low and hoarse.

Motiba looked up at him, tears working their way down his cheeks. "I know I should not blame you for this," he said, "but I do."

With that he turned and walked off, leaving Crane absolutely alone with his demons. No one came near. No one reached out a hand or asked if *he* were all right. To the people left on the plain he was as distant and as untouchable as the dead that surrounded him. But they were wrong. The dead, at least, knew peace.

ERUPTIONS

WASHINGTON, D.C.
15 JUNE 2024, 6:16 P.M.

The sun was lowering behind the Washington Monument and Mr. Li Cheun, head of Liang International in this hemisphere, knew that for the last couple of hours the little American bureaucrats who worked for him, though they didn't realize it perhaps, had been scurrying home. More important to him, the North American headquarters of Liang International was winding down for the evening. Liang Int, the Chinese star ascendant in the world of business, owned America. Ten years before, Liang Int had managed to get a toehold in America, wresting some business away from the Germans who'd owned the country then. The Masada Option had proved to be better than any business plan or ruthless tactics the Chinese might have devised, for the resultant radioactive cloud and fallout from the explosions had swept southern, central, and eastern Europe. When the Fatherland was devastated, suffering a loss of almost half its population, Liang Int was able to move swiftly and turn its toehold into a stranglehold, not only on America, but on German business operations throughout the world.

Now, standing in the secured boardroom, dim save for the glowing virtual map of the Earth that surrounded him, Li contemplated his empire. The diorama was transparent; he could look through it at the Moon, always full, inspiring the fanciful, but much desired, wish that the Liang Int diggers up there were always working.

There were no windows in this room, thus no day, no evening, only shifts. Every decision that mattered to the continuing business (most would say even the continuing existence) of Canada, the US, Mexico, and the Central American franchises was made right here. The rest of Washington—the mall outside running between the Capitol and the Lincoln Memorial, the White House and its occupants, the scores of departments, bureaus, agencies stretching to the beltways and beyond—all was show for the tourists. Liang Int owned it all and ran it all . . . including the so-called government of the United States of America. President Gideon, Vice President Gabler, the Cabinet, the members of Congress and the Supreme Court were little more than mere employees, figureheads and lackeys. Of course they maintained a pretty fiction of government, but that was all it was, a fiction.

Tonight Li was distracted, his thoughts turning time and again to the viddy-stract his staff had prepared the previous night and shown him first thing this morning on one Lewis Crane and the events on the Japanese Island of Sado. The Japanese. Upstarts all of them, fools most of them. They'd actually shared their ownership of America with Middle Easterners, back when there had been a Middle East. But their tenure was short. Still, from time to time a Japanese combine would try to take a piece of the business away. He sneered, glad that in response to just such an affront his predecessor at Liang Int North America had ordered the chopping down of the two thousand cherry trees around the tidal basin—trees that the Japanese had given to the Americans shortly after the turn of the last century.

"Rain in the midwest," said Mui Tsao from the soft darkness of his control panel. "It will delay the wheat harvest. I suggest we contact Buenos Aires and siphon their surplus until the harvest catches up."

Both men spoke English almost exclusively as a show of good faith to the natives, though American business people and officials were expected to speak fluent Chinese.

"Good," Li replied. "I saw a report of a major anthrax epidemic in the South American branch. See if you can trade them some cattle for the wheat. Bring them in through Houston."

"Where do we store?"

"We could store in the warehouses where we've got the headache chips."

"And what do we do with the chips?"

"We'll give them to the Southern franchises as part of the wheat repayment. By the time they've figured out what's happened, they already will have distributed the chips and be forced to try and follow through with a sales campaign."

Li heard Mui chuckle softly as the man punched deals into the keypad, and smiled himself. The "headache chip," as they called it, was an endorphin trigger; it sensed muscle tightness in the neck and immediately flooded the cortex with a shot of mood enabling dorph that stopped the headache before it got started. Only trouble was, the brain enjoyed the dorph hit so much it worked on developing headache after headache just to get the dose, wearing out the implant and leaving the user in the worst pain of his life. Once word had gotten around, Liang Int had been stuck with seven warehouses full of worthless chips.

"Done," Mui said, typing furiously, "and done."

"Good."

Li was in charge of the North American branch, and Mui was his control, his Harpy. Second in command of the decision making, the Harpy was responsible for constantly double-checking his superior, questioning his decisions. It could be irritating, but had a positive effect on business decisions, and business was what held all the world, all of life, together. Should Li fail to make the proper percentage of appropriate decisions, Mui would have his position—with his own little Harpy in place then to watch over him. It made for sleepless nights, but it was the very best thing for Liang Int.

And that was what mattered. Li was nothing if not a company man.

The map floated around Li, continents rising out of shimmering oceans, the trade routes of the world pulsing in pink, while areas of harvests and famines glowed in celestial blues. Food was always a problem since only filtered fields were able to withstand the full measure of the sun's wrath and produce.

Nuclear material storage areas glowed unblinking crimson in thirty different spots, leakage into ground water running like capillaries thousands of miles from their source. Movements of precious metals and ambulatory currency spiked metropolitan areas, while consumer spending showed up as gangs of small people, one per million, flashing their spending areas and products like dust motes dancing on sunlight. Production was tracked worldwide, immediate comparisons were made with other similar operations, and the interior of the office was filled with floating hieroglyphics decipherable only by a handful of Liang's top management. If any member of the team was to leave for a reason other than death, the entire code would be changed.

The Masada Cloud throbbed in dark black, its bulk covering Europe today, moving ever eastward on the jet stream. And the Masada Cloud led Li back once more to Lewis Crane.

Crane had won the Nobel Prize six years before for work that had flowed from his research on the exercise of the Masada Option, specifically its effect on earthquakes. That work also had led directly to the banning of all nuclear testing on Earth because Crane had showed conclusively that nuclear explosions could cause earthquakes hundreds, even thousands, of miles from the site of detonation. As the staff had pointed out to Li in their presentation, Crane had stated that the quake on Sado was, in fact, a direct consequence of the destruction of the Middle East back in '14.

Would it be possible, Li mused, for someone armed with Crane's information and programs to cause earthquakes in chosen, distant locations? He shook off the question. It was tangential to what really interested him about Crane at this time: politics and profits—and the question of why Crane was so eager to contact him through Sumi Chan. Indeed, Chan had left a message only hours ago about a meeting Crane wished to arrange.

Ah, these Americans were bold. But Li rather liked them and their country. It was a Third World country, as was Europe, both with real history. Its own corporate gods long dead, America had a cheap labor pool of hard workers who thought nothing of reinvesting all of their wages back into the company through consumerism. Americans were the world's best consumers. Except, of course, for the headache chip.

There had been nothing but success in Li's life, which was why he was having such a difficult time with the coming elections. In the past, Li had been able to tolerate America's fantasy of representative government because Liang's candidates always had won. But now, for some reason, its chief competitor in multinationalism, the Yo-Yu Syndicate, was making inroads with its own candidates. The off-year elections had cost Liang Int seven representatives. It was a nasty trend that Li needed to nip in the bud. But it was difficult because the fickle voters persisted in believing they needed "change" in government and that change was meaningful. With the American fantasy beginning to get in the way of corporate harmoniousness, Li had to act. Hence, Crane and his earthquakes. He could show the citizens how much he loved them by associating Liang Int and the government with earthquake prediction. That should fix Yo-Yu in the elections.

His diorama beeped and squeaked in a thousand different intervals and tones, Li recognizing them all. So, when he distinguished the delicate alto chirping of the telephone, he decided to make his move. He turned in Mui's direction, waved off the incoming call, and said, "Get Sumi Chan for me, scrambled and secured. Put him over the west coast."

While waiting, Li smiled. He knew Mui would be watching and listening very carefully.

Sumi Chan's disembodied face, five inches high, blipped to life, hanging in midair somewhere over the Sierra Nevada mountains. Li would not address the man face to face, however. He had a computer projection that stood in for him so as never to give anything away through inadvertent gesture or expression.

"Hello, Mr. Li," Sumi Chan said.

There was something expressed in the man's eyes that Li didn't understand. "Hello, Sumi," he said, the computer matching his voice to its projection's movements. "Are you well?"

"Yes, and I am also most grateful and most excited," Sumi replied formally. "You have honored me by your attention."

"As you have honored me by your invitation to meet with Dr. Crane." Li paused, allowing Sumi to begin offering up information about the meeting. When the man was not immediately forthcoming, he added, "I assume I am not to meet with him alone."

"Not unless you desire to do so. Dr. Crane wishes to present you and a number of other distinguished leaders with some of his ideas . . . and proposals."

Li nodded. "A very timely meeting. His exploits on Sado are being reported continuously and everywhere, I'm told."

"Yes, Sado. A great tragedy, but one whose human consequences could have been averted in large measure."

"Economic consequences, too, of course."

"Of course," Sumi echoed. "May we count on your attendance?"

"If my schedule permits, I should certainly like to be a part of such a gathering. I would ask, however, that you coordinate with Mr. Mui Tsao on the guest list, the arrangements, and so forth."

"That goes without saying, sir. May I tell you how pleased I know Dr. Crane will be?"

Li grunted and waved his hand dismissively. He'd had quite enough of this, and with a smile and a nod, he concluded, "Stay in the shade, Sumi Chan."

"And you also, sir."

Sumi's face instantly blipped off, and Li paced a few steps up and past the Arctic. He could walk freely within the body of his virtual world and literally feel the flow of capital and goods pumped through the beating heart of consumerism. The world was a living network of corporate deities and he was a demigod. Things were as they were supposed to be.

As an official of the Geological Survey, Sumi Chan actually worked for him. Tacitly understood in their conversation was the fact that he, Li Cheun, would call the shots on Crane's meeting. He would brief Mui on what he wished to accomplish. Yes, things were as they were supposed to be.

CONCOCTIONS
ON THE YACHT *DIATRIBE*, THE PACIFIC OCEAN
15 JUNE 2024, 9:35 P.M.

"Mr. Li Cheun is, of course, the one on this list who counts, the man to convince if you wish to succeed, Crane," Sumi said, smiling slightly, "and I trust you will dazzle him. I fear I'm going to use up all my chits on him." What he left unsaid was that he feared he'd already used up all his chits . . . with Mui Tsao, to whom he'd been talking until just ten minutes ago. There could be no doubt that Li Cheun had a definite use in mind for Lewis Crane.

"Oh, I'll dazzle him all right, do a veritable song and dance for him," said Crane, tilting back his chair and drinking directly from a bottle of very old Scotch.

"You've got copies of my paper for everyone who's agreed to attend?" Newcombe asked, trying to steer the conversation back to his concerns.

Sumi nodded. "There will be copies awaiting each of them in their cabins when they board."

Newcombe shook his head. Why Crane had chosen to spirit them away from Sado on this yacht to rendezvous with Sumi mid-ocean was beyond him. And out in the stratosphere were Crane's reasons for wanting to hold his high-powered meeting on a boat. Still, the *Diatribe* was a helluva craft, luxurious and crammed with technology. Who owned it and how Crane had come by it were mysteries Newcombe was fairly sure would not be solved for him.

"Let's review the politicos again," Crane said to Sumi. "We've got Kate—"

Sumi's laughter cut him off. "They're all politicos, every last one of them, the Vice President of the United States being the least political of them all."

"Gabler," Newcombe said scornfully, "a fool . . . a buffoon."

"And an important showpiece, Dan," Crane said firmly. "Just leave all this to Sumi and me."

"With pleasure," Newcombe retorted. "So let me get to the area where I am an expert. Why are you planning such elaborate maneuvers? We've got a pretty straightforward situation as far as I can see. The data on earthquake ecology is on paper—and proven. Sado came in so close to my projections that you've got to go five digits past the decimal to find divergence from the actual event. This is something concrete to sell, Crane. Sell it."

"I'll use it," Crane told him, smoothing his free hand over the bright yellow shirt covering his bathing trunks, "but I won't marry myself to it."

Newcombe frowned harshly and Sumi quickly refilled his glass with synthchampagne to which he added two drops from a small green bottle containing his own special dorph preparation. Newcombe knew Sumi urgently wanted him to ingest the dorph, but he didn't mind. Sumi's understanding of glandular chemistry was legendary.

"I'll tell you why I don't sell your EQ-eco, Danny boy," Crane said, slightly slurring his words. Crane didn't face living people very well straight. He put a hand over the mouth of his bottle when Sumi tried to bring the eyedropper of dorph to it. "First of all, you're out of line in making your suggestion."

"You hired me for my talent," Newcombe said. "Along with that comes my mouth."

"It's my foundation," Crane said, "my decision. Your calculations indeed worked wonderfully . . . *because*, Dr. Newcombe, you knew in advance where the epicenter was going to be. You knew it because I told you. Your work is only a small part of what the Crane Foundation represents. To focus simply on the EQ-eco limits the amount of grant money available to us. To be perfectly honest, however, I also see a basic flaw in your perceptions. You expect people to do the right thing. They don't. All the people in Los Angeles know they live atop faults held together by the thinnest of threads, yet they stay there. Would you convince the government to depopulate LA to the tune of thirteen million people? Where would you put them?"

"My system saves lives!"

Crane sighed and took a long pull from his bottle. "Few would consider that a compelling argument, doctor. Saving money is more to people's tastes."

"But it was so successful."

"Exactly why I want to use it, but de-emphasize it at the same time. I want nobody thinking in those terms alone. We're looking for much more."

"Like what?"

Crane leaned closer to Newcombe, Sumi automatically drawing near. He spoke low, dramatically. "Have you gentlemen ever thought about what it would be like if all scientific research in a given area were brought under one banner, in one unifying edifice, and properly coordinated?"

"You want everything!" Newcombe laughed. He couldn't believe it, the brazenness of the man.

Crane grinned. "Liang Int is omninational. Total control of tectonics is a real possibility. They just need the right sell job. I could run the whole show from the Foundation, have access to every bit of data extant. Suddenly, true prediction—along with a lot more—becomes reality."

Newcombe began to understand a great deal. "That's why you hired Lanie. You want her to sort through and make sense of all the data if you pull this off."

"And that's why all the support organizations that have vested interests are being invited to attend the coming meeting," Sumi said, sitting back and shaking his head. "Audacious! So, when I was speaking just moments ago of Li's importance, you were laughing at me, weren't you, Crane? Li Cheun was your target all along."

"Don't get mad at me, Sumi, please," Crane said, boyish and charming. He grew serious again almost at once. "Geological research blankets the Earth, but touches very few lives in an obvious way. Clearly, it should. And clearly Liang Int can amply fund our work, get much out of it, and never feel the slightest pinch. They'll only see profits from their involvement."

Newcombe stood, Sumi's dorph doing its work. Well-being washed over him like a summer breeze and there was a sexual edge to it—oxytocins, PEA?—that made him very glad he and Lanie were together again. The ship was rocking gently side to side. "We're dead in the water," Newcombe said, puzzled. "They must have put out the drag anchor."

"Yes indeed they did," Crane said, eyes twinkling with mischief. "Merely part of a little surprise I'm preparing for our guests . . . thanks to you, of course." He winked broadly at Newcombe, who shuddered involuntarily, feeling oddly cold all of a sudden.

"Why *do* you want so much power?" Newcombe whispered.

"Great power accomplishes great things," Crane said, the light of otherworldliness shining from his eyes. That the man was insane Newcombe had no doubt, but what he couldn't peg was the power of his vision. Crane's antics always had kept them funded, at least until now. Just how far could Dan Newcombe ride Crane's hellbound train?

He knew the answer: He'd take to the rails with the devil himself if he thought it would make his EQ-eco a reality.

MARTINIQUE
17 JUNE 2024, 9:45 A.M.

Raymond Hsu, a shift supervisor at the Liang Usine Guerin sugar mill in Fort-de-France on the Caribbean island of Martinique, was trying to place an emergency call to the franchise comptroller on Grand Cayman Island to report a work stoppage due to an attack of thousands of *fourmisfous*, small yellowish, speckled ants, and *bêtes-a-mille-pattes*, foot-long black centipedes—both species venomous enough, in large numbers, to kill an adult human.

They'd attempted to stop the invasion by dumping barrels of crude oil around the mill, the workers flailing away with sugar cane stalks, splashing insect blood all over the mill. At the supervisor's own house nearby, the maids were killing the ants and centipedes with flatirons, insecticides, and hot oil, while his wife and three children screamed. It wasn't helping.

The insect invasion was simply the latest in a long string of odd events traceable to Mount Pelee, twenty kilometers to the north. At the end of March there'd been the smell of sulfurous gas lingering on the air. Two weeks later plumes of steam were seen issuing from fumaroles high atop Pelee. The next week, mild tremors rocked Fort-de-France followed by a rain of ash.

The ash had gotten thicker, more unceasing, as the sulfur smell grew over the weeks. In the second week of June the rains had come, filling the myriad rivers that crisscrossed Pelee and its sister mountain, Pitons du Carbet, to bursting and sending boulders and large trees down the mountainside and out to sea in torrents, along with the carcasses of asphyxiated cattle and dead birds. Mountain gorges jammed with ash and created instant lakes in the drowning rains.

As Hsu's call was being placed in the early hours of June 17, Fort-de-France itself was coming under siege by thousands of *fer-de-lance,* pit vipers with yellow-brown backs and pink bellies, six feet or more in length and instantly deadly. The population was panicking, taking to the streets with axes and shovels to face the invasion, never realizing the snakes were fleeing in terror from the rumbling mountain. Hundreds would die, mostly children.

The comptroller, a man named Yuen Ren Chao, would tell Raymond Hsu to hire more workers and step up production, even though Pelee was thundering loudly, its peak covered by clouds of ash. Those who could see anything of the long dormant volcano were humbled by Nature's grandeur—two fiery craters glowing like blast furnaces near the summit, and above them, a cloud filled with lightning.

The mill would not make its quota today. Mr. Yuen would be forced to increase the cane quotas in Cuba while the citizens of Martinique fought the snakes instead of fleeing themselves.

Within two days of Raymond Hsu's call, an ash-dammed lake would break through its barrier, sending a monstrous wall of lava-heated water down the mountainside and onto the island, crushing the sugar mill and drowning everyone, including Raymond Hsu and his family, in boiling water.

MID PACIFIC
18 JUNE 2024, 10:13 P.M.

Newcombe climbed the ladder to the forward observation deck, enjoying the southerly breeze and the coolness of the night. He stepped onto the deck. Above, a line of twinkling ore freighters, probably from Union Carbide's organization, snaked toward the Moon like a conga line of traveling stars. The Liang logo, a simple blue circled L, was displayed in liquid crystal splendor on the surface of the three-quarter Moon.

"Catch your death up here," he said as he crossed to Lanie, who was moonbathing naked. He plunked down in the chair next to hers. Her eyes were twinkling like the stars as she smiled at him. "The mighty are gathering," he said, sorry he couldn't spend the evening up here with this glorious woman, "so Crane wants us to join the party."

"You look upset."

"Nothing a little homicide wouldn't cure—or a fast exit off this boat." He grimaced. "The ocean's a good place to meet the people down on the fantail, Lanie. Barracuda, every one of them. So what does that make us, bait?"

She regarded him thoughtfully. "Crane making you crazy?"

He nodded.

She got up and slipped into the party dress lying on the deck beside her. It was white, whiter than her skin, shining under the logoed Moon. "Do I look suitably dressed for cocktails with the Vice President of the United States?" she asked, turning a circle for him.

"Even if he wasn't a jerk you'd outclass him," Newcombe said. "You like all this, don't you?"

She cocked her head and stared at him. "What, the juice? Of course I do. Last week I was just another underemployed Ph.D. in a universe full of them. Today I'm part of the Crane Team, changing the world. In case you haven't watched the teev, we're the hottest thing on the circuit right now. Tell me you don't find that exciting? I can't sleep at night I'm so pumped up."

"I noticed." He stood up. "Just don't get lost in it. Now that I've finally gotten you to come out to the mountain, I want to see you from time to time."

"All you had to do was hire me," she said, fitting easily into his arms. She hugged him, her hair smelling of patchouli. "Oh, Dan. Maybe it will work for us this time."

"I always hope that," he said, wishing they hadn't both been worn down from five years of trying to tame their competing egos. "Come on. Let's get below. There's someone special I want you to meet."

"Who?"

"You wouldn't believe me if I told you."

They took the ladder, then the elevator, down to the main deck, and walked along the gangway to the fantail, where they found Crane. Half-drunk, he was holding court near the hors d'oeuvres table, recounting a story from the 2016 Alaskan quake that had sent Anchorage sliding into Cook's Inlet.

The fantail of the yacht was ringed with teev screens showing continuous feed on the tragedy of Sado, focusing often on Crane at the head of the cliff, presiding over the carnage.

Everyone wore clothing of the thinnest silks and rayons, putting as little between themselves and the night as they could. Dangerous daylight made night an obsession. Vice President Gabler was an empty suit, a ceremonial smiling face, his wife, Rita, giggling beside him as he took direction from Mr. Li, who, as always, had Mr. Mui at his side.

"There's Kate Masters," Lanie said, as Sumi slipped up beside her, thrusting a champagne glass into her hand.

Newcombe had already noticed. Masters was something else altogether. Chairman of the WPA, the Women's Political Association, she was a powerhouse. In a fragmented America, she could deliver forty million votes on any issue at any time. The WPA was second in power only to the Association of Retired Persons, which also had a representative on deck, a man named Aaron Bloom. He was fairly nondescript. Masters was short, with long bright red hair and indiscreet green eyes. She wore a filmy lime-green dress that seemed to hover around her like an alien fog. As she moved, parts of her body would slip into view for a second, only to disappear in a wisp of green. She smiled wickedly in their direction, Lanie smiling wickedly back.

"I'll bet she eats little girls for breakfast," Newcombe said. Sumi hovered, his eyedropper raised above the champagne glass.

"Something special for the pretty lady?" Sumi asked.

Lanie smiled and held up three fingers. "Private stock?"

Sumi nodded. "For making your own earthquakes, eh?" he said, then narrowed his eyes, studying her with surgical precision. "You don't like me, do you?"

"I don't know," Lanie said. "I've never met the real you."

"Sumi's the Foundation's best friend," Newcombe said, surprised at Lanie's reaction to the man.

"So I've heard," Lanie said, taking a sip of the synth and smiling at Chan as Newcombe watched Crane disappear into the cabin area. "What do you think of the success of the EQ-eco?"

"I think the Crane Foundation is very lucky to have Dr. Newcombe on staff," Sumi said, staring at Newcombe. "He is helping to advance science at a critical point."

" 'Critical' is certainly the word tonight," Newcombe said, regretting that he'd ever let Crane talk him into making one very special arrangement.

Sumi Chan smiled, then darted over to Kate Masters, who took an entire eyedropper full of dorph in her glass. Naturally distilled from the human's own glands, dorph was pure and impossible to overdose on.

Lanie leaned against Newcombe, snuggling, his arms going around her immediately. The PEA had kicked in. He nuzzled her neck just as Crane walked to the center of the deck.

"Friends," he said. "Thank you for indulging me in my secrecy by clandestinely traveling to Guam and boarding there. You are about to see why. But first I must ask that we meet a prearranged condition and shut down any and all transmission equipment." Crane pulled himself to his full height. The moment was replete with drama, as he intended.

Lanie wriggled away from Newcombe. She was entranced, all her attention on the scene Crane was creating.

Crane tapped his wristpad. "On my mark, Captain Florio." His voice boomed through the ship speakers and all the aurals. "Now!"

Diatribe blacked, every form of energy on the yacht dying—all fifty teev screens simultaneously going dead, all the lights and the music and everything else clicking off at once. The people on deck reached into pockets and onto wrists, concurrently shutting down their own devices of endless transmission and reception. In a world where communication was everything, they had all gone straight back to the Stone Age.

Lanie turned off her aural. Suddenly, she felt distressed, almost frightened, and realized she was beginning to hyperventilate. She tossed back the near-full glass of dorph-enhanced synth in her champagne glass, wondering if the others on deck, bathed in moonlight and cloaked in silence, were feeling, too, such profound anxiety at being cut off. If so, they weren't showing it.

"This is—this is so exciting," she whispered to Newcombe, whose deep responsive chuckle only tightened the string of her nerves.

"You haven't seen anything yet," he whispered back.

Her sharp stare at Newcombe was deflected by the sudden movements of Crane. He'd removed a small scanner from his shirt pocket, turned it on, and was whirling around in a circle.

"Nothing," he announced, stopping and smiling. "We're alone. And now, I beg your indulgence yet again. There is one more guest on board, a participant you haven't had the opportunity to encounter."

A door to the gangway off which the cabins were located slid open, and everyone on deck was caught in a withering blast of charisma as a tall Africk stepped out.

"Ladies and gentlemen," Crane said, "may I present Mohammed Ishmael."

A harsh collective gasp greeted the head of the militant Nation of Islam, outcast, fugitive, and some said, archcriminal and terrorist. Mohammed was well over six feet tall, and appeared even taller because of the black fez atop his head and the black dashiki that elongated his body in the shimmering moonlight. His stance was princely, the glance he swept over the participants majestic.

Riveted in place, the people on deck merely gaped, the silence astounding. But the tableau was short-lived. Turmoil erupted.

"My God!" Lanie exclaimed amidst the murmurs of outrage and surprise from the others, recovering now. "It's him!"

Two burly Secret Servicemen threw themselves in front of Mr. Li, who appeared to be laughing. Was it from shock, Lanie wondered, or in glee over the surprise to which he might have been privy? Vice President Gabler was waving his arms and sputtering, while other participants milled and muttered, with Kate Masters' throaty, nervous guffaws carrying over the sounds of all the others. Sumi Chan was, clearly, astonished, and only Mui Tsao of all the people on deck seemed entirely self-possessed.

Mui stepped forward. "I suggest a recess . . . a brief recess. Perhaps everyone could retire to his or her cabin?"

It wasn't a suggestion, but an order, Lanie realized, glancing quickly to Newcombe. She drew in a sharp breath at the expression on his face. Three hundred years of the hatred of the shackled Africk gleamed in his eyes. "I don't believe it. You're part of this," she said.

He looked down at her, his expression softening. "I helped to arrange to get the good brother to attend, yes, and I helped to spirit him aboard, just shortly after we picked up all our other distinguished guests in Guam. That cutting of engines, the anchor drag, remember?"

Lanie gulped. "After all—after everything—I mean, I—"

"Because of my past support of the Nation of Islam nearly destroying my career?" He nodded grimly. "I've got Crane's support on this now. And it's important, Lanie, very important—for the Foundation and for every Africk alive." He took her arm.

Guests were brushing by in the exodus from the deck and Newcombe was drawing her aft toward the spot where she saw that Sumi had backed Crane against the rail. Sumi's small fist pounded Crane's chest.

"Disaster," Sumi shouted. "The man's a wanted criminal, a total brigand. Such an affront to Mr. Li. . . . He will own me. Own me, I tell you. Why didn't you let me know about this?" he demanded of Crane, clearly beside himself with anger and fear.

"Would you have drawn the others here had you known?" Crane asked.

"Certainly not!"

Crane merely shrugged.

"Sedition, aiding and abetting—"

"Diplomacy," Crane said. "Peacemaking. And good politics. You will see, Sumi, you will see."

"I fear I will see nothing except my head on a plate held by Mr. Li Cheun."

"Your head? Not likely." Crane roared with laughter, then quickly sobered. He stared at Sumi, patted his frail shoulders, calming the man. "Is our other little surprise in place?" Sumi nodded. "Very well, then I suggest you start making calls on the occupants of each cabin with your synthchampagne in one hand and your little green bottle in the other, okay? Tell them we will reassemble here in ten minutes." He glanced at his wristpad. "Perfect timing."

"Yesss," Sumi hissed, turning abruptly and rushing across the deck. He got halfway before he said over his shoulder, "Maybe we'll get lucky and sink."

Lanie looked from Newcombe to Crane. She felt way out of her depth, a little lost. She needed her ten minutes alone . . . to think, and quickly excused herself to make her way back up to the observation deck. Actually, she fled, ran to the sanctuary high atop the ship. There, under the stars, she tried to digest the events of the evening so far. It was painful. She found herself unwilling, as always, to face the troubled world in which she lived. She dealt with the "realities" by trying to avoid them, by throwing herself into her work and personal affairs . . . or just blanking out. But Crane had launched her into a new orbit with a very high apex and, she knew, she had to face up to some very unpleasant facts, first and foremost, of course, this whole business with Mohammed Ishmael.

The Nation of Islam, the NOI, was dreaded and feared . . . and had been herded into the War Zones. She remembered that when the zones had first been created, her father had called them "ghettoes," a word that was chilling to the daughter of a Jew, openly discriminated against during her teenage years after the Masada Option. But she'd been prepared for the discrimination. She'd grown up with terror that had emanated from her father, no matter how hard he tried to hide it. Germans had run the country from the time she was scarcely more than a toddler until she was almost a teenager, and, though they bent over backwards to disassociate themselves from their ancient Nazi past, the Germans nonetheless exhibited the kind of authoritarianism that made her father fear a concentration camp was being built around every corner.

She winced, and kept her eyes closed. Ugly. So ugly, the ways of humankind in its prejudices and hatreds and violence. People had been divided and pitted against each other by racial, religious, or ethnic differences ever since she could remember. She rarely let herself think about all that she and Dan and others had suffered, because it hurt too much. Tears collected in the corners of her still closed eyes.

Dan had told her the worst of his suffering had begun with the Safe Streets Act of 2005, when it had become almost illegal to have dark skin. The Act freed ignorant, prejudiced white Americans from the hypocrisy of political correctness to allow them to express their hatred openly. The curfews, housing restrictions, and other indignities imposed by the law had confined Africks to certain areas of cities and towns throughout the country and curtailed their liberty to a few restricted daylight hours. Along with successive and even more oppressive laws, the Streets Act had been responsible for creating the Zones; the rise of the militant Africk Islamic fundamentalists had been responsible for the modifier before "Zones"—War. No one knew precisely what went on within the War Zones. The NOI was supposed to be indoctrinating Africks, arming them, training them, and, indeed, there were violent skirmishes with the Federal Police Force ringing the zones that gave credence to all the rumors about what went on within.

The most wanted "criminal" of them all? Mohammed Ishmael. The man's background of forceful resistance against the FPF, his rhetoric—well, everything about him, Lanie thought—made him one of the most wanted, hated, and allegedly dangerous men on the planet. Why had Crane brought him to this meeting? He should have foreseen the disruptive effect. More to the point, why had Dan made the contact with Mohammed Ishmael, who was known not to speak with any white person, and helped to get him here? Dan had supported the *idea* of NOI at the University of China, San Diego, been booted out, and very nearly ruined all his prospects. It made no sense. For Dan.

Lanie suddenly could see Crane's strategy. As well as Mohammed Ishmael, he had induced Kate Masters, the head of the Women's Political Association, and Aaron Bloom, the head of the Association of Retired Persons, to attend. Ishmael, Masters and Bloom represented *the* voting blocs in the United States of America. They were Crane's stick with Liang Int, the real power. And the earthquake prediction project was the carrot Crane offered them all, the opportunity to save lives and property and trauma among their constituencies, or at least appear to do so . . . appear to care. And Liang Int was, of course, interested in the man-hours and buildings and equipment to be saved . . . protecting profit. Lanie shook her head sadly. Profit was the motivator of almost everyone everywhere in the world. Everyone except Crane and the handful of people like him and like her and Dan.

A gong sounded.

Lanie levered herself out of the deck chair, feeling more ambivalent than she ever had. Part of her wanted to run away from the politicos below; the other half wanted to race toward the excitement that Crane generated and the potential he was gambling everything on to realize tonight.

THE GREAT RIFT, THE PACIFIC OCEAN

Chapter 3

18 JUNE 2024, THE WITCHING HOUR

A huge submarine, its bubbled-out glass foresection like a giant, staring eye, sat starboard of the *Diatribe*, dwarfing the yacht. Deckhands were slipping out of the conning tower to throw lashing ropes to their counterparts on the yacht as the guests reassembled on its deck. *VEMA II* was emblazoned on the hull of the sub.

"Prepare to spend the rest of tonight beneath the ocean," Crane announced. "I promise you an experience you'll never forget."

"Rift runner," Newcombe said beneath his breath.

"Rift runner?" Lanie asked.

"Yeah. We're going to see a mother giving birth."

"Mother . . . what mother?"

"Mother Earth," he replied.

Within minutes they'd all been herded into *VEMA II*'s

observation hall. Crane stood at the head of a long table and smiled at the aggregate of crooks and bastards sitting before him. In all the world, he had determined, these were the people who could best give him what he had to have, and a more intensely self-serving lot of rogues he'd never seen. Camus had said that politics and the fate of mankind are shaped by men without ideals and without greatness. So be it. If he couldn't talk sense, he'd put on a show. It was, after all, how he'd survived the thirty years since the death of his parents.

"I must ask that each of you stretch out your hands and touch the person next to you," he said. "We need to be sure that this is the real thing." Everyone reached out to perform the ritual, checking to see that the bodies on either side were real. Legal, binding negotiations could not be undertaken by holo projections.

The observation windows were locked down, shuttered tight as Sumi moved fluidly through the crowd, replenishing drinks doctored with dorph. Newcombe sat beside Ishmael, their heads together, talking low as everyone else stared at them.

"Civilization exists," Crane said, "by geological consent, subject to change without notice. With all the wonders we've created for ourselves, we're still terrorized by the world we live in. The question is why?"

The room was large, perhaps fifty feet long and thirty wide, by far the largest enclosed space ever put on a sub. It was bare, utilitarian, but met the needs of the scientists and sailors who worked this ship on the edge of the rift. Diffuse lighting glowed instead of brightening the room. The ship occasionally shuddered slightly to the sound of a tiny thump, which the audience assumed to be engine noises. Crane knew better; so did Newcombe.

Crane walked slowly around the table. "Our planet is nearly five billion years old and still seems to be primordially forming itself, tearing itself to pieces minute by minute."

"The nature of life is struggle, doctor," Brother Ishmael said.

Crane stopped walking and addressed the man. "And the nature of Man is to try and rise above the struggle."

"To deny God!" Ishmael persisted.

"To make a better world." Crane returned to his place, his good hand clasping his bad behind his back. His left arm was throbbing. He faced the group again. "There are over a million earthquakes a year, on the average of one every thirty seconds. Most are not felt, but about three thousand a year do make their way to the surface, of which thirty engender appalling devastation. The tendency is to say it has always been so and always will be." He looked at Mohammed Ishmael. "I disagree. How many of you really know what forces drive these quakes?"

"Please, just continue with the briefing," Mui, Li's associate, said.

"This is much more than a briefing," Crane replied. "The Earth we live on is made up of huge tectonic plates, twenty-six in all, six majors. The plates move fluidly on a cushion of hot, nearly liquid mantle. Ninety-five percent of all earthquakes occur in what are called subduction zones where the moving plates crash into each other, the plates that hold the oceans of the world literally crawling beneath the continental plates."

The sub shook again, this time more noticeably. "Is there some . . . problem with the boat?" asked Rita Gabler, a hand to her throat.

"No, none at all. Let me return to the subject. The oceanic plates are feeding themselves back into the core once they subduct beneath the continents," he said, his voice louder now to get over the nearly continual banging and shivering of the VEMA. He could feel the tension thick in the air, smiled at the sweat that had broken out on the faces of those in his audience. "Once the plate subducts, it begins a long process of transformation that results in . . . this."

He hit a console button on the table, the metal curtains sliding open immediately. Before them, the ocean glowed red-orange, brilliant. Belches of lava rose between the peaks of undersea mountains in an unbroken line as far as they could see in either direction, and they could see fire for many miles. The participants were hushed to silence in the face of magnificent turmoil on a planetary scale. This was how Crane wanted his audience—humbled.

"Rebirth!" Crane said loudly, moving right up to the window and pointing out with his good hand. "What you are looking at is the Earth repairing itself. Basaltic magma is rising from the asthenosphere and forcing itself between those incredible peaks and valleys beneath you only to cool in the ocean waters, form more peaks, then push the plate thousands of miles into more subduction."

VEMA shook hard, for the rebirth of the planet was accompanied by continual earthquakes.

"Is it . . . dangerous for us here?" Mr. Li asked, his even tone betraying no emotion.

"Only if we walk outside," Crane said, laughing. He turned to watch the beating heart of the Earth Mother that had indirectly killed his own mother. They were five hundred yards from the plasmic rift, the Pacific Rift. The sight of the orange-red liquid fire filled him with awe and anger, and he let his emotions spill over before turning back to the people he needed if ever he was to tame that fire.

"Come to the window," he urged them. "Come look at the open wound that gives much, but causes humanity such pain and heartache."

They rose tentatively. He wanted them to trust the sub, to trust Man's ability to control his own environment. It was sucking them in, he could feel it, the temperature rising in the room, bright red light from the eruptions dancing over their faces. It was the primal power of an entire planet unleashed.

"Incredible," Lanie said, her voice hushed. She moved around to face Crane, her eyes reflecting the fire from without and from within. He smiled, knowing what she was feeling, knowing that she would be the perfect tool to help forge his vision. She was a dynamo, a natural.

So, too, was Kate Masters, who'd moved close and was eyeing him. Finally, she spoke. "What has any of this to do with me?"

"You're my hammer, ma'am," he said. "To make these fine people do the right thing." He turned and pointed to

Brother Ishmael, then to the gray-haired Aaron Bloom of ARP. "So are you . . . my hammers."

"I'm not sure," Gabler said, "but I think we've just been insulted."

"Let me handle the business discussion, Mr. Vice President," Li said, making no effort to hide his contempt for his front man.

Crane continued around the table, stopping behind Newcombe and King. "With the help of these two able people, plus your assistance, I guarantee you that I can produce within a few years a computer program that will predict to the hour every earthquake that will happen on Earth. The program will tell not only where the quake will occur, but its magnitude, the strength of its P and S waves, the areas of primary, secondary, and tertiary damages. We will be able to tell you where it's safe to stand and when to get out of the way."

"Show me the profit," Li said, Mui nodding his Tweedledum agreement.

There was laughter farther down the table. "Excuse me," said a bald man with a red beard, a representative from the insurance industry who sat next to a brunette from the Krupp empire. "Such a program would render insurance companies able to write policies on earthquake damage that make sense. We've been studying the figures since we left Guam. With knowledge of the kind you could supply, we could deny insurance in major damage areas, perhaps even pass laws to keep people from building there. In the secondary areas we could legislate building regulation. In existing businesses, foreknowledge enables breakable items to be stored beforehand. It would save billions a year—billions, I might add, that are then available to be loaned to you industrial producers to expand your own businesses which will earn further billions. A perfect circle."

"Impressive," Li said.

"You'd know where not to build factories, dams, and power plants," Crane said. "Armed with my program, you'd lose nothing in a time of disaster, not man-hours lost to casualties, not downtime for rebuilding and repairs."

"That hurts the building industry, then," the Wang International spokesman said, and Crane thought of the *namazu*.

"Wait a minute," Newcombe said, standing. "You're stacking the building industry up against the loss of ten to fifteen thousand lives every year. How can you—"

"That's all right, Dan," Crane said, nodding the man back to his seat. "We all inherently care about the value in human lives saved, am I right?"

There was a low mumble of semi-agreement around the table. "There . . . see?" Crane said. "Everyone's heart is in the right place." He looked at Li and Mui. "Have you considered the value of exclusive rights to my program?"

"An exclusive." Li smiled. "An interesting thought."

"This would be meant for the world," Newcombe said, a hint of anger in his voice.

"Certainly it is," Li replied, "but at what price? If we held the cards, we could sell the information to competing countries on major disasters. Or not."

Mui laughed and took a drink. "We could make the Earth pay for itself."

"On the yacht you mentioned re-election," Gabler said, shifting uneasily in his chair.

"Think about it, Mr. Vice President," Crane said. "It would seem the ultimate humanitarian gesture. The people of the United States see that their government, the government they thought didn't care about them in this pay-as-you-go world, is willing to go all out to gather the knowledge to protect its citizens. It'd be worth a sweep in California alone."

"And what would you get out of the deal?" Masters asked.

"I get what it takes to do the job right," he said. "This sub we're riding in belongs to the Geological Survey. I want it. I need every bit of knowledge I can get my hands on. I want control of the thousands of seismographs we've planted over this globe, and absolute access to everyone else's. I want the Geological Survey's Colorado headquarters and their database. I won't fire anyone. They'll simply work for me. I want the entire Global Positioning System, satellites doing nothing but working for me for the next five years. And I want an open checkbook to fund my operations. No overseers."

"You've got guts, all right," Ishmael said. "What makes you think these power boys are going to share anything with you?"

"That's where you come in, Brother," Crane said. "You and Ms. Masters and Mr. Bloom. You three control millions of votes in the major metropolitan areas. With your backing, we could—"

"You don't have my backing," Ishmael said simply, standing. "We don't take handouts from white men. We don't vote for white men. We are self-sufficient."

"I'm not talking about handouts," Crane said, incredulous. "I'm talking about disaster planning. Can you imagine what would happen to the War Zone in LA if the San Andreas Fault—"

"You don't understand me," Ishmael said, his voice low. "We take nothing from the white animal and we give nothing. Your silly talk about earthquakes makes me laugh." He pointed to the window with its view of roiling lava. "This is the will of Allah."

"That's not sensible, Brother Ishmael," Crane said. "If it helps you to save lives, why not take advantage of it?"

"There are worse things than death, doctor. Submission is one. Submission brings slavery and degradation, life worse than any animal knows."

Crane looked sadly at the floor. "Death is pretty bad," he said. "It ends everything."

"We all live forever in the kingdom of Allah," Ishmael said. "But you wouldn't understand that."

"I try, sir." Pain choked Crane's voice. "I really do."

"Why are you here?" Gabler asked Ishmael.

"I came here because—" began Ishmael.

Alarms beeped loudly on the Secret Servicemen. "Sirs," one of them said, ripping a small scanner from his belt, "we're picking up some form of surveillance . . . microwave transmission."

"Isolate," Li said, everyone talking now, confusion filling the room as the jumpsuited men moved about, trying to read the signal.

"We scanned," Crane said. "There was nothing."

A whistle sounded, followed by the voice of Captain Long over the intercom. "Dr. Crane, we're picking up microwave generation from somewhere in the foresection . . . in your area."

"Must have been turned on in the last few seconds," Crane said, punching up the intercom on the table. "Thank you, Captain. We're isolating down here."

"As I was saying," Ishmael interrupted, "I came here so I could move through your government's webs of baffles and bullshit and present you, face to face, with our list of demands. Though your government does not recognize our government, we do exist. And we intend to be heard."

"What are you talking about?" Gabler said, his hands shaking as his men hurried their scan.

"Autonomy," Ishmael said. "Self-rule . . . an Islamic State in North America covering the areas now occupied by the states of Florida, South Carolina, North Carolina, Georgia, Alabama, Louisiana, and Mississippi."

"We're close!" one of the scanners called as he and his counterpart converged near the hatchway.

Ishmael, calm in a growing tempest, took a palm-size disc from his dashiki and slid it down the length of the polished table to Gabler. Li grabbed it.

"Our plan for self-rule is outlined on this disc," Ishmael said, "which is just now being shown to billions of viewers all over the globe. We demand secession, Mr. Vice President. We demand it now!"

"This isn't the proper setting," Gabler said. "I do not accept your words or your disc."

"Here!" one of the techs yelled, pulling something off the wall with a long pair of tweezers and running back to the table. He dropped the miniature camera, no bigger than a pinhead, on the table in front of Gabler, who promptly picked it up and swallowed it. "This . . . this scene was transmitted."

"It certainly was," Ishmael said. "The world now has

heard me and our demands—and seen you in action, Mr. Vice President."

"I doubt very much if the citizens in the states you mentioned would find your claims very legitimate," Gabler said.

"Perhaps your forefathers should have thought of that before they kidnapped my people from their homeland in slave boats and brought them here." Ishmael smiled, then walked to a silent Crane. "I don't care about you or your earthquakes, but I thank you for giving me the opportunity of meeting with Mr. Gabler and his, ah . . . handlers. Now, I believe I'll get some rest in my cabin."

"You are a cruel man," Crane said.

"No," Ishmael said, shaking his head. "I'm a dreamer like you. But I have different dreams."

"No dream, sir. A nightmare of bloodshed, anguish and uncertainty. Just remember one thing: Your issue is important for a time, mine for all time."

"This package you're trying to sell these fools isn't your game at all. You want more, much more."

Crane stared coldly at him. "Good night, Brother Ishmael."

The man strode from the deck, Sumi Chan hurrying to catch him.

"Well, this is wonderful, isn't it?" Gabler said, petulant. He took the disc from Li and stared at it as if it were a dead rat. "We could have had this meeting in Washington, under *my* security."

"At this juncture," Crane said, "you *must* take my suggestions if you want to survive. Ishmael just made a fool out of you, Mr. Vice President, before the entire world. You can either leave it at that or rethink the situation. All the latest polls I've seen show a large and growing segment of the United States population wanting some sort of closure with its own citizens in the War Zone. Caucasians now form only thirty percent of the total electorate. You can use my plan to make it look as if you have extended the hand of friendship to the Nation of Islam only to have it slapped away. If you follow through with my plan, it shows you have the best interests of all citizens at heart no matter how they treat you. If you don't, I take the issue to your opposition. *They* won't mind looking like humanitarians."

Gabler had cocked his head like a dog and was, apparently, thinking, or, Crane mused, trying to. "I'll just bet you Mr. Li understands," Crane added, the Chinese man smiling in return.

"We have reached a decision, Dr. Crane," he said.

Crane took a deep breath to calm himself, to not let the facade down. "Yes," he said.

"I would ask everyone to leave the room."

Crane nodded and looked at Newcombe, the man's expression revealing both irritability—he'd get over it—and excitement.

Within thirty seconds, Li and Crane were alone across the table.

"You are an interesting man, Dr. Crane."

"As are you, sir."

"You know, of course, that we could never give you carte blanche with the government checkbook."

"But, I—"

Li raised his hand for silence. "I've played with you this far. Now it's my turn. If, and I emphasize the word if, we're able to work together, you will need someone to oversee the project. I'm not averse to someone we're both comfortable with, say, Sumi Chan, for instance."

"Sumi?"

"We're not difficult men to deal with." His drink sat before him. "We like Americans. You're all so clever with your hands. You people make the most amazing gadgets. Quite extraordinary."

"You said *if* we work together?"

"Well, yes. Certainly." The man picked up the glass and drank, then poured the rest of Mui's drink in his and finished that also. "Everyone is very excited about your idea, but you are asking private industry and the government to turn a great deal of responsibility over to you, all on the strength of one demonstration."

"What are you getting at?"

"Simple, Dr. Crane." Li smiled, his eyes cunning. "You

may have everything you asked for. But we must know, for sure, that you are what you say you are."

"And how do I do that?"

"Once again—simple. Predict another major quake, something big, high profile. Do it before the election. This is May. It gives you six months. If, indeed, thirty major quakes occur a year, that should be plenty of time."

"Is that all?"

"No," Li replied. "Give us something close to home. Something the voters will really understand. And then, Dr. Crane, the world is yours."

THE *DIATRIBE*—OFF THE CALIFORNIA COAST 19 JUNE 2024 10:12 A.M.

"Of course we're under surveillance," Brother Ishmael told Crane.

Newcombe sat between them, listening intently. They were in the yacht's twenty-foot dining room, paneled and brass-trimmed. Ishmael had stayed on after everyone, including his own bodyguards, had left. Newcombe wondered why.

"Everyone's under some sort of surveillance all the time. It's the nature and the chief employment of your white man's world. People watch, and other people watch them. Machines watch machines. Why?"

"We're insufferably curious, I suppose," Crane replied amiably. "Plus, what gets invented gets perfected, then used. It's human nature. And not everybody gets watched. Those who can afford it hire people who can . . . outwit the technology."

Ishmael smiled and pointed a long finger. "Then *that* person watches you. And don't forget the person who watches him."

"You don't have survie units in the War Zone?" Newcombe asked Ishmael, who treated Newcombe with warmth and respect.

"Yes, we do," he said. "We use them on the whites, just as the whites attempt to use them on us. Like Dr.

Crane, we spend a lot of time outwitting the technology. My people tell me that this conversation is being recorded right now by a device called Listening Post #528, whose low space orbit carried it within our range until . . ."—he looked at his watch—"two forty-five P.M."

Lanie sat directly across from Newcombe, her eyes bright. "If we're being listened to, why are you talking?"

"It's part of our political agenda. We're prepared to present to the white population the reasons why we cannot share the same society. You, and the world, are listening to my reasoning. If I have anything private to say, I will say it privately."

"You are using me shamelessly," Crane said. He slugged heavily on a glass full of straight bourbon. "Look, Brother Ishmael. I have a great deal of respect for you. I don't even mind being used by you and your cause right now, but dammit, man, give something in return, a little support. I just want what's best for everyone."

"No," Ishmael said. "You don't want to help people; you want to slay the beast. I can see it in your eyes when you talk about earthquakes. You hate the earthquakes. God wrought their majesty, but you have the gall to hate His creation. I feel sorry for you and your windmills, and I pray to Allah you never get the power to vent your hatred."

"You're a hard kind of fellow," Crane said. "Sure, I hate the beast. I hate it the way the Cretans hated the Minotaur. Is it wrong to hate a monster? Wasn't it Malcolm X who said, 'When our people are being bitten by dogs, they are within their rights to kill those dogs'? I hate it because of the lives and dreams it destroys and I will find a way to blunt its sword with or without your help. There, I'm talking to the world, too." He snorted. "Do you really think you'll have your Islamic State?"

Ishmael nodded slowly. "We will have an Islamic nation," he replied. "In a fractured world, we are the dominant force."

"It didn't work that way in the Middle East," Lanie said.

"The Jewish entity chose to destroy itself rather than

face the reality of Islam," Ishmael said. "The Masada Cloud is the reminder of Allah's power over the Infidel. There are no more Jews in Palestine."

"There's nobody in Palestine," Crane snapped. "And there won't be. How can you presume to know who should live and who should die?" He stood. "I want everyone to live."

"Jungles don't work that way," Ishmael returned, "and neither do earthquakes. You can't bring your parents back, doctor."

"Please, don't try to analyze me." Crane picked up his drink, finished it with a scowl. "I'm going up to observation. Is it safe for you to be on board, Brother Ishmael?"

"I don't know, is it?"

"I'm not powerful enough to protect you. Anyone want to join me?"

"Sure," Lanie said, picking up her coffee and adding another spoonful of dorph to it.

As Newcombe started to rise, Ishmael put a hand out. "Stay with me, Brother Daniel. I want to speak with you."

Newcombe nodded. "Watch the sun up there," he said to Lanie. "I'll join you shortly."

Newcombe watched Lanie and Crane walk to the dining room hatchway where they donned coats, gloves, goggles, and hats, Crane pulling a tube of sunblock from his pocket to smear on their exposed faces. He opened the hatch, bright sunlight pouring in. Lanie waved at him and left.

Newcombe and Lanie spent a good deal of time with each other, and he was cautiously letting himself dream again of home and family, something—anything—besides Crane's relentless pursuit of his monsters. He'd even talked Lanie into moving in with him when they got back to the Foundation.

"Why are you with the white woman, Brother?"

"I love her."

"She is your oppressor. Not just a white woman, but a Jewess."

Newcombe's jaw muscles tightened. "She's a Cosmie."

"Judaism is a race, not a religion."

"I do not accept the philosophies of the Nation of Islam. I'm an Africk in America and I'm doing very well, thank you. I'm not oppressed; I'm the master of my own fate. Well educated, intelligent, I have risen to the top of my field—and I have chosen the woman I wish to spend my life with."

"Then why are you working for someone like Crane? Why don't you have your own labs, your own grants?"

Anger rose like mercury through Newcombe's body. "Who have you been talking to?"

Ishmael leaned close and spoke in a whisper so low Newcombe had almost to touch heads with him to hear. "I've stayed aboard to speak with you. The NOI needs you. Your brothers call out to you."

"I don't think so," Newcombe replied, uncomfortable now.

"Nation of Islam will need men of learning, intelligence and insight into the white society in order to build our new world. Our communities are fragmented, distanced from each other, surrounded in thirty different cities. We need room and we need physical unity desperately. We're engaged in a literal state of war. We will take what we must have—God's *sharia* and a wise caliphate will become a reality. Everyone will have to choose up sides."

"I've nearly destroyed my career once because of my public support for an Islamic state. Since our televised encounter on *VEMA,* I've taken a long step toward destroying it again. The cause of a homeland is just, but you've already drained my blood."

"You have no place in the white man's world except as his lackey," Ishmael whispered. "You want a better world. So do I. I'm telling you I can help you accomplish that goal far better than the evil man you work for."

"Evil? Crane?"

"He is of the Darkness, Daniel. I am of the Light."

"You're wrong. Crane's like me."

"You don't believe that for a minute. You know how crazy he is."

Shaken, Newcombe said nothing.

"Crane is a marked man with no real power base,"

Ishmael continued. "Our Jihad has begun. Political affili-ation with NOI will bring you power, recognition, respect. You can accomplish. You can call the tune. I will make of you an Islamic hero."

"Sounds like a jail sentence to me."

"Hear me out, Brother." Ishmael, majestic in his mid-night-slick dashiki, got to his feet. "Our world will come. It holds a place for you with people who love you. Believe me when I tell you there is no place in the white devil's world for an Africk with too much education. They'll make you a glorified shoeshine man. Crane is already do-ing it."

"You're wrong."

"Not about Crane, not about the woman. Brother, I'm the only one you can trust. The righteous anger of the Honorable Elijah Muhammad, Malcolm X, Louis Farra-khan, and Saladin the Prophet runs through my veins. Your 'friends' hate you and will always hate you. You will reach your full potential only within the Nation of Islam." He bent low and wrote on a pad of paper on the table: *Commit this number to memory. It's a safe line to me.*

Newcombe memorized the number, never expecting to use it, then tore up the paper on which it was written.

Ishmael walked over and stared out of a tinted porthole. The ocean was calm today, reflecting the sun in blinding sabers. He turned to Newcombe. "You think I do not know you," he whispered. "But you are wrong. I knew you in the jungle, and in the slave boats, and wearing the ox-yoke in the fields. I knew you when they wrenched you from your home and hung you from a tree or buried you in their jails to keep you off their streets. I knew you when they promised you freedom and gave you only the freedom to starve. I knew you, Brother, when they fed you their poisons of alcohol and drugs, and gave you guns to kill yourself. I knew you when they finally got tired of you and turned their backs completely, hoping you'd die in the jungle of concrete that *they* had built. Don't ever say I don't know you. I know you as you'd know yourself, if you'd open your eyes."

"They're going to arrest you, you know," Newcombe

said, his voice choked with emotion. "Can't you get out of here?"

Brother Ishmael merely smiled.

Sumi Chan's face blipped onto Li Cheun's screen. "I have called," he said, "to report, as you have asked, about Dr. Crane. He will be docking this afternoon and returning to the Foundation."

"Excellent. Have you seen to the planting of the surveillance equipment in his residence and laboratories?"

"Yes, Mr. Li."

Li watched Sumi's eyes narrow almost imperceptibly. "Are you having a problem with this assignment?"

"No, sir," Sumi said quickly. "It's simply that I have been a major supporter of Dr. Crane for many years and know him personally—"

"Let me be clear on this point, Sumi," Li said, gratified to see an element of fear creep onto the face floating a foot from him. "I can elevate or destroy you. If you work for the Geological Society, you work for me. If you issue grants it is I who is doing the issuing. If you do not want this job—"

"Sir, I condemn my thoughts. I am totally committed to you and to Liang International."

"Crane is your job, not your brother."

"Yes, sir. Excuse me, sir."

"Not at all. You're doing fine work. Please hold."

Li looked at Mui, who froze Sumi Chan's face in mid-grimace. "Tell me about Ishmael," Li said.

"General fear and negative reaction to demand for Islamic state," Mui said, reading directly from his screen. "*Very* negative reaction from the southern states he mentioned as location for a new Nation of Islam. Early analysis points to Yo-Yu candidates playing up the fear factor and using it to their advantage in the next elections."

"I see," Li said, an idea forming. "Put Mr. Chan back on."

Sumi's face re-formed, looking more relaxed. He'd hit the dorph hard while on hold.

"Sir," Li said, "I have great faith in you. Is Brother Ishmael still on board the *Diatribe*?"

"He was when I spoke with Crane a few minutes ago."

Li muted his wristpad and looked at Mui. "Put the Federal Police Force on this. See if they can arrest him while he's still on the boat. Charge him with sedition. We want him alive . . . tell them that."

Mui banged on the keypad, then pointed out of the darkness at Li. "Los Angeles elements of the FPF have been notified. The G is en route."

Li nodded curtly, then rewired Chan. "What I want you to do now is take a helo and pick up Dr. Crane, transporting him to the Foundation with our compliments. We will release enough money to you to keep the Foundation running on-line toward its goal. We'll give Crane everything he wants . . . for now. Spend a great deal of time at the Foundation. It is now your main obligation, and we will find someone else to handle your day-to-day activities with the Geological Survey. Understand?"

"Yes, sir. Thank you sir."

"Stay in the shade, Mr. Chan."

"Same to you, Mr. Li."

Mui blanked Chan's head as Li stared at California. Crane had bullied his way into the arena and made himself a player, Li thought. Fine. Now Crane would have to live with it.

Standing next to Lanie on the observation deck, Crane fidgeted, but not from the heat of his clothing and the brilliant sunlight doubling its force through reflection off the water. He was going stir-crazy, confined to the boat. And his arm throbbed dully. Action somewhere. Not close or the arm would have hurt. Still, there was a rising feeling of pain. He rubbed his arm.

Lanie's eyes widened. "What is it?"

"Something . . . just happened," he said, insides tight. "And I'm stuck here in the middle of the goddamned ocean."

"Is it close," Lanie asked, "a deep subduction trench quake, beneath us perhaps?"

Crane shook his head, his full attention on a flock of birds a hundred meters off the port bow. They were too big and were closing fast. "This part of the ocean isn't subducting. California lies on a transform fault, the Pacific Plate and the North American Plate rubbing against each other as they move in different directions. We'd know if something was going on there. But thanks."

"For what?"

"Not questioning my intuition."

The birds had attracted Lanie's attention, too. She watched them with a frown. "Dan says that you feel it in your arm."

"What else?"

She turned and smiled at him. "He knows it must work because he can feel your feelings as a sharp pain."

"In the ass?"

"Yeah. Those birds over there . . . aren't they awfully large for gulls?"

"Too big and too noisy. Hear the hum?"

"No."

He watched as they glided close, their little focus motors whirring—radio-controlled cameras disguised as gulls searching for them. "I think the press corps has ferreted us out."

The cams swooped low over the deck, news broadcast logos on their sides, then swung gracefully out to sea, making a wide circle around the *Diatribe*, then tightening the circle.

"We must be getting close," Lanie said. "Did you see the unmarked birds?"

Crane nodded. "FPF, the G. They're keeping tabs on Brother Ishmael. My bet is that they'll try and take him before we dock."

"There's nothing you can do?"

"He should have left when his bodyguards did, right after the meeting. I can't believe he stayed."

One of the unmarked birds buzzed the deck, Crane swatting at it as it passed within a foot of him. "Thank you for welcoming us back to America!" he called through cupped hands to the rest of the hovering cams. "We'll be looking forward to meeting with many of you upon our return." Then he whispered, "Bastards."

He waved with his good hand, urging Lanie to smile and wave also.

"Look at the clouds," Lanie said. Crane looked up to see his smiling, waving face projected onto cumulus clouds fifty thousand feet high.

"Those bulges make me look fat," he said, then raised a finger. "Let's have some fun with them. Stay here."

He hurried down the ladder, laughing, and to the lifeboat tethered on the main deck, grabbing the survival kit before hurrying back to observation.

"What are you doing?" she asked as he opened the aluminum box and sorted through it.

"Must be here somewhere," he said low, then, "Ha!" He pulled a flare gun out of the box and held it triumphantly in the air. "If the world is watching us, then let's give them a show they'll remember."

"You're not serious," she said, backing several paces away from him.

"I'm always serious," he returned and shoved a fat shell into the single chamber. He snapped it closed, and raised the gun with his good hand. He fired right into the midst of the fifteen gulls. A whump, then a pale red tracer tracked upward into the flock, the flare bursting bright red on impact.

"Bulls-eye!" Lanie said, clapping as two gulls, in pieces, went into the ocean, a third moving off, losing altitude by the second. The wounded bird was unmarked, FPF obviously. The bird disappeared behind a swell five hundred meters from the *Diatribe*, all the other cams turning in that direction to watch.

He reloaded and handed the gun to Lanie. "Want to try one?"

"Can I get into trouble for this?"

"Who cares?"

She pulled the trigger, bringing down a newscam in a white hot rain of shimmering magnesium. The remaining gulls scattered and put more distance between themselves and their hunters.

Crane could see boats dotting the ocean, converging, the curious or the professional turning out to see the earthquake man. Beyond the boats, the distant outline of land filled the horizon. They were home.

"Good shooting!" Crane yelled, the sky now covered with clouds, all of them showing television pictures, people tuning in through their aurals.

"I think you may be right about the FPF coming for Mohammed Ishmael." Lanie pointed to several innocuous-looking speedboats.

"I'm going to get down there and try and stop them." Crane dropped the box and hoisted a leg over the ladder.

Boats drew alongside, their decks filled with men in white jumpsuits with white hoods and standard issue facesaver masks with built-in goggles. They were armed.

Lanie caught up with Crane as he was about to enter the dining room. "Do you know what you're doing?" she asked, grabbing his bad arm.

"No," he said. She had beautiful, inquisitive eyes. They told the truth. "I've been making it up since Ishmael dropped his bombshell back on *VEMA*. I took a shot, needed all the cards to fall right. Ishmael screwed it up enough to queer things."

"But you've got the deal."

"I've got nothing."

Loudspeakers squawked from all around them. "This is the Federal Police Force," a pleasant female voice whispered like thunder. "We have been authorized to detain Leonard Dantine, a.k.a. Mohammed Ishmael, in accordance with the Safe Streets Control Act of 2005."

"I think this will play badly in the polls," Crane said, watching white-faced ghosts climb onto *Diatribe*'s main deck.

The galley door banged open, Newcombe sticking his head out. "Can't we do anything to stop them?"

"Is stopping them the right thing to do?" Crane replied, then waved off Newcombe's angry scowl. "I'll try."

The gangway was filled with men in white, coming at them fore and aft and from above. Lanie was right on Crane's heels.

"What do you mean you don't have a deal?" she asked. "I thought Li—"

"Li told me I'd have to do it again." He stepped up to address the uniformed person before him. The G was anonymous—the source of their strength and their power to produce fear.

"This ship is outside the territorial waters of the United States," Crane said. "You are, consequently, outside your jurisdiction and have no right being on board. Kindly leave now."

The G spoke into his pad, then nodded. "Two point nine miles," he said pleasantly, then gestured toward the door. "Is this the only way in or out of that room?"

"No," Lanie said, as Newcombe, angry, made to block entry. "There's a starboard door also."

"He won't run from you," Newcombe said, stepping aside. "He told me."

The G moved into the room in force. Brother Mohammed Ishmael sat calmly at the dining table, smiling beatifically. "Do you gentlemen have a reservation?" he asked.

"On your feet," the lead G said. "You're under arrest."

Ishmael stood. "I'm not of your country. Even so, I have broken none of your laws. You cannot place me under arrest."

"You may make an official statement to the booking robot," said the G, punctiliously polite. "These gentlemen are going to escort you. You may choose the degree of difficulty."

Six men moved forward. Seemingly unarmed, their sleeves bristled with electronic and microwave bands, deadly defensive weapons. They formed a loose cordon around Ishmael, then moved in quickly, grabbing.

They got empty air. Ishmael was transparent as they tried to take him, their arms moving through his body, flailing uselessly.

"A projection." Newcombe laughed. "It's not really him."

"Only since this morning," Ishmael called, walking right through the table and up to Newcombe. He whispered in the man's ear, "Contact me."

The G filed out without a word, the last one handing Crane a bill for the downed gull. Ishmael's laughing projection turned a circle for the remaining gull cams that were perched on the rails looking in through the portholes. "People of the world," he called, "this is how the white animal behaves. In savagery. In hatred. I wanted you to see why we must have our own homeland. Nothing will deter us. It is the will of Allah."

The specter vanished. Crane walked back outside, knowing the government types were going to try and set him up for something with Ishmael to take the heat off themselves. He had to get past it. He moved onto the deck, the gulls flying off, and leaned against the rail, staring out at the G climbing back into their boats. The professional news showed up with the amateur camheads. He sensed Lanie at his arm and turned. Newcombe wasn't with her.

"Li and the others, they made a deal with you," she said. "They have to keep it."

"If I can make another earthquake happen," he whispered, then winked at her.

Scores of boats of all sizes and shapes, a flotilla, surrounded them as they steamed closer to LA. People were waving and calling out to them.

Lanie and he drank in the celebrity, laughing and waving back.

He leaned over the rail and yelled to the closest ship. "Ahoy! What news of earthquakes? I sense something just happened."

A loudspeaker crackled from one of the news boats. "We received word a little while ago. Martinique has been leveled by an eruption of Mount Pelee."

"Don't unpack your bags," he said to Lanie, then put a foot over the rail and climbed down to the main deck, everything forgotten except the chase, the godalmighty, neverending chase.

Chapter 4

GEOMORPHO-LOGICAL PROCESSES

**LOS ANGELES, CALIFORNIA
20 JUNE 2024, 8:47 P.M.**

No one knew Sumi Chan was a woman. No one. The yi-sheng who'd delivered her in great secrecy had died five years ago. Her own parents, who'd engineered the deception after amniocentesis had revealed that their heir would be female, passed away in '22, victims of the St. Louis flu. The flu virus, brought from America by traveling salesmen, had been far more devastating than the flu of 1918, killing hundreds of thousands of people in cities throughout the Far East, while sparing the North American continent with a relatively mild epidemic.

So, for the last two years Sumi had been alone with the lie of her life. And she'd have to go on alone . . . even though her twenty-eight-year masquerade had failed completely in its objective: to inherit her ancestral land, a right forbidden to women. But her birthright no longer existed;

the land had been forfeited to bankruptcy; her parents had died destitute.

Being trapped was the operative experience of Sumi's life. She'd come to America to study science abroad, as was the custom. The U.S. Geological Survey position was a patronage job, simply meant to look good in the long-term corporate portfolio. Now it was all she had, and she feared desperately that her deception would come to light and she would lose her job. Dishonored, she would have nothing. All life was a lie. The only truth Sumi Chan really understood was the fear of exposure that ate away at her.

She sat in the denlike interior of a Liang Corporate helo, a silent eggbeater design favored for its smooth ride, and tried to hold herself together. Crane had been good to her, had given her status and generous amounts of credit for her contributions to his projects. She liked him, too, despite his eccentricities, sometimes even because of them. He didn't deserve what was about to happen to him.

She watched the crowd of perhaps as many as two hundred people approach the Long Beach Harbor dockside landing pad. The sun was down, a clear star-filled night just dripping onto the skyline of the largest city in the western hemisphere. Umbrellas were clasped firmly under arms now as citizens wiped sunblock off their faces and shed their coats and gloves. The freedom of night had arrived.

Newsmen swarming him like gnats, Crane led the long line down the well-lit docks toward her position. Most of the people following Crane were camheads, unemployed or bored citizens who lived to get on the teev, to see themselves projected onto the sites of buildings and clouds. So many people did it that it was no longer an obsession; it was a demographic.

Crane was flanked by Newcombe and the new woman. Why had Crane brought her in? Sumi didn't know what to make of Lanie King. She seemed to have Crane's drive and Newcombe's emotions, a potentially dangerous combination, but more importantly, Sumi feared the woman would see through her ruse, just as she feared all women would see through her.

The crowd arrived, and Sumi opened the bay door fully to admit Crane and his team.

"Hey, Dr. Crane," called a newsman in a gold mandarin jacket, "when's the big one going to hit LA?"

"If I told you it would happen tomorrow," Crane replied, grabbing the sliding door from the inside as Newcombe and King slipped in, "what would you do? That's the question you should ask yourself."

He slid the door closed and fell heavily into a padded swivel chair. He groaned, relaxing for just a second, his good hand coming up to rub slowly over his face. Then the second passed and he snapped up to the edge of the chair and looked at Sumi. "What the hell are we waiting for?"

Sumi touched the small grille in the arm of the chair. "Go," she said, the helo rising within seconds. She smiled at Crane. "Next stop, the mosque."

"The mosque?" Lanie asked as she wiped the rest of the sunblock from her face with a towel.

"It's what Sumi calls the Foundation," Newcombe said, stretching. "You'll see when we get there."

"Do you have updates on the Pelee?" Crane asked.

"Not with me," Sumi said.

"Give me what you know off the top. Martinique is in the Antilles Chain, right?"

"Yes."

Newcombe barged in before she could go on. "There could be more eruptions."

"Already have been," Sumi said. "Two others . . . smaller. The real problem right now is the weather. Twenty rivers run out of Pelee, all of them bloated, flooding. The mountain has been crumbling . . . coming down as mudslides, carrying away entire villages." Without pause, Sumi asked, "Can I get anyone a drink? Some dorph?"

"No," Crane answered, tapping his wristpad to connect his aural. "Sumi, call the newspeople. I want to take a few of them with me down there or they'll forget who I am by tomorrow. And get Burt Hill at the Foundation.

Tell him I want a dozen emergency medical personnel and a dozen big men."

"Big men?"

"Strong men . . . men who can dig. Good to see you by the way, Sumi."

"Yes, sir," Sumi replied, using the Foundation funded comlink on the chair to set up a forty-way conference memo to the major news organizations.

Crane punched up the exclu-fiber for Harry Whetstone on his key pad. He swiveled to take in the night show of Los Angeles through the bay window while waiting for the call to track down the man. He liked his benefactor, Old Stoney. A great guy. Damned shame his cash, all those billions, was being held hostage by the courts. Kill the lawyers, like Shakespeare said. Still, Stoney had things and people galore at his disposal, so he could provide what was needed.

"Whetstone," came a firm but friendly voice.

"Stoney, this is Crane."

"Hey, great to hear from you. So how the hell did it go with the Big—"

"No time for that now, pal. I want your plane and I need equipment."

"Pelee?"

"I should leave within the hour. Can you get the plane to my landing strip in the next thirty minutes?"

"Sorry, I can only give you a big bird. Old jet with no focus. I'll have to see if it's gassed up. If so, you'll have it on your timetable. If not, it'll take over half an hour just for fueling. I've got access to some heavy equipment I can send along if you'd like."

"God, no," Crane said. "What I need are picks and shovels. Can you get me those?"

"Are you sure you—"

"Picks and shovels, Stoney. Call me back on the Q fiber when you've got an ETA. Hurry."

The city was alive below him, teev pictures seemingly juicing in liquid crystal from every horizontal surface—buildings, billboards, walls and vehicles—the tallest buildings assuming the veneer of life as huge videos filled all twenty and thirty stories of them. They headed north toward Mendenhall Peak in the San Gabriel Mountains.

"Why did the G come on board my ship today?" Crane asked loudly.

Sumi answered with the obvious. She always had to be careful with the truth around Crane. "There is a great deal of negative reaction to Ishmael's demands. People want some sort of action taken. They fear what's stockpiled in the War Zones."

"How is this affecting us?"

"Too early to tell. There's damage . . . we don't know how much."

"But Li's not taking any chances, is he?"

"Mr. Li's a businessman," Sumi said immediately. "What would you expect?"

"I would expect him to protect me and the deal we made," Crane snapped, then waved it off. "This is no surprise." His mind drifted toward damage control. "I just need to run the action myself. I can survive Ishmael."

He sighed and shook off a wave of tiredness. He could sleep on the flight to Martinique. The horror was welling in him. He could feel the suffering. He knew the heart-pounding panic of those trapped within their homes under tons of mud and rock. Tears came and he wiped at his eyes, willing himself quickly into emotional detachment, vital to his getting through disasters like Sado and now Pelee.

He tried to focus on the nightshow below, seeing his Liang helo on many of the teev screens. There were reasons for the outside screens. They were mostly to keep occupied people who were waiting in huge lines for basic necessities. Electronics were cheap and entertaining; they kept a person's mind off the fact that the country's infrastructure was shaky at best. Dingy apartments, chronic food shortages from too few shaded fields in production, lousy wages made electronic consolation the next best thing to dorph.

Below, one of the helos chasing them had dipped too low, its skid catching on the side of a building, the machine smashing nose first onto the flat roof and tumbling, all the citizens running to the scene with their cams. Within seconds, they had passed the site and Crane followed the wreck on teev screens that filled the night.

Several men with crowbars jumped onto the hulk of the helo to steal the focus. Two pried on the ten-inch disc from three sides as another man squeezed into the smoking cockpit in search of survivors.

"Is there anything *good* happening?" Crane asked, his chair still turned facing the bay.

"Kate Masters," Sumi said, "has thrown unconditional support behind your earthquake plan in exchange for the government's allowing the Vogelman Procedure to be billed out on health insurance."

"Great," Crane replied, shaking his head at the thought of the no-pregnancy implant. "Now we're in the birth control business."

Of the hundreds of teev screens below them, half still projected the helo crash. As the vandals got the focus off the wreck, the other man emerged with the disoriented pilot in tow. Both men saw the vandals and attacked, fighting them for the focus. One of the powerful liquid electric cells that resided within could run a house for a year. Many would kill for a cell.

His wristpad blipped, and Crane activated his aural. "Yeah?"

"Stoney," came the response. "The bird is gassed and ready to take off. I've also got a couple thousand picks and shovels in a truck on its way to you from a north LA warehouse."

Below the lights were fading as they reached the blackness of the War Zone, the entrenched and heavily fortified two-by-four-mile stretch of real estate that had once been called East Los Angeles. Brother Ishmael's territory.

"You did good, Stoney," Crane answered. "My best to Katherine."

"Crane . . . about the plane. . . ."

"I won't give it away like the last one. Promise."

"Thanks."

Crane blanked as they passed over the perimeter lights of the troops surrounding the War Zone. The Zone itself was totally netted in thick mesh that covered roofs and sides of buildings. No one had seen inside for years. No one had any idea of how many Africk-Hispanics lived within the Zone or what they did to survive. Troops allowed trucks carrying non-contraband material to go inside; so few went in that many speculated the actual number of Ishmael's followers was quite small. It was a matter of some debate, for a great many children could be born in fifteen years, children with access to nothing but counterculture rhetoric. Young soldiers. The pilot immediately took on altitude when reaching the War Zone.

"We'll be leaving within thirty minutes of arrival," Crane said to Lanie. "You'd better call ahead and have them prepare any equipment you want loaded." He did a quick calculation on his wristpad. "I'm allowing you fifty square feet of storage with a two-ton weight limit."

"I'll make sure our bags are taken right from here to the plane," Newcombe said. "Then I'll get Burt to—"

Crane interrupted. "You're not going. I need you at the Foundation looking for another earthquake . . . any earthquake. The Central American franchises are always a good bet."

"You're taking Lanie and not me?"

Crane couldn't understand the puzzlement on the man's face. "She needs the crash course, doctor," he said, stern. "And you need to save our fannies. End of discussion."

He swiveled away from them, unwilling to deal with Newcombe's emotional life. He needed Newcombe happy, of course, but more than that, he needed him focused.

The helo banked slightly to the west, heading toward the Valley. They were crossing hundreds of fault lines now, LA itself riding atop the Elysian Parks system, a crisscrossed pattern of interconnected faults just powerful enough to bring down the whole city. He shook his head. How many of Brother Ishmael's people would die in such a quake?

The pilot had descended somewhat after passing the War Zone.

They were crossing other faults, too. Bigger faults— Santa Susana, Oak Ridge, San Gabriel, Sierra Madre—all capable of producing huge quakes. Then there was the famous one, the San Andreas Fault thirty miles to the east, an eight-hundred-mile slash. It marked the boundary between the Pacific and North American plates and the location where the buildup of pressure from two massive plates going in different directions would eventually rip apart and carry western California northward. It had been a short thrust fault, the Northridge Fault, that had shaped his life. After his Nobel Prize year, it had been renamed the Crane Fault.

He never understood people asking about the "big one." The earthquake that would destroy Los Angeles could come from any one of a thousand different fault ruptures, be they tectonic or stress from the tectonics. A thousand ways to rip the earth apart, a thousand ways to die. What was most interesting about California was not that it could die so easily, but that it hadn't died yet. That's why Crane had chosen to build his Foundation in the San Gabriel Mountains, mountains formed by thrust fault activity. He wanted to be dead center in the middle of the action. To slay the beast you had to go to its lair.

The helo banked into the Valley, hurrying them to Mendenhall. "Lanie," Crane said, pointing through the bay window, "come get your first look at your new home."

She moved up beside him and he smiled when she gasped in surprise. The Foundation could be reached only by air. Built halfway up the 4,700-foot peak on a rocky outcropping, the Foundation sat in the center of a honeycomb of ruby laser lines, ranging beams set to specific targets that could detect the most minute earth movements. It was science at its most beautiful. Clear red lines against a starlit night.

As they slowly closed on the grounds, they could see Whetstone's supersonic transport circle the mountain once, then dip to the long runway extending out from the working areas of the Foundation.

"My God," Lanie said. "It does look like a mosque."

"Told you," Sumi said, then looked at Crane. "Five newsmen are on their way up here now."

"How soon?"

"They're right behind us. The only people who could get here on your time schedule are the ones who followed us from the docks. Okay?"

"It'll have to be. Make sure they have landing clearance."

"Why does the main building look like a mosque?" Lanie asked.

"Architectural Darwinism," Newcombe replied.

"I don't understand."

They moved through the mesh of laser lines, zeroing on the pad near the main, stone building, massive and square, a large dome sitting atop it. "I built it like a mosque," Crane said, "because I've never known a mosque to get destroyed in an EQ. Some of the Middle Eastern ones stood for a thousand years. Only the execution of the Masada Option could destroy them. The sixteenth-century Ottoman architect, Sinan, used a system of chain reinforcement to earthquake-proof all the public buildings of the time. It worked."

The pilot set the helo down near the mosque, Crane immediately sliding open the bay door, then jumping out. The area was well lit and sprawling. The domed lab was three stories high and set off by itself in the open. A hundred yards away, nestled against the mountain, was the office structure, long and low, like a train. Above the offices, gouged into the side of the mountain, were a series of chalet-style cottages, Foundation residences, built on spring-loaded platforms. There were ten of them, connected up by a series of steel stairways and reaching perhaps a hundred feet above the Foundation grounds. The airstrip, a long glowing tube reaching into the darkness, sat on the other side of the lab. Whetstone's jumbo jet sat perched in its center, its back bay already open, workers hurriedly loading equipment and medical supplies.

Burt Hill came running up as they stepped out of the helo, others landing all around him. "Doc," he called, his full beard bushy, hanging to his chest. "We're getting everything taken care of except the medical people. The ones you took to Sado aren't ready to go back in the field yet."

"I'll bet," Crane said, already moving toward the massive front doors of the lab. "Here's what you do . . . call Richard Branch at the USC med school and tell him to send up stat a dozen of his top students. Tell him we'll give them the best training they've ever had. Got that?"

"Got it," Hill said.

Lanie had developed a soft spot for Burt on Sado, where his performance in the aftermath of the tragedy had thoroughly impressed her. Burt could have been any age between thirty and sixty, but his large, expressive blue eyes looked ancient.

"Oh, Burt," Crane said, "there's a truck full of picks and shovels on its way here. We're going to need to be ready to bring it up."

"We'll roll Betsy out of the hangar first thing. What time you figure on getting out of here?"

"It's nearly ten," Crane said. "Ten-thirty tops. Move."

"You want me to go?" Hill asked.

"Not this time, Burt. You stay here with Dr. Newcombe. Facilitate. The minute you get the chance, I want you to run a security sweep for surveillance gear. Do a class A sweep."

"You're not taking Burt?" asked Newcombe, angry. "What the hell kind of trip is this?"

"I'm not used to having my decisions questioned," Crane said, searing Newcombe with a look.

"Get ready for it, then," Newcombe said. "Because I'm not going to allow Lanie to—"

"You're what?" Lanie said, grabbing Newcombe's arm. Crane held back a smile as he watched the fire climb up her face and ignite her eyes. "You're not going to *allow* me to go? Since when are you my parent, my boss, or God?"

"You don't understand," Newcombe said. "This is much more dangerous than Sado. The last time—"

"Enough!" Crane said, opening the large double doors with the Crane Foundation plaque set in bronze right beside. Nothing mechanical, nothing that could lock up in an emergency. "We'll talk in the control room."

Lanie followed the men into the labs in utter amaze-

ment. The Crane Foundation was the most incredible piece
of property she'd ever seen, bar none. It was perched like
an eagle on a dangerous precipice, daring Nature to challenge it—Crane shaking his fist in the face of God. But
even the spectacle of the Foundation didn't prepare her for
the lab.

The lab was huge, wide open, its center and dome dominated by a three-story-high globe of the world. But it
wasn't just a map. In halos of showering sparks, workers
on cranes and tall ladders were welding at the top of the
shell. The sphere had terrain, complete with land mass
contours and oceans. It was only partially finished, and in
its innards she could see millions of tiny wires as well as
now empty vacuum tubes and flasks, obviously placed to
receive materials at a later date. A central core looked like
a small blast furnace. Lanie understood immediately.

"You're making the world," she said, and was surprised
to find her own voice raspy.

"This is all yours," Crane said easily. "This is why you
were hired."

"Mine?"

"You're going to duplicate the historical development
of our planet, Ms. King, the current conditions on it—"

"You're going to hinge your ability to predict on this?"

Crane's eyes were hard and playful at the same time, a
gambler's eyes, Lanie thought.

"No," he answered softly, "we hinge it on you. The
globe will be your tool, but you'll have help in forging the
tool. Too much help, I'm afraid you're going to think sometimes." His eyes were dancing with deviltry and exuber-
ance, and he took Lanie's breath away. "Ah, those helpers.
Now you'll have botanists, biologists, physicists—"

Newcombe interrupted. "We can talk about this another time. We have something to straighten out right
now." His tone was harsh.

"Certainly," Crane said, turning and walking off. Newcombe followed as if stalking him. Lanie trailed after,
walking backward, unable to keep her eyes off the monstrous sphere that was to be hers—hers to do what with?
She turned then and noticed that she hadn't seen glass

anywhere in the building. There was nothing on the walls that could fall and cause damage. It was straight stone top to bottom; small working labs full of seismographic equipment and computer gear had open doorways, no windows. Everything seemed to be bolted down, lighting provided by tiny, brilliant spots sunk in the block stone of the walls.

On the far side of the open room an entire wall a hundred feet long and two stories high was devoted to miniature seismographs that read out their peaks and valleys in both Richter and the more popular Moment Magnitude scales. There must have been several thousand of them, some beeping, some clanging bell-like. Lanie figured that the ones making noises were detecting the continual EQ's, the louder bells the signals of temblors that had made it to the surface. Far along the wall one of the machines was wailing constantly, almost like a baby. It sent a chill through her—Martinique.

A set of metal stairs marked Off Limits to Everyone was built into the wall beside the scales. Crane and Newcombe already were climbing them to a small blockhouse jutting out of the stone near the ceiling. She hurried to join them, looking up, not down—vertigo was her weakness.

She squeezed through a small doorspace and into the control room. Like a wartime bunker it was small and cramped, the walls covered with control panels that, she guessed, could access and run most of the machinery in the labs. A cutout, rather like a large window in the foot-thick stone wall, looked onto the globe.

Newcombe handed her a set of muffling headphones—both he and Crane were already wearing them—and indicated she should put them on. She did so. Crane, seeming none too happy, punched a button, and a piercing horn blared, the sound painful even through the mufflers. If anyone was listening, they no longer had eardrums.

They removed their mufflers, Crane hitting a button on the panel that energized the room with static electricity to jam any attempted surveillance. The air around them crackled with tiny blue lightning flashes that occasionally tickled Lanie's skin and that made her hair stand on end.

Crane sat heavily on the only chair in the room, then thought better of it and stood. He looked at Newcombe with a blank face. "What?" he said. "Spit it out, Dan."

"You're not taking Lanie to Martinique," he stated flatly, then turned to her, putting a hand up for silence. "Hear me out. You're new to this. You're not trained in lifesaving or survival skills." He jerked around to face Crane again. "She's going to get in your way more than she's going to help."

"Don't be so patronizing, dammit." She was having a hard time controlling the rage at Dan that threatened to overwhelm her. "How else do I get the experience unless I participate?"

"Just listen for a minute, all right?" Newcombe told her, his face set hard. "The last time Crane did a volcano we lost seven people."

"You mean—"

"Yeah. Dead. Half the team didn't come back. We weren't looking for publicity then, so it never became a big issue."

She looked at Crane. "Is that true?"

"True," he said without hesitation. "It was in Sumatra, a new volcano that had risen on the island in a month. We were evacuating from the other side of the crater, away from the flow, because I feared a parasitic crater when the main flue collapsed." He returned her stare and she could detect no regret or sadness in him. "We weren't fast enough. The new cone blew out half the mountain. We never even found bodies. Still want to come along?"

She shook with the rush of a momentous and life-changing challenge. "Will I really be able to help?"

"Working an active volcano will give you more knowledge of tectonics than reading all the books in the world on the subject," he answered simply. "If you can dress a wound, you'll be able to help."

"Then I'm coming," she said without hesitation.

"If she's on the plane, so am I," Newcombe said, hard.

"No," Crane snapped. "You'll spend all your time trying to protect her, which will make both of you useless. Besides, I already told you I need you here."

"Don't do this to me," Newcombe said low, moving up into Crane's face.

"To you," Lanie repeated. "Why does everything come back to you?"

"I'm just utilitizing my employees to their best advantage," Crane said. "Maybe you should think more about the program than your love life, Dan."

"I resent that," Newcombe said. "I didn't ask you to bring her here. I didn't—"

"Enough!" Lanie said, her arm trailing blue lightning as she moved it in front of her to point at Newcombe. She nodded at Crane. "May we have a moment alone, please?"

Crane glanced from one to the other, and she could see in his eyes the fear that he'd made a huge mistake in hiring her. If she were to make this work, it would have to happen right now.

"Certainly," Crane said at last. "I'll be down making sure the loading is going all right." He started for the door-space, turned back around and said, "Settle this *now*."

There were several seconds of silence after Crane left, Lanie and Newcombe regarding each other from three feet away. "Don't screw me on this," she said finally.

His face took on a pained expression. "I don't want you hurt . . . maybe killed," he said. "You're untrained. Crane doesn't care. He'll do anything when he's confronting one of his goddamned demons. To lose you like that . . . I couldn't stand it."

She moved to him, let him take her in his arms. "I want this job, want it desperately," she said fervently. "This is the greatest challenge, the greatest opportunity, an imager could ever hope for and I don't want to lose it."

He gently stroked her hair. "It's not worth dying for," he whispered, the electricity charging slightly wherever their bodies touched.

"You know me. You know my drives."

"Yes."

"Then listen, better for me to die in the flash of discovery than to live knowing I've missed the chance of my lifetime."

"Don't say that."

"It's true, Dan, and you know it. If you kept me from doing this, you'd lose me forever."

He pulled away from her then, turned his back and moved to the opposite side of the tiny room. There was nowhere to go, no escape from the truth. When he turned back around, there was confusion in his eyes. "I-I don't want to lose you . . . that's all."

"You won't lose me," she said softly, and knew she was manipulating him the way Crane would. "I'll be back before you know it. Do this . . . have my luggage and all my stuff in storage sent up to your bungalow. Make sure I'm all moved in. When I get back, we'll start our life together."

"You mean that?"

She nodded. "I'm all yours, lover." She stuck out her hand. "Deal?"

He shook it vigorously, then grabbed her up off the floor, swinging her around and kissing her. He set her back down, his eyes getting hard again. "You just watch your fanny out there," he said. "Nothing crazy. Promise?"

"I promise," she said, then moved quickly to the door. "I've got to tell Crane. Catch up with me at the plane."

She was out the door, her feet practically floating down the stairs, her eyes fixed on the globe, her globe. Excitement filled her, the danger only adding fuel to the fire of her drive.

She found him outside, machinery and people moving all around him as he gave orders and pointed, like a conductor directing the symphony of real life. She walked up beside him.

"When do we leave?" she asked.

"In about five minutes," he answered, one eyebrow raising slightly. He stared out over the edge of the mountain. Lanie heard a slight whine and a huge helo crested the precipice not twenty feet from them. It was dangling a two-and-a-half-ton truck beneath it full of picks and shovels. Crane pointed it toward the transport. In the world of Lewis Crane, nothing was impossible.

Chapter 5

FADE-AWAY

THE FOUNDATION
21 JUNE 2024, 1 A.M.

"I guess once a week isn't good enough," Burt Hill said, not for the first time. "Now we gotta do special sweeps on Friday nights. It don't matter that I been here since seven yesterday morning, no indeed. His majesty says to do a Class A sweep on a Friday night."

"Saturday morning now," Sumi said.

They stood in a shuddering cherrypicker as Burt slowly guided the crane around the top of the globe. He held a palm-size machine with a coil of wire looping from it out in front of him, the debugger bleeping every ten seconds.

"You say you do this once a week?" she asked.

"You bet," Burt said, his brows furrowing as he watched the meter register on the debugger. "Seven in the A of M every Monday of every week." He turned the meter away from the globe, pointing it back toward the labs.

"Every Monday?"

The man looked up at her through a hedgerow of facial hair, reacting warily to the question, Sumi smiling pleasantly to allay suspicion.

"Starts things out fresh for me," Burt finally said, "gets the routine going. I like the Foundation to run smooth as an engine, smooth and predictable. Guess that's what Doc Crane appreciates about me."

"I think he appreciates you for many reasons, especially because you're dependable." Sumi hated that she was going to have to come through every Sunday night and remove whatever she planted. Her arms hung loosely at her sides. Ten transmitters were stuck to her hands, one to each finger and thumb tip.

"How so?" They finished the circle. Hill hit the down button, and the gondola swayed silently toward the floor.

"Crane's not here. You could have put off the sweep until Monday. No one would have been the wiser." The gondola shuddered slightly as it reached ground level. They climbed out, Sumi walking over to admire Patagonia on the globe, her hand resting on the Malvinas Islands. She could feel Hill's eyes on the back of her head, tearing at her.

"Couldn't do that. Wouldn't do it. Being foreman for Doc Crane is the best damned job . . . the best damned *time* I've ever had in my life. I'm embarrassed to tell you how much he pays me. Hell, he gives me a bungalow on the mountain free of charge . . . and it's just as good as his. I'll tell you, Sumi, when Crane sides with a man, he sticks with him. That means something to me. He's done the same for you. How do you think you got moved up to Senior Grant Advisor? A Nobel Prize opens a lot of doors. Crane went and talked to the Board for you."

At his words Sumi's hands tightened involuntarily. Damn! She accidentally left three transmitters on the globe, two on Gran Malvina and one on Isla Soledad. The size of dust motes, they'd never be seen, but the transfer activated the units. She hoped Hill wouldn't turn the debugger on again in here. She coughed, turning to him. "Did that not also benefit Dr. Crane?" she said quietly.

"My new position certainly enabled him to get grants, and quickly."

"And what the hell's wrong with that, Mr. Chan?" he said, now offended and reverting to formality.

Sumi looked at the floor, and despite all rationalization, she was ashamed.

"Here," Hill said, handing her a dorphed lemon drop. "Even out."

"Thanks," Sumi said, tossing the thing in her mouth as Hill turned and walked toward the west wing of labs and storerooms. She'd have to be selective as to where to plant successfully in the west wing. She wanted the places Crane frequented the most.

The dorph took hold quickly, her mood stabilizing as she caught up with Hill, but there were some things even dorph couldn't cure. One of them was the bitter sting of guilt.

"You want to slug down a couple when I'm done here?" Hill asked as they walked, and she knew he was suspicious. "The view's pretty goddamned spectacular from my porch. On a really clear night, you can see the Late Show on the side of the Moon."

"You've got a deal, Burt. But may I suggest that we do our slugging from a special bottle I've got in my suitcase?"

"A man after my own heart," Hill said, and Sumi wondered how far they'd get pumping each other for information.

Hill touched his wristpad. "GET OFF YOUR WIDE LOAD ASSES AND GET BACK TO WORK!" his voice boomed, graveyard-shift welders, programmers, and housekeepers jumping up and hurrying to their workstations.

"Crane usually takes you on his trips, doesn't he?" Sumi asked.

Hill frowned, genuine concern on his face. "Yeah. Don't like it when he goes alone." He shook his head. "Hope somebody reminds him to eat."

Sumi looked at her watch. "I should imagine that he's in-country by now."

The man laughed. "By now he's in-country and running the whole goddamned show."

At that exact moment, Lewis Crane stood up to his knees in the midst of a nightmare of ash and mud in what had once been the coastal city of Le Precheur, Martinique, screaming in lousy French, *"Silence, s'il vous plaît . . . silence!"* to the townspeople who were trying to dig their families out of the mud.

The mountain still rumbled and lightning flashed overhead as Lanie planted her sensors into the side of Pelee, banging the poles in herself with a ball peen hammer.

They were on the eastern face of Pelee; lava flows still bubbled over the southern face. Light and heat reached through the dense curtain of ash that hung over everything. It was sometime before morning; but day or night didn't matter here. It would be perpetual night until the next big rain washed the ash from the skies. Farther to the south, Fort de France was in flames. Liang Int people were blowing buildings with dynamite trying to re-establish firebreaks.

Though Crane had been pumping data through the SISMA net, he knew it would be days before the international community mobilized to send aid, days before the citizens of Le Precheur had anything but their own meager resources to depend upon. But he also knew that local resources were the heart of all disaster management, local citizens taking care of their own. The fade-away time, the mortality rate for people trapped in collapsed houses under tons of mud, was fifty percent at six hours. Every minute beyond that increased the percentage. Le Precheur already had been buried for nearly eight hours. His guidance was essential if they were to take any of the victims back from the belly of the beast.

"Écoutez donc!" he called out. The area resembled a junkyard of broken mortar and skeletal wooden beams thrusting out of a sea of oozing mud. *"S'il vous plaît!"*

This whole chain of islands was volcanic in origin, all born of the fire of the earthquake. They'd been called the West Indies at one time, then the European Community had gotten Martinique from the French and called it For Sale. Liang had owned it outright, along with its citizens, for a number of years.

The living ran helter skelter all around him, some digging into the mud with their hands, others using construction company earthmovers. They screamed and cried while their buried loved ones fought for breath.

A man, crazed, talking to himself, hobbled past dragging the remnants of a bed through the pumice-laden sludge. He was covered with soot and caked mud—like all of them.

Crane moved to the man, bumping him away from the bed, the man continuing on without it, oblivious. Crane pulled a lighter from his pocket, flicked it, then tossed it onto the bed. Flames rose immediately. He turned and motioned for the trucks of equipment he'd had ferried from the landing strip on Dominica Island to the north.

Five huge trucks literally plowed into what had once been the town square, Crane yelling at the drivers to start beeping their compressed air horns. They did, raising an earsplitting din that turned all eyes toward the man beside the burning bed.

"Écoutez donc!" he screamed again; this time the dazed and distraught people listened. "I am here to save you," he shouted in French, "but you must listen to me. You are making too much noise. You cannot hear the cries of the survivors. You must stop talking. You must shut off the bulldozers; they will only bury your loved ones. My trucks are full of picks and shovels. Get those. Dig where you hear voices—we must all be quiet and listen. If you hear a voice, verify it with someone else, make sure of the location, then dig carefully. Those trapped in the rubble will die if you don't do what I say. The men should dig. Women and children should help carry away the debris. Use wheelbarrows, planks, doors, anything you can pile up with mud and rock. Move quickly, but silently. Medical personnel are here to help with those who have been hurt. If you find an injured person, don't pull him from the wreckage until a doctor has checked him out. You are

good people; you will understand the wisdom of my words."

He repeated his message in English, then in Chinese. When he was finished, he was so hoarse he could barely speak.

Wide-eyed Americans climbed out of the trucks. Crane loved and hated people. They were capable of gallantry and ignominy all at the same time. "You were briefed on the plane," he croaked. "You know what to do. Get with it!"

The area calmed to an eerie silence as the truck drivers turned on their high beams to illuminate the area. Lanie joined Crane in the center of the pantomime.

"The sensors are in place," she whispered. "And you were right. The information we're pulling out of the ground will be the best education I or your computers could ever have. We're standing on a living, breathing seismic heart."

He nodded, looking skyward. "Make sure the data is transmitting to the computers," he whispered in return, "then see to the satellite transmission back home."

"You keep looking up," she said.

He was shaking his head. "My arm," he whispered. "This bastard's not finished with us yet. The people have got to be taken from here as soon as possible. We'll load trucks with the injured and get them right down to the docks."

"J'ai entendu quelqu'un," someone called excitedly from farther down the square. Then someone else, *"J'ai entendu!"*

"Dig!" Crane called through cupped hands. *"Bêcher!"*

They worked diligently, quietly, everyone pulling together. Crane moved over the face of the cataclysm, trying to take back the lives that the monster would have for its own. As he went, he spoke with his workers, explaining void-to-volume ratios for air in collapsed buildings and the likeliest places to find survivors. He helped with the unloading and placement of the amplified listening equipment, thermal-imaging cameras, and fiberoptical visual probes stuck directly into wreckage that helped find more people, the living and the dead. Surveillance technology sometimes came in handy. He felt neither good nor bad about what he was doing, only urgent. His obsession brought him here; his anger held him fast.

Soon people—remarkably, many of them alive—were being brought out of the rubble. Her computer work on line, Lanie joined the others to help with the triage of patients, field-dressing wounds, then getting them into the trucks. Weary hours passed. She looked up once and saw Crane through the confusion, giving orders like a general. A woman following two stretcherbearers and their burden, broke away and ran to Crane, throwing her arms around him and hugging and kissing him in gratitude. A look of horror swept over his face and he stiffened, pushing her away as if afraid of the contact.

Lanie labored under the most intense fear she'd ever known. She'd been too naive to be scared at Sado. Here, she knew what they were up against. She felt on knife edge. She wanted to trust Crane's good sense to see them through, but she had begun to learn that the man had no sense at all, only cunning. His continual looking toward the sky didn't help her feel any better.

Then she saw it, and her whole body tensed in shock. Lightning, pale pinkish lightning, was jumping from the monolith of the mountainside to the clouds and back again. Suddenly it seemed to be springing from everywhere, crackling loudly, like cannon fire.

She ran through the confusion of increasingly desperate and tired workers, finding Crane amidst the partially cleared wreckage of a large house whose top floor was simply gone, its staircase leading to nowhere. A teenage boy lay at the foot of the staircase, his legs pinned beneath a wooden beam. Several workers were improvising a hoist to raise the beam while Crane and a USC intern knelt beside the boy.

"Crane," she said. "The sky—"

"Not now," he said, then turned to the workers who were in the process of levering up the beam with another crossbeam. "Don't take it off!"

"Why not?" the intern asked. "His injuries seem minor. We can get him on a truck and—"

"Good lesson, doctor," Crane said. "Ever heard of crush syndrome?"

The young man, smeared with mud and soot, just stared. "In a case like this," Crane said, "we've got to treat *in situ* before we risk moving him. He's had almost ten hours under this beam to build up toxins where the blood flow was cut off. You pull him out of here now, he'd walk away fine and be dead of a heart attack in an hour."

"What do we do?"

"We flood him with fluids and antitoxins intravenously, pump him up. When we move the beam, his body's prepared to deal with the toxin rush into the system."

"I'll get the gear," the young man said, hurrying off.

"Okay, talk to me," Crane said to Lanie as he bent to the boy, brushing strands of hair out of his face.

"J'ai peur," the boy whispered.

"Moi aussi, mais pas trop," Crane replied, then looked at Lanie.

"The lightning," she said. "It's jumping up from the island."

Crane, his face a mask, rose without a word and moved out of the debris to look upward as the intern hurried back into the wrecked house to start an IV.

Lightning crackled all around them, played up and down the rumbling mountain like fiery rain. "Everyone's got to go," he said.

"What is it?" Lanie asked as he walked off.

"St. Elmo's Fire," he called over his shoulder. He began shouting at his people to gather up whoever was left and get them to the docks.

Lanie ran to catch up.

"The whole atmosphere's charged with static electricity," he said. "Something's going to happen."

Suddenly, Le Precheur was all motion; people climbed onto the trucks or simply ran in panic. The rumbling got louder, more intense as heavy ash rained down on them. Lanie focused on Crane to avoid thinking about the danger and ran to keep up as he darted back to the house they'd just come from.

They moved into the wreckage. "Get out of here, doctor," he said, taking the IV from his hand.

"But my patient—"

"Get the hell out of here now!" He turned to the workers as the doctor left. They were busy propping the lever beam atop a rock, making a fulcrum.

"*Sauve qui peut!*" he yelled, and the men, frightened already, hurried out.

"What the hell are you doing here?" Crane said to Lanie, his eyes intent on the plastic fluid bag he held. "Go . . . go!"

"Not without you."

"I'm giving you an order, lady."

"You've probably seen how well I respond to orders," she said. "Look, you may as well save your breath."

His jaw muscles tightened. "Get on that lever. When I give you the word, push with all your strength and I'll drag him out, okay?"

She moved in the confined space to the crossbeam and waited, listening to the sounds of trucks roaring off for the docks and the mountain snarling and spitting.

"So why are you staying behind?" he asked as he held the boy's hand.

"I don't know," she answered honestly. "Maybe I wanted you to see how seriously I take the job."

He laughed then, deep and genuine. "You've convinced me. But I don't think I'm the person at the Crane Foundation you need to convince."

She ignored the reference to Newcombe. "Are we going to die?" she asked instead.

"Yeah . . . probably. Okay?"

"You're the boss."

They waited for the slow IV to drain. Crane spoke softly to the boy as the ground rumbled menacingly beneath them, and as soon as the bag was empty, he ripped it out and tossed it away. "Go! Go!" he yelled.

Lanie strained on the beam. The smell of sulfur was overpowering. There was no panic within her, only professional detachment. She'd do her job. It's why she came. She surprised herself with her calm. Amazed herself.

She heard Crane grunting even as she strained on the lever and the ash was choking her, making her gag.

"Got him," Crane yelled, using his good arm to hoist the slight young man over his shoulder then stagger up in the debris. Lanie released her lever and stumbled with him, the square empty as they slogged through sucking, knee-deep mud.

"Now what?" she asked.

"Now we . . . oh my." Crane was looking up again, his eyes wide with wonderment.

Above them, the summit of Pelee was suffused with a dull red glow that became brighter and brighter as they watched. Total darkness lit up to brilliant daylight. Without warning the glow broke away from the peak and rushed down the mountainside a hundred yards from them. It wasn't lava, but a red-hot avalanche of rock with a billowy surface. There were boulders and the remnants of trees within the pulsating destruction, huge rocks which stood out as streaks of throbbing red tumbling and throwing off showers of sparks.

The velocity was terrific, the avalanche rushing down the entire mountain and into the sea in seconds, narrowly missing them.

"I've heard of this but never seen it," Crane said low, his voice hushed with awe, and perhaps with exhaustion too, for he still held the young man on his shoulder.

"Is it over?"

"No."

Just as the crimson glow from the avalanche faded, it was replaced with a monstrous cloud shaping itself against the now visible sky over the landslide's site. The cloud rose from the path of the avalanche and moved along its course, gaining momentum, as if lighter particles of volcanic material had begun to rise slightly and continue forward as the heavier particles settled to earth.

The cloud was globular, its surface bulging with masses that swelled and multiplied with a terrible energy. Lanie was hypnotized by it, barely feeling Crane's bad arm pushing at her. The cloud rushed forward, directly toward them, boiling and changing its form every instant. Ground hugging, it billowed at them in surging masses, coruscating with lightning.

"Back inside the wreckage!" he yelled at her over the terrible hot gale force wind that led the cloud. "Now! Move!"

She moved.

They were being pelted with a rain of stones the size of walnuts. The hot roar moved nearer, nearer. Crane knew he had about twenty seconds to figure out how to protect them from two-thousand-degree temperatures that would suck the oxygen right out of their lungs.

The workers had opened a ten-foot clearance cave to rescue the boy, but it was giving in now, collapsing in upon itself. A beam squeaked loudly, creaking, then snapping. He saw it in terrible slow motion as it swung at them, catching Lanie full force on the side of the head, knocking her to her knees. She began weaving from that position, gagging loudly.

"Come on!" He grabbed at her, but his bad arm didn't have the strength to pull her up. He lay his burden down; the young man shakily got to his own hands and knees and crawled farther into the collapsing darkness of his house.

Crane seized King around the waist and pulled her up his hip, bearing most of her weight. Behind them, outside, the square was brilliant fire. He could hardly breathe. *"Salle de bain,"* he shouted to the boy. "Tub! Tub!"

"Ici," the boy called weakly and continued to crawl.

"Good," Crane said, pulling a moaning Lanie with him as he squat-walked through the wreckage, the heat unbearable. "Are you still with me?"

Her head lolled on her shoulders, her eyelashes fluttering, trying to bring back the eyes that wanted to roll up into her skull. "I'm f-fine," she mumbled weakly. "I just need to . . . need to . . . lie down, I—I—"

"Yeah, yeah," Crane said, dragging her now. "Dan's going to kill me if this damned volcano doesn't."

The boy had crawled behind the stairs to nowhere and pushed weakly at a splintered doorway half squashed by its own frame. Crane, working at sucking air, dropped King and threw himself against the remnants of the door. It gave way with him, and he tumbled into a bathroom that was half caved in from the side facing the mountain but remarkably intact otherwise.

He reached back and pulled the young man in with him. A freestanding bathtub waited majestically in the middle of an ash-covered floor. He scrambled back over the splinters and took Lanie by her collar to drag her into the room. "You stay awake!" he yelled at her as she bumped over broken mortar and wood. "Do you hear me! Don't go to sleep!"

"Aye, aye, Captain," she said, her voice raspy. Blood flowed down her neck, soaking her hair and shirt.

He dragged her to the tub and placed her flat next to it. "Don't move," he said, then pulled the boy by the arm and put him close beside her. He lay atop them both and tipped the tub over them, hoping it would hold enough of an air pocket to keep them alive and be strong enough to protect them from falling debris.

The rumbling got louder, all-encompassing in the stifling darkness beneath the tub. *"Retenir votre respiration,"* he told the boy, then to Lanie, "Take a deep breath and hold it."

They did, to the roar of the cloud washing over them, the rest of the house giving way under the heat and mud, falling in on top of them, screaming as it died, screaming as his parents' house had.

His body cooked dry, robbing him of fluids. He couldn't breathe or swallow. He could hear Lanie and the boy gasping for breath. Dammit, Pelee would not take his life or the lives of those with him today! By God, the monster had had enough.

"Easy," he whispered through parched lips, and he found himself stroking Lanie's hair in the darkness, the terrible roar a distant storm now. He felt her relax under his hand. "It's over."

She groaned loudly. "Then c-could you . . . get your . . . knee out of my *back*. You're . . . k-killing me."

"Sorry," he said, finally able to draw a strong breath as fresh air rushed through the crack around the bottom of the tub, filling the vacuum created by the cloud. Air meant some sort of passage to the outside. A beginning.

He shoved out with his good hand, the tub budging, but stuck. It was pinned under something heavy. The boy reached up and helped, the two of them straining the tub up far enough for Crane to roll out and clear the ceiling off the thing and roll it away from them.

It was black as a deep cave. Crane touched the sloping underside of the staircase. It had collapsed in an inverted V atop them and had probably saved their lives. Unfortunately, it was now their prison.

They were trapped.

The boy moaned. Crane reached for him as he fell heavily to the littered ground and searched for his carotid artery. There was no pulse.

"No!" Crane screamed, the darkness swallowing his words. "You can't have him!"

He began administering CPR, knowing instinctively that they'd taken the boy off the fluids too soon and that the strain of the fear had sent his heart over the edge.

"Come on," he pleaded, then pounded the boy's chest. "Come on!"

He didn't know how long he'd worked on the boy. He only knew that at some point even Lewis Crane had to give up. His breath was coming in gasps as he fell back atop a pile of masonry. He smelled gas, not knowing if it were real or a memory flashback in the darkness. He felt the heat of flames, but couldn't see them. Then he cried softly and wished, as he had every day of his life since the Northridge quake, that he'd stayed inside the house with his parents. The peace of death eluded him, but its agony was his constant companion.

"He's gone, Lanie," Crane finally whispered into the darkness to no response. He stiffened. "Lanie . . . Lanie!"

He crawled to her. She was limp. He gathered her to

his breast and rocked her gently in their mausoleum of mud and stone. And even as his mind spun into a numbed vortex of falling buildings and bright orange fire, every part of him, rational and irrational, was willing life into the body of Elena King.

Chapter 6

PANGAEA

**THE FOUNDATION
21 JUNE 2024, 11:15 A.M.**

Newcombe sat before the thirty-by-forty-foot wall screen in the dark lecture hall where Foundation briefings were held on missions. Pictures streamed in from helos hovering above Le Precheur. He saw an ocean of mud, a desert of slime with skeletal signs of civilization poking from its innards. Somewhere, buried beneath the ooze over the crumpled city, were the two most important people in the world to him. He refused to accept their deaths. Refused.

There were lots of people working the site—the Foundation's people were there out of obligation, the townspeople out of gratitude to the demon saint who'd saved their loved ones. He could see mud-covered workers picking at the wreckage in thirty different places. Damn, it was too loose, too widespread an effort to be truly effective. Those rescuers would never get to Lanie and Crane in time if they kept to that strategy.

"H-hello?"

"Yes, who is this?" Newcombe returned, noting the tension in the man's voice.

"M-My name is Dr. Ben Crowell and I'd really like to get back to the digging, I—"

"Doctor," Newcombe said. "We don't have much time, sir. Were you the last one to see Dr. Crane and Dr. King before the eruption?"

"Yes . . . I—"

"Have someone put a camera on you, Ben. I want to see . . . ah, good."

The grim face of a haggard, filthy man blipped as an insert onto the huge screen.

"You know where they are, Ben?"

"I know where they *were*, doctor," Crowell said, "but everything's shifted. Nothing's where it was. I can't seem to get my . . . bearings. I'm sorry."

"Calm down," Newcombe said, his own resolve solid. "Crane's alive. We're in contact with him. They still have a little air. We just need to pinpoint them. Are you in the town square?"

"I think so."

"Did this happen close to the town square?"

"Yes!" the man said, brightening.

Newcombe inserted a detailed satellite photo map in the lower right-hand corner of the excavation shot, showing Le Precheur as it was mere days ago. "Have someone give you a monitor . . . we're transmitting from this end."

"Just a moment . . . I . . . yes, I see the map."

"Look at it carefully and draw conclusions."

He zoomed in on the street leading up to the square, focusing on the masonry houses with the red thatch roofs, French colonial influence.

"This one, this one," Crowell shouted. "The fifth house from the square on the west side of the street."

"How can you be so sure?"

"There were stairs going up, but no second floor. Your

map only shows one two-story house on the block on that side of the street. It's got to be the place."

Newcombe overlaid a ruler on the map. "The square had a flagpole in the center."

"It's still there."

"Due east from the flagpole, 113 feet four inches, is the front door of that house. Measure accurately—okay?— and have everyone dig there . . . but slowly, carefully, very carefully."

Crowell darted away and was off-camera for a minute or more, though in audio contact the whole time.

"You've got enough diggers there," Newcombe said brusquely. "I need your attention, Crowell, got to get some more information from you." Crowell's tired face popped up again. "Good. Now, tell me, what exactly happened? How was it that the two senior members of the expedition were left behind during an eruption?"

"We were evacuating the city quickly because of the St. Elmo's Fire. I was giving a patient with crush syndrome an IV, when Crane came rushing in with Dr. King and ordered me and the men on the lever to get down to the docks. Crane took the IV from me and we ran. It was a nightmare, trying to run through the deep mud, getting bogged down in it. . . ."

"Take a deep breath, Ben. Better now?" Crowell wearily shook his head. "Go on," Newcombe said encouragingly.

Crowell's expression darkened as he relived his time in hell. "We . . . we somehow got down to the docks, lightning, pink lightning, was everywhere. There were fires . . . rocks were pelting us." He rubbed his eyes. "Confusion at the ferries, mass chaos with trucks and people shoving. We somehow all got on board, but we couldn't have been a mile or two from shore when the top blew off the mountain and the damned cloud formed. It came right for us, reaching for us, full of lightning. It roared and flung rocks. I knew we were all dead. Then, it started slowing down. The cloud got kind of pale, then just sailed over us, raining ash. But it started to sort of, well expand . . . until it filled the sky . . . except for a sliver of horizon. I've never seen anything even remotely like that."

"Hold it, Ben," Newcombe said, seeing the diggers making some progress. "Tell them to get optical sensors in there," he said, Crowell disappearing from the screen for several seconds. He came back frowning.

"They sent me back. Everyone's afraid to talk to you. Most of the surveillance gear was lost in the . . . did you call it, eruption? It didn't seem like—"

"Please, Ben."

Crowell nodded apologetically. "They're trying to rig something now."

"If they can hear me, then they know, they'd better hurry! Come back with my people alive or don't come back. Now tell me, how much time passed between you leaving Crane and King and the eruption?"

The man opened his eyes wide. "Maybe ten minutes, barely enough time to finish the IV."

"And what time of day was this?"

The man reached into his pocket, pulled out a watch, and held it close for Newcombe to see. Its face was cracked, the time frozen at 7:26. "I smashed it on a truck getting onto the ferry. Can I go now?"

Four hours. Oxygen was the problem—if they'd survived the mud and fire. "One more thing, Ben. You say there was a staircase in the house?"

"Yes."

"Okay. Thanks. We're finished." He blanked Crowell's insert from the screen, replacing it with a revolving tour of the news feeds on the scene. He let his head fall back on the seat and closed his eyes. They'd find them now, hopefully before the air ran out. Crane stayed with the house, the area under the stairs a decent place to trap oxygen and as good a place as any to be. They were there. He refused to let himself think about anything except the prospect of finding them safe, sound.

"Would you rather be alone?"

Newcombe opened his eyes to see a hologram of Brother Ishmael, ten inches high, floating in the air before him, an angelic glow around the image. "I'm not even going to ask how you did this," he said.

The image looked sheepish. "I planted a homer on your hand back at the boat. It's that thing that looks like a pimple on your left thumb. Pull it off and I'm gone."

Newcombe looked at the thumb, noted the device, left it alone. "Have you seen what's happening?" he asked.

The image nodded. "I thought maybe you could use some support, Brother. Crane's foolishness has put your woman in danger."

"Foolishness," Newcombe repeated. "They dug forty-two living people out of that mud. I'd call that courageous, Brother Ishmael."

"It takes courage just to live," Ishmael replied. "I'm not here to argue with you, only to wait with you . . . to grieve with you if it comes to that."

"Let's not worry about the grief yet."

"Indeed. Are you involved in the S and R mission?"

"In a small way," Newcombe said, looking past the holo to the diggers.

"What happened on Martinique? They haven't been able to explain that cloud or anything else on the news—"

"They'll figure it out eventually," Newcombe said, angry that no one had taken charge of the surveillance gear on site. A good optical sensor could save them hours. Burt Hill would have seen to the equipment. Damn Crane for not taking him. He looked again at Brother Ishmael. "This kind of eruption happens from time to time. The French call it *nuée ardente,* 'glowing cloud.' A hundred and twenty years of refinement has settled the term at 'glowing avalanche.' It's happened on Pelee before."

"What is it?"

"A kind of lateral eruption with just enough force to blow the top layer of crater scum straight down the mountain. It acts as a heavy liquid, a mixture of gas, steam, and solid particles. As the heavier particles settle, the gas and steam are free to continue onward, only the smaller particles holding the cloud earthbound. As those are dispersed, the cloud ascends."

"What's the thing they're bringing to the dig now?" Ishmael asked.

Newcombe looked at the screen, his insides tightening up for the big one. An optical sensor. Now they'd see.

Crane and Lanie sat side by side in their muddy tomb, leaning back against the tub that saved their lives. The boy whose name they hadn't learned lay beside them in the darkness.

It was completely black. Crane had no idea of how much mud separated them from the outside. What air they had, he feared, was dissipating quickly. It was foul and musty.

He tapped his wristpad. "Dan . . . you there?"

"I'm here, Crane." There was relief and happiness in Newcombe's voice. "I think we've isolated your location. We're coming at it with an optical sensor."

"Get an air tube in here."

"Okay. Let me talk to Lanie."

"She's indisposed," Crane said, tapping off and sagging against the tub. Beside him, Lanie slid in and out of consciousness. She'd had a nasty cut on the temple; he'd stopped the bleeding by applying mud. He'd torn off the sleeve of his shirt and tied it tightly around her wound, loosening it every few minutes, then retightening. He'd gone through medical school for the field knowledge, never carrying it any further than on-site emergency treatment. Lanie needed a real doctor.

She moaned, regaining consciousness, just as she had fifteen times already. She had the damnedest type of concussion, one with trauma to the deep section of the frontal lobes involving recent memory. She could not capture and hold on to a new thought. Every time she became conscious, the experience was brand new to her. Crane prepared to start with her again at Square One. He heard her sudden intake of breath, knew she was reacting to the darkness and the pain, and quickly put a hand on her shoulder.

"Don't panic," he said low, soothing.

"Crane?"

"Take it easy. You've had a blow to the head. Try and relax."

"Where the hell are we?"

"Trapped," he said, "in the debris of a house . . . under a mudslide. In Martinique. They're coming to rescue us."

"You're kidding? Martinique? Is Dan all right?"

"He's fine . . . though a little worried. He's back in California."

"He is? Why don't I remember?"

"It's normal," he said calmly, patting her shoulder again. "Don't worry about it."

"What happened to me?"

"A blow to the head."

"Really? And Dan?"

"He's all right. He's not here."

"We're not in California, are we?"

"No." If the circumstances weren't so grim, he knew he'd find it difficult to keep himself from laughing.

"I'm fine now."

"I know."

"Where are we?"

"Martinique."

"Really? And Dan's not here, right?"

"Right."

"We got trapped here, but we're going to get rescued."

"That, dear lady, is my sincerest hope."

She grunted. "I'm fine. Really okay now. My head feels like hell, though. I think there's some dorph somewhere . . . I never travel without—"

"I've got it," he said. "You've already had some, but if you want some more. . . ."

"Only one," she said, holding out her hand. He retrieved the dorph from his work shirt pocket and gave her a tablet. They'd repeated this particular scenario six times.

"You take one," she said, swallowing the pill.

"You know I don't take dorph."

"How come? Ow! That hurts."

"Don't touch your head." He drew his legs up. "You know, it just occurred to me I can tell you anything, because you won't remember it."

"I'll remember." She laughed. "I told you I'm fine. I simply need to know . . . is Dan all right?"

"He's fine. He's back in California."

"Did I take a dorphtab?"

"Yes," he said, the most wicked, thrilling sense of freedom stealing through him: no surveillance and perhaps a ton of mud for soundproofing insulation; a listener who would immediately forget what he said. If this were to be his last conversation, he'd make it a winner. "I was about to tell you why I don't take dorph."

"Why?"

"I tried it once. It stopped the pain."

"That's what it's supposed to do."

"That's why I don't take it."

He felt her stir beside him and looked in her direction, imagining her face in the darkness, her wide, inquisitive eyes. "I get it," she said. "You're going to be honest."

"And you'll forget everything I say. By the way, what's the last thing you remember?"

"Well, we're talking . . . I remember that. I remember being on a boat. Why is it so dark?"

"We're trapped under a mudslide, but they're coming to rescue us."

"Dan's fine, though. Right?"

"That's right. You know I'm attracted to you?"

"Whoa . . . hold it. I'm not looking for a quickie in the rubble."

"I've never met a woman like you. Passionate . . . intelligent. I can see your mind working as I look into your eyes." His fingertips came up to brush her face. She pulled away slightly, but only slightly, he noted.

"Right," she said. "How many times have you trotted that line out?"

"What line?"

"That . . . you know, whatever you said."

He smiled. "I'm going to tell you my story. You're my perfect audience for it. I lived with my mother's sister, Ruth. My aunt and her husband didn't have much money, and he didn't like me. Her own kids came first, so I had to perform to get noticed. I'd read every book ever written on seismology and plate tectonics by the time I was ten. Got my first college degree at age fifteen and went on fast from there."

"What about your emotional life . . . friends . . . girl-friends?"

"I was the outsider," he said. The rubble shifted and planks fell to the floor nearby. Lanie scooted closer and clutched his arm. "I grew up around people years older than myself. It strengthened my performing, but got me no friends. Nothing was ever expected of me emotionally."

"Women?"

"None. Not even close. Never been kissed. I'm thirty-seven years old and I've never even held hands with a girl I liked."

"Well, I'll tell you what," she said, laying her head on his shoulder. "If we ever get out of here, I'll give you a first-class kiss to get you started on your way."

"Promise?"

"You bet, I . . . it's so dark. Why are we here?"

"We were trying to save a boy trapped by the vol-cano—"

"Volcano?"

"—and we got trapped ourselves. And yes, Dan's all right. He's not here. Here is Martinique."

"Have I asked you these questions before?"

"A time or two."

"Guess I forgot. But I won't forget now. What happened to the boy we were trying to save?"

"Put your left hand out beside you."

"Okay, I—Oh God!" She practically jumped onto his lap. "Is that . . . ?"

"The boy. He didn't make it."

She went limp, then slumped against the tub. "We're going to die, aren't we? We're going to die in the dark."

"The possibility exists. I'm sorry. They're looking for us now. We did get the city evacuated in time, though."

"City . . . evacuated?" He heard her take a deep breath. "Can we do anything from in here?"

"Not really," he said. "In the dark, I'd be afraid to pull on anything for fear of bringing the house down on us."

"Maybe there's a lighter or—"

"We've already looked . . . even in the boy's pocket. Besides, I'm beginning to worry about the oxygen."

"Scare me, why don't you?"

"It's all right, you'll forget."

"I resent that. I will not. Is Dan here?"

"No . . . and he's fine."

"Good," she said, then took a long breath. "Did we predict this one?" she asked.

"I can't predict anything," he said, then stared in her general direction. "You want to hear the whole story?"

"What story?"

He drew a deep breath of the fetid air. "I'd been tracking Sado," he said low, "since the day the Israelis saw the Iranian helos overhead and blew their whole nuclear stockpile, thirty multimegaton bombs. Fifty million people vaporized instantly, ten million more within seconds." Tears rolled down his cheeks; Lanie was shuddering. "The blasts not only irradiated the entire Middle East and its oil, but it had profound effects below ground—first on the Arabian Plate, which in turn had an effect on the Turkish-Aegean and Iran Plates. It was like watching dominoes fall. By the time the Indo-Australian and Eurasian Plates started to buckle, I was predicting the quakes with a fair degree of accuracy, within, say, a month or two. Finally, years later, the Indo-Aus, Philippine, North American, and Pacific Plates collided roughly, which had a small, but devastating effect on a zone near Sado." He shrugged. "It was laid out like a roadmap."

"What was?"

"The EQ's connected to the Masada Option."

"Why didn't you predict other quakes before Sado?"

"Two reasons. First, nobody listens anyway. Second, if I was going to take the chance of being wrong and being forever labeled as a crackpot, I'd take the best odds. Sado was the plum, the shot heard round the world."

"Now . . . we're not at Sado now, are we?"

"We're in Martinique. Dan's not here. He's fine. Ask me the next question. If you've been listening, you're probably wondering what I'm selling since you now know that I can't really predict earthquakes."

"Yeah. Tell me that. I'll remember this time."

"I'm selling the dream of a perfect world," he said. "This kind of suffering is needless, wasteful."

"I'm sorry . . . I lost something back—" She flailed her arms, squealing. "Crawling on me. A thing's crawling on me. Get it off! Off!"

His hand felt her thigh, running its length. He felt it then, cold, metallic.

"Ha!" He grabbed the optical sensor that had slithered into their lair and held it up to his face. "It's about time you got here. Dig us out slowly. We've got a pocket here, but the whole place is about to go. Tunnel in easy. Try and get us an air tube first. And for God's sake, get me a drink! They have sugar mills here; there must be rum. If you can get to the air hole, shove a bottle through."

The sensor slithered away. He relaxed at the sound of the rescue workers pounding a pipeline of fresh air into their musty tomb.

"Is Dan out there?" Lanie asked.

"He'd better not be," Crane said. "He's supposed to be at the labs looking for quakes."

"If you really can't predict," she said, "what's the point?"

He took her hand in the darkness, kissed it. "Dear lady, you don't give up your life's dream just because it has no reality."

Suddenly the barest light shone in the cavern, brightening it to a sickly haze. A rush of fresh air followed, and with it, hope.

"Dr. Crane," a voice called down the five-inch tube.

"I'm here! Where's that rum I ordered?"

"Coming!"

The bottle was shoved through the tube, followed by a bottle of water. Crane handed Lanie the water and unscrewed the cap on the rum, taking a long drink. "How far away are you?"

"Ten to fifteen feet," the voice returned. "We'll have you out quickly."

"Are we the only ones?"

"Everybody alive got out . . . except you three."

"Two," Crane said, taking another long swig of rum. "There's only two of us here."

He sat back, glancing sadly at the corpse. Lanie had been staring at it ever since the light had entered.

"What happened?" she asked, reaching for his bottle of rum after she finished the water.

"We tried to save him. He died. End of story."

"Was this an earthquake?"

"A volcano . . . we're in Martinique."

"You're kidding. Where's Dan?"

"Back home." He liked having her this way. He was able to be honest without ramifications, sincere without recriminations. "Do you remember your promise?" he asked.

"Promise. . . ."

"Never mind." He sagged close to her, pressing his lips to her ear. "I love you, you know," he whispered.

"Don't say things like that," she said sternly. "We have enough problems in our lives."

"Say things like what?"

She took another drink and passed him the bottle. They looked like people made of clay. "You know," she said, "there's something I don't understand."

"Yes?"

"You want all this funding, all this . . . power to predict quakes. Didn't we just talk about that?"

"Yes, we did. You're probably wondering what I really want."

"Yeah. Predicting to save lives is a noble cause, but Dan's the person working those fields. Why not go his way? Define areas likely to be affected and rewrite building codes or make them off limits. You don't need the detailed information you want to do that."

He said what he'd never had the guts to say to another human being. "I don't give a damn about earthquake prediction," he whispered. "It's a means to an end."

"What end?"

"I cannot coexist with the world the way it is," he said.

"So I intend to change it. I intend to stop earthquakes from happening."

She laughed and reached for the bottle again. He took another long drink before giving it to her. "And how do you intend to stop earthquakes?"

"By fusing the plates," he said fierce and low. "This world was once one continent, named Pangaea. It had no earthquakes, no volcanoes. I'm going to make it that way again."

Lanie drank deep, Crane grabbing the bottle from her and finishing it. She giggled. "You said you wanted to fuse the plates, didn't you?"

"Yes."

"How?"

He winked at her before murmuring directly into her ear, "By exploding huge thermonuclear bombs right on the fault lines."

"What?"

Light flooded in, the sound of excited voices echoing all around them. "Come on, Elena King," he bellowed, grabbing her around the waist with his good arm. "We live to fight another day!"

"Is Dan here?" she asked as hands reached in to pull them to safety.

"No."

"What about the boy?"

"Leave him. Nothing mars a triumphal rescue like an untimely death. PR, Lanie. We live and die by it."

Dan Newcombe sat staring at the screen, fists clenched, keeping his mind clear and controlled as he watched the SAR team digging gingerly in the gray-green mud that had once been a two-story house. The image of Ishmael floated just beside him, quiet, contemplative. He could see the icon, but it could not see him. "Are you watching the dig?" he asked, his voice choked.

"Yes," Ishmael said. "I have a very positive feeling about it."

"How so?"

"Crane is a madman. He will walk unscathed through tragedy. It is his blessing, Brother, and his curse also."

"The first time I've ever heard you speak well of him."

"I am not speaking well of him. He is not a man in the normal sense. He is a force moving through my life as I am a force moving through his. We're glaciers, Crane and I, slowly creeping, rolling over everything in our paths. Crane is beyond definition. Do you see the man in the bright blue coat by the truck?"

Newcombe looked. It was the tech working the monitor for the opticals. He appeared to be excited as he turned the dials.

"I think he's got them," Newcombe said, watching the man dance an impromptu jig in the mud. "Look at him jumping! They're alive!"

The lecture hall door banged open. Burt Hill and several programmers charged in, whooping. A similar scene was being monitored on the huge screen by the crew in Martinique.

"Go," Newcombe whispered, Ishmael disappearing on Hill's entry. Newcombe made a mental note to call and thank the man for his friendship during a bad time.

"I ain't *never* letting him get away without me again!" Hill shouted. He charged happily down the aisle to watch the excavation with Newcombe; the others scattered through the theater. "They must have lost all the surveillance gear. That thing they used is jury-rigged outta spare parts."

Newcombe nodded. "Believe me, next time Crane goes into the field, I'll personally chain him to you."

"Gawd," Hill said, shaking his head as the workers shoved a bottle of rum through an air facilitation tube. "He's getting a drink before he gets out. That's Crane."

Newcombe continued to stare as they dug, the workers handing bucketsful of mud along a human chain, shoring up the wreckage as they went. There was life. Now to see if there were injuries.

The team broke through within minutes. The crew in the theater and in Martinique cheered as Crane stumbled out of the debris under his own power, smiling wide for the cameras. He was carrying Lanie in his arms, his good arm taking most of the weight, the nearly empty bottle of rum dangling from his bad hand.

Newcombe's stomach lurched. Lanie's head was bandaged, blood covering her entire left side, matting her hair. She appeared to be only semiconscious. Crane didn't look any the worse for wear.

"She's hurt," Hill said.

Newcombe grunted. "They'd better have someone more experienced than interns down there." He banged on the wristpad, reopening the contact between him and the team. A muddy figure, barely recognizable as human, blipped onto his screen. "Get Crane over here," he told the man.

Just then, on the main screen, he saw Lanie throw her arms around Crane and give him a long kiss as she was lowered onto a stretcher. His insides knotted and he clenched his teeth to keep from cursing out loud. Crane seemed more startled than surprised at the kiss. What was happening?

Crane waved heartily at the cameras, holding up his bottle of rum and laughing, one more sumptuous meal at the buffet table of his exciting life. Damn the man. Brother Ishmael was right—he wasn't human.

Swallowed up by his rescue team, Crane slithered off the screen and disappeared for half a minute, only to blip up on the insert box, finishing the rum.

"Crane," Newcombe said low.

"Danny boy!" Crane dropped the bottle to wipe his face with a towel. "Did you miss us?"

"Where is she?" Newcombe said. "I'm hoping you haven't killed her."

"This is an open line, Danny boy."

"Where is she?"

Crane had put on his public face and it wasn't going to budge. He smiled. "We're getting set to vac her over to Dominica for some doctoring. I think it's only a concussion. She'll be fine. Keeps asking for you, by the way."

"Put her on."

"Can't do that, Dan." He looked off camera for a second. "They're getting her ready to go. Besides . . . you don't need to be having any reunions over an open line. Save it for later."

"For the love of God, Crane, put her on. I have to know if she's all right."

Crane shook his head, the smile still on his face. "Not on an unsecured line," he said. "We don't want to give away any trade secrets."

"Crane—"

"Got to go, Danny boy. My public awaits." Crane walked away from the screen, leaving dead air behind.

Newcombe fell back heavily in his chair, staring at the screen and the workers preparing to leave the site.

"I got to set up for them to come back," Burt said, standing, quickly putting distance between himself and Newcombe. He got everyone else out with him.

Newcombe sat alone, feeling stupid, feeling used. He hated Crane at this moment, would hurt him if he could. Ishmael had been so right about so many things. He saw with a clarity that defied rationalization.

The Q line was the secure fiber. He tapped it up on his wristpad and pegged in the number he had memorized in the *Diatribe*'s dining room.

Sumi Chan sat before her surveillance terminal, juicing right into the wall screen in her Foundation chalet. "Are you receiving the transmission, Mr. Li?" she asked, the wall screen rerunning a scene of Newcombe speaking with a small projection of Mohammed Ishmael.

"Yes, quite clearly, Sumi. Thank you."

"I felt the subject matter might be of interest to you."

"More than in passing. Pursue whatever connection between Dr. Newcombe and the outlaw that happens your way. We will do the same. Mohammed Ishmael's provocative behavior and poor public ratings have forced us to condemn his actions and the existence of the Nation of Islam as an entity."

"I see," Sumi said, but she didn't see at all. "Is there anything else for now?"

"Keep up the good work. We have big plans for you. *Zaijian,* Sumi Chan. Stay in the shade."

"*Zaijian,* Mr. Li."

Contact broke from Li's end, though his computers had dumped the entire conversation between Ishmael and Newcombe into its memory. Sumi shut down and pulled the green dorph bottle from the desk beneath the full 3-D wall screen.

She moved to the front door. The chalet was huge and roomy, basically one open room with a loft bedroom beneath an A-frame roof. The entire front was open to the outside and a magnificent vista. Under different circumstances she could have known complete peace here.

She stepped out onto her balcony, the wind warm and playful this high up. A lone condor flew beneath her. She felt Mr. Li was making a mistake in condemning the Nation of Islam whose members were consumers, at least to some degree, and in their own way a part of mainstream life in America. Condemnation set them apart and drew attention. That attention could lead to derision, certainly. It could also lead to support. Americans were used to diverse, individual thought patterns. Unchallenged, they would absorb NOI. Forced to choose, however, Americans were likely to opt for freedom, a concept unknown to Mr. Li.

Feeling suddenly melancholy, she uncorked the green bottle and drank directly from it. Her breasts hurt beneath their bindings, a monthly problem. Her special dorph, containing high concentrations of both oxytocin and euphoric PEA, seemed to help, even if it did burden her with a certain sexual yearning that could never be satisfied. No sexual partner could be trusted. Sex itself could not be trusted.

She let the feelings spill over her, warming her, evening her out. Bilious clouds filled the sky, running tapes of Nation of Islam supporters being arrested by the G just outside the beefed-up security checkpoints into East LA. Below, Burt Hill was supervising the setup of a buffet under a large awning for the returning team. There was also a bar, a small aid station, and a stage for a press conference.

Sumi would skip the press this time. All she wanted to do was unbind and hide under the covers in the loft bed. She drank from the dorph again. Maybe today, for once, she could lose herself in bliss.

Chapter 7

BIG BANGS

THE FOUNDATION
3 SEPTEMBER 2024, 3:45 P.M.

A condor flew high above the defensive perimeter of the Crane Foundation. Keeping lone watch over the intruder alarms and electromagnetic jammers, the compound and its occupants, the bird circled and swooped endlessly, perched and glided continuously. The condor's sleek beauty was surpassed only by its complexity, for it was completely electronic and its ganglia were connected directly into the brain of Mohammed Ishmael. Fitting, he thought, that a huge black American vulture should be his spy from above. Soon, if all went as he believed it would, he'd have another spy, almost as reliable, within the Foundation itself.

In Brother Ishmael's opinion, Lewis Crane needed careful watching, for he was the only person on the planet who presented a serious threat to him. Crane challenged Brother Ishmael's apocalyptic vision of the world. He'd known the first moment he'd set eyes on Crane that somehow their fates were linked and, so, it did not trouble him overmuch that his intense preoccupation with the man and the work of his foundation might be entirely irrational, wholly personal . . . and far too time-consuming. It was necessary, though he could not be at all certain why or how.

The eyes of the condor zoomed in on the helo landing zone near the primary building in the Foundation complex. Crane called it "the mosque," which did not amuse Brother Ishmael at all, though it did amuse him considerably to note that the guests arriving at this minute had been at the meeting at sea in June. Everyone had been invited back except him. He threw back his head and laughed.

Lanie King was spectacular in every way, Crane thought as he looked around the central lab or, as he was encouraging everyone to call it now, the globe room. The last three months Lanie had proved herself time and time again. She lived computers, breathed them . . . and she wholeheartedly shared his goal for the globe. She'd hired the programmers, moved them out of the dank back rooms and into the main room so they could be close to the object of their work and appreciate at all times the immensity of the project. Good management that, Crane reflected.

The only thing with which he was dissatisfied was his public role. He ricocheted from one performance to the next . . . song-and-dance man, comic, P.T. Barnum and Cecil B. deMille. By nature introverted, he was depleted by these performances, though he doubted anyone guessed how much they took out of him. This little show today was one of the most crucial of his career. The politicos and money people wanted to see progress; most importantly, Li demanded a quake, and by God he was pretty sure he had one to deliver.

The work of Newcombe and Lanie showed that ground-based radon levels were up by nearly thirty percent all through the Mississippi Valley. Electromagnetic charges were also occurring in the region. Both phenomena possibly came from fault-line stress on rocks: When rocks cracked, radon escaped; when they fractured, they allowed electricity to flow more easily through ground water. Precursors. Probably.

In July, Lanie's computers had used the seismic gap theory of rate of return to predict a major quake on the New Madrid fault line in Missouri. The last big one there had occurred in 1812. He was going to tell all his guests about that historic quake as a preview of coming attractions. His divided soul felt glee and despondency. He needed the quake to go on with his work and, ultimately, save millions of lives. He felt utter dejection, deep grief at the thought of a quake along the 120-mile New Madrid fault line which could destroy everything from Little Rock to Chicago—including Memphis, St. Louis, Natchez. He needed to be right; he hoped he would be wrong . . . at least about the extent of the devastation.

He looked around the dramatically lighted room. A small stand of plush stadium seating had been built near the front doors for the VIPs. They were there, chatting and drinking Sumi's enhanced champagne. Even Mr. Li seemed in good spirits, as did Vice President Gabler, sans wife today, and President Gideon. How these people could be so cheerful was beyond Crane. There had been riots for the last two months in the War Zones, backing the NOI demand for a homeland. Heightened security and the curtailment of food shipments were doing little to keep the occupied territories in line. The Islamic fundamentalists in Paris, Lisbon, Algiers, and London supported their American brethren with rioting. Boycotts of Liang Int products were forcing Mr. Li to capitulate in many areas, particularly relenting on withholding food.

A new sex plague was sweeping the Indian subcontinent, once more confounding dire predictions of overpopulation. Genetic plagues and antibiotic-resistant strains of viruses and bacteria—as well as the ancient enemy of mankind, famine—were proving the Malthusians wrong every day. The food supply was dismal. Very little grew well in the wild anymore; the UV bleaching of crops destroyed everything that wasn't grown beneath the cheap sunshields developed under exclusive patent by Yo-Yu, Liang's major competitor.

In July the President had announced that the government—that is, Liang Int—was funding a major study into the possibility of ozone regeneration, prompting Yo-Yu officials to accuse the administration of attempting to destroy competitive marketing by attacking them directly on the sunblock and sunshield fronts. They called the government study "political terrorism." Crane could only shake his head at the antics of Man. In opposition to the antics of Nature, however, he was prepared to act . . . even now. He stepped up onto the platform where Lanie sat at a computer console and Newcombe at the long table with imbedded microphones that projected even a speaker's whisper through the vast room.

"Ladies and gentlemen," he said, his voice godlike and booming theatrically from dozens of speakers burrowed into the walls.

The room darkened. Crane waited until his audience grew silent, then said simply, "The universe."

Brilliant light flashed for ten seconds. "The universe," Crane continued, "began with a clap of hydrogen and helium, vomiting fiery matter at fantastic speeds in all directions."

The globe burst into holoprojection flame, vibrant reds and yellows swirled about the globe. "Our planet was born into fire about 4.5 billion years ago. Spinning, its contracting clouds of dusts and gases gradually congealed." The globe changed as Crane spoke, holographically showing the formation of the planet from gas to solid. The massive scale of the sphere and the changes it demonstrated overwhelmed the people sitting in the darkness. Crane could hear their appreciative muttering.

"At first we were a planet of molten rock. Slowly, the heavier elements, nickel and iron, settled into a dense inner core. Some of the lighter rocky materials, such as basalt and granite, melted, floated upward, and cooled into a thin crust. There was mantle around the core."

Lanie's fingers flew over the keys of her computer, and

the globe projection transmogrified into a barren, rocky sphere.

"Then it began to rain. . . ."

Thunder reverberated through the room. Holo rain fell on the globe from dense clouds filled with lightning.

"It rained for thousands of years until the planet was covered completely by water. At last the sky cleared."

The globe became a ball of spinning water.

"Cooling at a leisurely pace, the water evaporating, the planet developed land, floating land."

Continental chunks appeared on Lanie's globe, all of them slowly navigating the water world. Everyone watched, rapt, as the continental masses moved toward the equator, finally joining together in a mammoth, still-barren supercontinent.

"Pangaea," Crane said, "Greek for 'all lands,' the starting point for the world we know today. The breakup of Pangaea due to unknown forces, probably convection, brought volcanoes—and the gases of the volcanoes brought the beginning of biological life." Crane paused. "And the breakup of Pangaea brought earthquakes."

Crane looked down at Lanie. "Program the last New Madrid quake into the globe," he said quietly. Newcombe scribbled on a piece of paper, and Lanie hurried to her programmers. She needed more input than she could manage alone to pull this off. Newcombe held up the paper. It read: *Don't stick your neck out!* Crane merely shook his head, smiling wryly.

When Lanie signaled that she and her crew were ready, Crane said, "I call your attention to the United States and the Mississippi River." All the lights went out except for one spot, focused on Middle America.

"It is May of 1811," Crane went on. "The rainfall is bad this spring and rivers overflow. Although people hear a lot of thunder, they note that, strangely, there is no lightning. In the fall, the citizens of New Madrid, in southeast Missouri near the border with Kentucky and Tennessee, are surprised to find tens of thousands of squirrels leaving their forest homes and moving in phalanxes to the Ohio River where they drown themselves. In September, the

Great Comet of 1811 passes overhead, shedding a brilliant and eerie glow over the forests—an omen to many."

Crane walked slowly down the stairs. The globe was no longer spinning, but had stopped before the grand-stand, showcasing the Mississippi Valley.

"America is a lawless frontier. Tecumseh rules the Indian tribes near New Madrid and all through the fall leads many a battle against the forces of General William Henry Harrison. Pirates and robbers ply their trade on the river, forcing cargo boat captains to form convoys for mutual protection. But in the early morning hours of December 16, a Monday, all that becomes secondary."

Crane stepped into the spotlight. "At 2 A.M., Hell comes for a visit."

A loud crack echoed through the room as a huge scar appeared on the globe. "The ground shakes violently, knocking down log houses. A hideous roar, mixed with hissing and a shrill whistling sound, emanates from the ground which opens. Noxious sulfurous odors envelop the surviving settlers. Flashes of light burst from the ground as it rolls. The ground erupts like a volcano, spray-ing water, rock, sand, and coal as high as the treetops. Twenty-six of these events occur during this one night. Horrendous. But only foreshocks. The twenty-seventh is the day of the quake and its power is felt in thirty states. Entire forests are leveled. The ground sinks, reforming it-self, as huge fissures open up, swallowing everything. The Mississippi River reroutes hundreds of times; caught in huge groundswells, it turns into a nightmare of whirlpools and waterfalls, killing everything alive on the river. At one point it flows upstream. As the banks collapse, the river rises, flooding the whole valley, drowning anything not already dead.

"In Jackson, Mississippi, fifty miles from the epicenter, trees snap and buildings fall. In St. Louis, far upriver, light-ning shoots up from the ground, chimneys topple, houses split in two. A thick haze envelops the city for days. Ruin is extensive in Arkansas. Memphis is devastated by land-slides. As far away as Nashville, buildings rumble and quake. A lake just north of Detroit bubbles like a boiling pot. The shocks are felt heavily in Richmond and in Washington, D.C. The statehouse in Raleigh, North Carolina, is rocked during a late-night legislative session. In Charleston, the church bells clang and residents experience nausea from shaking."

Lighted branches on the globe extended out from the quake zone to include most of the United States.

"What has this to do with us, doctor?" Li called.

"A great deal, Mr. Li, because our calculations indicate that another major quake on the New Madrid fault line is years overdue. Many of the precursors of such an EQ are already in place and we are attempting to pinpoint an exact time for this catastrophe. Dr. Newcombe, do you have anything to add?"

Newcombe sat for a moment. He wasn't sure it was time to sound the alarm, but he couldn't very well keep silent after Crane's presentation.

"The Rocky Mountains tend to soak up western quakes," he said at last. "Any quake to their east is going to be devastating. Our initial findings put the death toll at over three million people and the damages somewhere in the vicinity of two hundred and fifty billion dollars. The inherent chaos would affect the country's ability to provide goods and services well beyond the quake areas and onto the international stage. The blow to the economy might doom it, and the country might never recover, much as Great Britain was unable to recover from its Twentieth Century wars."

The entire room fell into a deep, hushed silence. Newcombe took a long breath. "Does that answer your question, Mr. Li?" he asked without rancor.

Crane liked the looks of President Gideon. His concern seemed genuine and he gazed into your eyes when he talked to you. He had an air of command about him that the Vice President lacked. Of course, that didn't make him any more autonomous than Gabler, just easier to deal with.

"I hope you were merely trying to scare us all, Dr. Crane," Gideon said, a drink firmly lodged in his hand. "I surely don't know that I would want to preside over a disaster as all-encompassing as the one you describe."

Mr. Li, standing beside Gideon, leaned up close to the President. "The good doctor doesn't have that kind of a sense of humor," he said. "I think he truly believes the prediction he made today."

"I'm not conjuring spells, gentlemen," Crane said, "if that's what you mean. We're merely building a reasonable scientific hypothesis."

The President cocked his head. "You're not sure this will occur?"

Crane raised his glass, Burt Hill hurrying over to refill it with bourbon. "Oh, it will occur, Mr. President. The Earth will not be denied."

"But the timing, Crane." Li smiled. "This is all about the timing."

"We're working on it," Crane replied, watching both men carefully. "The signs are there. We're trying to put a date on it now. If the globe were finished—"

"But it's not," Gabler said. "And your predictions are so much talk."

"Like Sado was just talk, Mr. Vice President?" Crane replied, staring the man down. "My team is filled with highly skilled professionals who have spent their entire lives building to this moment. What are *your* credentials, sir?"

Gabler's face turned red as Gideon put a hand to his mouth to hide his smile.

"We really must pin this down," Mr. Li said. "The election is only two months away."

"I'm doing my best," Crane said. "To hurry into a wrong prediction wouldn't do anyone any good."

"True enough," Li said. Sumi walked up to pour enhanced champagne into his glass. "Remember that it's in your best interests to come up with something before election time."

"Could you see it?" Gideon said, holding his own glass out to Sumi. "We announce, in advance, a major disaster . . . save millions of lives and billions in property. The Yo-Yu people wouldn't have a chance."

"Unfortunately, Mr. President, I fear that precisely the opposite might happen," Li said, catching Sumi by the arm. "We announce a major disaster, evacuate, shut down factories, protect inventory, only to have it never happen."

"Bite your tongue," Gideon said.

"Those are the stakes," Li said. He turned from the President to Crane, his sober expression changing chameleonlike to one of warm affability. "Is Sumi working out to your satisfaction, Dr. Crane?"

Crane and Sumi shared a smile. "Sumi Chan is the best overseer a project could ask for," Crane replied. "He's on site most of the time, understands the priorities, and writes the checks accordingly. A first-rate associate."

"Excellent," Li said, smiling broadly. He put an arm around Sumi. "Liang Int could use more men like Sumi. You know, doctor, I'm fascinated by your globe. I have one, too."

"I've heard," Crane said. "You'll have to show me sometime."

Li laughed. "I'm afraid that would be impossible. Regulations, you know."

"Of course. Sumi, President Gideon seems to have emptied his glass."

"We can't have that," Sumi said, bringing the bottle around to give Gideon a refill. "At the Foundation, no glasses are allowed to go empty."

Gideon nodded happily. He seemed loose and comfortable, his bodyguards, too, at ease. He raised his glass. "To you, doctor."

They all drank, then Gideon said, "What are the chances of getting a tour of your facility? I find it amazing. If someone's free, I'll—"

"No one knows this place like I do," Crane said. "Come on. Anybody else interested?"

"You two get acquainted," Li said. "I have some business to discuss with Mr. Chan."

"Fair enough," Crane said, leading Gideon off.

Li turned to Sumi. "How close are they really on this New Madrid thing?" he asked, sharp, the foxlike smile with which he'd gifted the others completely gone now.

Sumi shook her head. "I'm not sure. There's a lot of information coming in. I know they've settled on it, but they're still in the process of pinning it down. They might find it won't happen for years."

Li frowned. "I want them to find a quake that's going to happen before the election."

"They can only do what they can do."

"No, Sumi. They can find a quake—if Crane's theories are at all on the mark. But to do so, these people must apply themselves to getting what I want—not indulging themselves playing with their data and their toys—" he sneered "—their basic research. Speaking of research, how is yours on Dr. Newcombe? Is his little journey still on for tonight?"

Sumi nodded, feeling that the net that had fallen over everyone at the Foundation was being tightened. "He'll be traveling under the name Enos Mann. He'll leave with the dark."

"Hmm, gone all night then. The Masada Cloud is scheduled to run in around midnight."

"Are your people in place?"

"Don't worry about my people," Li said, a frown settling on his face as Mui approached. "You take care of pushing these people to get me that prediction. Now I suggest you circulate so that we do not make people suspicious."

Sumi bowed slightly, holding in the tension and the anger. She moved toward Newcombe, wishing there was something she could say, some subtle way she could get across to the man that he should stay at home tonight. Newcombe's actions could doom Crane, the Foundation. Kate Masters, dressed in a bright red body stocking and trailing cape, was talking as Sumi arrived, champagne in hand.

"Oh, Sumi," Masters said, her red hair in tight curls hanging to her shoulders. "You simply must give me the secret of this sometime." She held out her glass.

"Old family recipe," Sumi said, giving Masters the kind of leer she'd seen men do. "Good for your sex life."

"Honey, I got no problems in that department, but fill

me up anyway." She held out her glass, and Sumi poured. In a lot of ways, she felt that Masters played a game of hide-and-seek similar to her own, a game designed for a man's world. There was more, much more, to Masters than she revealed.

"Hey, save some of that for me," Newcombe said, holding out his own glass.

"I want all of you to know," Masters said, taking a long drink, "I think what you're doing here is important. I know that Crane has to sell it to the powers that be and that by its selling it becomes cheapened. But not to me."

"We appreciate that," Lanie said, smiling at her. "We really only want to help people here, but it seems we always have to have an angle."

"Nature of the game," Newcombe said, frowning. "It's a game I hate, but it's the only one in town."

"You scared me to death, you know, with your speech today," Masters said.

"I hope so," Newcombe said. "It's got me scared to death."

"For what it's worth," Masters said, taking another long drink, "we traded the Vogelman Procedure for backing the Crane Foundation, but had the administration declined, we would have backed you anyway. Some things are more important than politics. You people have class."

"Hail fellows well met, huh?" Sumi said. "Good for you. I must go get another bottle now. Stay in the shade."

Sumi left quickly, Lanie following him with her eyes. There was something terribly lonely, terribly sad about Sumi Chan. She didn't trust him, but that didn't stop her from feeling sorry for him. She looked at Masters. "What's involved in the Vogelman?"

"You interested, honey?"

"No," Newcombe answered for her. "We'll just—"

"Yes, I am interested," Lanie said, looking steadily at Newcombe. "I have a lot to do in the next couple of years and I don't want to have to worry about children."

"Single implant," Masters said. "Outpatient stuff, over in fifteen minutes. It stays put forever and keeps you from ovulating—no cramps, no periods." She looked at Newcombe. "A *lot* of women are having it done."

"So much for the world's population," he said.

"You want to get preggie, you take a pill. No sweat. Mothers are having it done on their daughters at puberty. It takes care of one headache."

"It's unnatural," Newcombe said.

Masters flashed her toothy smile. "Easy for you to say, buster. Nature is as nature does. There's a couple of really good doctors in LA who do the procedure, Lanie. You want me to set something up for you?"

"Yes," Lanie said.

"No," Newcombe said.

Masters took a long breath, finished her glass of enhanced. "So . . . maybe you two had better talk it over, eh?"

"I'll call you," Lanie said, glaring at Newcombe. Why did he have to be so overbearing?

"I'd better mingle," Masters said, theatrically tossing her long hair. "They don't pay me to stand here and drink."

"Like hell they don't," Newcombe said.

The woman shrugged. "So I know when to make a graceful exit, okay? Thanks again for the show today. I'll have nightmares for a week." She shook hands with Newcombe and gave Lanie a lingering hug.

"I'll call you tomorrow," Lanie whispered. When Masters was well away, Lanie turned angrily to Dan. "I don't know that I've ever been more embarrassed," she said. "How could you do that?"

"How could I? Isn't something like this a decision both of us should make?"

"Not from where I'm standing. It's my body, my life. And next week I'm going to have the Procedure done whether you like it or not."

"We're not kids anymore," he said. "Your childbearing years won't last much—"

"Childbearing," she said, taking a long breath to relax herself. "I'm not some earth mother just waiting for fertilization, Dan. Why do you always have to spoil—"

"It's a great day!" Crane interrupted. "We set 'em on their asses, didn't we?"

"We promised them something we can't deliver," Newcombe said harshly. "What's so great about that? At the very least you should have waited until we took stress readings on site before announcing the quake to the world."

Crane looked at Lanie. "What's his problem?"

"Babies," she said.

"Babies," Crane repeated, then shivered. "What a horrid thought. Never mind. We'll have all the loose cannons out of here in a tick. I want to invite both of you up to my house for dinner, a little celebration."

Lanie brightened. "That sounds—"

"I can't," Newcombe said.

"What? You got another invitation?" Crane asked.

Lanie watched Dan avert his eyes. "I've got to go down the mountain," he said. "I've been putting off checking the calibration on our San Andreas equipment. It needs to get done."

"Tonight?" Crane said. "It's a Masada night."

"I'll take a burn suit."

"Take two," Lanie said. "I'll go with you."

He shook his head. "You stay here. Enjoy dinner. I'll be back first thing in the morning."

"I really don't mind, I—"

"I want to do this by myself," Newcombe said, Lanie surprised at how mad he was. "Nothing personal . . . I-I need some time to think."

"Think about what?" Lanie asked, suspecting that his behavior had nothing to do with her having the Vogelman Procedure, that it was something else he was hiding from her.

"Doc Dan!" Burt Hill called as he trotted toward them. "It's getting dark. I got the helo out for you if you still want it!"

"Coming!" Newcombe said. "I'll be back in the morning. Enjoy your dinner."

With that, he turned and strode across the globe room without a backward glance.

"What the hell was that all about?" Crane asked.

Lanie shook her head. "I don't know, but it had nothing to do with the San Andreas Fault."

"What do you mean?"

"He sent one of his techs to recalibrate that equipment last week."

9:10 P.M.

"Are you ready yet?" Crane called from the cherrypicker as he sped around the globe on the thing, thirty feet in the air.

"Come down from there!" Lanie shouted. "You're going to kill yourself." The crazy man was hanging out of the gondola and waving a bottle of rum at them.

"I'm too ornery to die!" he yelled through cupped hands. "Get your people's asses in gear and let's crank this thing up."

"We're working on it!"

Sumi was at Lanie's side. "Crane seems . . . exuberant tonight."

"That's one word to describe him, I guess." Lanie was starving. Crane's dinner invitation never quite materialized once he got hung up on the idea of trying out the globe for real. Between Dan's absence and Crane's childishness, she was beginning to feel more like a mother than an associate.

She turned to her programmers, then rolled her eyes at Sumi. "Come on, people. You heard the man. Let's get the thing online."

Groans and complaints came from all down the row. Lanie looked at Sumi. "Can *you* get him down?" she asked.

"I wouldn't even try."

"That's what I thought."

She moved away from the terminals set against the wall and out near the globe, the thing rising majestically into its contoured ceiling. They were so small beside such a large dream. "Get yourself down here!" she called up to

Crane as his hoist made another circumnavigation. "Or I'll shut it down!"

He banged the controls, the hoist jerking to a stop, his gondola swinging wildly. His bottle crashed on the floor near Lanie. "Oops," he said.

"Down, Crane . . . now!"

He brought the gondola down to the floor and stepped out of it, his face boyishly contrite. "My bottle fell," he said.

"I'll get you another," Sumi said, hurrying off.

"Great," Lanie said, looking at Crane. "How much more of that have you got?'

"Cases," Crane said, wiggling his eyebrows. "Cases of rum from the grateful citizens of Le Precheur. What's the holdup on the test run?"

"As you may or may not know, doctor," she said sternly, "we've been feeding info, not programs, into the computers. A task, I might add, that we haven't finished yet. We're having to open up all the pathways for your little test run tonight. These people have been at work all day and they're tired. Give them a minute, okay?"

"You're angry with me," he said, pouting.

"I'm angry at Dan," she said. "You're here. One thick-headed geologist is the same as the next."

"Dan's a big boy. He's got business or something, that's all."

"His life is here. He's got no business below."

"One bottle of Martinique rum." Sumi said, hurrying up to them and giving Crane the bottle. "Unenhanced."

Crane unscrewed the top and took a long drink, turning on his heel to stare at the magnificent globe. "I'm going to go nuts soon if we don't get this thing running."

"You're already nuts," Lanie returned. "Look, you can't expect much this first time out. The intangibles are—"

"The intangibles are the reason I hired you," he said, his smile gone. "That's why the imager is here, to talk to my globe, to synnoetically communicate, to synergize."

"It's not simple, you know. We're getting in all the his-torical data, but we're talking about the life of the planet itself. Somebody digs a pool in Rome, lubricating an unknown fault: Two years later there's a major earthquake in Alaska. We can't program in chaos and we don't know how large, how pivotal, a role it plays."

Crane looked at Sumi. "What do *you* think?"

"I think you need to predict something before the election or we're going to lose our funding. If this will advance that cause, then I'm all for full speed ahead."

Lanie ignored Crane and looked at Sumi. "What the hell good would it do any of us to mispredict? I don't get you. You're as bad as Mr. Li. We can't make the earth perform to our specs."

"We can't survive without funding either," Sumi said, then looked at Crane. "You all but predicted an EQ in mid America within the next few months. I didn't say it, you did."

"We were on the spot," Crane said. "Needed to come up with something, that's all. The signs are there, but not complete signs."

"What else do you need?"

Lanie felt a chill go through her when Sumi asked the question and she wasn't sure why.

"We're going to the site next week to take stress readings. That will tell a more complete story." Crane drank. "Some increased activity after the period of dilation or a foreshock would be nice. More ground-based electrical activity wouldn't hurt either. Though with the dilation process, I'd be willing to do some speculation if the seismic activity picked up again. It's a pretty good sign that lubricating activity has moved the serpentine, the olivine and water mix, into a position to make a major fault slip."

"You'd predict on that?" Sumi asked.

"If push came to shove," Crane said, then pointed to Lanie with his good hand which also held the bottle. "And I want to tell you something. First of all, I want no negativity. We've gotten this far by being positive and bold. Secondly, we're fulfilling the dream of a lifetime here. Your computers are becoming crammed with more knowledge about planet Earth than any other single source encompasses. Answers will lie there. Maybe, once we've assimilated all this knowledge, you might possibly discover a great many things we've never realized before, *including* the notion that there might be a pattern to chaos."

"Don't you ever run down?" she asked.

"Never!"

"I think we're online!" one of the programmers called, a small cheer going up from them all.

"I thank you one and all." Crane turned to Lanie. "Would you like to do the honors?"

She felt it then, the mixture of fear and excitement that she'd held at bay ever since he'd suggested trying the program. She nodded, unable to speak, and walked to the master board, a double-tiered profusion of winking lights, rheostats, and buttons with a single, controlling keyboard below a large monitor.

She juiced the monitor to a flashing cursor and wished that Dan were here, no matter how things came out. She hesitated at the keyboard.

"We don't have any brass bands, Ms. King," Crane said, and he was staring straight up at the monstrous globe.

Fingers shaking, she typed: Advance from Pangaea. Then she took a deep breath and hit the enter key.

With a low groan, the globe started spinning, the continents reforming themselves to the single, great continent of enormous weather variations. It split apart quietly, the continents running red veins of EQs where they broke and sheared against one another.

"Beautiful," Crane said. Lanie was far too involved in watching for glitches in the process to appreciate it. She was a bundle of nervous energy as she walked up to join him.

"What's our first historical interphase?" he asked, his voice hushed.

"The Chicxulub meteor, five miles wide," she said, "sixty-five million years ago."

"The K–T boundary," Crane said.

She stared, shaking, at the globe. "Yeah. Beginning of the Tertiary, end of the dinosaurs. Look for volcanoes on the antipode. There."

The holoprojection of a huge meteor burning in the atmosphere flew through the globe room, slamming into the Yucatán peninsula. A mammoth dust cover rose and spread over the entire globe, the faintest trace of throbbing red lines extending from the impact site showing through the dust as volcanic activity began on the opposite side of the sphere.

Crane reached out and grabbed her arm, his face transfixed as he watched Earth history create itself before his eyes. "Yes," he whispered to her own growing excitement.

And then she heard it: a small bell sound from a distant programming station, then another, and another. The system was shutting down.

"No," she said, breaking free of his grasp and turning to her console, error messages flashing, bells clanging loudly all over the huge room. She turned her back and looked. The globe had shut itself down completely. Crane's head jerked from side to side, and a deep growl issued from his throat.

She reached for the console, her hands ready to type in damage control, but she stopped when she saw words written on the monitor that she'd hoped never to see:

No Analog—System Incompatible.

Her hands fell to her sides in utter confusion, Crane striding quickly to stand beside her.

"Get on with it," he said. "Work the inconsistency."

"I can't," she said, pointing to the screen. "I wouldn't know where to start."

He read the words, then spun her by the shoulders to face him. "What does it mean?"

A horrible confusion took hold of her as other programmers walked slowly to form a loose cordon around her and Crane. "It means that the Mexican crater cannot be made to fit historically with anything else we've programmed into the machines. It's telling us this is impossible."

"No," he said, then louder, "No! I will not accept that. Reset it and let's do it again."

"Look, Crane," she said. "There are two possibilities. One is that we misprogrammed, which is understandable considering you gave us no time to double-check ourselves. To fix that, we'll have to go back over everything we've done tonight, checking it every step of the way. These people are too tired for that."

"What's the other possibility?"

She took a long breath. "Events before Chicxulub, perhaps the breakup of Pangaea itself, had already altered the world so much that the meteor's impact had a different effect than the one shown on our globe."

"You told me that the machine could define and correct such inconsistencies by running through the limited possibilities of missed events."

She watched him tilt the bottle to his lips and drink half of it in one long pull. He was, as always, a time bomb ready to explode. "That's between known event and known event," she said. "Between, say Chicxulub and the walls of Jericho falling. But Chicxulub's as early as we know about. Anything before that is pure speculation."

He pointed at her again, his finger shaking with drunken rage. "Still within a limited scope of possibilities," he said, turning from her to walk to the globe, staring straight up at it, as if concentration could give him the answers of his life. For the first time since she'd come to work for Crane, she began to wonder how much of his energy carried this project. It wouldn't be the first time that a crazy man had talked people into believing nonsense.

He turned to her. "Crank it up again," he said. "We'll check the program as we go."

"No," she said. "My programmers are tired. *I'm* tired. Let's try it again in the morning."

"I gave you an order!"

"And I refused it."

"Damn you!" he yelled, flinging his arm up. The half-finished bottle went flying into the globe, smashing on Siberia. Acrid smoke rose where the rum had drenched the wiring. "You're fired!"

"Fine," she said, and turned to the group of

programmers huddled around her. "Go on home. We're through here for the night. Your new boss will tell you what to do tomorrow."

"I think we need to get him home," Sumi said.

"The hell with him."

"Lanie. . . ."

Lanie nodded wearily and moved to take Crane by his bad arm while Sumi took his good. "Come on, we'll get you home," Sumi said. "You need sleep."

"I don't need sleep," Crane said, reluctantly letting them lead him out, watching the globe as they dragged him away. "I need to sit down and work." He turned and kissed Lanie on the cheek. "Ah, perhaps it's a matter of weight. How much did you add to Earth's total?"

"A thousand short tons a day because of meteor impacts."

"Try adding in more weight than that in earlier times. Meteor activity is far less now than it was a billion years ago."

"Whatever you say," she returned, and they got him outside, Crane brushing them off to stand on his own.

He looked up at the sky, the Moon three-quarters full, running scenes of bloody car wrecks on its side. "That's where I need to live," he said, pointing, then looking at both hands for a bottle that was no longer there. "Up there I could watch the lunacy rise in the morning and set in the evening." He guffawed.

They walked toward the staircases set into the mountainside. "At least you wouldn't have to worry about earthquakes on the Moon," Lanie said.

Crane and Sumi laughed. "The Moon has earthquakes," Sumi said.

"Really?"

"About three thousand a year," Crane said, weaving.

"Is there a core?"

"Yep," Crane answered. "A nine-hundred-mile diameter. They're little quakes though, Richter 2s. Very seldom break the surface. Almost like a quake memory."

"A memory of what?" Sumi asked.

"I don't know." Crane stared again at the Moon. "A

man could build a world to suit himself up there. Not like the mining companies, the takers, but a world of truth."

"You're starting to sound like Dan," Sumi said. "There is no truth."

"Science is truth," Lanie said quickly. "Love is truth."

"There is no such thing as love," Sumi replied bitterly, the first time Lanie had ever heard the man expose anything of himself. "Love is simply a disguise for pain."

"That's not true," Lanie said.

Sumi looked at her, eyes inscrutable. "Then where is your man tonight?"

"The lie of freedom," Crane said, quoting Newcombe. "The lie of security. The lie of politics. The lie of religion." He turned to Lanie. "You're not fired."

"Thank you . . . I think."

"You must make the globe work. Do you understand what I'm saying? This can't stop here; it just can't. The dream . . . the dream. . . ."

Lanie shuddered, thinking of dreams and realizing why she was so upset that Dan was gone. She'd have to face the night alone. "I'll do everything I can to make the globe work," she said. "Trust me."

"I do trust you. I trust you as much as I trust Dan . . . or Sumi, here." He patted the small man on the back, Chan looking uncomfortable. It made Lanie sad to think Crane's world was so small he had to trust Sumi Chan, though she could think of no reason for the feeling.

A bell sound drifted on the warm breeze across their plateau, followed by the compound computer's voice saying: "The radiation levels have risen to an unacceptable range. Please take shelter and appropriate precautions immediately."

The immediate response was the sound of closing doors and snapping windowshields.

"The cloud," Crane said, pointing to the west. The Masada Cloud. "We'd better get indoors. Let's go up to my place for a drink. What do you say?"

"Crane," Lanie said, "if you'd ever open your eyes you'd realize that I can't go up to your place."

He stared at her, face slack, then his eyebrows shot up.

"Vertigo," he said. "I remember now. You're afraid of heights."

"Petrified, is more like it," she said. "My knees weaken and I simply shut down physically."

Crane laughed. "I always wonder why you and Dan never come up to visit me. You're just full of surprises."

They had arrived at the stairs; Lanie walked up to the first landing, the lowest level where the bungalow she shared with Dan was located. Crane, using Sumi for support, straggled behind. "If you think that's something," she said, "wait until you hear about the nightmares."

"Nightmares?" he said, reaching the landing.

"I dream about Martinique every time I go to sleep."

"What are you dreaming?" he asked.

"I'm remembering little things," she said and shivered. The wind blowing in with the Cloud was cold. "Pieces. I remember sitting in the dark and touching that poor boy's body. I remember . . . rum."

"What else?"

She frowned. Crane seemed upset about her dream. "You're in the dream," she said slowly. "You're wearing a big, bulky suit . . . all white like a burn suit, only bigger . . . more solid. You're all excited about something, but I can't hear you through all the bulky clothing, I . . . I'm not sure. There's screaming and explosions all around me, and that dead boy is there . . . and all the men covered with mud. I-I guess the worst of it is the feeling it makes me have."

"What feeling?"

"Like I'm waiting to die." Tears came rolling down her cheeks. She reached for the knob on her front door.

"Lanie, I—"

"I've got to go in," she said abruptly. She went inside quickly before Sumi and Crane could see her fall apart.

"Dan," she cried softly, burying her face in her hands. "Where the hell are you, you son of a bitch?"

She went to bed and cried herself to sleep—and had the nightmare again, only this time Crane was reaching for her in his bulky suit, trying to make her take his hands. This time, she could hear the word he was yelling: Pangaea.

Chapter 8

CHAOS THEORY

THE LA WAR ZONE
3 SEPTEMBER 2024, 9:20 P.M.

Newcombe walked slowly through the carnival on the edge of darkness, two blocks from the leveled ground surrounding the Zone. The sidewalks, even the streets, were clogged with people rushing to beat the Cloud and with off-duty federal cops killing time.

Lines were long at the dorph and food markets, customers nervously watching the skies while residents bolted steel shutters and doors to their homes and business establishments, preparing for Masada. Everyone was hoping it wouldn't rain. As always, the broken streets were camouflaged with the eye candy of swirling light and color as teev played on the blank walls and holoprojections wandered aimlessly through crowds or talked to their owners, keeping them company in line.

Newcombe was, quite literally, looking for trouble. Brother Ishmael had finally talked him down off the mountain. He was excited. Being with Brother Ishmael, even if it had been only his projection and only twice a week, had made Newcombe feel a part of a larger life force. But the meetings had intensified his internal conflict. He wanted success and acceptance in the white and Asian world, while he also wanted the wholeness of identity and comfort that came from solidarity with his Africk brothers and sisters.

He stopped a dorph street vendor, a little white man, and bought a liquid dose.

"You know where the Horizon Parlor is?" he asked as he took the small bottle that the vendor had poked a straw into.

"One block . . . right down there." The vendor pointed into a kaleidoscopic mass of bright light and motion. "You don't look the type."

"What type is that?"

"Head jobs . . . chippies, whatever you want to call them." He narrowed his eyes and looked at the sides of Newcombe's head, trying to spot interface ports. "First time?"

"What're you, a cop?" Newcombe asked.

The man's eyes widened. "You don't have to insult me!" He marched away with his cart, and Newcombe started to work his way through the mob. Security cams were everywhere, but he always wondered who monitored their output. There were ten times more cameras than people in Los Angeles, with the G there to back them up, their smiling face masks making them look like benign Golems, their small booking robots toddling along with them. But there was to be no trouble tonight. The crowd was polite, evened out. Business as usual.

"There!" someone called. Newcombe tightened up, but was immediately relieved to see that people were pointing upward at the night sky. The first wisps of black cloud were drifting overhead. He needed to get indoors.

He picked up the pace, relieved to see the word HORIZON in blood-red Gothic print, drifting in the air in front of an unmarked steel two-story building. He hurried to the sole door he could see in its windowless facade and got inside.

He'd never been in a chip club before, had no idea what to expect. Liang had condemned the use of direct access brain chips long ago because chip addicts didn't consume much except chips. But free enterprise was not to be denied and Yo-Yu had moved in to fill the void left by Liang, opening chip clubs despite bans against advertising and aggressively restrictive zoning laws.

He passed through a narrow, dark foyer, then through another door into a wide white beach looking out into an endless ocean. He could smell the ocean and feel the hot, salty breeze. He could barely hear the noise of the outside world, the warning horns bleating, telling the citizens to get off the streets.

A Chinese man in a swimsuit was walking toward him from way down the beach. Newcombe sat on a canvas chair and waited.

The man came close. "Excuse me . . . sir!" he called.

The man stopped and turned. "Lovely day, isn't it?"

"I'm wondering if you could help—"

"I've got to go. I've lost my dog," he said.

A gull flew down to perch on Newcombe's shoulder. "Sorry," the gull said. "I was tied up in back. Someone didn't want to vacate when their time was up. Waiting long?"

"I'm supposed to meet someone here," Newcombe said carefully.

The gull took to the skies, flying circles around Newcombe. "If you don't have a reservation," it said, "you won't be doing anything. We're always booked solid on Masada nights."

"My name is Enos Mann."

The bird squawked, then landed on his head. "Ah, Arabian adventure," it said. "We've been expecting you. Follow me."

The gull flew out over the ocean. Newcombe followed, stepping into the water without getting wet. He felt a curtain in his face, and parted it to find a hallway filled with doorways. A man was staring at him. "This way, please," he said in the gull's voice.

Moans and cries issued from behind the closed doors. Newcombe had seen chippies on the teev, but Liang always had them portrayed as emaciated shells, living only for the brain fix. He had no idea of what it was really like to interface directly with a computer, though the thought of joining with the Foundation's machines struck him as a marvelous notion.

The man opened the next to last door, ushering him into a bare utilitarian room containing a bed and a recliner, with a small table set between them. An inch-square chip sat in the center of a tiny red pillow. Alongside on the Formica of the table was a box with flashing numbers, its meter.

"You heard the horns?" the man asked as he slid the bed aside to reveal a manhole cover in the floor.

"Yeah."

"You're here for the night." The man stomped twice on the manhole, then left, the steel door clicking locked behind him.

His heart beating fast, Newcombe stared around the room. He picked up the chip, studied it, wondered about the moans and laughter he'd heard. If he were to change his mind, this would be the last possible instant in which he could get out. He looked at the door, then at the manhole in the floor.

It moved. Newcombe jumped back as it lifted, a smiling face peering out of the darkness. "Brother Daniel!" Mohammed Ishmael said and chuckled, "How pale you've turned."

"You make a grand entrance." Ishmael climbed out of the hole and hugged Newcombe. Two young men eased over the rim and into the room. They had scanners and came close to examine Newcombe.

"I see there was a big meeting today at the Foundation," Ishmael said, straightening his dashiki.

"How did you know that?" Newcombe asked, raising his hands up so they could scan under his arms.

"I keep tabs on my brother," Ishmael said. "He moves in elite circles. How is President Gideon? What's he like?"

Newcombe shrugged. "He's a politician."

"Who isn't? Is Liang still insisting on a quick prediction?"

"Very quick."

Ishmael fixed him with bright eyes. "It's a rollover, Brother. Remember I told you that. Watch out."

The scanners were buzzing. "Two transmitters," one of the young men reported. "One on the right hand, the other on the left sleeve."

"The one on the hand is mine," Ishmael said, moving to look at Newcombe's sleeve.

"I don't know anything about this," Newcombe said, suddenly frightened at the position he'd put himself into. "I would never—"

"Of course you wouldn't," Ishmael said, pulling the bug, scarcely bigger than a mite, off his sleeve and stomping on it. "This could have come from anyplace. They float on the breezes outside."

"We must go," one of the bodyguards said.

Ishmael nodded and moved to the manhole. "Follow me, Brother." He started climbing down.

Newcombe was really scared now. The bug queered everything. Not only was he consorting with the enemy, but also there was someone who knew about it. Gently pushed from behind by one of the bodyguards, he realized as he walked to the opening in the floor that he was no longer in control of his life, and wondered if Ishmael had planned it this way.

A metal ladder led down into darkness. He looked over his shoulder at the bodyguards, one climbing down on his heels, the other locking the manhole over them. He reached ground about thirty feet later, Ishmael right beside him, his face glowing faintly in the haze of a red dry cell light in the brick sewer.

He started to speak but was interrupted by a menacing buzzer. "Uh-oh," Ishmael said loudly over the noise. "The G is at the door. Come on, you'll get to see what it's like to be a revolutionary."

They strode through a long tunnel, lit with the same bloody haze. It seemed to stretch on forever. They were moving fast, the bodyguards always right behind.

"This doesn't look like the sewer system," Newcombe said as they hurried along.

"It's not. We built it."

"How?"

"Prisoners dig. That's what they do." He took a sharp right turn and walked into, then through, a wall. Newcombe followed, the wall a projection. He found himself in another hallway, this one tiled and well lit. It branched off to either side at ten-foot intervals. "We will fight in these tunnels and escape through them, should it come to that," Ishmael said.

He turned into another wall, and Newcombe, confused, followed closely. They were at the top of an ornate winding staircase. They descended. Or was it an illusion?

"I didn't mean how did you dig them," Newcombe said. "I meant how did you *afford* to dig them?"

"Money is not a problem for us. Space is. We have many benefactors, people like you who have found their way to us and are sympathetic to an Islamic State on this continent. There is much you don't understand."

"Apparently. And, by the way, I really didn't lead the G here intentionally. I have no idea how that—"

"Nature of the white man's world," Ishmael said, waving it off as he reached the bottom of the stairs.

They were in a vast echoing cave honeycombed with tunnels. It was lit by torches, hundreds of them. Ishmael moved quickly across the chamber.

"Are we going to be caught?" Newcombe called from behind as he hurried without prompting now.

"Hope not!"

They ran for nearly a minute before reaching rock walls. Ishmael pulled on a ground-level boulder, the cave face creaking open to reveal an elevator within.

Once they were all inside, Ishmael pushed a button to close the rock doors. They moved through the virtual back of the machine and into another hallway whose walls, ceiling, floor were tiled in ceramic squares of the palest blues and yellows. There were no doors. Ishmael slowed his pace, Newcombe realizing they were close to their destination. The beauty of the elevator was that its function motor could disguise the virtual projection equipment.

"Does the elevator go down?" he asked.

"And up," Ishmael said. "It leads into a myriad other passages, even into the *real* sewer system. You're the one who's in trouble, you know."

Newcombe knew. "Whoever owns that bug owns my ass," he said bitterly. "You didn't do it, did you?"

Ishmael looked Newcombe dead in the eye and shook his head. "We're on the same side, Brother."

"I hope so," Newcombe said. The hallway was well lit now and twisted sharply to the right.

The hallway was cracked all the way around, the walls out of line. "How far down are we?" Newcombe asked.

"Fifty . . . seventy-five feet. The earth shifts a bit, eh?"

"This is part of the Elysian system of faults," he said, excited to look at a transform fault. He ran his hand over the jagged, angry crack. "How long has it been like this?"

"Maybe two years. Gets a little worse each day."

Other people were walking toward them along the hall. "This isn't going to stop," Newcombe said. "It will eventually destroy this whole section of tunnels."

"Allah protects," Ishmael said easily. A crowd of about twenty people, mostly men, surrounded them. Some of them were teenagers. And all of them were armed. "We've lost other tunnels."

A young woman in a black jumpsuit was at his elbow, her face inquisitive, her eyes were Ishmael's eyes. "You must be Khadijah," Newcombe said.

"Well, you've brought us a mind reader, my brother," she said, the group laughing.

"This is Daniel Newcombe, the man I've told you about."

"Oh?" Khadijah said. "The man who doesn't have the courage to join with our Jihad?"

"Yeah," Newcombe said, staring her down. "That's me." He turned to Ishmael. "Have you ever checked the radon levels down here?"

"No."

"I'll send you some equipment. Radon can be deadly. Best to know what we're deal—"

"I trust there are no Elysian Faults and radon emissions in North Carolina," Ishmael said.

Newcombe stared at him, the true zealot at home with his inventions. Or a visionary. Like Crane. "You want me to butt out . . . I'll butt out."

"I want you to butt in," Ishmael said, smiling widely and slapping him on the back. He pointed toward the ceiling. "But up there, Brother, not down here. Up there. Come on."

They went to a pale green door with a crescent moon and single star of Islam painted on it. Ishmael ushered Newcombe inside what looked like a large briefing room with chairs, a stage, small kitchen and break area.

"We'll meet my brother Martin," Ishmael said, leading him toward a far door. Khadijah walked with them, a frown on her face, as she sized up Newcombe.

Newcombe saw guns. And ammunition. Everywhere. Boxes of ammunition stacked high against the walls.

He hadn't seen a gun in fifteen years, ever since personal security had become the national priority. Everyone who could afford bodyguards and security systems had them. Offensive weapons had become easily detectable by X-raydar, automatically marking anyone carrying them as a criminal and, consequently, fair game for legal defensive retaliatory response. Offensive weapons, not surprisingly, had fallen into disuse.

Ishmael took him into an office where a middle-aged man dressed in a white robe and small white fez smiled through his salt-and-pepper beard. He was lean, coiled like a snake.

"I have just heard the reports," he said. "Allah, in his infinite wisdom, has declined to let it rain on the War Zone tonight."

"Good news," Ishmael said. "Brother Daniel, this is my brother, Martin Aziz. It was Martin's idea to approach you."

"*Asalaamu aleycum,*" Aziz said, leaning over a desk

that separated them to hug Newcombe fiercely, then kiss him on both cheeks. He pointed to miniature security teevs covering the far wall. "I noticed you had some trouble tonight."

"My doing, I'm afraid," Newcombe said, stealing a glance at Khadijah, who was rolling her eyes.

"Don't worry," Aziz said. "They never got past the phony sewer system. They found another manhole and climbed back out, chasing several projections we planted for them. Sit down, Brother Newcombe. It's you we must worry about now, since the FPF knows you are with us."

"What will they do to me?" Newcombe asked, taking a hard-backed chair near the desk, Ishmael and his sister sitting on a couch across from him.

"Impossible to say." Ishmael shrugged. "They do what they want. Make up the rules as they go. Have you ever known anyone to come out of an FPF jail?"

"No," Newcombe said, "but I've never known any criminals . . . I mean, not until now."

Everyone laughed, even Khadijah.

"I think you're safe," Aziz said, "as long as you're associated with Liang. Away from their protection, who knows?"

"Could Crane have planted your bug," Ishmael asked, "to keep you under control?"

"That's very unlikely. Brother Ishmael, he and I are scientists. All we're trying to do is make life a little better on this planet. Is that so difficult to—"

"That's all *you* want," Khadijah said. "From what I've heard, Crane is a complex and devious man."

"He's a driven man."

"But driven to what?" Ishmael asked, getting off the sofa and walking over to Newcombe. "Don't answer. Just think about it."

"If your association with us becomes public knowledge," Aziz asked, "what will happen to you and the Crane Foundation?"

"I have no idea. . . . You asked Brother Ishmael to approach me?"

"Correct," Aziz replied. "You see, my brother and I

have a very different way of looking at things. You may have noticed that I chose Martin, the name of nonviolence, when I rejected my slave name. I believe that the world is ready to hear our righteous demands. We simply need African and Hispanic men of stature in the white world to present them for us. Unfortunately, my brother is the only public symbol we have. People fear him. I want to show America a different side."

"Whites never give up anything without a fight," Ishmael said. "Even though outnumbered by other races, they *still* control the country through the Chinese overlords. The only thing they will listen to is Jihad. We make enough trouble and they will give us what we want to shut us up."

"Can't people just vote them out of office?" Newcombe asked. "The teev is right there. Its voting button—"

"Where have you been?" Khadijah asked. "The Chinese will only let whites run for office because they know that whites will maintain the financial status quo. They control the government with money, keeping the whites rich, everybody else beholden."

"But why should the Chinese fear you?"

Ishmael laughed and returned to his seat. "We are the next wave, Brother. They will have to make way for us. They should be frightened. They walled us up to end their 'crime' problem and still our numbers grow, our influence expands. We do not ingest their poisons. We are strong and incorrigible. The Koran is our guide. We are of the world. They are of history."

"While Leonard rants," Martin Aziz said, glancing with a slight smile at Ishmael, who was looking angry at the use of his slave name, "I've been thinking about your position. You know, Crane is keeping you down, second to him. I've learned about your EQ-eco system and wonder why you don't use it to elevate yourself a bit. Celebrity makes it much easier to absorb controversy such as you find yourself in."

"Crane doesn't want to publish yet," Newcombe said. "What can I do?"

"You're a free man," Ishmael said. "Do what you

choose. You tell me this will help the world. So, help the world. Achieve your potential."

"And become a better spokesman for you," Newcombe replied. "It's a moot point. I work for the Foundation, which owns intellectual property rights over anything I come up with. My hands are tied."

Aziz reached out. "Here, Brother. Let me untie you. Your slavery is not becoming."

"Go against Crane?" Newcombe said.

"Why not?" Aziz asked. "He'd go against you in a heartbeat."

"He's done a lot for me, I—"

"No!" Ishmael shouted, pointing a long finger. "*You've* done a lot for him. Don't you see? What has Crane ever done but use you to make himself look good? Do you think it's wrong for him to deny the world your discoveries?"

"Yes, it's wrong," Newcombe said. This was something he'd stewed about for weeks. "Of that I'm sure."

Ishmael leaned down close from his perch on the desk, his voice raspy with anger. "You grovel to a man like Crane because an Africk can't survive in the white man's inner world without an owner. Are you too lost in the white woman or tied up in your own webs to see that?"

"Damn you," Newcombe said, standing, pacing.

"But from me," Ishmael said, "it makes sense, doesn't it?"

Newcombe took a long breath, tried to repress his anger at Crane . . . and couldn't. "Yes," he said, "it makes sense."

"Then I've convinced you?"

"No, but you've made some inroads."

Ishmael slid over to the office door and locked it. He turned back, grinning. "I'm in no hurry."

GRABENS
THE MISSISSIPPI VALLEY—NEAR NEW MADRID
10 SEPTEMBER 2024, LATE AFTERNOON

Gary Panatopolous was a contractor with the Geological Survey. A digger, he was paid by the job, not the depth of the hole he gouged into the earth. He'd been fighting Lanie, Crane, and Newcombe for three straight days up and down the Mississippi about how deep to make the holes. He did not want to dig so much or so deep. His five-year-old son was with him today, standing like his father with hands on hips, scowling at the Foundation team.

His machine, which he called Arthro, was large and black, crouching on eight legs like a spider over a hole that was five feet in diameter. His drill bit was bigger than several men and powerful enough to throw the sediment a mile back up and out of the hole. The digger was two stories high and a block long and sent geysers of dirt and mud heavenward. As it finished each section of digging, its spider legs placed pipe to secure and stabilize the hole. Long after Crane and the team were gone, Mr. Panatopolous would be filling the hole in again.

Newcombe walked between the legs of the digger to join the others; the drill was moving up and down, sucking at the lifeblood of the Earth.

"You people are crazy!" Panatopolous was saying as Newcombe arrived, confirming his status as an honest man to Dan. "What'd'ya think you're gonna find that deep, huh? Buried treasure?"

"If we're lucky," Crane said, his hood pushed back while they stood in the shade of the digger's underbelly. "Dan, have you had any contact with Burt?"

"He supervised thirty seismo setups," Newcombe said above the eerie growl emanating from the depths of the hole. "Everything's up and running. All we need is Nature's cooperation."

"Nature never cooperates," Crane said. "Tame it or live with it. Those are the only options."

"Yeah," Lanie said, while tapping her wristpad. "It's me. What?"

"I'm gonna lose money on this whole deal," Panatopolous snapped.

"Got it," Lanie said. "Keep juicing." She glanced from man to man. "Get on the N channel and take a look at this."

Newcombe punched his wristpad, the inside of his goggles instantly showing a chart of the numbers of known earthquakes in the Mississippi Valley by the months of the year. Fully seventy percent of the earthquakes in this area occurred between the months of November and February.

"We're on with research," Lanie said. "Want to ask a question?"

"See what you can find about relationships to lunar phases and solar flares," Crane said. He turned back to Panatopolous, speaking low. "You do what you can for me, and I'll do what I can for you. Fair?"

"Fair," the digger said, nodding firmly just as a horn bleated, signifying completion of the digging of this hole. "We have reached six thousand and . . . fourteen feet. I'll get the gondola."

Newcombe kept the N channel on his aural and listened to the response from research.

"We find no correlation between lunar phases and Mississippi Embayment quakes. However, there does seem to be a close relationship between sunspot activity and Reelfoot displacement. Major quakes have taken place during periods of low sunspot activity. Observe the graph."

Newcombe didn't bother putting it on. Instead he watched the hole; the thick cable of the digger rewound quickly, whistling, spooling up inside the digger itself—the spider retracting its web.

"What about this year's solar activity?" Crane asked.

"Few sunspots," the researcher said, "the fewest since . . . 1811."

Crane was not surprised, but Newcombe's mouth went dry, and Lanie sucked in her breath.

"There's the gondola," Newcombe pointed out.

They cut transmission and hurried to the digger which was wheezing bright white smoke from its open belly fifteen feet above.

Newcombe put on a backpack containing a water drill and climbed into the elevator-size car, followed by Crane and Lanie. Crane cradled the spike like a baby.

They journeyed quickly down the tube, freefalling, interior lights coming on. They pulled off their goggles and headgear. A mile passed, brake skids slowing their descent the last several hundred feet. Finally, the gondola clanged against the rock of the graben.

Lanie knelt to pull off the floor round, so like a manhole cover, Newcombe thought, smiling wryly. They stared down at five-hundred-million-year-old rock.

They sat on the edge of the opening, planting their feet on the rock. It was smooth and flat, polished by the digger. Newcombe got out the drill and attached the gauging armature to the front. "Turn me on," he told Lanie, who flipped the switch on the backpack that juiced the compressor.

Pressurized water shot from the nozzle in a pencil-thin line, drilling easily into the rock, the nozzle then moving down the armature until it hit bottom after about ten inches.

He released the pressure and pulled away the drill. Crane unwrapped the ten-inch spike and its toy hammer. The spike had a hairlike appendage on the end, the brains of the machine. He looked at Lanie. "Would you like to do the honors?"

She smiled and took the apparatus, leaned forward and slid the spike into the drill hole until barely a half inch protruded. She used the hammer then, tapping the spike gently. An activation hum sounded immediately.

"I'm already tied to the van's system," Newcombe said, pulling the tiny interface out of his wristpad to hook to the top of the spike. He married the units, then hit enter, the wristpad bleeping as it measured the amount of compression stress being exerted on the rock of the graben.

He ran some of it through his goggles as it fed to the van. "What's the slippage on this a year?"

"Couple inches," Crane said, "accumulated over two hundred years."

Numbers in red and blue flashed past Newcombe's eyes. "That's over thirty-three feet in slip built up. A lot of pressure. I'm looking at stress numbers here that exceed anything I've ever seen. We're getting damned close to the rupture threshold."

The numbers stopped. "There's going to be an earthquake here," Newcombe whispered, "and soon."

"I know," Crane said, holding his left arm and grimacing.

At that moment a wall of noise rumbled through the rock, their cavern shaking for several seconds, dirt cascading down and coating them.

"Real soon," Newcombe said. Lanie clutched his shoulder.

Crane calmly tapped his wristpad. "Take us up, Mr. Panatopolous," he said. "We're finished."

Sumi listened to the down link bleep on her console and knew she was hearing a grace note in the long sonata that had begun several months before in *VEMA*'s observation deck at the bottom of the Pacific. Her swan song.

Outside it was raining. Most of the crew at the Foundation had taken the day off since both Crane and Burt Hill were in Missouri. Everyone from techs to department heads were outside, their voices drifting happily up to Sumi's perch.

Dutifully, she tapped the R line, Mr. Li's open emergency line. He answered immediately.

"It's Sumi Chan, sir," she said. "You asked me to inform you when the New Madrid party started sending back data. I've used security access to divert it to me instead of the Foundation's computers." Sumi felt ashamed.

"Good initiative, Sumi," Mr. Li said in an almost humorous tone that was quite unlike him. Something was happening. "Are these the stress readings you told me Crane thought so important?"

"Crane said he'd do a prediction based on the results of the stress tests, yes." She could feel it coming, the decision of her lifetime. She always had engaged in situational ethics, and she felt she had no inner reserves of strength to draw from in making this decision.

"What are your recommendations?" Li prompted.

Sumi drew a long breath. "I have none," she said finally.

"You've stolen their numbers, yet have no recommendation?"

"Sir," Sumi said, "any recommendation I could make would be cancelled out by adverse conclusion."

"Hold on," Li said, clicking off. A second later, he materialized beside her desk in projection.

"Come . . . sit with me, Sumi. It's time we talked."

She rose from the computer and followed the projection to her sofa. Li, a wicked glint in his eye, offered her a seat before sitting himself. He hovered two inches above the lowslung couch.

"Now," Li said. "Suppose you tell me what the recommendation is, then let *me* judge the 'adverse conclusion' for myself. Please."

Sumi's mind was melting down. Generation equipment had to be hidden somewhere in her chalet in order to bring off his projection. And he knew that she knew. The noose tightened around her neck. Who watches the watcher?

She cleared her throat. "If you want to have Crane predict before the election, simply change the stress numbers, making them infinitesimally larger, increasing the notion of the stress, making the problem seem more immediate. I know enough about the EQ-eco to work the math and bring the numbers up to rupture point."

"Wonderful," Li said, smirking. "What could possibly be the downside of that?"

"You don't see?" Sumi asked, and reached into the pocket of her work pants for dorph gum. "These people, Mr. Li, are on the verge of predicting the most devastating earthquake in the history of the United States of Liang America. I trust their judgment." She stuck two pieces of gum in her mouth. "If we intentionally mispredict, you're leaving a large population base at tremendous risk for when the quake really *does* come."

Li shrugged. "We're trying to win an election here. There have been several destructive quakes in different parts of the country since the last election. People are afraid and they'll be grateful for our concern whether the prediction turns out to be correct or not. They'll vote for our candidates."

"Didn't you hear what I said?"

"I can limit Liang's exposure to damage and loss in that area, if a quake does occur later. I'll be prepared." He stared at Sumi. "Has it ever occurred to you that if the government really got into the prediction business in a serious way that it would end up in court? A mess. That's what the whole thing is. But as a device for achieving results in the election? Excellent. So, change the numbers."

"Sir," Sumi said, bowing slightly. "I mean no offense, but I can't implement an order I find immoral, dangerous to so many people."

Mr. Li grinned, his cosmetically whitened teeth gleaming. The projection put a ghostly hand on Sumi's shoulder. "Look what I have here."

A holo of her bathroom appeared in the center of the living room. Sumi watched herself emerge from the shower. No doubt about her gender. She flushed with embarrassment. "So you know."

"You are a fine-looking woman, Sumi," Li said, his hands trying to run down her body, but disappearing within her instead. Somehow that made the violation worse. "Does anyone else know?"

"Just you," she said, "which I fear is enough."

Li laughed. "I do not wish to expose you to public and private humiliation. I wish only to keep using you as my instrument. Now I have the knowledge to hold you. I have many plans for you. I ask you again, will you do as I ask?"

She frowned heavily. "I've worked side by side with these people. They're good, I like—"

"I've now got the Geological Survey on the line. I am prepared to tell them you're a liar and a pretender—and to give my recommendation to terminate you immediately. Decide now."

Sumi bent over, face in her hands. "I'll do it," she said finally, her voice muffled.

"What?"

"I'll do it," she said louder. She stood and went to the console, sat, and began typing. She finished within a minute and dumped the altered numbers into the mainframe. She had cheated people her entire life. Now she was cheating the purity of science.

"Done," she said, turning around. The projection was gone. Sumi went into the bathroom and washed her hands.

Chapter 9

SOUND WAVES

**THE CRANE FOUNDATION
1 OCTOBER 2024, 6 P.M.**

Crane's office wasn't really an office. It was a hovel—a large hovel to give him plenty of space to pile his junk. Printouts were stacked all over the floor, many of the stacks wobbled or collapsed and were left as they fell. Books filled cases and overflowed onto the flood of paper. His desk was littered, its wood surface completely obscured. Coffee cups and food wrappers were strewn everywhere, computer terminals and printers crammed onto any surface that could take them. He had a bed in the office, several empty liquor bottles lying beside it. Crane knew exactly where anything he wanted could be found.

On the wall was a smoke-damaged photo of his parents and a melted toy airplane was stuck on one of the bookcases. They had been the only things recovered from the firestorm that had eaten his childhood home and the only personal items Crane owned. He was a man possessed by his past, a human being only in the biological definition of the word.

There was a hole cut right through his cinderblock wall so that he could look at the globe whenever he wanted.

An edge of excitement jangled the room. He had assembled most of his senior staff, who'd dutifully shown up carrying their folding chairs and coffee while he half reclined on the bed. He was about to make the decision of his lifetime and wanted their input, not to help him make the decision of course, but to reinforce what he'd already decided.

Lanie and Dan hadn't arrived yet. Newcombe was trying to hurry out his EQ-eco chart, and Lanie was supervising the globe through another attempt at defining the planet beyond Pangaea. But Crane couldn't see her through the cutout and had heard the failure bells earlier when the system had shut down.

There was something truly wrong with their conception of the birth of the planet, he had decided. If Pangaea were correct, then everything between it and the Yucatán Comet that began the Tertiary Age would be of finite dimension— some relative form of world, wrong or right, could be set up to connect the two events. But the machine continued to deny the truth of Pangaea, which could mean that their mistakes lay in the far distant past.

It was troubling to him, but something he couldn't deal with at the moment. He'd spent thirty years biding his time. Tonight would be the night he'd stick his neck out. He'd always known it would come down to a decision like this, but he never realized the fear connected with it. If he were wrong when he went public in a big way, it would ruin him. It frightened him, but didn't deter him. Now, he needed to know the extent of the loyalty of his staff.

"Sorry we're late," Lanie said, stumbling through the open doorway, helping Newcombe carry a four-by-four-foot poster board. "The chart held us up."

They got the chart in, a pie graph in rainbow colors, and set it on the open easel before a camera. They plopped down on the floor and leaned against the wall in unison as if joined at the hip. Newcombe watched Crane carefully. The man seemed more agitated than usual. A truly frightening concept.

"I assume we failed with the globe again?" Crane asked, eyes dark.

"Fifteenth try," she said sourly. "Beginning to get discouraging."

"The answer's there," Crane said dismissively. "We're just not seeing it. Keep trying." He dare not look at her as he talked. In their four months of working together, he'd allowed her closer to the real Crane than he'd ever imagined he could allow anyone. He was petrified at giving that kind of power over him to anyone, especially a woman. But he couldn't help himself, she seemed to understand him so completely.

"As most of you know," he said, sitting up straight, his bad arm numb, tingling, "we've been seriously considering making a public statement announcing a quake for the New Madrid Fault."

General confusion broke out then, everyone talking at once. Crane put his good hand up for silence. Newcombe could see it in all their eyes—the fear. A real prediction meant real commitment and real failure if they were wrong. To outcasts like these it meant the threat of the money train coming off the tracks. They had nowhere else to go.

"I'll listen to everything you have to say," Crane said, "but one at a time. Dr. Franks?"

A tiny man with short curly hair and a drawn face stood, shaking his head. "We're hearing a lot of rumors."

"Such as?"

"Such as the Ellsworth-Beroza tests are not in line with a prediction at this time."

"That's true," Crane said, "and please, sit down, doctor." Crane looked around the room. "Until the globe is truly operational, I believe all our attempts at trying to use standardized testing procedures will lead to inconclusive, even contradictory data."

General turmoil erupted again, Crane once more raising his hand.

"Let me say this: No test is perfect. That's why prediction is so difficult. But listen to what we do have. Electrical activity is up, helium emissions up, radon emissions up, foreshocks are occurring, though not directly within our nucleation zone. There has been evidence of dilation. And we've got powerful evidence in our stress readings. Dr. Newcombe?"

"We took a core sample from the rock of that region," Newcombe said, "and put it in the lateral compression chamber to see how much stress it could take before rupturing. The rock broke apart at 4033.01435 pounds per square inch. The readings from the Reelfoot Rift came out at 4033.01433. The rock in the Embayment, according to our calculations, can't possibly survive any longer than twenty-nine more days."

"What magnitude of quake are you predicting?" asked Sumi, who'd come in a few moments earlier.

"Because of the location of the stress and the estimated return times," Crane said, "we're looking at a Mercalli Level XI quake in the immediate area, which translates to 8.5 Richter, over 9 Moment Magnitude."

Franks was on his feet again. "An 8.5. That's . . . that's unimaginable!"

Crane looked grave. "Memphis . . . gone. Saint Louis . . . gone. Nashville . . . gone. Little Rock . . . gone. Chicago heavily damaged. Kansas City heavily damaged. Indianapolis . . . gone. The list is scary. All farmland in the grain belt destroyed. Firestorms that will cut the Eastern US off from the rest of the country. Communication and power out over two thirds of the country for God knows how long. Take a look at the chart."

Everyone crowded Newcombe's chart, talking and pointing. "We figure the hypocenter at about thirty miles below the surface," Newcombe said, "and the above-ground epicenter on the rift fifteen miles north of Memphis. If the pinpointing is correct, my chart will be as accurate as the Sado specs."

One of the tectonicists, Loreen Devlin, turned and stared at Crane. "You'll set off a panic. What if you're wrong?"

"What if I'm right?" he returned. "I can't, in all conscience, keep this knowledge to myself. In four thousand years of recorded history, thirteen million people have died as a direct result of earthquakes."

"You waited in Sado for weeks," she said. "How are you going to do it in Memphis?"

"I believe I learned something in Sado. This time I'm going to give them a specific date, not an approximation, not a range of dangerous days. I'm saying October 30th, at sometime after 5 P.M. when the late afternoon chill seeps in."

"You realize what you're letting yourself in for?" Sumi asked. "Who's responsible once you speak? The government? The media? What should businesses do—shut down and lose their revenue, or stay open and risk lawsuits by those hurt within that business when it collapses? If you're wrong, are you financially culpable for socioeconomic downturns in the affected areas? Will your prediction start a panic, Loreen's scenario, complete with National Guard troops and looters?"

"A little late in the game for cold feet, isn't it, Sumi?" Crane said. His voice had taken on an odd timbre.

Sumi approached him tentatively, like a penitent. She got right beside Crane and whispered, Lanie straining to hear the words. "I simply worry about you, Crane."

"I have to make this prediction," Crane answered, "and you know it. Don't desert me now. It doesn't have anything to do with funding anymore. I can't keep this information to myself."

Sumi nodded, a bit sadly Lanie thought, and moved to the far end of the room.

"Does anyone have any suggestions or comments?" Crane asked.

"Yeah," Franks said. "Don't do it. I sure as hell wouldn't want to be the bearer of tidings this bad. Besides, do you really think people will pay attention to you?"

"I can only lead them to the trough, doctor," Crane said. "I can't make them drink. The whole point of Sado, of all the publicity, has been to build my credibility as a predictor in order that people will listen seriously to me. The moment is never going to get more ripe."

"Are you going to disseminate through a government agency?" Mo Greenberg, the resident vulcanologist, asked.

"No," Crane said. "I'd still be fighting red tape long after the quake had hit."

He moved to his desk, scattering junk, to retrieve a CD the size of a large faucet washer. "I've put it all on here," he said, voice hoarse, expression somber. "We'll broadcast from here, cutting back and forth between my talk and Dan's graph. We'll rebroadcast every hour."

"I'd like to put this before the Geological Survey," Loreen Devlin said.

"No!" Crane yelled. "You want to bury it because you're weak! I will not have divided loyalties. We have a quest, a mission, one that we are not going to shy away from. What I demand is your hearts and souls bonded to me. We're entering the fight of all time, Man against Nature. I will have no quavering allegiance, no equivocation. You will support me now or leave. Are we on the same page, ladies and gentlemen?"

There was halfhearted response, Crane's face turning red with anger. Newcombe felt Lanie's hand tighten on his arm.

"Join me now or go!" Crane yelled. He grabbed an open bottle of rum from beside his bed, waving it around as he spoke. "I will slay this beast! Are you with me?"

He went to each person in turn, burning them with his eyes and asking the question. One by one they fell into line. Then he reached Newcombe, who said, "I will not act your slave by vowing this form of allegiance."

"You're no different from anyone in here," Crane whispered harshly. "Commit to our cause or walk out right now."

"I stood with you on the plain in Sado. I need to prove nothing to you now."

"Damn you," Crane said low. But he shut up then and turned back to the desk. He dug the transmission panel out from under. He slid the CD into the slot and without hesitation hit the transmit pad.

"It's done," he said. "Now get out, all of you."

• • •

There had never been banging in the dream before. Lanie lay sweating in bed, her mind enflamed with the vision of Crane in the white suit with the bubble helmet. He was yelling, trying to reach out to her, but the banging was so loud she couldn't hear him . . . couldn't hear—

"What the hell?" Newcombe said. Jerking awake, Lanie sat up straight. The banging continued.

"Open this door!" yelled a drunken Crane. "Traitor! Open it!"

Lanie shook her head, glancing at the bedside clock. It was nearly four in the morning. "What does he want?"

"How the hell should I know?" He stood up and walked naked down the stairs.

"I know you're in there!" Crane screamed. "Open the door!"

"Go away!" Newcombe yelled back. "Go sleep it off!"

As Lanie slid her legs over the edge of the bed, Crane threw himself at their door, the structural aluminum not giving. He tried again.

"Oh, for heaven's sake," Lanie said, turning on the bedside light. She walked to the loft railing. "Would you let him in before he hurts himself?"

"Monster!" Crane yelled, throwing himself against the door again.

"You're crazy!" Newcombe yelled back, Lanie hurrying down the stairs, naked herself. She opened the door.

He brushed past both of them, jerking his good arm away when Lanie tried to take his sleeve.

He moved across the room and juiced the full wall screen there. "You've betrayed me," Crane said, his eyes flashing at Newcombe.

"I don't know what you're—" Newcombe began, but stopped when he saw his own face on the television screen.

Lanie moved close to take his arm but, as Crane had done before, he pulled it away. "Oh no," he said low, moving to the couch to slump on it. "They promised me they wouldn't run this for months."

"Well, I guess they changed their minds." Crane's eyes widened at Lanie's nakedness. He grabbed an afghan draped over a chairback and tossed it to her. "Cover yourself."

Embarrassed, she flushed, then wrapped the cover around her and looked at the teev. Dan was presenting a detailed dissertation on his EQ-eco equations, giving up publicly every detail that Crane had kept secret. Newcombe turned off the sound.

"Have you read your contract, doctor?" Crane asked.

"I know the terms of my contract. I give proper credit to the Foundation all through this speech and all monies received from it go to the Crane Foundation."

"Who cares?" Crane yelled. "This is all part of our package, the thing that is supporting us. When you give out free information, it destroys everything else we're building."

"The world needs these theories," Newcombe said. "I took it upon myself to do the right thing."

"That's not your decision to make," Lanie said.

"Stay out of this," Newcombe snapped, then looked at Crane. "If you calm down, I'll talk to you."

Lanie watched Crane's face. He was totally out of his depth on issues such as these. He sat on a straight wooden chair. "Why?" he asked, his voice low and uncertain.

"You have a dream, Crane, a dream that failed earlier today for the fifteenth time."

"My dreams go beyond that globe," Crane returned.

"To where? What are they? What *exactly* are you looking for?"

Crane just stared at him.

"See?" Newcombe said. "You won't tell me, or you don't know, or . . . what? Well, I've got a reality instead of a mere dream. I've spent ten years studying and classifying the waves put out by EQs. Maybe it's not glamorous by your standards, but dammit, after ten years the figures came together and they were right and they've enabled me to predict damage areas around fault lines. The equations stand on their own and need to be shared with the world. So, I wrote them up and sent an article to the scientific journals. The Foundation gets credit and royalties. My dream is reality."

"Your dream is owned by me," Crane said, pointing to the screen, "which makes this . . . nothing but stealing. I am under no obligation to share my vision with you, Dan, nor will I until I choose to do so. You don't have the power to define me *or* my dreams. If you're so unhappy with the way I run things, why don't you quit? I won't make a man stay with me who wants to go."

"I don't quit because I need your money! Why don't you fire me?"

Crane took a long breath and stood, all the anger drained out of him suddenly. He shuffled slowly toward the door, turning to them when he'd opened it. "I can't fire you," he said. "I appreciate you too much. You're too damned good. Sorry to have disturbed you."

"Crazy bastard." Newcombe locked the door after him. He strode back to the sofa and struck it with a closed fist. "Dammit! They promised me they wouldn't run the story without first informing me."

"I guess Crane's prediction has made EQ-eco too hot to pass up," Lanie said, the afghan still wrapped tightly around her. "Cheer up. You're going to be famous now, too."

"Are you saying I did this deliberately?"

"I don't know if you did or you didn't," she replied. "I only know you had no right to steal Crane's property just because he wasn't handling it the way you wanted him to."

"I gave it to the world, Lanie," he said, walking up to touch her shoulder. "You're going to have to get used to that."

She twisted away from him and turned her back. "You like to steamroll over everything, don't you? If you want to know the real reason I had the Vogelman done, it's because I knew, once you got it in your head, that you'd steamroll me into having babies and doing what you wanted me to do."

He turned her around. "Wait a minute. I thought we'd decided you weren't going to have that procedure."

"It wasn't your decision to make," she said, jerking away from him again to face the screen, the wall now filled with a close-up of Dan's face. "Like that wasn't your decision to make."

"You did it without telling me."

She was still looking at his giant face, the eyes so sincere. She had to laugh. "Seems as though you've done a few things without telling me, too."

"Oh, hell," he said, softening. "Turn that thing off and let's go back to bed."

She couldn't face him, knew she couldn't sleep with him tonight. "You go on," she said. "I'll be up later."

Lanie stiffened when he touched her. Newcombe grunted and moved away. "Fine," he said, starting up the stairs. "Do me one favor, though. Don't let yourself get too caught up in Crane's fantasies. He's only a crazy man, that's all!"

"My globe is not crazy!"

He ignored her, moving up to the loft, the light clicking out to the sound of the bedsprings.

She turned and stared at the front door. "It's not crazy," she whispered to the man who wasn't standing there any longer.

RUPTURES
GERMANTOWN, TENNESSEE—NEAR MEMPHIS
27 OCTOBER 2024, 10 a.m.

"And then the guy tells me," Newcombe said, swinging the mallet to pound Lanie's sensor pole into the black delta soil, "that he's going to put my name up for the Nobel Prize."

"A touch early to open the champagne, don't you think?" Lanie was good and tired of this subject—in fact, Dan was so full of himself these days that she was getting a little tired of him. "Usually the science prize is given many years after the discovery."

"It happened early for Crane." Newcombe helped Lanie pick up the long brushlike antenna and slide it into the hole. "Give me the opportunity to get a little excited, okay?"

"You're the doctor."

"Damn right, doctor."

She smiled and locked the focus on the top of the apparatus. The red light came on, indicating that data was being transmitted, and she turned and looked back down the line. This was the fiftieth pole, the final one in a neat row that defined the edge of Dan's calculated zone of destruction. Half a mile beyond lay the tent city, filling many acres of cotton field. Thousands of people had fled here already, and they were preparing for thousands, maybe even a hundred thousand, more. Not that they'd had much help from the authorities.

Praise be for Harry Whetstone's lawyers, Lanie had thought a dozen times over the last two weeks. Crane's benefactor and friend, good old Stoney, had been able to come through for the Foundation because his lawyers had gotten the case against him dismissed, thus freeing up his billions from escrow. The poor performance of the government and of Liang Int in alerting people, providing information, guidance, and assistance to the population, had been nothing short of astonishing at first. Then it had become so frustrating that Crane had said he was going to start howling at the logoed moon every night.

Still, people poured into their camp, which was now ten times the size of the one on Sado. And there were unending teev pictures of clogged roads and air lanes as people tried to get out of the area. With whole sections of Memphis and nearby towns abandoned, the looters had come, of course, and the FPF was responding. In fact, the FPF seemed to be the only arm of the government that was doing its job properly.

Lanie shook her head and looked up. The sky was bright, the sun hot for late October. She was sweating in her long coat and heavy gloves; her floppy hat dropped down around the top of her goggles. Clouds floated lazily overhead, broadcasting pictures of the traffic jams all over the Mississippi Valley. Still other pictures showed the hardcases, those who didn't believe the prediction—all the way down to those who didn't even know what an earthquake was. Crane had hired a whole staff of historians to document this series of events so that he could draw up a sound set of plans for future quake predictions.

"Is that it, then?" Newcombe asked.

"All I've got," she replied, wishing that she, too, could dash around in a T-shirt and no hat. "It's going to be interesting taking readings in antediluvial mud. Everything's going to rearrange itself."

Newcombe smiled. He went over to the flatbed truck on which they'd hauled the sensors in and got into the operator's seat. "The earth turns liquid. You'll see things, whole houses sometimes, disappear beneath the surface and other things long buried rising back up. Believe me, I wouldn't want to live in New Orleans right now—they're going to have the dead rising right out of their graves, both those few still buried in the ground and all those in the mausoleums above ground."

"A cheery thought," Lanie said, climbing into the passenger seat and closing the door. "I wonder how the Ellsworth-Beroza is looking this morning?"

Newcombe opened the focus, programmed the truck, and it plowed through the black field, the skeletons of stripped cotton plants jutting from the ground all around them. "I'm worried about the E-B," he said. "Every goddamned rockhead in the world has descended on the Rift and all of them say the same thing: Without the E-B showing positive results, the quake can't happen."

"We were down in those holes, Dan. We saw the stress readings. We felt the tremors."

"I agree. So why isn't the Ellsworth-Beroza showing us some activity?"

"Maybe this one won't give any more warnings."

Brow arched, he said, "Yeah . . . maybe. And maybe we stuck our necks out at the wrong time. If that's the case, Crane's finished. It only reinforces my decision to go public with EQ-eco. I can cut myself loose from him if I have to and still survive."

"Yeah . . . maybe," she said sourly. "Somehow I find it difficult to believe that Crane would ever be finished. Only when he's in his grave. Maybe not even then."

"He's a psycho. They'll put him away one day."

She sat back and watched the clouds and their never-ending teev shows. As smart as Dan was, he had absolutely no handle on Crane, on the man's greatness. Crane might be a psycho, perhaps even delusional, by the definition of ordinary men and women who could not understand or appreciate him. But Dan? He should be the last to label Crane anything but brilliant.

Dan's luck had been extremely good lately. Not a week after his public release of the EQ-eco equations, a Chinese team of tectonicists on the verge of discovering a quake in its early Ellsworth-Beroza stage applied Dan's theory to their estimated epicenter and talked the citizens of Gui-yand, the capital of the Guihou Province, into evacuating. Two days later, a 7.2 Richter rocked the area to great devastation, but no one was killed. The scientists credited EQ-eco for helping them define areas of evacuation. And his success was feeding his ego—no, stuffing his ego, making it fat . . . and rather ugly, she thought. As his own re-gard for himself grew, his regard for Crane diminished. There was something obscene about Dan's disdain for Crane now.

She'd put distance between herself and Dan the night of the prediction and he seemed not to notice. She'd kept it up beyond reasonableness to see if he'd respond; then it simply had become routine. There was no way to breach the emotional gap. They lived every moment now under a microscope, public pressures extinguishing their personal flames. She simply consigned everything to the wind and was living day to day.

Except for the dreams.

The dreams were a constant, the swirl of Martinique growing larger to the point that she now thought the nightmares significant in some way beyond simple remembrance, though remember she did. Sections were opening up—the terrible mud, the triage of the wounded, the sound of the trucks all honking at the same time—though the actual event that caused her memory loss was still hazy. She wasn't even sure if she wanted to remember that part.

"Would you look at the people?" Dan said, driving into

the middle of the tent city, no colorful, jammed-together tents like Sado. These were all in military olive drab and spaced in rows wide enough to accommodate passing trucks. And there were thousands of them. A projection of an American flag waved against a perpetual electronic wind above the compound.

People were everywhere, being directed by tan uniformed employees of Whetstone, Inc., the billionaire's gun-for-hire service organization.

Dan pulled up to HQ just as a busload of students from a local boarding school was arriving.

"Tech kids," he said, climbing out.

Lanie watched as the youngsters, from preschoolers through high-schoolers, got off the bus. They looked frail and frightened.

"Learning" was being reevaluated, and the tech schools represented a new direction in education. Their primary subject was Wristpad 101. It taught children how to manipulate the computer net through their pads, how to access absolutely anything they'd ever need or want to know. The proliferation of voice lines on the pad even precluded the need for reading and writing. The power of the pad was the power of absolute knowledge. But what about discipline? What about memory storage and retrieval? Stealing one last glance at the line of twenty children, Lanie followed Newcombe into HQ. Tech kids—they had a poor ability to synthesize and react to physical demands and emotional situations. They lived in the pad. They thought it gave them everything, all the answers. The problem was, they didn't know the questions.

Housing block leaders were moving in and out of the tent, bringing requests and questions. Crane was frowning heavily, shaking his head as he talked to Sumi and white-haired Stoney Whetstone, dressed in the same uniform his men wore. Teevs filled the sides of the thirty-foot-square room, showing the same things the clouds were showing.

"You're a boob, Parkhurst," Crane said as they approached. He shook his head and tapped the man off.

"Got a busload of tech kids outside who are going to

need special handling," Lanie told him. Crane looked at Sumi.

"Would you take care of it?"

"Of course," Sumi said, immediately moving off.

"What about the E-Bs?" Newcombe asked Crane, who was staring vacantly at the floor.

"No activity," Stoney said.

Stoney was impressive, Lanie thought. Tall, commanding, and down-to-earth, he had a weathered, still-handsome face. He was enough of a man at sixty-seven to make her wonder what he'd been like at forty.

"Something very strange is going on around here, I think," Stoney added.

This wasn't new. Stoney had been frowning more as each day passed, voicing suspicions and questioning everything that was going on with the government and Liang Int. "What do you mean this time?" Lanie asked, somewhat wearily.

"The government is dragging its heels on what aid it's providing—which is damn little. And wasn't the whole point of them buying into Crane's prediction how much hay they could make for the electorate—the publicity they'd get for being good guys? I assumed this place would be a madhouse of pols and newsies, with Li and his buddies trotting every one of their candidates through here, giving each of those clowns a chance to sound off for the electorate. Do you see any of that? In fact, have you seen a single candidate or elected official or Liang Int big shot around here?"

Lanie slowly shook her head.

"No, of course not, because something's fishy, that's why."

"Let's not add paranoia to our list of problems," Newcombe said. "We've still got a couple of days until Q-day. Maybe something will—"

"My arm isn't hurting," Crane said. "This close to a quake my arm should be throbbing."

The teevs flickered, casting eerie images over all their faces. The pictures died, then the Presidential seal blossomed on every screen. Lanie tapped her pad to the K channel, though it wouldn't have mattered which fiber she chose. They'd all been pre-empted.

"—ident of the United States," came the voice through her aural. President Gideon sat at his desk, Mr. Li by his side.

"My fellow Americans, I address you today to right a terrible wrong. With great effort and at enormous cost, your government has undertaken a massive investigation and uncovered an egregious fraud. Lewis Crane is a charlatan. Unprincipled, publicity hungry, he is misleading the country into believing the entire middle and southern area of the United States is on the verge of catastrophe. Thankfully, we have discovered this is not the case, and denounce his prediction of a quake on the 30th of October as fantasy. Further, we are immediately cutting off all federal grant money to the Crane Foundation."

Crane was standing now in front of the largest screen, shaking his head. "What are they doing?" he whispered. "Why?"

"Couldn't you smell the screw job in the air?" Stoney asked. "I knew something was up."

The President continued, "We have proof that the Crane Foundation has continuing contact with Nation of Islam leader, Mohammed Ishmael, since Ishmael proclaimed an Islamic State while in Crane's company. We, the people, are victims of some kind of conspiracy."

A viddy came up of a man walking along a city sidewalk, arms swinging, everything from the viewpoint of his coat sleeve. The man stopped at a dorph vendor and bought a bottle. When he swung his arm around to pay the man, the face of Dan Newcombe filled the screen.

"What is this?" Crane whirled on Newcombe. "What the hell are we about to see?" he shrieked.

"Me and Ishmael," Newcombe said, his face blank as he stared Crane down.

"What else?"

Newcombe nodded at the screen, the tape blipping pictures in rapid succession of him being led down a hallway in what seemed to be a chip parlor. Lanie watched in amazement, her pulse speeding up and a sense of dread making her stomach queasy. Dan had gone to the Zone the Masada night that he'd disappeared . . . that was perfectly clear now. Betrayal. Personal and professional too, she suspected. She began to tremble. Tense, Dan avoided her gaze, steadfastly looking at the teev. He was being taken into a cubicle, a bed moved to reveal a manhole, Ishmael coming out of the hole to embrace Newcombe like long-lost, beloved kin. Lanie glanced around. Everyone was rapt—and horrified.

Newcombe and Ishmael were staring intently, malevolently out at the audience through the lens of a camera that must have been in Ishmael's palm.

"Stoney," Crane said, a shocked expression on his face, "would you get a couple of your biggest men to guard the tent flap? I don't want any reporters around until we're ready for them. And get Sumi back in here."

Whetstone nodded, then grasped Crane's shoulder consolingly before leaving the tent.

"Look, Crane," Newcombe said, "that trip to the Zone had nothing to do with you or the Foundation. It's personal. It's about me."

"And me?" Lanie asked. "It sure as hell has something to do with me. I know how the NOI feels about race . . . about what they call the 'purity' of the races."

Wristpads were bleeping on every arm as media tried to communicate with the members of the Crane team. They'd have only a few minutes, tops, before they were overwhelmed by outsiders.

"Lanie," Dan said. "I didn't tell you for the same reason you didn't tell me about the Vogelman—"

"Please," Crane said, trying to calm himself with long, slow breaths. "Let's worry about the immediate problem first." He pointed at Newcombe. "Do you promise me your contact with Ishmael is not related to your activities with the Foundation?"

"My word," Newcombe said.

"Your *word*," Lanie snapped, feeling her whole world slipping away.

"How did they wire you?" Crane asked, nodding to Sumi who'd returned with Stoney.

Newcombe showed empty palms. "I have no idea. It may have been random."

"Freelanced to Liang," Sumi said. "It happens all the time."

"Does that really matter now?" Stoney asked.

"No," Crane answered, his gaze going to the burly guards stationing themselves at the tent flaps. "As long as there are no other surprises."

"I had a visit and a personal chat with Brother Ishmael," Newcombe said. "We talk sometimes, ask each other for advice."

"Did he give you 'advice' about illegally going public with your paper?" Lanie asked, unable to check herself.

"Not now," Crane said, walking closer. "Do you *swear* to me that you don't know anything about Gideon canceling the program?"

"Of course not!" Newcombe said, indignant. "I've got as much to lose in this as you do."

That's not what you said earlier, Lanie thought.

"You saved *your* program," Stoney said.

Newcombe turned to face him. "What is that sup—"

"No," Crane said. "Low blow, Stoney. I don't . . . I won't question Dan's integrity. What we've got to do now is figure out what's going on and how to counter it."

Newcombe laughed ruefully. "What's going on is that we've just been shot down. They lasered us from stem to stern, Captain." He saluted, then turned to Sumi. "What about you? Why didn't you see this coming?"

Sumi looked startled. "When our relationship began with Mr. Li, I was assigned to an onsite job. I have no contact with the government. I've been here with you."

"We need to stop blaming one another," Crane said, Lanie startling at the sound of a crowd gathering outside, yelling. "We've still got the prediction."

"Your arm doesn't hurt," Newcombe said.

"Sir!" came a man's voice from the tent flap. One of the guards had stuck his head inside. "This is turning into a situation out here."

"Tell them we'll talk in a minute," Crane said, the guard looking to Whetstone, who nodded.

"The stress readings don't lie," Crane said. "The other signs don't lie. That's what makes no sense here."

"What about the Ellsworth-Beroza?" Newcombe asked. "Maybe we're all fools."

"No, doctor," Crane said. "We're not fools. Suggestions?"

Everyone stared at him.

"Crane," Whetstone said at last, "are you going to stand behind your prediction?"

"My arm doesn't hurt," Crane said, smiling slightly. "It doesn't lie to me. But you see, it doesn't matter. We're married to it one way or the other. We have no choice but to proceed full steam ahead. It's our roll of the dice, don't you know? Once the pronouncement is made from on high it cannot be rescinded." He walked toward the tent flap.

"Where are you going?" Lanie called.

He stopped, then turned abruptly, mechanically. "I'm going to go out there and convince those people and the press to ignore what they just heard and believe me instead."

"You're going to deny everything?" Newcombe asked.

"Easy to do," Crane said, smoothing his rumpled hair with little result. "I don't know anything. All of you stay in here and don't come out. I've taken the glory. Now it's time to take the flak." He looked at Newcombe. "I'll protect you as best I can."

"Don't do me any favors," Newcombe replied.

Crane narrowed his eyes, selected a wide-brimmed hat from those on the rack standing beside the flap, and went into the Tennessee morning. Lanie looked around, realizing all the teevs were showing Crane from the viewpoint of the crowd outside.

Hundreds of people, most with cams, were filling the dirt street in front of HQ. Crane had moved just outside the tent, Whetstone's people forming a cordon around him and pushing back the bystanders.

"I want to talk to you for a minute," Crane said, putting up his hands to silence them. When the noise level didn't abate, he padded himself into the tent city's speaker system.

Lanie turned to stare at Dan. "I don't know you any-more," she said.

"Maybe you never knew me," he said, his eyes fixed on the screen. "I realize how all this looks. I simply want to say I'm sorry. I love you. I did what I had to do."

"Friends!" Crane said, voice booming. "Despite what you may have seen and heard moments ago, the Crane Foundation's prediction is still active and online. We, here, have no idea what the President was talking about. What I do know about is earthquakes. And you're going to have one."

Lanie pursed her lips angrily. "Destroying my work by connecting yourself to a man who'd as soon see me dead. Is that what you *had* to do?"

"*Your* work?"

"Good morning, Dan! Surprise! Wake up! The globe is my baby, *my* EQ-eco. And guess what, I think it could be even more important than your work."

"That globe," he said with a look of distaste, "is simply the physical manifestation of Crane's insanity. It's mean-ingless."

She slapped him so hard her hand stung. "Go to hell," she said, turning on her heel.

Outside, people were shouting questions at Crane about the Nation of Islam.

"Nation of Islam is not connected with our earthquake research in any form. Dr. Newcombe has a long-standing friendship with Mohammed Ishmael and has every right to visit the man on his own time."

The shouting got louder, Crane still trying to maintain order.

Newcombe growled. "I don't need him to defend me."

"Don't—" Whetstone said, but Newcombe was already going out the flap.

"I'm a free man," Dan said to the crowd. Proud, the fire in his eyes flared as if he were a lion in a world of hyenas. "Yes, I've visited Brother Ishmael. I can visit whomever I damned well please."

"Did you talk to him about his call for an Islamic State?" someone in the audience asked.

"Yes, I did, as a matter of fact."

People were shouting at him, trying to drown him out. Lanie watched his pride turn to anger and feared for the outcome.

Crane spotted real trouble brewing and elbowed his way back to center stage. "If there's nothing else—"

"Do you support the forced disenfranchisement of southerners to support an Africk homeland?" came a voice, clear as a bell.

Lanie took a deep, steadying breath. Dan's answer would force her to make a decision.

"For many years," Newcombe said, "we have kept eight percent of our citizens locked up in ghettoes. Did they do anything? No. Do they deserve the same freedoms and liberties most Americans take for granted . . . life, liberty, the pursuit of happiness? Yes."

"But what about forced eviction?"

"Brother Ishmael wishes to move no one. He only wants an Islamic State where the wisdom of Allah and the Koran prevail. The people who live in the Islamic homeland will be free to do as they choose."

Crane walked wearily back into the tent, Sumi rushing over to comfort him. As Lanie listened to NOI rhetoric coming out of Dan's mouth, she felt as if she were being pushed to the edge. She had waited a long time to let herself love him. And now what was there but pain in the loving?

"Are you a member of Nation of Islam?" one of Whetstone's people called, the security force slowly melting into and becoming part of the crowd.

"That is a decision I have been grappling with," he responded. "At the moment I'm a citizen of the world. I'm merely speaking my mind and will continue to do so."

A cold hand clutched Lanie's heart. As Dan went on shilling for Brother Ishmael, she went deep into herself. Segregation . . . the veiling of women . . . the espousal of violence. Could Dan Newcombe—the man she had lived with and loved—really align himself with a movement that advocated those things? She was very much afraid the answer was yes. Suffused with pain, she clenched her jaw and held herself rigid. She could scarcely bear it. . . . Crane! She had to concern herself with Crane.

The moment Crane had realized that with every word Dan spoke the Foundation was losing more and more of its support, he'd located his stashed bottle of bourbon and gone to work on it in earnest. Camheads started to cut away from Dan's face to show pictures of people leaving the tent city on foot and in vehicles, vandalizing the place as they went. By the time Dan was finished, most of Crane's dream of saving lives and of positive, collective action at a quake site was either smashed to the ground or stolen. The red tent stood in the midst of rubble. Two days before the date of his prediction that the quake would hit, it was all over. . . .

Lanie went to Crane's side. There were tears streaming down his face, and he cradled the bourbon in his bad arm. When she touched his shoulder, she awakened him from some dream of horror. His eyes opened wide.

"All I ever wanted to do was help people," he said, his voice low and very small.

She hugged him. "Maybe we should think about leaving this place."

"No. Not me. You. Get Burt and tell him to pack it all in and get himself and the rest of the team back to the Foundation grounds as quickly as possible."

"What are you going to do?"

"Stay here. Do my job. I've still got an earthquake coming that I need to warn people about. Just because the government decided it wasn't going to happen doesn't mean it won't."

They stared at each other for a long moment. "Crane, I can't—I won't let you stay on alone. I'm with you—"

"No. You've got to leave. Get everybody back as fast as you can. Work on the globe. Work hard. We'll do what we can at the Foundation until the money runs out."

"Are you going to be all right?"

"I've never been all right." He took a drink. "Go on. Get out of here. I don't need my people getting arrested in Tennessee."

"Arrested?"

"I'm a charlatan, remember? I've perpetrated a fraud. Charges and arrests are just around the corner no matter what happens with the quake. I'll probably be in jail when it hits." He looked hard at her. "I'm counting on you . . . on *you*, Lanie. The globe is everything. Only you can carry on with that work."

Tears filled her eyes. Finally, she nodded and was rewarded by one of Crane's warm, broad smiles, all the more beautiful because it was so rare. "That's my imager," he said and patted her on the shoulder. Then he looked away, his gaze on a far horizon no one else would be able to see.

Lanie stepped back, feeling an alien yearning to embrace Crane, to hold him close and promise that everything would be all right. But that would be an empty promise, a lie. Nothing might ever be right again. And Crane. He was so alone. Alone and crushed by treachery, its origins and at least some of its perpetrators a mystery. She shook herself. The only positive action she could take was to do as Crane wished. Purposeful then, she crammed a hat on her head and raced out of the tent.

Dan was standing alone in the middle of the road, people streaming around him, fleeing the camp as quickly as they had made their way to it. Several hundred yards off, the leveled compound was burning steadily. She walked into the human river and waded toward Dan. When she reached him, her mouth gaped in surprise.

"You're crying," she said.

"It was wonderful! I spoke my mind without fear and without remorse for the first time in my life. It felt good, Lanie, so good—and so free."

She glanced at the devastation all around, the fire threatening to blaze out of control as Whetstone's people tried to put it out. "It freed all of us," she said, doubting that Dan even would notice the irony of her tone. "You're going to join them, aren't you?"

His answer was a mere shrug. "I want us to spend a lot of time together. It's all in the open. I can promise you no secrets from now on," he said, putting his arm around her shoulder. She slipped from under it.

"No, Dan," she said, backing away from him. "I can't. I simply can't. . . ."

"But I love you."

"Whether or not you go back to the Foundation, I am going to move into my own house."

"But, Lanie—"

She spun away then and started off. Dan called her name, but she didn't turn back. She walked farther into devastation. The site was in ruins. Crane's reputation was in ruins. The Foundation might be gone in weeks, a month or two at the most. All the bright and wondrous things she'd been envisioning for herself and Dan personally, and for herself and Crane professionally, were extinguished.

Suddenly, Lanie saw none of the devastation around her. She saw only Crane as she'd left him in the tent, alone, slumped in a chair, swilling bourbon straight from the bottle. The late-afternoon sunshine was brilliant, but for Lanie King and for Lewis Crane the day had turned black as pitch.

Book Two

Chapter 10

THE FAILED RIFT

THE FOUNDATION
6 NOVEMBER 2024, 8:47 P.M.

"What do ya think, Doc?" Burt Hill asked as he guided the helo through the gloom up the steep side of Mendenhall to the shelf on which the Foundation stood. "Exactly like ya left it."

"It's the sweetest sight I've seen in two long weeks." Crane drank in the sight of the grounds, the mosque. The ruby laser lines welcomed him back from a trip to hell in the outside world. It was Tuesday night, election night, the night that was supposed to have marked his triumph. Instead he'd had to sneak back into LA in disguise lest camheads recognize him and go on the attack. The first thing he'd done when the helo was far from the City and over open country was throw off that disguise.

He turned in his seat and looked full at Burt, whose face had a warm glow from the ruddy light rising from the Foundation. "How many have I lost?" he asked in little more than a whisper.

"A couple. Everybody else is hanging on. They feed you okay in that Tennessee jail?"

He waved the question away. The local police had stuck him in the Memphis city jail early on October 31 when the quake had failed to materialize on the previous day. He'd been transferred to the Shelby County jail two days later and held without bond on felony fraud, charged with reckless endangerment of millions of lives. He was only thankful that the FPF hadn't gotten involved. He'd sat it out, all the charges miraculously disappearing this morning, election morning. He had apparently served Mr. Li's purposes, so he could be set free.

"You look skinny to me, Doc. I'm gonna make sure you get something in you before the night's over. And I don't mean rum. Solid food."

Food in jail? Crane didn't remember eating . . . or not eating. "I was thinking in jail, Burt. Time passed."

The helo rose over the shelf, then banked down toward the mosque through buffeting crosswinds. "Is Sumi here?" Crane asked.

"Nobody's seen him since it all came apart," Hill said, flashing a concerned glance at Crane. "We hear he's got a cushy administrative job with the National Academy of Science. Sounds like blood money to me, a payoff."

"Give him the benefit of the doubt," Crane said just as Hill set the helo down gently about thirty feet from the door of the mosque. "Sumi's been a good friend."

Hill only grunted.

Crane hated to think that any of the people near him had been treacherous, but his time in jail had given him opportunity to think, to put it all together. The paths along which his thoughts had led were thorny . . . his final destination a mean and barren place.

"Newcombe still here?" He was out of the helo, walking fast.

"Far as I know." Hill hurried to catch up with Crane. "Wondered when you'd get around to asking."

Crane hit the wristpad on the P fiber, his line to the tectonicist. "Where are you, Danny Boy?" he asked.

"Crane?" came the startled response. "Are you out?"

"I'm down," Crane said, "but I'm not out. Where are you people hiding?"

"We're in the briefing room watching election returns."

"Well, I haven't voted yet. I think I'll join you."

He padded out and walked into the mosque, his breath catching at the sight of the globe. God, it was good to be home. When he'd been in jail, he'd spent the first day or two contemplating suicide, but the Foundation and all its unfinished work pulled him back. He wasn't through yet. Despite Mr. Li. Despite the other people who'd betrayed him and the cause. There was so much to do and he'd barely started. He might be broke, he might be a pariah, but he still had his brain and all that beautiful, beautiful data he'd collected. Besides, death wasn't an option. It would end the pain that was his heritage and the sole origin of consciousness. His pain could be relieved only by experiencing his pain fully.

He'd lost everything, had taken the worst, and was still on his feet. He knew now that nothing could stop him or turn him aside. There was power in that insight.

He hurried through the globe room then, and hit the theaterlike briefing room at a trot. Fifty heads turned toward him; a hundred pairs of eyes focused exclusively on him. He'd either get them or lose them right here and now.

Smiling, Crane waved and hurried down the aisle to take the stage. The huge screen behind him ran a collage of coverage from twenty different sources, always changing, always devoted completely to the election.

A "Vote Now" light was flashing at the bottom of the screen. Crane logged on via the pad and entered his voter's code. He accessed, pushed one button, then transmitted.

"Straight Yo-Yu ticket!" he announced loudly to the audience, scattered laughter coming back to him. He could see by the constantly tallying numbers on the board that Liang had won the major national races. Interestingly, though, Yo-Yu had made considerable inroads in local elections, which the teev analysts were downplaying as a fluke.

Crane held his arm high above his head, made a fist, and shook it. "I will fight anyone who has the guts to walk up here and tell me to my face that we're through." He looked around. "I'm still alive, so I'm not through. You're still sitting here. If you're through, get out. I don't want to see you again."

He waited. No one left. "Here's what I can do: If we cut worldwide ops and hunker down, I can keep us going for about ten to twelve months with everyone at full salary. That gives us another year to get respectable again. We gathered a great deal of information before the government pulled the plug. Now we can put it to good use.

"My areas of interest are twofold: getting the globe online and getting a blanket reading on the tectonics of southern California. To that end I am reassigning all our field personnel to in-state sites."

He walked toward the stairs at the end of the stage. "If you still work for me, get to it. Don't sit around here." He forked his thumb at the screen. "Somebody turn that damned thing off."

He took the stairs down from the stage as almost everyone left the room. Lanie sat in the first row, smiling up at him, confidence still strong in her eyes. Newcombe was walking toward him from several rows back. Interesting, Crane thought, that the two hadn't been sitting together.

Lanie came up and gave him a quick hug. "Welcome back."

"I appreciate all you did in trying to get me out of jail," he said. "I heard you were dogged."

"I just hope it wasn't too horrible for you."

He smiled. "I had some very personable cellmates in the county jail," he said, loving the liveliness in her eyes. "They taught me how to make a shiv out of a spoon."

"I figured they'd throw away the key with you," Newcombe said, moving closer and offering his hand.

Crane shook it. "I did a structural analysis of the building the first day I was there. On the second day I issued a report through the lawyer Lanie sent in saying the building was unsafe and should be condemned. The lawyer sent the report to every state agency in Tennessee, plus all the legit media. Then he filed a class action suit on behalf of the inmates. By the third day the cops were ready to get rid of me. Could you two join me for a few minutes? I want to talk about what happened."

They nodded, Crane noticing that Lanie was carefully keeping distance between her and Newcombe. They walked to the globe room. Burt Hill joined them with a faux-chicken sandwich for Crane.

"Stay with us," Crane said, as Hill literally fed a piece of the sandwich into Crane's mouth.

"How long since you've had a decent night's sleep?" Hill asked.

"I'll get one tonight," Crane answered, chewing, wondering what was happening between Dan and Lanie.

"I've got something for you," Newcombe said. He pulled an envelope out of the cinched waist of his trousers and handed it to Crane.

Crane opened it, pulling out a check made out to the Foundation in the amount of half a million dollars. It was drawn on a Liang Int account out of Beijing.

"It's a royalty check on EQ-eco," Dan said. "As promised, it's for the Foundation."

"And we can use it," Crane said, handing the check to Hill, who juggled the sandwich to get it into his overalls pocket. "I'm glad . . . and surprised to see that you haven't moved on. I'm sure you've had offers."

"Yeah . . . some. So far you're still the best job in town."

"What my ex-roommate is trying to tell you," Lanie said, "is that after his little tirade about the Nation of Islam, he's in as much disrepute as the Foundation."

Crane looked at Newcombe. "I want you to know I don't blame you for any of that."

"I'm not going to stop talking."

"Fair enough," Crane said. "Just keep me out of it."

"Done."

"That's it?" Lanie said. "Everything's in ruins and you two simply move on?"

"Politics is a shifting breeze," Crane said. "It's not real, not substantial. I remember times before Mr. Li, and I remember times before that. I'm still here. Most of them are gone. As for Dan, he's a man of integrity."

Hill stuffed another piece of tasteless sandwich into Crane's mouth as he sat on a chair in front of the computer banks. Lanie and Newcombe also sat, rolling into a loose circle.

Crane swallowed, waving off the offer of another bite. "Talk to me. What . . . exactly happened?"

"They continued to use tape of me with Brother Ishmael," Newcombe said. "Liang Int and government officials decided to go on the attack against NOI, talking openly about some unnamed conspiracy between the two of us, making everyone look guilty of something."

"Me . . . it was fraud. But those charges depended upon us actually *being* frauds, the quake not occurring," Crane said. "Why would they take a chance like that?"

"They didn't take no chances," Hill said. "When the President read that message he *knew* there wasn't going to be no damned earthquake. He was too cocky."

"Then where did we go wrong and how did they know about it?"

Newcombe reached for Crane's sandwich, but Hill pulled it away. "Maybe the government listened to the other geologists and tectonicists who came down and said we were crazy."

"I'm tellin' you," Hill said, "Gideon was surer than that."

"Where does that leave us?" Crane asked.

Lanie had been quiet, listening, but Crane could tell she wanted to say something. Finally she spoke.

"Think about this for a minute," she said. "It's been making me crazy ever since it happened. The only thing we predicted on, really, were the stress readings on the failed rift. Everything else certainly pointed to a potential quake, and still does. It's the stress readings that were out of line."

"Equipment failure?" Crane asked.

"No," Hill said. "We tested the spike two days ago in the Foundation's compression chamber. It reads true."

"Rules it out, then," Crane said. "We fed the Reelfoot readings directly into the Foundation's computers."

"Not exactly," Newcombe said, pointing to his wrist. "We fed into my pad, which fed into the computer in the van. After all the tests at all the sites were completed, I uploaded everything into the Foundation's computers at the same time from the van."

"Two transmissions," Crane said. "Maybe there was a glitch in the transfer. Do you normally doublecheck data feed?"

"Not if human intervention isn't a factor," Lanie said. "Machine to machine we only check file size."

Crane frowned and looked at Newcombe. "Is the file still in your pad?"

Newcombe nodded.

"Let's have it, then," he said, holding out his hand. "We'll match up your files with the Foundation's. If they're the same we rule out the stress readings as a factor."

Newcombe removed the three-inch-wide pad, tossing it to Crane, who bobbled it with his bad hand, the thing falling to the floor. Lanie retrieved it.

"What's the filename?" she asked while attaching the interface to one of her globe computers.

"Reelfoot."

She typed it in, the file coming up on screen as she scanned the index for the Foundation file.

"Put them up next to each other," Crane said. They rolled their chairs to get a better angle on the screen.

Numbers scrolled beside one another: material density numbers, material type, tensile strength, degrees of dilation. The lists were long, with a separate list for each type of material the spike had touched. The last number in each line was PSI—pounds per square inch. These were the stress numbers that showed exactly how much strain the material was taking.

"Well," Crane said, "everything seems to be—whoa!

What's this? Just pull the stress numbers from the two files."

Everything disappeared except for the stress numbers. "Do you see anything?" Crane asked.

"At the thousands place," Newcombe said, "each number on the Foundation's computer is one number higher than those on my pad."

"You're right," Lanie said, excited. "With higher stress readings, no wonder we came up with the wrong conclusion. How did this happen?"

"Only two ways," Hill said. "It's either a glitch or somebody changed the data on purpose—and I'll be damned if I can think of a glitch that would affect a whole series of numbers so selectively."

"Well no one else got near them except me," Newcombe said. "I loaded it all myself."

"Yeah," Hill said. "It was right around the time you were puttin' together that paper of yours, wasn't it, Doc Dan?"

"Yes it was, Burt," Newcombe said, angry. "Do you find some particular significance in the timing?"

"Since you ask me, I'll tell ya," Hill said, putting the sandwich on the console, then on the floor when Lanie scowled disapprovingly. "You're jealous of Doc Crane. You saved your own work just before everything went up in smoke. You controlled the numbers that went haywire."

"Enough," Crane said. "Dr. Newcombe told me he didn't manipulate the numbers and that's all there is to it!"

"Could the signals have been intercepted before they got here?" Lanie asked.

"Yes," Crane said. "But it would take someone who not only knew our systems intimately, but also had code access to them."

"Someone on the inside," Lanie said.

"It was Sumi," Hill said, slapping his leg. "Had to be Sumi."

"A minute ago it had to be Dan," Crane said. "Let's worry about a viper in our midst later. Right now let's try an experiment. Dr. King, would you be so kind as to enter the correct stress readings into the Reelfoot files?"

"My God," Newcombe said, falling back in his chair. "This means that we may have been right all along. The timing was just a little off."

"Only now," Crane said, "no one will listen to us when we warn them."

"Got the readings," Lanie said, swinging her chair around and nodding toward the globe. "I've put it up there. Ready?"

"Go," Crane said. "Take it from the day, from the minute, we made the readings. If we hit a quake, slow it to real time."

"Working," Lanie said, all eyes on the huge globe. A spotlight triggered the motions. For a moment nothing happened, then a rumble issued from the innards of the analog Earth, Lanie calibrating the speed to real time.

Crane watched the red line form on Reelfoot, just as they'd thought, the quake emanating from the thirty-mile-deep hypocenter and extending upward and out.

In amazing detail they were watching a preview of a power so destructive as to render even the imagination weak in comparison. The sound, the rumbling, came from the P waves, the Primary or pressure waves, acting like sound waves pulsing through the ground, compressing and dilating the rock, pulling and pushing the earth, manifested as the ground moving violently up and down.

The Secondary waves moved slower than the P waves and whipped through the rock, shaking the ground sideways. On the globe, the earth was rocking hundreds of miles from the thin red line of Reelfoot, the Mississippi and Ohio rivers reforming over and over, looking like huge writhing snakes.

Then came the two L waves, the surface originating waves, counterpointing what was going on deeply underground. Raleigh waves rolled across the planet like ocean waves while the Love waves vibrated wildly at a right angle to their path, the two waves in unison creating a corkscrew motion that no building, tree, or dam could withstand. With nothing to absorb the waves, they spread farther and farther outward. The ground on the globe buckled. Fissures opened; hills rose only to sink again; the Mississippi continued to jerk wildly, a living thing. They called it a failed rift because it had never succeeded in breaking apart from the continent. Now that small geologic notion was getting ready to cause untold suffering two hundred million years later.

Crane heard Lanie gasp as the area of destruction grew wider and wider. Inside of him, tension knotted his muscles, his arm aching involuntarily. He was staring into the sallow mirror of his own fears and anger. It was happening here and it would happen in reality. He could see it, right before him, but he was powerless to stop it.

"Give me a day," he said low, in almost a whisper.

Lanie turned her body to the console, her gaze glued to the globe. An aftershock rocked the land again no sooner than the first had stopped. She typed with one hand. A second later, blood-red letters five feet high hung suspended in the air before them:

27 February 2025, 6:00 P.M. + or −

"Oh, my God," Newcombe said. "Three and a half months. Crane, I . . . dammit, this is scary."

"Yeah," Crane said, standing, pacing. "And we've got zero credibility. They've threatened to arrest me if I even set foot in Tennessee or Missouri."

"What do we do?" Lanie asked.

"Cry wolf again," Crane said. "Make enough of a pest of myself that if they don't listen to me at least they'll remember that I said it." He paused. "It will re-establish me so they'll listen next time."

"Trouble is," Burt Hill said, "everybody thinks you're crazy, Doc. Nobody's gonna listen to you."

"You think I don't know? Wait a minute." Crane ran to Hill and hugged him. "You've just given me the idea of a lifetime."

"I have?"

Crane punched up the Q fiber on his pad, hoping that Whetstone hadn't deleted him from the preferred list. "Come on, Stoney," he whispered. "Come on."

"Am I going to be sorry I answered this call?" came Whetstone's voice through Crane's aural.

"You're a good man."

"I'm a laughingstock."

"Maybe. But are you also a gambler?"

"Crane. . . ."

"Meet me tomorrow. . . . Can you?"

"I can do anything I want."

"Then meet me. I can make you a hero."

"Not tomorrow. Day after. But tell me something, Crane, why do I listen to you?"

Crane chortled. "Because you're as crazy as I am."

Li stood inside his globe, basking in election night victory. Numbers flickered all around him like electronic fireflies. They'd held the presidency easily and won the contested Congressional seats, though some of those races were closer than he'd wished. The bottom ledger line: Liang had retained complete power for another two years at least. He credited the last-minute attacks on Crane and Ishmael—the conspiracy theory—for his success.

"So are you satisfied?" Mr. Mui asked from outside the glowing world. Only the COO was allowed inside the sphere.

"Of course I'm satisfied," Li said, surprised at the question.

"Then you found tonight's results a success?"

"Why are you asking me these questions? We were victorious, were we not?"

"According to my figures," Mui said, "we lost over three hundred seats in state houses around the country. Yo-Yu now has a major foothold."

"Inconsequential. We retain the power."

"The political power springs from beneath in this country . . . through local laws, local statutes. Yo-Yu has outright control of fifteen legislative houses, which means fifteen venues from which to attack our economic base and expand their own."

"You're making too much of this," Li said.

"My reports will mirror my thoughts. Others will judge.

Also, my polls show you made a major mistake with the Islamic issue."

"How so?"

"In the local elections, Yo-Yu candidates took a soft wait-and-see line on the issue of an Islamic state as soon as we came out strongly against it. They favored negotiations over confrontations. Their success in state races is directly attributable to that factor."

"I disagree."

"You gave them fear," Mui said, "but that simply tied them to the greater fear of the global Islamic movement, which people feel is too large to challenge."

"I did what had to be done to win the election. All I need to do to remedy the situation is to sacrifice someone on the altar of Islam, put the blame on him, then become more compromising. By the time the next elections come around, this will no longer be an issue."

"Who shall you sacrifice?"

"President Gideon has let the Vice President make most of the anti-NOI speeches. Perhaps it's time for Mr. Gabler to step down." Li smiled. "After all, we can't have a racist as Vice President, now can we?"

"And who would you put in his place?"

Li smiled again, thinking of the frames of Sumi Chan in her bath. With Sumi, control would never be a problem. "I've been thinking that it might be time for an Asian-American to step into the forefront of American politics," he said. "I'll study the issue in the next few days."

"Do you have someone in mind?"

"Perhaps. Are you finished attacking me?"

"Sir," Mui said respectfully. "It is my job to question your decisions, just as it was your job to question your predecessor's decisions. I respectfully submit that you owe me an apology. Your attitude must also go in my reports, I'm sure you know."

Li nodded. All they needed were knives to make the bloodletting more public. "I am sorry to have offended you. Is there anything else that will go into your report?"

"Yes," Mui said, and Li could see the shine of his smiling teeth in the outer darkness. "I'm going to tell them that your deliberate falsification of earthquake prediction figures could potentially destroy the economic viability of this entire sector."

"Oh, come now," Li said. "You cannot really believe that clown Crane can predict earthquakes?"

"Why not?"

Li felt anger well up. "Because it's impossible, that's why!"

"Ah," Mui said easily. "Your knowledge and certitude are obviously much more advanced than mine. I would say, wait and see, just like Yo-Yu. But you, Mr. Director, are willing to bet your life on the impossibility of Crane making predictions. Bravo."

"You're mocking me," Li said.

"Yes, sir," Mui replied. "I am doing just that."

Chapter 11

THE WAGER

THE FOUNDATION
8 NOVEMBER 2024, 4:45 P.M.

"You know," Lanie said from the doorway to the living room of Crane's chalet, cleaned and spiffed up for the occasion, "we've all got to drink rum because that's what Crane has stocked."

Newcombe smiled at her. Her eyes were glinting. She was pumped up, energized by her success in lobbying Kate Masters all day. When Kate had heard from Stoney that he was coming to the Foundation, she'd decided they should meet up there. But she'd come early, way early, and sought out Lanie immediately. Newcombe wasn't thrilled. He didn't like Kate Masters. Something about her showy clothes, her brashness, her mouth bothered him. And he hated the fact that she'd struck up a friendship with Lanie. The Vogelman Procedure was Kate's fault . . . and it had been the first rupture in his renewed relationship with

Lanie. She came closer to him now. "I'm glad you've decided to talk to me, Lanie," he murmured.

"I had a couple drinks. Makes things easier. I don't mean to avoid you, really. I just don't handle this kind of thing very well."

He wanted to reach out and touch her hair, but wouldn't allow himself to do it. "Maybe, if it bothers you so much, it means you've made a mistake."

"No, Dan, really. Things are better this way."

He closed the distance between them and seized her by the arms, the drink she held spilling on them both. "Things are not better and you know it." He put his arms around her, but she stood stiffly in his loose embrace. "Dammit, Lanie," he whispered, "come home. We'll forget everything that's happened and start over."

She pushed away. "And forget everything that's going to happen? You've chosen a path for yourself, Dan, that I can't travel with you."

"We'll just see. We—"

"Everybody!" Kate Masters called from the living room. "Quick . . . gather around. I've got some news for all of you."

"I wonder what's going on?" Lanie asked, turning quickly to avoid Newcombe and walking back into the living room.

He followed dutifully, not able to gauge the intensity of her words. He didn't mind her being angry at him. It was the pulling away that hurt. Things had been so good this time. What had happened to drive her so far away? He couldn't believe it was the NOI stance. She knew he had a big mouth. And the publication? Didn't his giving the big check to Crane show the goodness of his intentions?

Crane and Whetstone, who'd arrived only minutes before, joined the group, drinks in their hands. Burt Hill lay half asleep on a sofa near where Masters stood.

"I've been conferencing with my board for the last half hour," Kate said. "And we've made an executive decision."

"Let's hear it," Whetstone said.

Kate ran her hands through her red hair. "I'm waiting for the drum roll."

Burt Hill pounded rhythmically on his stomach.

Kate turned to Crane. "As president of the Women's Political Association, I am pleased to announce that we have reconsidered our decision to take your grant money away and are awarding you, for calendar 2025, a sum of five million dollars for earthquake research."

Crane roared with pleasure as everyone applauded. Masters turned to Lanie. "And you have this woman and her eloquent plea to thank for it. I used some frames of Lanie's talk with me today to show the board. It passed unanimously."

Lanie hugged Kate, then turned to Crane, who had made his way to her side. The two of them shared a long, meaningful look before hugging fiercely. Newcombe felt dark vibrations.

"My thanks to the Women's Political Association," Crane said. "You have shown great wisdom."

Standing in a loose circle around Kate, everyone laughed, Crane smiling broadly. The jubilation subsided in moments. Whetstone cast a shrewd glance at Dan and Lanie. "Crane tells me," he said, "that you tracked the sabotage on the Memphis quake. Hard to believe anyone so closely associated with the project would be that malicious, isn't it?"

There was an uncomfortable silence. Lanie sighed heavily, Newcombe was scowling. Crane's expression was unreadable. The three of them had talked off and on in the last day and a half about the meaning, the possible impact of the sabotage, and the conversations had served only to make them weary and depressed. Finally, Kate spoke up.

"Do you think Sumi Chan had anything to do with your problems? I like him, but there's something quite odd going on with that man."

"Doesn't matter," Crane said. He'd fought a hard battle with himself on the subject of the saboteur, triumphed over his rage, and wanted to move on. "The question now is how to repair the damage and make people listen to us again."

"Not possible," Whetstone said with authority. "All you are to people now, Crane, is the crazy man who fooled everyone. You don't recover from that."

"They'll have to listen," Crane said, almost shouting.

Whetstone's bushy brows arched high. "You've recalibrated your figures? You've got another date?"

"February 27th," Newcombe interjected.

"You're kidding," Kate said, looking sharply at Crane.

"Unfortunately, no. We're dead—I repeat, dead—serious," Crane said, his expression somber.

"Yes, but are you dead certain?" Kate asked impudently.

"Dead certain," Crane bit out.

"So that's why you got me here," Whetstone said. "Okay, what do you want from me?"

"Check your liquidity lately, Stoney?" Crane asked.

"I don't have to check. If I need hard cash, I can get hold of about three billion dollars, give or take a couple of hundred million."

"I want to borrow it," Crane said.

Whetstone laughed. "I imagine you do. And what would you do with it?"

"Place a bet."

"A bet! I think your jail time has left you completely unhinged. What sort of bet?"

"I want to place a bet with the American people that an earthquake will take place on the Reelfoot Rift on February 27th, 2025. I want the wager to be run through a third-party accounting firm that will verify the numbers and insure impartiality. We'll give two-to-one odds. People can take up to fifty dollars of that bet, to be paid off the day after the earthquake is predicted if it doesn't come off."

"You want to bet three billion dollars of my money that you have correctly predicted the day of the quake, is that right?" Whetstone asked.

"It'll look like a sucker bet," Crane said.

"*Look* like!" Whetstone said loudly. "It is!"

"We're not wrong, Stoney. We can't miss. At fifty bucks a pop, a lot of people will get in on the action. The teev will love to cover it because you stand to lose so much. We'll get our exposure again, maybe even convince some people we're right and get them the hell out of the danger zones. Once we win the bet, our credibility is restored, plus we won't have to play politics—the Foundation won't need government funds to keep running."

Whetstone just stared at him. "You're mad."

"Am I?" Crane returned. "The stress readings don't lie, and this time I'll bet we even have the Ellsworth-Beroza to back us up as we get closer to the time."

"Look, Crane. I'm as altruistic as the next person, but I didn't manage to make billions of dollars by being an idiot. Why should I risk almost all of my cash on a scheme you've already failed at once?"

"Because it's the right thing to do," Crane said.

"There's nothing right about gambling my money away. I'd be ruined. Couldn't you do it with a million or so?"

"No. The numbers need to be enormous in order to get the exposure and keep interest alive."

Whetstone shook his white-haired head. "I respect you," he said, "but this time—"

"May I say something?" Lanie asked, everyone turning to stare at her. No one shut her up, so she continued. "I've been working the project for over six months now, taking Crane's idea for the globe and trying to make it reality. It's forming before my eyes. My job is to talk to it, to make it understand what it's trying to accomplish, and as I do so, I'm continually struck by the amazing possibilities beyond EQ prediction."

"Such as?" Masters asked.

"Such as long-range weather prediction. The Earth, for all of its largesse, is really a totally closed, self-sustaining system on a huge scale that operates under its own set of rigid principles. The globe can make them understandable. It may be the most important piece of machinery ever devised. If we can predict weather patterns long range, it means we can plot areas of famine and plenty, and we can do it years in advance, planning for them, knowing where and when to grow food, where relief will be needed, when hurricanes, floods, and tornados are going to cause destruction.

"Mr. Whetstone, do you understand the implications of what I'm saying? You can help make the globe a life-sustaining, nurturing reality. It has the capacity of changing forever life on planet Earth in the most positive of ways. We may never be able to control the Earth, but we can understand it, which is the next best thing. Don't take this away from the people of the world."

"But your globe hasn't gone online, young lady," Whetstone said. "It may never work."

"It already does to an extent," Lanie shot back. "I've had success going from known event to known event. I believe our problem is a basic one."

"Pangaea," Crane said.

She pointed to him. "Correct. We've based the globe on a possibly erroneous assumption—that Pangaea happened the way scientists have speculated it happened. If that speculation is incorrect, then there's no way our globe will connect with the realities that we do know about for sure. I've thought about this a great deal, and I believe we need to go back farther, beyond Pangaea, for our answers."

"Back to where?" Masters asked.

"All the way, I suppose."

"The beginning of time?" Masters asked, amazed.

"If that's what it takes," Crane said. "We can let the globe tell us about Pangaea."

"Sounds wonderful," Whetstone said, "except for the fact that starting with the totally unknown could mean that you create an earth that doesn't really exist, one simply invented by the globe."

"No," Lanie said. "Not possible. My job as a synnoeticist is to communicate with the globe, to talk to it, to form that symbiotic relationship that makes the sum of the parts greater than the whole. We know where our globe ends up. We have real events that must conform. All I have to do is explain to the globe that it must design a world that ends in conformation with what exists. The rest will take care of itself."

"You can really do this?" Whetstone asked, his voice hushed.

"She's the best," Crane said. "Of course she can do it."

"Mr. Whetstone," Lanie said, "you can help mankind see the dawning of a new day in which Man and Earth work in conjunction, not opposition. If you turn us down now, you are destroying the hope of humanity rising above its bondage to Nature's unfeeling destructiveness. You sit in a historic position, sir. How much money do you really need to finish the rest of your life, and how does that stack up against the salvation you can bring?"

"You can really do this?" Whetstone asked again, his voice small, childlike.

"I can," Lanie said. "And with your help, I will."

Whetstone was staring at her, his lips quivering soundlessly, his eyes locked on some faraway, internal place. He looked at Crane. "When do we do it?"

"Right now," Crane said without hesitation. "Tonight."

"Thanks to your imager," Stoney said, "you've just got three billion dollars."

"*Borrowed*," Crane said. "Borrowed, not 'got.' You'll have every cent of your money back on February 28th."

"Let's shake on it," Stoney said, extending his hand.

Burt broke out a small bottle of the cache of Sumi's famous dorph, and everyone started to celebrate with it except Crane and Newcombe.

Newcombe felt out of place and wondered what Brother Ishmael was doing right now. He'd stopped drinking alcohol and given up dorph after his visit to the Zone. It was a revelatory experience. He found himself having to deal for the first time with depressions and the kind of minor irritations dorph would take away in an instant. He guessed that he seemed surly to those around him, but inside he felt in touch with his true self at long last. He might suffer petty emotional discomfort, but at least what he felt was for real.

"What are we waiting for?" Stoney asked. "We've got the terms of a wager to figure out, an accounting firm to line up, and, I assume, a broadcast to plan, right?"

"Right," Crane said. "Let's go down to my office."

They were off then to pats on the back from Kate, Burt, and Lanie.

Newcombe couldn't take his eyes off Lanie. She and Kate had hit the dorph pretty hard and were refilling their glasses with rum. He didn't like that one bit. It wasn't like Lanie. That thought encouraged him. He missed her terribly, wanted her in his life and his bed; maybe she was suffering, too. He walked over to where she was standing with Kate.

"Don't you think you'd better go a little easy on that stuff?" he asked, taking the glass from Lanie's hand.

"I think it's none of your business how much I drink," Lanie said, snatching the glass and draining it.

"Do you mind, Kate, if I steal her away for a couple of minutes?" Newcombe asked rhetorically. He took Lanie's elbow, none too gently steering her toward Crane's bedroom.

"I'll be right back!" Lanie called over her shoulder. "Don't get ahead of me!"

He nudged her into the room and closed the door.

"What the hell do you think you're doing?" Lanie asked. "You embarrassed me back there."

"We weren't finished with our talk."

"We were as far as I was concerned. Don't you get it, Dan? We've been tearing each other to pieces for five years now. It's time to stop the pain, to staunch the bleeding. Dan, it's over."

"It's him, isn't it?"

She sat heavily on the bed. "What are you talking about?"

"Crane," he said. "You've got something going with that madman."

"You're wrong," she said. "But even if you weren't, it's none of your business."

"You've completely sold yourself out to his insane program," he charged. "I couldn't believe the words that were coming out of your mouth a few minutes ago. How could you say them with a straight face?"

She jumped up and stared him down. "I meant every

word of what I said. How dare you belittle my life and my work!"

"Look, you're good with computers," he said. "Kudos. But Crane is selling fantasy. How can you possibly believe that globe will ever work?"

"It *will* work. I'm going to make it work."

"Then you're just as crazy as he is."

She glared at him, and for the first time he saw meanness there, focused anger. "Are you finished?" she asked quietly.

"No, I'm not finished. I'm just getting started."

"Well, I've heard enough, Dr. Newcombe. You've got to excuse me. There are two people in the other room who don't think I'm insane. I'd prefer to be with them."

"I'm not going to let you go that easily," he said. "Crane's infected you somehow with his insanity. I can wait, Lanie. I love you and I'll always be there for you."

"Do yourself a favor, Dan," she said. "Move on."

Newcombe's gut was on fire, dorphless rage and despair settling over him as he watched Lanie leave.

Sumi sat at her new desk at the National Academy of Science and tried to concentrate on the grant requests stacked up before her. She was having a difficult time keeping her mind on the job. They'd put Crane in jail—jail!—and it was all her fault. He had always treated her with respect and friendship. And how had she repaid him? With the basest deceit. She wondered how much of herself she could give up and still remain human.

"You seem deep in thought," came a voice, jerking her back into the here and now.

Mr. Li stood before her desk, smiling beatifically down at her. "Sir," she said, rising. "Is it you or a projection?"

He reached across the desk and touched her arm, his touch lingering. "I'm real and I'm here. What I'm going to say is very private."

"Sir?"

"Sit down, Sumi." She did as she was told.

Li moved fluidly, snakelike, around to her side of the desk and sat on its edge. "Sometimes," he said, "life has a way of altering our...circumstances in the most astounding fashion without our having to do anything to precipitate the changes. Do you know what I'm saying?"

"I assume my new position here is an example," she said, not liking the look in his eyes.

"On a small scale, yes. Do you mind if I ask you a personal question?"

"Yes, I do mind."

Mr. Li laughed. "I'm finding myself intrigued by your lifestyle. What's it like to masquerade for some twenty-eight years as the opposite sex?"

In absolute defensive mode, she answered carefully. "It's not like anything, really. I've always done it, so it's...natural."

"Do you feel like a man or like a woman?"

"I feel like what I am."

Mr. Li stood and moved behind Sumi, his hands coming up to massage her shoulders. "You know what I mean," he said softly. "Sexually. What are you like sexually?"

"Sir. I do not wish to answer questions of this kind."

His hands moved down to her arms, rubbing softly, as she fought back feelings of nausea. "You will do whatever I tell you to do," he said. "Answer the question."

She sighed deeply, her body rigid as he caressed her. "In order for my deception to work," she said, "I gave up all thoughts of sexuality many years ago. I couldn't risk exposure. I simply control those feelings."

"You've never had sex?"

"No, sir."

"My goodness." He leaned down and kissed her on the top of the head, then walked away from her. Sumi relaxed immediately. In front of the desk again, he looked at her with raised eyebrows. "I think we're going to have a very interesting association."

"How so, sir?" She hoped he couldn't see her shaking hands.

"I have a new job for you, Sumi. How would you like to be Vice President of the United States?"

Sumi Chan laughed out loud. "You are joking."

"I'm perfectly serious. It soon will be time for Gabler

to resign—and time for the face of China to shine forth in American politics. It will bind the cultures closer together."

"You must surely realize, Mr. Li, that the American Constitution provides that a Vice President be a natural-born citizen of the United States."

"Ah," Mr. Li said, reaching into his pocket and withdrawing a small disc. "But you are such a citizen, Sumi. It's all right here." He dropped it on the desk. "You are the son of an American Marine, an embassy guard, who married a Chinese national. You were born on a Navy ship that was en route to the US. Unfortunately, your parents died in the flu epidemic several years ago—that much is true, eh? The record is complete. I did an excellent job on it."

"Even greater lies added to my life," Sumi said. "Mr. Li, I cannot do this. My ancestral lands—"

"I have acquired them. They were lost to you in the bankruptcy action of your parents. But I knew you would be working to reacquire them, so I did. They are yours when our business is concluded. If you refuse, you will have nothing."

"Why are you doing this?"

"I've already told you. I like the idea of an Asian being a heartbeat away from the Presidency. And this will also give us the chance to work . . . closely together. However, we will not make this change for a month or so. I wish you to prepare yourself."

Mr. Li's wristpad bleeped insistently. "What?" he asked crossly. He listened glumly for a moment. "Thank you, Mr. Mui," he said at last and blanked the man. He touched the pad again, Sumi's wall screen coming up, bringing with it a shot of Crane and Whetstone. She smiled involuntarily. Crane was out of jail.

"People call me a fraud," Crane was saying. "Well, this is your opportunity to profit from my so-called fraudulent nature."

Whetstone spoke. "We have put three billion dollars cash into an escrow account. That money talks: It says there will be an earthquake on February 27th in the Mississippi Valley that will cause massive devastation. We are betting on Mr. Crane's formidable knowledge and scientific genius. We will give two-to-one odds. If anyone wants a piece of the action—"

"What are they doing?" Li asked.

Sumi shook her head. "You never believed it, did you?"

"That Crane could predict earthquakes? Certainly not."

"You were wrong, Mr. Li. I tried to tell you about it when you had me sabotage their program, but you wouldn't listen."

"But what's happening now?"

She was laughing, with relief and with the irony of it all. "Don't you see? They've discovered my treachery and have corrected their calculations. You are going to have your earthquake, Mr. Li. You are going to know the horror of getting what you asked for."

"But that . . . that changes everything!"

"Yes. Everything." She laughed. "Life, sir, is change."

THE KING PROJECTION
THE FOUNDATION
23 JANUARY 2025, 2:00 P.M.

Running, Crane circled the programmers within the newly built stationary orb around the globe. "Worthless!" he shouted at the globe. "You're useless. I'm going to sell you for scrap."

"Turn off the atmosphere inducers, run in to that globe, and kick the damned thing for me," Lanie called wearily to him from where she slumped at her console.

He stopped running after he'd caught sight of her. She was dejected. He was only angry. He trotted over to her. She was staring at her keyboard. When the last of the shutdown bells quieted, he said gently, "It's just something stupid. Don't give up."

She didn't even look at him. "Better be something stupid, because we're fresh out of smart ideas."

He turned and stared through the thick ahrensglass at the huge globe. It had shut itself down this time somewhere before the formation of Pangaea during the planet's watery stage. Some progress at least. Before, during the first two weeks after the bet, they'd reset it twenty times. Twenty times they'd recalibrated, making slight adjustments to the fiery birth of the Earth Mother. And twenty times they'd failed. Then the globe had made a request direct only to Crane—and he'd responded quickly. The globe was transforming itself . . . Crane knew that, Lanie did, too, though neither of them could predict to what sort of entity.

The globe had urged Crane to reposition its magnetic poles and to reconform its environmental surround to match Earth's gravitational field through and beyond the ozone layer. In response to the request, Crane had ordered all the openings of the globe room, the window and door apertures, to be sealed. Then vast numbers of machines had been brought to the Foundation. Huge vacuum tubes and force field impellers, under the direction of the best physicists Crane could hire, had been placed at dome and base to transform the globe room into a chamber that was a piece of the universe in which the globe-Earth revolved on its axis.

And now, this afternoon, they'd at last been able to test again. And for all the changes—the time, the money, the hard work—they'd got nothing but failure . . . again. It was maddening.

"You know, the sad thing," Lanie said, popping a dorph tab, "is that the damned globe doesn't even hold out any hope of ever constructing itself. It finds no way of getting from point A to point B."

"We're just not doing something we should be doing."

"It's so simple, though." She got up and joined him. "We've got known factors—a weight of around six and a half sextillion tons of rotating fire. It contains elements we can discern. It rotated faster at the beginning, but we've allowed for that."

"Known factors. You said, known factors." Something was eating away at Crane, something right in front of his face that he could almost see.

"Maybe Dan was right," Lanie said. "Maybe both of us are nuts and this is just a fantasy."

"Dan says a lot of things I don't agree with." Newcombe had come out again publicly in support of an Islamic State. True to his word, he'd kept the Foundation's name out of it both times he appeared on the teev. Instead he billed himself as "the inventor of EQ-eco."

It had been a strange month and a half since the night he and Stoney had gone on teev with the wager. The government had viciously attacked him and the bet, calling it a con game meant to bilk the citizens of America. Despite that, the wager had been covered within three days, actually two and a half. It was already out of the news, but that didn't matter. The closer to the time they came, the bigger an issue it would become. It was a self-generating concept.

To a man, the scientific establishment rang with condemnation, referring to Crane as a "lunatic bent on making himself famous no matter what the cost." Actually, he'd been glad to hear that. It meant they'd stay away from Reelfoot and leave it to him.

"Cheer up, people," Newcombe said, moving up to Lanie's console, a printout in his hand. "It can't be that bad."

"The Earth has been keeping her secrets secret," Crane said amiably. "In line with your speculation."

Newcombe shrugged. "I'd love to see you succeed. But we're talking about five billion years of earth history, most of which we know nothing about. It really isn't possible to expect—"

"You're wrong in a great many respects," Lanie said, pointing at her line of programmers, all working fast, inputting data, increasing the globe's knowledge. "Current data is simply a reflection of the ancient past. In every instance where I've worked backward from a known event, I've been able to connect it to an unknown event that began the chain. It's time-consuming, but it works."

"Then why not apply that to the whole globe?"

"Can't," Crane said. "To go backward, an event at a time, would consume the rest of our lives and then some.

Each event would be judged independently because we don't know inherent connections. And when we were done, we still would have made a globe based only on what we know about. What about the geologic eccentricities we haven't even uncovered?"

"Besides," Lanie added, "even with the single events I've been able to trace backward, I can go only so far. At some point hundreds of millions of years ago, the machine shuts down and says, 'You can't get there from here.' "

"In other words," Newcombe said, taking a seat himself, "you can't go either way with it. Your globe is telling you that the world we *have* is not the world we *had*."

Crane snapped to attention. "That's *exactly* what it's telling us," he said, staring through the ahrensglass and up the three-story height of the globe. "It's not the same. Something happened to this planet that changed it drastically, altered it forever. So, what could have happened, what—oh my God. I've been so stupid." He turned to Lanie. "Crank it up. We're going to go from scratch right now."

"What?"

"Just do it. I've got an idea and we're going to try it out."

The globe went dark as the computers reset themselves. Within a minute Crane stared at a ball of fire, spinning wildly in its youth. "All right," he said. "I want you to increase your six-and-a-half-sextillion-ton mass by one eighty-first."

"One eighty-first," Lanie said. "One eighty-first?"

"Do it," Crane said.

Newcombe laughed. "Crane, you're batty."

"Only if I'm wrong."

"The machine refuses to take the extra weight," Lanie said. "It's telling me the increase is unstable by its very nature. The globe can't support the increase in mass and still hold together."

"Perfect," Crane said. "Talk to it, Lanie. Explain to it that it's all right to build to an unstable state."

"It's not going to want to hear that," she said.

"Tell the globe that the instability will resolve itself."

"It will?"

"I think so," he said, as Lanie turned to the computer and opened a line of discussion with its higher reasoning functions.

Crane walked up to Newcombe. "What's the printout?" he asked.

"Ahh." Dan smiled, handing him a small stack of seismograms. "Almost forgot. We've begun to get Ellsworth-Beroza tremors on the Reelfoot grabens consistent with the beginning phases of a major quake. Also, levels of radon, carbon monoxide, and methane are continuing to rise along with electromagnetic activity."

Crane nodded, not surprised. He'd make his three billion dollars, but it would be at a cost beyond belief. It was happening, a cycle of real horror beginning its relentless harvest of life and property. And no one was going to listen to his warnings.

"Got it," Lanie said, swinging her chair around. "However, the globe will only do it if you tell it to, Crane. Would you step over here?"

Crane moved to her console as Lanie typed the command that would start the globe. "The machine refuses to take responsibility for what happens," she said. "It's looking for authority from higher up."

He looked at the screen. It read:

Initiate Globe (Y/N)

He hit the Y. The screen faded, then read:

Project Leader Confirm

"Speak your name into the C channel of your pad," Lanie said.

Crane did so, and the globe lights immediately came on. The sequence was initiated.

The globe spun quickly, but off balance. All the lights went down. Lanie's programmers stopped work to watch the spectacle. The Earth is not perfectly round, but this one was obviously way off, its equatorial bulge huge and moving, throwing the planet on a wobbly orbit.

"You're going to break your toy," Newcombe said.

Warning lights were flashing up and down the consoles, the screens warning of imminent breakup.

A huge lump of fire now appeared on the globe, threatening to destroy it as centrifugal force drew the fireball slowly away from the globe.

"We're going to have to shut it down, Crane!" Lanie called.

"You do and you're fired!" Crane yelled over the warning bells sounding up and down the line.

"It wants to go into shutdown sequence."

"But it hasn't, has it?" he returned. "It's smarter than we are. Let it go!"

The globe was wobbling horribly. It creaked as it tore itself apart, but Crane watched it with a satisfied smile.

Then it happened. The globe, now a lopsided dumbbell shape, was no longer able to sustain the hold on itself and the bulge broke free, spinning off, only to get captured in the larger mass's gravitational pull. What was left began to spin normally again, all the warning bells and flashers shutting off up and down the line.

They were looking at a planet and its moon, a real chunk of the globe, dancing in synchronous orbit, and the globe was just as happy as it could be.

Newcombe sat staring, his mouth hanging open.

"Is that the Moon?" Lanie asked.

"Well"—Crane shrugged—"now we know where that came from. Bully. Let's keep watching."

"It seems to be orbiting so closely," Lanie said.

"I think we'll find," Crane answered, "that as the Earth's rotation slows, the Moon will move farther away. Right now, imagine not only the effect the Moon will have on sea tides at this distance, but land tides as well."

"I can't believe it's still working," Lanie said as the planet cooled and holorains began, the Moon now a bit farther away.

"This is weird," Newcombe said. "This isn't some kind of trick, is it, Crane?"

"This is history, my fine fellow," Crane said. "Earth history as no one's ever seen it before. If this thing keeps working, we may all be obsolete."

And work it did, half holo, half "real." Land emerged from the evaporating waters, the closeness of the Moon causing major havoc on land and sea—quakes, tsunamis, and tidal waves rattling the globe in ways none of them could have anticipated. If there had been a Pangaea as such, they never saw it. For an hour that was hundreds of millions of years, the continental masses seemed to form and reform in a continual dance with the Moon, which moved ever so slowly away.

The globe stopped many times during these early periods, adding holo comets, asteroids, and meteorites to the mix in order to conform to known life later on, but it didn't shut down—it continued. The farther it went, the more excited the programmers became, until they were shouting and cheering every time the machine hit a glitch and reset itself to continue onward.

The Moon finally distanced itself enough to lose its major impact on sea and land. Here, they saw the beginnings of a stable world, more stable, at least, than the frenzy of its earlier years. The seas calmed. The continents emerged in roughly the same form as today.

For Crane, time did not exist during this exercise. First to last passed in an instant for him. He thought of all the men of science from its beginnings who had measured, timed, and speculated about the nature of their Earth. Without their observations, the globe would not have been possible. For thousands of years, scientists had meticulously recorded their findings with no notion of where those findings would lead. This was one of the places. There would be others.

Five hours later, he emerged from his thoughts to the sounds of cheering. The globe stood proudly online, up to date, turning slowly. Dead even with them.

Everyone was still there, including Newcombe, and they had been joined by the rest of the staff. It was a spectacle none of them could pull away from. The addition of new information would continue, but this was the core unit from which ever more knowledge would spring.

"Do you realize what we've just done?" Crane called to the applauding group. "However much information we've put into this system is merely a grain of sand on the seashore in comparison to what the globe has invented on its own to make our data compatible. Every hairline fissure, every graben, every underground stream or unconfirmed nuclear explosion that has occurred on planet Earth is now ours to know. Information is power, ladies and gentlemen. And we have the power."

Another cheer. He turned to Newcombe. "Still think I'm crazy?"

"Crazy for trying," the man said. "Brilliant for succeeding."

Lanie moved to the two men. "I'm still in shock." She put her arm around him as Newcombe stiffened.

"You did it," Crane said, hugging her close then moving away when it felt too good. "We're going to call your globe the King Projection."

"You're naming it after me?"

"You're its mama," Crane replied, then raised his voice for all of them to hear.

"We've done the impossible," he said. "Now let's try the unthinkable. Dr. King, would you be kind enough to program ahead on the Reelfoot and see what it gives us? Take us forward to a quake, a big quake."

Lanie hurried to the keyboard. As if it were a monstrous crystal ball, they were using the globe to try and look into the future. It was heady and scary. This was different from the prediction they'd made on the stress readings. This was the Earth simply winding out the certitude of its own history. To the sound of a loud buzzer the globe stopped turning, the spotlight zeroing on the Mississippi Valley, the familiar red lines of a Valley quake jagged as a gash.

"Time," Crane said, his mouth dry.

Lanie punched up the blood red numbers again. This time they read:

27 February 2025, 5:37 P.M. + or −

Twenty-three minutes sooner than their earlier calculations.

"We've done it," Crane said. "We've conquered the future."

He looked to Newcombe again. "This is our research source," he said. "All our answers lie here."

Newcombe looked hard at him. "All we need now is the guts to use it. Do we really want the responsibility of knowing the future?"

"It's moot," Lanie said from the console. "Want it or not, it's here."

Newcombe stood and walked to Crane. "Now that you've got it," he whispered, "what are you really going to do with this goddamned thing?"

"Anything I want, doctor."

The Masada brought rain that night, which meant radioactivity flushing down the streets and into the water supplies. Some sickness and death would result, the greatest toll taken on outdoor life. But it used to be worse, and would continue to be a decreasing threat until it would dissipate in the mid-2030s and be remembered ultimately as a scourge falling somewhere between the Black Plague and the Spanish Inquisition on the scale of suffering of humanity.

This particular night, it was a godsend for Crane. He had celebrated the globe with his people, then drifted to his office when the alarms had driven everyone to shelter. Now, as the rains fell outside, he would have the globe to himself for a while.

He sat at Lanie's console, explaining exactly what it was he wanted to accomplish. As he finished inputting, Burt Hill came over his aural.

"Where the hell are you, Crane?"

"I'm staying in my office tonight," Crane replied on the P fiber. "Don't worry about me."

"You're only wantin' to play with that globe."

"Can you blame me?"

"Not at all. Got to tell you something, though. An announcement just came through all the teev stations—Vice President Gabler has resigned. Everybody thinks it's because he's got blamed for all the problems with the War Zone."

"Interesting," Crane said, not finding it interesting at all.

"That's not the juicy part, boss," Hill returned. "Gideon has appointed Sumi Chan to fill out the term."

"Sumi?" Crane said, very interested now. "Wonder how they got around the citizenship requirements."

"Never mind that," Hill said. "This clinches it. Sumi's nothing but a traitorous, slimy—"

"I want you to find a private fiber to Sumi," Crane said. "I want to talk to him. And when you get to him, be sure to give your most hearty congratulations."

"But he's—"

"A powerful man who can help us," Crane interrupted. "Call me back on this fiber."

He blanked and looked at the console. Over the last year, he'd fed every morsel of info he'd ever learned on the effects of under- and aboveground nuclear testing on faults. By now the globe knew much more than he did.

He typed his question and hit enter.

The globe hesitated only slightly before revealing a series of flashing red lights all over the Earth, Crane running to it to check locations. All the lights were centered on or near rifts. His heart pounded as he counted them—fifty-three.

This was it, the reason for his existence.

He broke down and cried then, not stopping until he had Sumi on the line and more business to be done.

CONTI-NENTAL DRIFT

THE FOUNDATION
25 FEBRUARY 2025, 7:30 P.M.

Lanie finished the last of her packing, then stepped out onto her porch to watch the final preparations for the pilgrimage to Tennessee. Their condor dropped momentarily into view, Lanie calling to it before it swept past and majestically retreated to higher ground. The sun was gone now, freeing everyone to get out of doors. There were as many as fifty helos, private donations, stacked up on the plain below, being filled with food, water, and medical supplies.

It had been Crane who'd solicited the helos, thinking they might come in handy for evacs and emergency medical. She'd been amazed at how many people still believed in him and were willing to contribute. Besides the supplies, he had a crack medical emergency team in each bird—people, good people, donating their time. Maybe there was hope for the planet after all, she thought.

She saw Dan come out of his chalet, four houses away, carrying his bags. Since the night of the wager, they'd been near strangers. It was amazing how someone who had once been so important to her could simply move into a different role in her mind and heart. She knew that he wanted her to let him back in but, thankfully, he wasn't pushing it. She did want to be his friend, though, so when he came over, she gave him an affectionate hug. He responded enthusiastically. "I'm sorry I've been so standoffish," she said, looking him in the eyes. "I didn't want to give you the wrong idea."

"The wrong idea," he echoed.

She watched him compose himself. He leaned on the rail, looking down. Burt Hill was directing the loading-up operations, one of Stoney's jumbo jets taking the bulk of the Foundation's gear and personnel. Dan shook his head. "What would we do without Burt?"

"Starve," she answered, leaning on the rail beside him. "Run out of materials. Chaos would ensue."

He smiled at her. "Undoubtedly." His lips tightened. "I'm not even sure what happened between us."

"You want the truth?"

"I think so."

"Okay," she said calmly, although her heart pounded like crazy. "I found myself not trusting you. I found myself noticing jealousy between us. I found myself wanting you to be different. One time you said maybe we were finally growing up. I think that's what happened. We grew up and apart. Besides, you have a whole different life now."

"I'd give it up in a minute if—"

"No," she said, putting her hand over his mouth. "You'd feel trapped and miserable. There's no hope for it, Dan. We've just moved on."

"I can't stop loving you," he said.

She nodded, swallowing hard. "We'll always have that. Let's remember it that way."

He stared at her for a long moment. "I'll be there for you if you change your mind. Crane can't make you happy."

"This has nothing to do with Crane."

"You need to be needed," he said. "Maybe Crane needs you more than I do, though I think that's impossible."

"I'm not relating to this discussion, Dan."

"I know."

"Friends?" she asked, putting out her hand.

She didn't understand the smile he gave her. "Friendly adversaries," he said, shaking her hand. "You going below? I need to check my equipment manifest and make sure they got everything."

"Aren't you flying down with us?"

He shook his head. "I'm going to spend the night in LA. I'll meet you on site tomorrow."

"Then I'll walk with you." They moved down the metal stairs, Dan carrying his suitcases, Lanie unsure as to how she felt about the previous conversation. As with most things concerning Dan, nothing ever seemed to be truly settled. And what did he mean by "friendly adversaries"?

"You look tired," he said. "Having the dreams again?"

"Again? They've never stopped."

She shivered. It had been rough the night before, the worst yet. She could literally feel the fire burning her as it rose from a pit, while Crane kept reaching for her hand. And that boy was there, that dead boy, only he was alive and she feared for him more than for herself. She'd awakened in terror, drenched in sweat at 2 A.M. and hadn't even considered the notion of going back to sleep.

"Still think it's connected to Martinique?"

"It's got to be."

They walked into the confusion of helos and support personnel, all running human chains as manifest lists were verbally checked off. "Have you ever asked Crane to help you with it?" Newcombe spotted Hill and waved him over. "He *was* there with you."

"He always changes the subject," she said. "And that's too bad, because I think if I could simply remember Martinique, all the dreams would go away. It's right there in front of me . . . yelling at me."

"What's up, Doc Dan?" Hill said, winded from exertion.

"I've got to go down to the city tonight," Dan said. "Is it possible?"

"If you're willin' to go now, it is. At the moment, I've got three dozen pilots standing around with their thumbs up their butts." He took Dan's bags. "Something'll be waitin' for you on the main pad in about ten minutes."

"Thanks, Burt."

"Stay in the shade, Doc."

They moved on to the mosque. Dan was looking good tonight, wearing all black, a suit with a turtleneck. He looked like the Atlantic City version of Brother Ishmael. She wondered if he were going to the War Zone.

They walked in, then through to her station. They peered through the ahrensglass at the globe. Lanie always was excited when she saw her handiwork alive and pulsating with information. They were running a full slate of programmers tonight who were dumping weather data into the computer.

"Martinique," she said, her eyes fixated on the globe. "The answer to my memory loss and to the dreams. I must remember what happened . . . and I think I'm close. It's like a fog dissipating." She watched the West Indies slide past, followed Martinique as it turned, saw its volcano.

"Dan," Crane called down through a new hole in his office wall that let out into the programmers' area, "I need the EQ-eco on downtown Memphis!"

"I'll bring it up." Dan went to his labs.

Lanie drifted toward Crane's office. Time was such a strange commodity. It had its own organic structure that worked on people without their consent. Like her and Dan. Sumi Chan, for instance, had gone from valued ally to traitor and back again to friend within the space of a few months. As Vice President, he was once again supporting Crane behind the scenes, and it was support that Crane cheerfully accepted.

She walked into Crane's office, smiling at all the teevs running his exploits on the walls. He'd been right about the bet. It seemed the entire world was waiting for the events to unwind. It was the money—the bet—right now that counted to the world. Soon, it would be the horror.

"How will they judge me, do you think?" Crane asked her, all but reading her mind.

"Some will blame you. Just like on Sado. Some will praise you, some love you, some hate you. You'll be a magician and a scientist, a monster and a savior. But none of that matters to you, does it?"

He smiled, his jumpsuit sleeves rolled up as he stuffed a briefcase full of cash. Bail money. "As long as we can keep the funding rolling in, I'm happy," he said. "People don't know what's good for them; they only know what they want. I learned to keep my expectations low a long time ago. It's good advice for anyone."

"Dan's going down the mountain tonight."

He grimaced but didn't respond.

Lanie looked through the new window at the globe. "I never get over it," she said. "The damned thing's still running."

"And will continue to," he said. "King's Projection will be in use millennia after we're gone."

"Unless they come up with something better. Now, why haven't we taken it any farther forward than February 27th? I'm sure there are other quakes to predict. But we haven't done it. Why?"

"I'll tell you why," Newcombe said from the doorway. "Now that he's got the power, he's afraid of it."

"Not far off," Crane said, reaching for the printouts in Newcombe's hand. "I just thought it was time for a little reflection before moving forward. Besides, there's Memphis. . . ."

He took the schematic Newcombe handed him and stared at it. "Here's the Memphis jail," he said. "I'm sure they'll arrest me and take me here."

"It's going to be close," Newcombe said.

"Yeah. The east side of the building looks like it won't make it, but the cell blocks are stacked on the west side."

"That's a narrow ribbon of safe territory. Too narrow."

"I trust your calculations."

"I'm not so sure about the river," Newcombe said. "I know what will happen to the land around it, but things are going to shift and force it to change course. I've got no real eco on that."

"We'll take our chances."

"Will you have access to teev?"

"Yes," Crane said, Lanie finding herself watching a wall show about the quake on Martinique. As she watched, lights began flashing in her head, recognition. God, she could feel the mud getting through her clothes. She itched.

Crane was still talking, but it was coming to Lanie as something from far away. She held her head, pain flashing. She could feel the scar under her hair, then the heat, the darkness, the overpowering fear of suffocation, the house collapsing all around them, everything else fading away. . . .

Hands shaking her, a distant voice in her ear.

"Dan? Is Dan all right?" she said, but something was wrong. Tears were streaming down her cheeks.

"Lanie! Get a grip. . . . Lanie?"

Dan was in front of her. They were in Crane's office in the Foundation. She was gasping for breath, the sadness all over her as she began crying again.

"What is it?" Crane asked gently.

"That boy," she said, sobbing. "That poor boy. We never even . . . even knew h-his name."

Dan moved to comfort her, but she turned instinctively to Crane, who put his good arm around her.

The doorway opened fully to her then, her memories drifting lazily back—the fear, the interminable questions, the rum. And Crane. A smile spread slowly over her face. "I remember," she said to him. "I remember everything."

"What's to remember?" Newcombe asked.

"The rum bottle . . . being pushed down the breathing tube. That's right when you were telling me about your plan for ending earthquakes."

"*Ending* earthquakes?" Dan asked.

She looked at Crane, instinctively realizing she'd said something wrong, something meant to be kept private.

"If you've got a plan for ending earthquakes," Newcombe said, "I'd sure love to hear it."

Crane merely looked at him. Newcombe turned to Lanie. "Okay, *you* tell me."

"I-I'm still confused," she said. "I'm just not sure what I . . . what I. . . ."

"You're a lot of things, Lanie," Newcombe said, "but confused isn't one of them. What are you holding back? *Why* are you holding back?"

"Dan," Crane said quietly. "Ask me, not Lanie. I'm the one with the secrets."

Newcombe stared angrily at him. "You're nothing but secrets. From the first you've had some sort of game plan you kept from the rest of us. We've had to pick our way through your self-generated darkness. How about a little truth for a change?"

"Come on," Crane said. "I'll show you. I don't suppose it would do any good to swear you to secrecy?"

"There's been too damned much secrecy," Newcombe said, following Crane out of the office.

Lanie trailed behind, tense. She'd not meant to blurt anything out. God, why did she have to go and open her big mouth? She was surprised to find Crane moving to her controller's console. "Ladies and gentlemen," Crane said to the programmers working at their stations, "you may take a thirty-minute break beginning now. I want all of you out of the building. Go."

Lanie joined them at the console, Crane's fingers already busy on her keyboard. There were, apparently, things about the globe that even she didn't know.

"I've been studying quakes my entire life," Crane said, taking the globe offline and reprogramming. "I'd decided early on that I wanted to heal, not just to define. That's why I entered into the study of the effects of nuclear testing on surrounding strata."

"We all know your old news, Crane," Newcombe said. "You're still credited as the man whose work made the politicos see the light and stop all nuclear testing."

"Gave me the Nobel Prize for it," Crane said, and laughed. "But I never earned, nor wanted, that award. And I certainly never wanted to stop nuclear testing."

"I don't understand," Lanie said. Crane hit the enter

key and the globe stopped dead, red lights flashing all over its surface.

"Heat," Crane said, walking to the globe, "enough heat to melt rock . . . to weld rock."

"You want to fuse the plates back together," Newcombe said, his voice hushed, his eyes narrowed in deep suspicion.

"I asked the machine," Crane said. "I postulated a temperature of five thousand degrees centigrade and asked if it were possible to reconnect the plates through spot welding." He pointed to the globe. "This is what it gave me. Fifty-three spot welds that, if done properly, will fuse the continental plates and end drift forever."

"That's what the globe was for," Lanie said. "You wanted back-up for your theories."

"Correct," Crane said. "We can end the destructive reign of the earthquake in our lifetime."

"You want to explode fifty-three nuclear bombs?" Newcombe asked, incredulous.

"Fifty-three gigaton bombs," Crane said.

"You're crazier than I thought."

"Am I?" Crane asked. "Think about it. The world sits on enormous stockpiles of nuclear materials, old warheads, waste matter. Done properly, my bombs could eliminate those stockpiles by exploding them back downward, toward the core, which is simply a decaying radioactive process anyway. We could end EQs and volcanoes, and get rid of our nuclear mess all at the same time."

Lanie cocked her head. There was sense to what he said. Deep underground explosions right on the rifts, if handled properly, could relieve all the push-pull pressure. If the bombs were planted deeply enough, they'd pose zero threat to life above ground.

"Has your ego no limits?" Newcombe asked. "Has it occurred to you that earthquakes are a natural part of our world? That the planet may exist because of them? There would be no life on this planet at all if the volcanoes hadn't pumped life-sustaining matter into the atmosphere. What you're proposing is nothing less than destruction of the processes which made us what we are. They're natural, Crane. Leave them alone!"

"What's natural about an earthquake?" Crane asked. "People are always so quick to judge. Just because it's always been this way doesn't mean it has to stay like that. The globe thinks it will work fine and the globe knows far more than we do."

"It does not!" Newcombe said loudly. "The globe knows nothing of humanity or of ethics or of common sense. You're talking about interfering with a basic process of the Earth. God only knows the catastrophe you could cause by trying to make this insanity work!"

"Ask the machine," Crane said. "See what it thinks."

"I don't care about the goddamned machine!" Newcombe shouted. "It's an extension of your insanity."

"Wait a minute," Lanie said. "The globe works. You've seen it work. It can be a very useful tool in—"

"You're as bad as he is," Newcombe said. "Listen carefully to me: It's the entire planet you're putting at risk here. It's unnatural, Crane. It's wrong."

"Strange words from a scientist," Crane said. "Dams change the course of nature's rivers. Medicines interfere with the natural process of sickness. Genetic manipulation changes everything from the food we eat to the children we bear, again by going against the nature of life. This is no different."

Newcombe tapped his wristpad for the time. "There's science, Crane, then there's egotistical arrogance. Who the hell do you think you are?"

"I know who I am, doctor," Crane said. "You should ask that question of yourself."

"I have," Newcombe said, "and here's the answer: I'm the man who's going to keep you from destroying the Earth."

With that, he turned and strode quickly out of the mosque.

Lanie moved to Crane, put a hand on his good arm. "I'm sorry," she said. "I shouldn't have blurted out—"

"Don't worry about it," Crane said, watching Newcombe leave the building. "He would have found out soon enough anyway. I'll be going public."

He idly reached out and patted her hand. Lanie feared that this might be the last quiet moment of their lives.

Looking down on the Zone from the roof of the two-story warehouse Brother Ishmael had converted to his home, Newcombe felt as though he'd stepped into the past.

The inner city was clean but crowded, people everywhere on the streets. There were no teevs on the buildings, no projected dinosaurs or camheads running around desperately looking for the visual that would change their lives.

Young children were parading the streets, though, all carrying weapons as the onlookers cheered them on. Newcombe was uncomfortable with the weapons.

Above, blue lightning crackled across the black top of the Zone, a protective electronic jam for a city within a city. They existed inside an electric cocoon totally cut off from the white man's world. Looking at the huge numbers of children and young adults, he concluded that over half the population of the War Zone had probably never even seen the outside world.

He sat with Ishmael, Khadijah, and Martin Aziz. They watched a small teev showing the scene just outside of the gates, in the cleared area that stood as a free fire zone. Several hundred Muslim children were out there charging the FPF positions, throwing rocks and chunks of concrete. The FPF responded with low-frequency infrasound, meant to disrupt the thinking processes, and with nausea gas. The children were going down, writhing and crying, a show for all the world to see.

"Why don't you bring them back in?" Newcombe said, "before they're taken away . . . or worse. They're just kids."

"They're martyrs to Islam," Ishmael said quietly. "Their suffering will open the hearts of the people to our cause. They are the first wave of our Jihad."

"What's the second wave?"

"My brother is talking about bombs, about terrorism, about killing," Martin Aziz said.

"My brother does not have the heart for revolution," Ishmael said.

"You're wrong," Aziz said. "It's the stomach I lack. I believe that cycles of killing and revenge and more killing will add years to our struggle."

"And what has inactivity brought us?" Khadijah asked.

"I'm not speaking of inactivity," Aziz said, Newcombe listening to a sibling patter that was as natural to this family as breathing. "Brother Daniel's more considered approach through the media has already brought us endorsements from prominent citizens."

"Endorsement." Ishmael snorted, standing to look over the rail to the streets below. The demonstrators, seeing their spiritual and political leader, broke out in a thunderous cheer, thousands of voices calling his name.

Smiling, Ishmael turned back to Aziz. "And what has my approach brought?" he asked. "In the last month our spiritual brothers all over the world have risen up and demonstrated against Liang Int, boycotts are in progress in thirty countries, and the lands living under Islamic Law already have refused to do business with Liang until we are given a homeland. Our visibility and the suffering of our children have touched billions of hearts and, more importantly, we are hitting Liang in the pocketbook, the only place they feel pain."

Aziz simply shook his head and stared at the teev. "Behold the fruit of Islam," he said sadly.

A large FPF force had broken from behind their barricades and were wading with electric prods into the sea of vomiting children, indiscriminately swinging fifty thousand volts at anyone not quick enough to crawl out of the way.

Grimacing, Ishmael turned from the teev. "That's enough," he said. "Call them back."

Aziz hit the pad. "Open the gates," he said. "Now!"

On the screen, Newcombe could see the two large gates to the secret city swinging open, the children retreating, screaming and crying, back into the Zone, FPF chasing them, swinging their clubs, stopping thirty feet short of the gates themselves. No one had ever tried to breach the Zone.

The G retook their positions behind a six-foot wall a hundred yards away from the Zone. As they went, they dragged the bodies of dead or unconscious children with them.

"Turn it off," Ishmael said.

"This is horrifying," Newcombe said, his stomach in knots. "This can't be allowed to go on."

"You're right," Ishmael said, patting him on the shoulder, "but all wars have casualties. Understand that. We may bicker among ourselves, but we must be willing to pay the price in blood to have our freedom."

There was nothing Newcombe felt he could say. He looked up at the crackling blue fires and realized the sky always looked the same here.

"How do you power all this?" he asked as Brother Ishmael's wife, Reena, served cardamom coffee and cookies. "It would take a focus the size of a small building to generate a web this big."

"You know the Pan Arab Friendship League building downtown?" Ishmael asked.

"Of course I do," Newcombe said. "It's shaped and faceted like a jewel. People come—"

"The whole building is a giant focus," Khadijah said. "We've barely tapped its power."

"No one has ever suspected," Ishmael said. "The cables that connect us are in the sewers. You will find something similar in every city that has a War Zone."

The cheering grew louder, and they all stood to watch. Leaning over the rail, Newcombe saw children as young as six, bloody and battered, some being carried on stretchers, returning home from battle. The procession stopped beneath them. The crowd roared now. Ishmael picked up a bullhorn to address them. Newcombe was startled to realize that most of these people probably didn't have aurals. It was exciting in its very primitiveness.

"Heroes of the Revolution," Ishmael said, "we salute you! You are the future! You will live to raise your own

children on your own land, with Allah as your guide! Go
now . . . home to your parents who love you!"

To thunderous applause Ishmael returned to his seat,
delicately picked up his demitasse cup, and sipped. He sat
back and said, "Soon, other cities, other War Zones will
join the children's revolution. We'll schedule the riots in
shifts so that there's always one going on someplace." He
looked over at Newcombe. "Do you go with the others
from the Foundation to Memphis?"

"I leave tomorrow."

"There's a small War Zone there," Aziz said.

"Yes, I know," Newcombe said. "That's one of the
things I wanted to talk to you about." He pulled out the
EQ-eco he'd drawn up for the city of Memphis. The War
Zone there was circled in black. "Do you see this area?
It's downtown Memphis."

Khadijah and Martin walked over and joined Ishmael
in peering at the paper Newcombe held.

"This jagged line shows an area where the earth will
sink by as much as fifteen feet. Here, on the other side of
the jagged line is an area of uplift that will tear the city in
two."

"It goes right through the War Zone," Khadijah said.

Newcombe looked at her, their gazes holding. "Yes,"
he said, then turned his head to Ishmael. "Do they have a
way out of there?"

"Underground . . . like we have here."

"Will they listen to me if I warn them?"

"If I tell them to."

"Tell them."

"Where would they go?" Martin Aziz asked.

They all stared at one another, Ishmael's face slowly
cracking into a wide smile.

"They'll go south," Ishmael said. "Into Mississippi."

"The promised land," Khadijah whispered, eyes alight.
She clapped her hands.

"They will be the first to make the pilgrimage to our
new homeland," Ishmael continued. "There are hundreds
of traditional Africk townships in Mississippi. Our people

will locate in one of them and take it over. It will be our beachhead."

"Perfect." Newcombe smiled, and Crane's words from Sado fell out of his mouth unbidden. "What drama!"

"As long as the government of Mississippi doesn't object," Aziz said.

Khadijah laughed. "It certainly presents an interesting problem for Mr. Li," she said.

"If he should allow us to settle," Ishmael said, on his feet now and starting to pace, "our people will immediately demand separatist status."

"And if he decides to stop the pilgrimage?" Aziz asked.

Ishmael shook his head. "More martyrs. But I've noticed something about businessmen. They dislike killing consumers."

Aziz nodded, smiling slightly. "Brother Daniel has provided us the impetus to make our revolution active. I approve."

"Excellent!" Ishmael said, hugging everyone in turn. He laughed after kissing Newcombe on each cheek.

"What is your boss going to think about all this?" he asked.

"He's too busy trying to blow up the world to notice," Newcombe replied, surprised at how much anger came out in his voice.

"What?" Ishmael asked.

"You remember you told me the first time we met that Crane had a secret agenda?" Ishmael nodded. "Well, he does. He wants to fuse the continental plates by exploding fifty-three gigaton bombs at key points where the plates intersect. He wants to stop earthquakes completely."

"He shakes his fist at Allah," Ishmael said. "Crane puts himself above everything. Just amazing."

"It's only amazing in that he wants to," Newcombe said. "I can't imagine a government in the world that would consent to a scheme as obviously misguided as his."

"I cannot believe, Brother, that you underestimate Crane so very much," Ishmael said, putting an arm around his sister, both of them staring hot fire at Newcombe. "He's already come back from the dead and is returning to the scene of the crime. No, he's probably more than capable of convincing people to go along with him."

Newcombe was puzzled. "You seem almost happy about it."

"I've been waiting for the connection," Ishmael said, "the collision point between Crane and the Nation of Islam." He shrugged broadly. "And now I have it. Our greatness will be tested. This is the mountain upon which Dr. Crane and I will take tea."

"I want to convert," Newcombe said, watching amusement show on Ishmael's face. All of them laughed.

"You are a godless man," Ishmael said. "Why would you wish to become Muslim?"

"Why do you care? I believe you'd want me to convert if I worshipped inkblots. Correct?"

"More than correct, Brother," Aziz said quickly, rather than let the words pass through Ishmael's mouth. "By having you go through a public conversion we'd reap major public relations benefits—an intelligent and successful man chooses NOI because he believes in it. The gentle side of Islam balances out the necessarily violent revolutionary side."

"It also makes him an insider," Ishmael warned. "He would rapidly become our official voice without meaning to." He pointed at Newcombe. "You haven't yet told me why you wish to convert."

"No mystery," Newcombe said. "I'm doing it for the Cause. And I'm doing it because it will put me in direct opposition to Lewis Crane when this bomb business becomes public. He's a madman. I wish to stand against him as one of you."

"Liar," Khadijah said. "It has something to do with that white woman."

"No," Newcombe said, lowering his head. "Lanie and I are . . . no longer together. We haven't been for some time."

The woman laughed and took a step closer to him. "So maybe you want to teach her a lesson, huh?"

"God, I hope there's more to me than that."

• • • •

Rum bottle between his legs, Crane watched the satellite viddies of the Masada Option. He felt a shameful exhilaration at the monstrous beauty of thirty multimegaton bombs going off all at once. The blast cloud rose, amazingly high from the vantage point of outer space, its crown branching off and flattening out, spreading.

It had been one of those stunning events in world history that forces everyone to remember where he or she was when it happened. Crane remembered that he'd been getting his first aural implanted at that moment. The news of Masada were the first sounds he'd heard through the device. He'd been horrified at first, in shock, along with the rest of the world. But things once done could not be changed, and he'd realized the inherent importance of Masada as field research for his studies on the relationship between nuclear testing and EQs.

He'd been in a burn suit in Sudan by the next afternoon with a truckload of seismos. It was the day after that, standing in Saudi Arabia, that the notion of fusing the plates had come to him. The Rub Al Kali desert was a solid sheet of glass unbroken to the horizon. The intense heat had melted the sand. Under roiling gray clouds and thick rains of radioactive ash, he had skated on the desert.

"Crane," Lanie called. "You in there?"

"Go away," he said, taking a drink, watching the Masada cloud beginning to drift eastward, China and The Russia Corporation gradually disappearing beneath a haze of gray.

"It was beyond belief," Lanie said from right behind him, her voice soft. "I was twenty-two, starting grad school. I remember feeling cheated that I wouldn't have the chance to inherit the world. There was speculation that everything might go. Plus, Jews were being killed in many places. It was scary."

"Is that when you became a Cosmie?"

"No." She laughed, moving around to sit beside him on the couch. "My father was Jewish by birth, not my mother, which left me nowhere in a matrilineal culture. I always remember my dad as a Cosmie. He converted when I was very young. Guess that's why I gravitated that way.

Cosmies are friendly enough folks, like Unitarians with vision. It didn't stop me from losing a scholarship because they said I was Jewish, though."

"There was a lot of anger for awhile," Crane said. "I remember the backlash. That's why most of my staff members are Jews. Can I ask you a question?"

"Shoot."

"Do you think I'm crazy?"

"You're a visionary," she replied immediately. "All visionaries are thought of as crazy by the people they want to serve."

"You didn't answer my question."

She tilted his face to hers, staring at him. Crane was tense, her touch was electric to him. "Yes, you're crazy," she whispered. "You're just crazy enough to survive the madness we live in."

"My plan can work. It can."

"You don't have to convince me."

He nodded grimly. "Thanks." He looked away, then back at the screen.

"Why," Lanie asked, "do I have such a hard time making eye contact with you?"

He looked at her for a second, looked away. "I have a . . . difficult time thinking when I look at you. I don't know what it is. It's never happened before. I get, I don't know . . . lost in your gaze or . . . or something. Stupid, huh?"

She moved into his line of vision. "It's the sweetest thing anyone's ever said to me," she answered, and this time he forced himself to hold the eye contact. "You know," she went on, "you said a lot of things when we were trapped in that house in Martinique. Do you remember?"

He started to look away, held on. "Yes, I do."

"Did you mean them?"

"I thought you'd never remember."

"Did you mean them?"

"I meant them," he said, looking down, her fingers lifting his face back to hers. "I'm sorry, I . . . didn't mean to compromise our professional—"

"Oh, the hell with that." She scooted closer and put her

arms around his neck. "You have greatness in you. It excites me."

"But I'm a cripple, I'm—"

"Just shut up and kiss me."

In the next few minutes Lewis Crane discovered, for the first time in his life, that communication need not be verbal to be understood and meaningful.

MERCALLI XII

**MEMPHIS, TENNESSEE
27 FEBRUARY 2025, EARLY AFTERNOON**

The barn smelled like wet horses and manure. Newcombe hid in the corner behind bales of hay to make contact with the War Zone.

"There is no doubt," he was saying into a monitor-cam sitting in his palm and pointing toward his face, "that the quake will happen today. I am speaking under Green Authority. Repeat: Green Authority. Your pilgrimage must begin within the hour if you are to survive. You may have to fight your way at first, but the way will be clear soon enough. You must leave within the hour. Go now!"

He blanked and hoped for the best. He'd been transmitting on the ultrahigh-frequency infrared band that nobody used because of the cost of the reception equipment. But it would be picked up in the War Zone's focus building in downtown Memphis to be rebroadcast through the connecting cable to the Zone.

His hands were shaking. He had just committed an act of sedition, one that Brother Ishmael had made sure *he* would have to accomplish. "If you're convinced of the quake," Ishmael had said, "if you're sure, send the message when you know."

He knew.

The Ellsworth-Beroza nucleation zone was now constant, showing ever-building seismic activity. They had measured hundreds of temblors, undetectable on the surface, but growing to the Big Slip. Cracking rock had released large amounts of trapped gases while dilation occurred throughout the Reelfoot, cutting off the S waves that were unable to move through the water seeping into the cracks. It was classic, all the physical signs coming into line. The horses were kicking nervously against their stalls, neighing and whinnying in fear. Dogs bayed in the distance.

"Dan!" Lanie called. "Dan? Are you in here?"

He slipped the cam into his shirt pocket and moved out of his hiding place. "You caught me," he said, smiling sheepishly.

"What are you doing in here?" she asked, moving through the barn doors. She was wrapped head-to-toe, hatted, and block gleamed on her face.

"I had to get away from the madhouse for a few minutes." he said. "I needed some time alone."

"If you'd take a couple of dorph—"

"Why are you looking for me?"

She moved close. "They've come for Crane," she said, her voice quavering. "They're arresting him."

"Calm down," he said, hands reaching out to take her arms. "We knew this would happen. Everything's being done that can be done."

"I'm scared, Dan. The crowd's ugly, and the—"

"We've got escape routes. Don't worry. Come on, let's go give Crane some moral support."

They went out into the madness of the soybean farm. A man named Jimmy Earl had donated this ten-thousand-acre farm, south of Memphis in Capleville, to Crane for use as a refugee center. His motivation wasn't altruistic;

he was making a viddy about Crane and his prediction from the inside. But none of them had anticipated the reaction of the public. Above, hundreds of helos swarmed like mosquitos through clouds that ran continuous loops of a speech by President Gideon condemning Crane.

Angry over the debacle of the October folly and whipped into near frenzy by the government and the teev schmoozers, people were descending on Jimmy Earl's farm like a locust plague. Thousands of people had shown up in the last two days to jeer and demand Crane's head. Electrified fences had been hurriedly erected around the tent city, and Whetstone's people, instead of being able to help the refugees, were forced to form security details around the perimeter.

Newcombe pulled his goggles over his eyes. They moved through the barnyard and into the tent city just as the front gates opened and the police cruiser slid in, display lights strobing.

"The command post?" Dan asked. Several members of the crowd rushed in before the gates closed, security massing to beat them back.

"Yeah . . . giving interviews up to the end."

"They taking Whetstone, too?"

"Both 'perpetrators,' " she said sarcastically. "By the way, other seismic stations around the world are beginning to pick up our foreshocks. I think some minds are changing."

"Too late," he said. "Nobody's going anywhere, not with the President on the teev calling us everything but child molesters."

"You're tense."

"Yeah, I'm tense. I've been going over the Memphis EQ-ecogram and I'm still afraid I haven't paid enough attention to the river. It's possible to get in a range with a river that changes course, but my calcs were never designed to deal with a situation like the Mississippi. It needs more refinement."

"Does Crane know you're still worried?"

"Yeah. He says he trusts me. I've got to work more on this type of situation."

The rows of tents were empty except for volunteer workers. Not one person had accepted the offer of help, not yet. As they reached the centrally located command tent, the cruiser, lights still flashing, turned into the row, churning dust behind.

Newcombe jerked his goggles up as he entered the tent. Other teevs filled the tent sides, some showing EQ-ecograms of metropolitan centers that would be affected by the quake. Still others showed emergency EQ supply lists, another a list of safe evac locations.

Crane and Whetstone stood together at the front of the room, before an alarming seismogram display showing an almost constantly increasing amplitude on all crests. A crowd of ten camheads was around them, private broadcasters working around the government's jam of the airwaves. Jimmy Earl, of course, stood in the center of it all, making his viddy.

Crane was speaking. ". . . in Memphis, because Memphis is going to take the brunt of the quake. We have an observation scale that's been used for nearly a hundred years called the Mercalli Intensity Scale. I'm predicting Memphis to fall within the range of a Mercalli XII, Damage Total. Practically all buildings damaged greatly or destroyed. Waves seen on ground surface. Lines of sight and level distorted. Objects will be thrown into the air. Please, anyone in Memphis who's listening right now: Get out of the city. Come south to Capleville. We can help you here."

"Crane," Newcombe called. "They're here."

Crane frowned and looked at Whetstone. The two shook hands and walked toward the flap just as the police entered.

"You're in charge now," Crane told Newcombe. "I'll get back here as soon as I can."

"I don't trust the river," Newcombe replied. "Can't they—"

"No," Crane interrupted. "It's too late. We'll have to take our chances."

"I'm Chief Hoskins of the Memphis PD," the man cuffing Whetstone said, then nodded to his partner. "This here is Mr. Lyle Withington, the mayor of our fair city. I have a warrant for the arrest of Lewis Crane and Harry Whetstone."

"It will give me great pleasure, sir," the mayor said to Crane, "to watch you being put away where you can do no more harm."

"Do you live outside of the city, Mr. Mayor?" Crane asked as they put the cuffs on him.

"Why, no . . . I have a house right in—"

"Then get your family out before they're hurt."

"Now, really . . . sir."

"Is there a Jimmy Earl here?" Chief Hoskins called.

"Right here!" Jimmy, a big country boy with rosy cheeks and a fatback smile that never left his face, elbowed his way to them. *Inherited money,* Newcombe thought.

"You can come along, too," the Chief said. "The mayor's given you permission to videotape in the cell."

"Thanks, Uncle Lyle," Earl said, pumping the man's hand.

Crane turned to the other camheads. "People of Memphis," he said as Hoskins led him to the door, "go to your main power boxes and shut down the focus. If you have anything that runs on natural gas, cut the valve at the source. Do it now."

They moved through the tent, Newcombe following, pulling his goggles back on with the rest of them as they got out in the sun, the crowds jeering loudly when Crane was spotted.

"Chief Hoskins," Newcombe said, pointing to the crowds, "can't you disperse those people? They're trespassing on private property."

"No!" Crane said as they shoved him into the car. "They're safe here and they'll be able to help after the quake."

Lanie leaned through the window to give Crane a long kiss as the cams pulled in tight, Newcombe feeling a flush of rage that he fought down.

She stepped back, Crane sticking his head out the door and talking into the lenses of the cameras held by the camheads. "Take heavy objects off your shelves," he called. "Take down glass and chandeliers. Get flammable materials out of your home. Now! Right away!"

Hoskins slid behind the wheel as Whetstone and an excited Jimmy Earl climbed in back with Crane.

Mayor Withington stared hard at Newcombe. "I'd advise you to pack up your belongings and get out of here," he said. "There's not a cop in Tennessee who'll protect you from those people out there."

"You'll be blessing us for being here before the day's out, Mayor," Newcombe said, turning from the man and walking back into the tent, Lanie on his heels. He padded onto the P fiber. "Burt . . . Burt, are you there?"

"Yeah, Doc Dan."

"You keeping track of that lawyer Crane dragged down here from Memphis?"

"Yeah . . . he's right here."

"Crane's been arrested. Give the lawyer his retainer from the cash box. Tell him to go into town tomorrow and work the bail—that's if the jail's still standing tomorrow."

"Got it."

"What the hell?" Lanie said. Dan blanked Hill and turned to her. She was watching the screens. Africks and Hispanics were pouring out of the city's sewer system, firing guns into the air. They were hotwiring cars on the streets and driving off. Cars were bumper-to-bumper on State Highway 51, Elvis Presley Boulevard.

"What the hell's going on?" Lanie asked.

"The start of the revolution," Newcombe said, his mind screaming, *And I did it!*

"What time is it?" she asked.

"3:45," he said without looking. "We've got less than two hours."

The Memphis city jail was part of the new law enforcement complex built on the old station house at 201 Poplar Street in the aging section of town, five miles from the Mississippi River and down the street from U China Tennessee State and the tree-lined splendor of Audubon Park. Of course, the park's trees had mostly died. The city fathers undertook a campaign years before of filling the dead branches with artificial leaves so that the city's ambience could remain intact. And they constantly reminded everyone that it was beautiful winter or summer.

They took Crane and Whetstone into the station amidst confusion. The War Zone had just exploded from its nest and flowed into the city proper, the entire force mobilized to fight. But the Zoners appeared not to want to fight—only to flee.

Dozens of Muslims were being dragged into the station, all demanding they be given the right to leave the region. Crane was thrilled that somebody was listening to him.

By the time they were booked and thrown into the tank—the huge holding cell that was filled to capacity with angry Zoners yelling for freedom—it was 4:00 P.M. When the tank was filled to capacity, people were jammed into other cells, then the halls, the whole block being locked down tight.

And during the entire procedure, Crane had never stopped talking, never stopped speaking into Jimmy Earl's camera, rigged not just for recording, but also for broadcast.

"Time is running short," he said. "The people in here with me are from the War Zone. They are trying to escape the disaster.

"You must listen carefully to me if you want to save your lives. It's too late, I fear, for you to escape if you haven't already. So, get shoes on. Wear heavy clothing and pack a bag. Take dry goods, canned goods. Fill water bottles. Fresh water will be the thing you most need in the hours to come. Your biggest problem right now, though, is your home. Your home is full of death—flying glass will kill you; objects hanging on your walls or sitting on your mantels are deadly projectiles; chimneys will crush you; your water pipes are explosives; the roof of your own home could fall and bury you. Bricks are bombs; splinters are swords. Get out of your house.

"There are dead trees everywhere. Avoid them. Stay off the roads. Look for open ground. Remember, emergency services are set up in Capleville. If you can see the EQ-eco on your region, gravitate toward the less dangerous areas.

There will be aftershocks, several hundred of them in the next few days, so keep moving toward the safe areas.

"Fresh water . . . fresh water. Please . . . fill bottles now. There's not much—"

He heard it then, the low rumbling roar coming from beneath them. It suddenly got deathly quiet in the cell block as the noise increased.

"It's here," Crane said. "It's here! Out of your homes! Now! Now!"

The roar was upon them, the cell floor buckling, throwing them all to the floor as the sidewalks, streets, and lawns outside began exploding.

Jimmy Earl screamed and grabbed the bars for support. The entire line of bars fell outward, on top of the men in the halls as the building shook, plaster dust raining down on them. The lights went out.

"Stoney!" Crane shouted. The floor rolled and pitched like a ship on stormy seas. The wail of human beings joined the sickening roar in a stentorian cry of despair. "Stoney!"

"C-Crane!" came the pained response. "Here . . . here!"

Crane cursed the cops for putting too many people in the holding tank. He crawled through the writhing mass of flesh on the rocking floor. Pieces of the ceiling were falling all around. He was alert, not scared. Death would toy with him for a long time before taking him.

"Crane!"

He found Whetstone in the corner of the cell, his face bleeding so much his white hair was bright red. His arm was broken, maybe his shoulder. Pieces of ceiling had crushed his rib cage.

"Your legs!" Crane screamed against the roar that seemed to go on forever, though he knew only half a minute had passed. "Can you stand?"

"Oh, God . . . Crane! The pain!"

"Can you use your legs?"

"I . . . I think so. . . ."

"Then hang on." Crane threw himself over Stoney, covering the man's body as more of the ceiling fell in. But the rocking was less, the sound more distant. The first shock had passed.

He struggled to his feet; others did the same. He dragged Stoney while screaming, "Get out! Get out now! There'll be more shocks."

Huge holes were gouged through the walls. The prisoners straggled toward the light coming in from outside, Crane's wristpad was bleeping. He kept hold of Stoney and opened the fiber with his nose. "What?"

"C-Crane?" It was Lanie. "Are you all right?"

"Barely," he said. "It's a mess here. I'm trying to get out of the jail now. What's it look like?"

"All we can see is smoke on the helo views," she said. "Nothing else. Smoke."

"It'll clear. I've got to go. I'll get back with you. Tell Newcombe we cut it a little *too* close."

He blanked and kept moving. It was difficult not to trip. Bodies littered the floor.

They made it into the middle of the hallway, jammed with people piling up in front of a hole in the wall. "We've got a safe exit," he called to the crowd. "Nothing to worry about. We're all decent people. Help one another through. We're all right. We'll stay all right."

Jimmy Earl caught up with him just before he got through the hole, the man still framing CD, still making his "movie." He helped get through the hole and out with Whetstone.

"Hang in there, you bastard," Crane said to Whetstone, who was moaning. Crane was afraid for his friend, whose breathing was ragged. "I owe you three billion bucks, Stoney. Don't conk out on me."

They got onto Poplar, a few cops walking around in a daze, their entire station house, all ten stories of it, collapsing, dust rising from the debris, the air tasting dirty.

Smoke rolled through the area. A haze of smoke, fires and dust burned their eyes. As near as Crane could see, Memphis was gone. The elevated roadways had crumpled like paper, the hospital that had blocked his view on the drive in simply wasn't there anymore. He couldn't see the fairgrounds, the smoke was too thick. What was left of the university was burning out of control. The streets, the sidewalks, the lawns had buckled under the Slip, then cracked, opening huge fissures all around them. There were geysers of city water shooting high into the air from broken mains.

An aftershock hit then, everyone going to the ground again as a hydrant exploded and shot a hundred feet into the air.

There was a roaring sound that Crane couldn't identify. He and Jimmy Earl lay Whetstone gently on the ground and went to investigate.

They carefully picked their way across the broken street, moving toward the west and the impenetrable smoke that blocked their view. They hadn't walked fifty feet into the smoke, when Crane realized it wasn't smoke at all, but a fine mist, a spray, like frothy drizzle.

"Oh, my God," Jimmy Earl said.

They were standing on the bank of the Mississippi River, looking out over a raging torrent that used to be Memphis, Tennessee. The skeletons of dead buildings poked through the raging waters, bodies and homes floating past. Memphis had been a city of a million people. Now it was river bottom. A little farther upstream, where the fairgrounds had stood, was a sight magnificent in its beautiful, deadly symmetry. A waterfall a hundred feet high now occupied what had been downtown Memphis and as they watched in amazement, the incredible span of the Memphis-Arkansas bridge floated over the edge of the falls to crash, in slow motion, into the river below.

It was beyond imagination—even Crane's.

Jimmy Earl fell to his knees and began retching into the river. "No time for that now," Crane said, pulling him up by the collar. "You wanted this and now you're going to get it all on tape."

"Time," he said to his pad, 4:39 coming through the aural.

He dragged Jimmy Earl back to Whetstone, the man pale, but conscious. He hunkered down.

"You're something, Crane," Whetstone said weakly. "We walked into a lulu, didn't we?"

"Save it," Crane replied. "You'll need your strength. Dammit, we've still got work to do on the globe. The quake hit fifty-eight minutes early."

"That's not so bad in f-five billion years."

"Yeah," Crane said, preoccupied. He looked up at Jimmy Earl. "Anyone who can still hear me right now, you need to remember two things. Get away from anything that can fall on you and try to administer first aid to those who need it. Worry about your losses later."

Heedless of the sun, he pulled off his shirt and slid it under Whetstone. "This is going to hurt," he said, knotting the shirt over the man's ribs and jerking it tight. Whetstone grimaced.

Crane addressed the cam. "People are going to be in shock. They're going to be wandering around dazed. Take these people under your wing, protect them." He yanked on Stoney's shoulder, slipping the ball joint back into place, and Whetstone sighed with relief.

Screams came from the remaining cell blocks, the ones on the higher levels. Men were hanging out of windows and rents in the walls. "You men!" Crane called to the Zoners who were standing, watching the end of the world. "Grab debris, steel and concrete. Start piling it up securely against the side of the block. Make a platform to bring those people down!"

He pulled off Whetstone's belt, doubled it over and jammed it into the man's mouth. Without a word, he jerked hard on the elbow, working the broken bone. Stoney bit down hard on the belt, blanched and passed out.

Jimmy Earl stood before him, recording it all, tears streaming down his face. "Just keep doing what you're doing," Crane said softly. "This is important."

"I-I never t-thought—"

"Not now!" Crane said sternly as he checked the gash on Whetstone's head.

He stood and moved to a plot of ground wet from the gushing fire hydrant, taking Jimmy Earl with him. He spoke to the camera. "If you have injured people who are bleeding," he said, "Nature provides her own remedy."

He dug his hands down into the ground. "Mud," he said, holding up two handfuls. "Pack the wound in mud."

He hurried back to Whetstone, demonstrating the mud technique on the injured man, packing his head in it. "This will stop the bleeding. Worry about infection later."

A huge explosion from the university complex punctuated his sentence, followed by another shock, a strong one that hurled people to the ground.

He pulled the belt out of Stoney's mouth and ran it around his shoulder to make a sling for the broken arm. Behind him, the Zoners were working quickly to build the tower to get the people out of the top of the rubble of the jail. Everyone was fighting against the darkness of despair.

Jimmy Earl had backed up and was framing the action as men formed a human chain to hand up pieces of debris, the cops pitching in to help. Humanity was happening, petty hatreds and politics crumbling in the face of danger to the family of Man.

There was life; there was hope.

Stoney came around, groaning, then smiled up at Crane. "I'd thank you," he said, "but you'll probably find a way to charge me for this."

"Charge you? Hell, man, I'm saving you money."

"How's that?"

"The whole police station's gone." Crane smiled. "We don't have to bail ourselves out."

Book Three

Chapter 14

AFTER-SHOCKS

WASHINGTON, D.C.
13 APRIL 2026, MID-MORNING

Mohammed Ishmael's condor glided gently on the thermals high above Constitution Avenue, following Crane and his motorcade as it tracked through the ghost town of Washington, DC, toward the Capitol building.

Much had changed during the past year—and each change brought surprises. When Li Cheun had told the President of the United States in February of '25 there would be no quake on the Mississippi, he could not have guessed that he would be dead within thirty-six hours. And by his own hand.

The cataclysm on the Reelfoot had been so devastating in so many areas—and so much more so because of Mr. Li's connivance—that within a day it had been obvious Liang Int America would show a loss for calendar 2025, a first in its North American history.

Upon seeing the financial projections and being a man of honor, Mr. Li had doused himself in Sterno, stepped within his beloved diorama, and set himself ablaze. Most considerate of Mr. Li, Mui Tsao thought. His death made it possible to carry on without having to change much of anything. Had Mr. Li gone into exile or been imprisoned, company rules would have compelled a change of every code.

Mr. Mui then survived a corporate inquisition by bringing forth all the records he had sent to the home office in Beijing concerning what he had termed Mr. Li's "increasingly foolish" behavior. He also accused the dead man of "egotism and intractability" in his business dealings and vowed to be a more levelheaded, compromising manager who would put Liang America back in the black within a year. That last part was, of course, a lie and everyone knew it, but optimism is fundamental in business theory.

Mr. Mui immediately acquired his own Harpy, a young and ambitious corporate man named Tang. The new Harpy was pushing hard for Liang to compete with Yo-Yu in the mind chip business, an area in which he had great interest as he himself was a double-ported chippy.

Truth of the matter was, the Liang Int empire was slowly collapsing under its own weight and the Reelfoot quake, along with its associated eight hundred aftershocks, simply had accelerated the process.

In 2011, Liang had bought up all of America's debts, all its chits. Basically, it owned the country, with most of the taxes collected going to interest payments on the huge debt owed to Liang, although a small amount of tax dollars had to be applied to various programs for the people. Liang Int not only owned and exploited America, but also didn't want to maintain its investment. Since the company was the de facto government, however, it was left holding the bag when Reelfoot hit.

Reelfoot *had* been big enough to fell a giant. The main shock was an 8.5 on the scale, about as high as the scale measured. Memphis never got out from under the Mississippi, though the river continued to change course for three months after the quake. It was simply the memory of a city now, a place for divers to search for lost treasure.

Little Rock and Paducah were rendered all but uninhabitable. Nashville was severely damaged, as were Louisville and Evansville and Carbondale. In St. Louis, the river swamped the city under a huge wave, knocking the Arch onto the city itself and leveling buildings. In Kansas City, the Quay River left its banks and drowned more people than were directly affected by the quake. Lake Michigan also overflowed, and flood waters along with aftershocks in Chicago toppled the twin black Liang office towers on Dearborn.

Knoxville, Lexington, Frankfort, Indianapolis, Fort Wayne, both Springfields (Missouri and Illinois), Jefferson City—all towns suffered Mercali VII or VIII damage.

Four dams in the TVA system collapsed, flooding Tennessee and cutting off hydroelectric power to a region of the continent that still used it. Levees in Mississippi and Louisiana crumbled.

The death toll reached nearly three million; a staggering ten million were left homeless. Damage ran into the hundreds of billions of dollars.

Liang was a streamlined operation that matched production to natural resources. Hundreds of chemical plants, paper mills, auto factories, food processors and distributors, focus factories, and shield manufacturers went down with the quake, to say nothing of the retail outlets Liang owned to sell their products. People turned to their government for financial help, and Liang Int was put in the unenviable position of demanding restitution from itself.

They couldn't afford it. Neither could their insurance carriers.

Corporate decided simply to try and get the flow of goods and services moving back through the area and rebuild slowly. To that end the company declared the quake region a total loss and walked away from it, leaving the Midwestern United States a poverty-and-disease-ridden dead zone of collapsed buildings and broken dreams. Revenue loss was staggering, public relations destroyed.

President Gideon had become the most hated man in

America. He refused to step down because he needed the paycheck, and he was unable to put the blame on Mr. Li, where it rightfully belonged, because that would be admitting that Mr. Li had told him what to do in the first place. Gideon had become a prisoner in his own White House.

Brother Ishmael's condor dropped to treetop level for closeups of the motorcade as it pulled up to the Capitol. Its occupants hurried out of their vehicles and into the building.

The edited version of Jimmy Earl's viddy, *The Last Best Hope,* had been the most watched show in the world in 2025, bringing him awards and fame and, parenthetically, turning Lewis Crane into the most beloved and recognizable man in the country.

Then there were the Zoners who had escaped the cataclysm in Memphis. They'd gone south and taken military control of a small town named Friars Point, Mississippi. Renamed New Cairo, the city had attracted fifty thousand refugees.

The Mississippi had always run right by the town. Now it was several miles away, but it had left behind the richest silt on the face of the planet. Quickly enough, the initial fifty thousand had been joined by a million others, disaffected southern Africks, escapees from the Zones, or any Muslim wanting a start on a new life. The original boundaries expanded, taking in more and more land, pushing out the previous landowners until finally Mr. Mui was forced to step in.

Mui regarded the spread of Islam as an inevitability. Besides that, he was not about to undertake the expense of a full-scale war to roust them from the land. What he did, in effect, was create another War Zone, larger than any other. Immense, in fact. He built a wall seventy feet high that completely surrounded New Cairo, though several miles from its front lines and not a direct threat. People were allowed to travel freely, unarmed, in and out of the walled area.

NOI set up immediate contacts with other Islamic States worldwide that supplied them with food and materials while they got on their feet. Soon after, Brother New-combe went to Yo-Yu and struck a trade deal that gave NOI enough shields to cover the delta crops it would need to raise to allow New Cairo to become self-sufficient.

It worked. What also worked was violence, ever-escalating guerrilla and economic warfare with unrelenting confrontations with the FPF and threats or actual boycotts of Liang Int products. In the deepest inner sanctum of NOI leadership the split was more profound than ever. Martin Aziz and Dan Newcombe versus Mohammed Ishmael . . . neither side able to prove itself conclusively. Stalemate.

Sumi Chan sat on her lofty perch in the Senate chamber and presided over the bumptious gladhanders who called themselves congressmen. Currently they were "debating" whether or not to pass a nonbinding resolution that would, in a miracle of complex rhetoric and dazzling il-logic, blame the Yo-Yu Syndicate for the tragedy at Reel-foot Rift.

"Mr. President," said the congresswoman from New York, "I would like to allot three minutes of my time to the Honorable Senator from Arkansas/Oklahoma."

"Noted," Sumi said automatically. "You have the floor, Mr. Gerber."

"Thank you," said the gentleman, with the aplomb of a snake oil salesman.

As he began to speak Sumi drifted. She had yet to com-pletely figure out why she was here. And the only man who could tell her was long dead. She had managed to avoid Mr. Li from the time she had taken the job until his death because she'd feared him sexually. Now here she sat, bored and alone, symbol of American political leadership since Gideon had hidden himself away in the White House.

"Mr. President!" The voice startled her. A Senate page tugged on her sleeve. "Someone wants to see you. He says it's important."

"Who?"

"Lewis Crane."

"Crane's here?" she said loudly enough to be heard in the chamber.

"He's waiting out in the corridor, sir."

"My God," Sumi said. She'd had no personal contact with Crane since Reelfoot. She turned to the page, a pimply-faced federal judge's son, and said, "Put him in the old Supreme Court downstairs. I'll meet him in a moment."

The page hurried away, Sumi fully alert now and excited. Crane may have been many things, but he was never boring. She turned the gavel over to the sergeant at arms to call the majority leader, and slipped out of the chamber and into the hollow, echoing halls. She'd heard that once six million visitors a year had come here to listen to proceedings and see democracy in action. No one came now. They were all anachronisms, living out their lives in a two-hundred-year-old building that was crumbling because of George Washington's nepotism in choosing his own inferior rock quarry for the materials to build the damned thing.

Lewis Crane had come to her territory. He must want something. But then, Crane always wanted something. Now he wanted something before Yo-Yu took power. In a government where the votes were purchased, Liang's rival had more purchasing power. Yo-Yu could get control of the government without taking one seat in an election. *She'd* even been approached with bribes . . . and had considered the possibility. America tended to have that effect on people.

Crane waited with Lanie in the gallery of the tiny preserved eighteenth-century courtroom while the rest of his entourage toured the entire facility. The room was an incongruously small space for producing the big decisions that had been handed down there—Dred Scott, Marbury vs. Madison—remarkable precedents in jurisprudence. Modern American society had been formed in this place, then deconstructed in the large faux Greek building across the street.

Lanie put her hand over his. "Don't worry," she whispered as if she were in a Cosmie church. "It's going to work out."

"We haven't seen Sumi for a long time."

"I have faith in you," she said. "You're coming to the right place at the right time."

Crane hoped she was correct, but was skeptical—and, he felt, appropriately cynical about politics. He would make his judgments about Sumi after they'd talked. His bad arm ached terribly. There was going to be a major quake this afternoon on the Cocos Plate where it met the Caribbean Plate. Later tonight, in Africa, the Great Rift would separate a little bit more as part of it pulled away from itself, creating grabens and opening huge fissures. There would be mudslides tomorrow in California. Evacuations of the affected areas were already underway, thanks to the Crane Report, his monthly newsletter about the state of the Earth. He gave populations a two-month lead time on any impending quake.

"Crane!" came a voice from the doorway. He turned to see Sumi Chan, in black silk pajamas, standing with arms outstretched, smiling broadly.

Crane jumped up to hurry over and give Sumi a bear hug. "You're looking well."

"Looks can deceive," Sumi said, walking past Crane to greet Lanie. "Congratulations on your impending marriage. I hope I will be invited to the ceremony."

"That's why we're here," Crane said, as Sumi kissed Lanie on the cheek. "We wanted to invite you personally."

"Right," Sumi replied, turning back to Crane and smiling. "And maybe do a little business while you're at it?"

"I can always do business," Crane said, the three of them taking seats. Crane noticed a slackness to Sumi's features. The man needed a challenge. He pulled a magazine out of his back pocket and gave it to Sumi. "Here, the new Crane Report, hot off the presses."

"I've already got one. Required reading for any acting head of state. When is the big day?"

"July twenty-third," Lanie said. "At exactly two thirty-seven in the afternoon."

"In the Himalayas," Crane added.

"The Himalayas." Sumi smiled. "Your fortunes have risen since last we met, my friend."

"As have yours."

"No. I am simply doing what I did when you first met me, hype and PR, only I'm doing it in another place. I feel like a caretaker, just watching the office until the real Vice President shows up."

"Then it's true what we've heard about Yo-Yu?" Lanie asked.

"Probably more true than you realize," Sumi replied. "The Syndicate scored big with new chips that I hear are better than dorph. People want Yo-Yu. Once they started their ozone regeneration project, I knew Liang was finished. Yo-Yu has managed to replace five percent of the ozone layer this year alone. People like that. They vote for that."

"Is your power completely gone?" Crane asked.

"Not completely," Sumi said, her eyes already sharpening. "How's Dr. Newcombe?"

"Haven't seen much of him in person the last few months," Crane replied. "He's on a sabbatical, trying to fine-tune his EQ-eco to better fit soil liquefaction. We see him on the teev all the time, though."

Sumi nodded. "He's in Washington more than I am. New Cairo is still news to people and he's the NOI spokesman. I think his public conversion has had a lot to do with the people's greater acceptance of the Nation of Islam."

"He's a geologist, not a politician," Crane said, not troubling to hide his contempt. "He needs to spend more time on the important things."

"Have we hit a sore spot?" Sumi asked.

"Dan's talented." Crane shrugged. "Wasting his talent on nonsense is incomprehensible to me . . . no disrespect intended to you."

"There are those who find the notion of an Islamic State in America something other than 'nonsense,'" Sumi replied. "I know the people at Liang look at it as a top priority."

"The people at Liang can—"

"Crane," Lanie interrupted as she pointed to her wristpad.

He nodded, then smiled, surprised to find himself nervous. "Have you wondered why I haven't tried to contact you for so long?"

"I assumed you were angry with me," Sumi said, bowing slightly.

"Oh, Sumi, no. Think about it. Who better than I to understand how one can be pressured, tormented, ultimately coerced to do things he does not really want to do? Who better than I to understand the rationalizations that lead one to conclude the end justifies the means?" He shook his head, an expression both wise and compassionate on his face. "I have put the past behind us. Please believe me, and do not think of it again."

Sumi and Crane looked intently at each other. They connected and there was understanding and forgiveness between them.

Crane cleared his throat. "I've spent the last year working on a special project, something really big. But to put it over, I need your help."

"It pains me to admit it, Crane, but government R&D money is pretty tough to come by these days. Sadly, someone in Beijing will have the final word on any funding—"

"I don't want funding. I want permission and sanction. The Foundation's rich. That three-billion-dollar bet, you know. Also, we started publishing the Report and the world has paid—for the Report itself, for the EQ-eco in predicted areas, for the core assessment of possible damages, and for general advice. We are prosperous beyond my dreams."

"No funding?" Sumi asked, frowning. "But what can you want from me, if you're off the teat? What could I possibly have to offer a man who has all the money he needs?"

Crane's mouth was dry. He reached into his pocket and pulled out a tiny disk. "Take a look at this," he said, handing it to Sumi. "It will explain a lot."

Sumi slipped the disk into her wristpad, then looked around for a screen. "May I borrow your goggles, please?"

Lanie handed Sumi the extra goggles from her tote bag,

what she called her everything-Crane-needs-to-survive-on-the-road bag. Lanie took a deep, nervous breath, her eyes wide. This was it.

"Try it on the L fiber," Crane said as Sumi pulled down the goggles and padded on.

"Once you're through with this job, I could use a good public relations man," Crane joked.

"Bribery, Crane?" Sumi asked with echoing humor. "This must really be important."

"It is. But, seriously, a job is always open to you. I hope you know that."

"The globe," Sumi said, smiling.

"Yes," Crane said like a loving father. "We've missed you at the Foundation, Sumi." The globe was spinning quickly. If Sumi only knew, Crane thought, what had transpired with the globe during this past year! It had evolved at an astonishing rate into something beyond his wildest imaginings when he had hired Lanie all those months ago. The globe's cognitive function was beyond reproach, but more, it was developing awareness and—he forced his attention back to the image of the spinning globe. Its spotlight found and highlighted California as the rotation slowed.

They were staring at California, the view filling their entire vision in the goggles. The world was green and brown, the oceans blue, the cities vibrating in pale, friendly yellow.

"Okay," Crane said, "you remember where the San Andreas Bumper is?"

"Just south of Bakersfield, right? Mount Pinos."

"Yes."

The San Andreas Bumper was an S-shaped bend in the Fault Line, a flangelike protuberance or kink where the northbound Pacific Plate and the westbound North American Plate were stuck. Inexorable movement continued, the Plates monstrous, unstoppable Titans shoving against each other, the pressure squeezing ever tighter on the Bumper, straining the rock ever harder.

"There," Crane said. "Do you see the red zone opening up on the base?"

Bright red blinked just south of Bakersfield and began creeping through a fault line that ultimately encompassed a huge slab of the Pacific Plate, all the way to the Philippines. Los Angeles was on the wrong side of the ripping fault. So was San Francisco. The tear went all the way south, into Mexico, cutting off the Baja Peninsula at the northern end of the Gulf of California.

"The red spot is so large at the Bumper," Sumi said.

"That's because the entire Bumper is getting ready to come apart. Watch."

Sumi gasped.

The entire flange was now throbbing red, straining. Then it simply crumbled as all the strain was relieved at once. The Pacific Plate moved. There were no people pictured on the globe, but as the yellow cities began pulsating in ugly red, any human watching could have heard the screams of hundreds of thousands of hurt and dying people.

"What we're looking at is the true detachment of Southern California from the North American Plate," Crane said. "It is becoming an island, containing the carcasses of two of the world's major cities, not to mention that all of oceanside California, so heavily developed, becomes a cadaver. See? A new minicontinent is born, pushing north."

The chunk of continent slowly crept toward eventual subduction beneath the northern ridge of the Plate.

"Amazing," Sumi whispered. "And the year?"

"Keep watching."

Crane tapped Lanie, who yanked her goggles up to stare at him. He shrugged, she returned the shrug, then blew him a kiss before jerking her goggles back into place.

He pulled his on again just as the numbers 6–3–2058 came up on the screen. "I want to remind you, Sumi," he said, "this is no simulation or set of speculations. You are looking into a crystal ball and gazing directly into the future, the real future."

"Thirty-two years." Sumi pressed the pad to pause the disk. They all raised their goggles. Sumi's face was strained and pale. "What a sadness it must be to watch such horror all the time, to know how inescapable it is."

"But is it inescapable?" Crane asked, watching Sumi's eyes narrow.

"You just told me we were gazing into a crystal ball."

"A crystal ball that shows a future that is real only when it arrives."

"I don't understand."

"Turn your disk back on. I want to show you another future."

The globe relit inside the goggles. Time rewound. "Look farther south on the Fault, down in the Imperial Valley. Watch for a small red zone to open up."

As he spoke a small spot along the San Andreas Fault's southern arm blazed red for several seconds. Then it was gone.

"What was that?" Sumi asked.

"Watch," Crane said. "The globe is going to pick up speed."

It spun wildly, chasing the years, finally stopping on California. The numbers 6–3–2058 again, but everything appeared whole and placid. The show ended; its viewers removed their goggles.

Sumi stared at Lanie, then back at Crane. "All right. What happened . . . what made the difference?"

"I asked the globe," Crane said, pausing dramatically, "if it were possible to avoid the destruction of California by fusing the plates."

"How do you fuse tectonic plates, Crane?"

"Heat. Heat so intense it would melt solid rock and bond it together."

"And how would you produce such intense heat?"

"A thermonuclear reaction is the only way I can think of. In this particular case a five gigaton explosion along a six-mile stretch of underground twenty miles beneath the Earth's surface right on the spot indicated by the globe."

"You're talking about an explosion thousands of times more powerful than anything previously detonated."

Nodding vigorously, he said quickly, "But deflected downward, into the thermonuclear core. It wouldn't even cause a ripple on the surface. We've simulated it. It works."

"But how could you know it would result in anything other than a major break in the fault and the hastening of catastrophic destruction?"

"Sumi, didn't you tell me that the Crane Report is required reading for heads of state? Well, the Crane Report is based on the globe's functions and it hasn't been wrong yet. We're just using it here in a slightly different way. Think about this: Fusing the plates farther down the fault where there is no strain at the moment will take all the pressure off the Bumper. In fact, this one weld actually slows down the rate of continental drift by joining the two plates back together. For fifty years after the event, we show an eighty percent decrease in drift in these two plates, with a concurrent decrease in EQ activity."

Sumi jumped up and started to pace. "You're sure the strain doesn't come out someplace else? Maybe we'd be destroying South America to save LA."

"I went forward 250 years on the globe and found no activity that wasn't already destined to happen. Perhaps farther on there might be, but how much insurance do you want? We've learned that this one weld decreases worldwide temblor activity by seven percent."

"You mean it?"

"I mean it."

Sumi walked out of the rows of seating to stand at the end of their aisle. She pointed at Crane. "This is bigger than California with you, isn't it?"

"Yes," Crane said simply. "The globe has shown me fifty-three weld spots that, when completed, will halt continental drift completely, along with their associated EQs, volcanoes, and tsunamis. I figured that talking the world into doing it will be one hell of a lot easier once we've shown it works in one place."

"Thirty-two years is two lifetimes for a politician! That presents problems."

"It's tougher than that," Crane said. "We've got only a five-year window, at the most, on the San Andreas weld. By September of 2033 the pressure will have increased enough all along the fault that the weld won't be possible without starting a major quake."

Sumi moved along the aisle and sat beside him, staring up at the justices' bench. "And what would you need, exactly, from the government?"

"A lot of things except money. First off, we'd have to figure out a way to get around the ban on detonating nukes. I'd need the right permissions to dig down into the Imperial Valley in the Salton Trough. And, of course, I'd need access to nuclear stockpiles."

"Maybe," Sumi said, "it wouldn't be quite so difficult as you think."

"What do you mean?"

"You're an expert on nukes," Sumi answered. "Do you remember the development of the first atomic bomb?"

"The Manhattan Project," Crane said. "So what?"

"It was done in utmost secrecy, the government treating it as a national security measure, not telling anyone about it until it was dropped on the Japanese."

"Are you suggesting we could do this whole thing secretly?" Lanie asked.

Sumi nodded, then looked at Crane, and touched his arm. "I've always had faith in you. If you say to me, this is possible, then I believe it is possible. You're a gracious man. I've wronged you badly and I owe you, and you know I do. It's an obligation."

"No, Sumi, I'd never—"

Sumi put her hand up for silence. "Please. Allow me to retrieve my honor and gain face. Liang Int has suffered a severe blow. They would ultimately approve the project if we could run it right near the next election and succeed—especially if it won't cost them anything. That's the ringer here."

"I understand," Crane said.

"It would be in absolutely no one's interest to let this leak to the world. I can just hear the outcry now, especially with the Masada Cloud circumnavigating the globe every seventeen days to remind people of the nuclear terror. This may be an historic period for you, the chance at last to realize your dream. I assume this is what you've been aiming for all this time?"

"You assume correctly."

"It will be the greatest sell job in the history of the world, but I'm ready to undertake it. The aspects are as good as they'll ever get. I'll need more from you than this disk to sell the program, though. You'll fund it all, every cent?"

"I'm prepared to do that."

"Then I only have to convince the right people of its feasibility. Get it all on paper. I assume you've red-teamed it?"

Crane nodded. "That's what I've spent the last year doing. I know every argument against it and each counter-argument." He reached into his pocket and pulled out another disk. "It's all on here."

Sumi took the disk. "You are a feared and respected man at Liang Int. They landed on your wrong side once and paid the price. They'll want to listen." She pocketed the disk and stood. "I'll get on it right away."

Crane also stood. "You'll do it, really do it?"

"Absolutely. It may be why I was put on this planet . . . solely to do this job."

Lewis Crane, hard as rock and focused as an epicenter, fell back in his seat, stupefied. "I-I don't know how to thank you, I—"

"No," Sumi said, shaking her head vigorously. "It is I who thanks you. I may recoup my honor now."

She bowed and hurried out of the chamber. Crane was shaking, nearly delirious.

Lanie squealed and threw her arms around his neck. "You did it! You . . . did . . . it! How do you feel?"

Crane wiped his eyes and kissed his bride to be. "I feel like the weight of five billion years has been lifted from my shoulders."

RECOMBINATIONS
NEW CAIRO
16 JULY 2026, 2:00 P.M.

Abu Talib, also known as Daniel Newcombe, stood in a huge cotton field with representatives from the Islamic republics of Algeria and Guatemala. Daily, Islamic dignitaries came to pay their respects or to negotiate trade deals with New Cairo. Right now, cotton was king.

Upon conversion to Islam, Newcombe had taken the name of Abu Talib. It was the name of Mohammed's uncle and greatest lifelong supporter, who also had not believed in the prophet's mission, as Newcombe/Talib did not believe in the tenets of Islam or in the philosophy of Brother Ishmael. It was the godless man's way to embrace religion.

The field stretched out for hundreds of acres, the Yo-Yu screens, ten feet overhead, casting a slight bluish glow over everything. In the far distance Liang's wall split the horizon. Hundreds of people worked in the field around them. Right now the cotton plants resembled small dead bushes, but the earth was black and rich, the spring rains mere weeks away.

Ali Garcia, the trade rep from Guatemala, was kneeling by a plant, frowning at it. "This will be American Upland cotton?" he asked, his fingers playing with a twiggy branch.

"Best in the world," Brother Talib said. "It doesn't look like much now, but the flowers will start forming after the rains come. Once they wither, the boll forms and matures in a couple of months. You'll be able to take delivery in mid-August."

"What can you produce from a field like this?" asked the Algerian, Faisal ben Achmed.

"We got eight hundred thousand bales of cotton from these fields last year without knowing what we were doing. This year we'll double that. Interested?"

"Of course we're interested," Garcia said. "What are you looking for in return?"

"Investment capital, farm machinery, livestock, and building materials," Talib said. "We're digging in, entrenching until the rest of our people are welcomed to the homeland. We want to establish a strong base from which to grow."

"*Kwiyis.*" Faisal nodded. "Your people are strong, your soil blessed. You will make a good addition to our international family."

"We must go," Garcia said, standing, "if we wish to catch the shuttle to Belize."

"Sure you can't stay and have a meal with me?" Talib asked. "The food is delicious, and all raised right here in New Cairo. Let me extend my full hospitality."

"*Alfshukre,*" Faisal said. "But no, and with regrets. Abu Talib's hospitality is renowned."

Talib nodded, then led them toward the main road through the fields, the three of them climbing, under a fat, warm sun, into the vehicle waiting there.

"How large are the occupied territories?" Garcia asked as the driver opened the focus and sped off.

"We are the northwestern corner of the territories," he said. "The Mississippi divides us from Arkansas and Louisiana, and provides us a natural boundary all the way south to the Gulf of Mexico. We will extend east to the Atlantic Ocean. There will be enough room."

"For now," Faisal said, all of them laughing.

"Will the Americans capitulate?" Garcia asked.

"I hope so," Talib answered. "I truly hope so."

They drove through the cotton fields, then the soybean fields . . . the rice fields . . . past the dairies . . . past the chicken farms. Housing was mixed throughout the fields, workers living close to their jobs. The housing came in the form of three-story blocks of apartments made from brick fired in New Cairo. Building was a major concern and always on full throttle. Lacking the proper equipment early on, the building industry was nearly biblical in its methods, something Talib wanted to rectify as quickly as possible.

He loved the respect with which he was treated these days. With Crane he had lived in the shadows. Here, he cast the shadow, and it was a large one. Most everyone thought of him, not Brother Ishmael, when the Islamic State was mentioned. It put the two men on a strange footing, especially since Talib didn't regard Ishmael as his spiritual leader.

Dead magnolia trees and live people lined the roadway leading up to the pre–Civil War plantation house that served as the governmental and religious headquarters for

New Cairo. Yo-Yu had been given permission to build a
shield plant in the walled state and in exchange they were
designing tree shields so that regeneration of the thousands
of magnolia and cottonwood trees in New Cairo could get
underway.

He wished his guests *sahbah innoor,* had the driver
move them along, then began to push his way through the
crowd thronging the front entrance to the government
house. There were always crowds, either people complain-
ing or, most often, refugees seeking asylum. As soon as he
was able to put up another building, he was going to have
Immigration moved to the farthest geographical point in
New Cairo from where he was standing.

The people parted for him the moment they recognized
him. He was a Presence, thought of as Ishmael's word
made flesh, and was treated accordingly. And he was
NOI's only statesman. Brother Ishmael refused to assume
that role and refused, even, to visit New Cairo until, as he
said, "all my brothers are free to journey home."

So, to the citizens here, it was Abu Talib who ruled
New Cairo. To date no request of his had been denied, so
his overlord status was unchallenged. New Cairo's first
year had been full of hardship, emotional, physical, financial. But they had survived and the colony was succeeding,
and he had been a large part of it.

It had made sense, when he'd decided to go on sabbatical, to come here. He was close to the action and respected, and he could work with the very soil that had
thrown his EQ-eco out of synch to begin with. Also, Crane
and Lanie were far away. He was working hard to forget
both of them—with little success.

His lab had been a large bedroom with a wide veranda.
He worked and slept there, leaving the French doors open
to the breeze all night. Now he coded in and locked the
door behind him.

"*Assalamu ahlaykum,*" came a voice from amidst his
computers and seismos.

He turned in surprise. Khadijah was staring at him.

"*Wiahlaykum issalam,*" he said, crossing the distance
between them to kiss her on both cheeks. "What brings

you down here to Africktown? You're a long way from the city, girl."

"My brother has sent me. He wants me to 'get used to the alluvial plain.' Is it always this hot?"

"Most of the time," he said and laughed. "I hate to say it, but it's good to see you."

"Thank you. I'm actually glad to be here."

"Well, if you intend to stay for a while," he said, "remember to wear a veil when you go outside. This is an Islamic state."

She smiled. "I found out the hard way. Someone threw a rock at me when I was coming in."

"What did you do?"

"Threw it back."

He chuckled. "You'll have to be put to work, too," he said. "That's the rule here. You gotta work."

"In the fields?" she asked, horrified.

"Or construction, or plumbing, or shield maintenance—"

"Enough. Let's talk about it tomorrow." She pointed into the liquefier. "What's that do?"

"When I'm finished inputting data," he said, "I'm going to duplicate last year's EQ. This is an exact geologic map of this area. I've filled it with tiny sensors to read changes. With luck, the river will alter its course and ultimately end up where it is today. If it does, it means I've calculated correctly. If it doesn't, it's back to the basics."

"How many times have you tried this?"

He raised his eyebrows. "A dozen or so. There's no instant gratification in science. But I'm getting closer."

She put her hand over his mouth. "I hear the white woman is going to marry the earthquake man."

He shook his head, freeing his mouth from her hand. "I like your subtle approach, Khadijah. Yes, it's quite true that Lanie and Crane will marry," he said, adding sardonically, "next week as a matter of fact and at a lodge in the Himalayas with a superb view of Mt. Everest. I'm sure Crane chose the location. He's nothing if not dramatic."

"The tone of your voice makes me believe you are free of her."

Talib merely shrugged.

"She will not be yours?" Khadijah persisted.

"No."

"Then I have a proposition for you."

What now, Talib wondered, smiling wryly. "Does a proper Muslim woman proposition a man?"

She made an exasperated sound. "Look, you have no woman. I have no man. I am of the right blood. It's a perfect political alliance."

"What is?"

"Our marriage! What do you think I'm talking about?"

He laughed loudly. "Our marriage? Are you joking with me?"

"Oh, do shut up and listen to me," she said angrily. "This is hard enough for me to do without you making fun. I know you are a . . . good man. You would be kind to me."

"And keep you near the top of the power curve, huh?"

"What's wrong with that? If you haven't noticed, it's kind of genetic . . . anyway, traditional with me and my brothers. I like excitement as much as the next person. I'd also make you a good wife and keep an Islamic home. I could give you children; I'm strong." Her voice lost its power and she stared down at the floor. Speaking in almost a whisper, she added, "You would have my heart and my dedication forever."

"Stop," he said, quietly but sternly, taking her shoulders. "Don't . . . do this. We can't marry. We won't. I'm flattered and you're wonderful. Soon, some man will—"

"I'm too headstrong for Islamic men."

"Well, yeah . . . there's that."

"You will need to wed and father children. We'll make future leaders together. Don't you understand how right this is, how destined?"

"Khadijah, I don't love you."

"We're not talking about love," she said. "I could never love an egotist like you. Marry me. Your woman belongs to someone else."

"That doesn't mean I can just stop loving her!"

"Love again. What is this? Life goes on, Abu Talib, with or without you."

His hands were trembling on her arms. "Leave me alone," he said. He turned from her and walked through the French doors. He leaned on the veranda rail and looked at the bustle below, a neverending river of people snaking into history. He had accomplished so much. God, why did he feel such pain?

Khadijah was at his arm, touching lightly. "I'm still a virgin," she said. "I will give that to you right now, if you'd like. I know I can please you."

"It would please me," he said, "if you would forget this discussion ever took place. Don't sacrifice yourself on the altar of Dan Newcombe."

"Abu Talib," she corrected, stepping very close and pressing her body to his, "that is your name. And I am your future."

Slowly, she pushed away, turned and, head erect, strode from the veranda. He watched her go through the room and out into the hall, then looked back over his domain, a blue sea of shields stretching in all directions as far as he could see. And he thought about Lanie.

It was bad enough that she was marrying Crane so fast, and when he'd heard the rumor she was pregnant, it had been a true punch in the gut. Marrying and having a family had been a major issue between him and Lanie for so many years—but with Crane, she'd been instantly ready for full commitment.

He cursed and slammed his fisted right hand into his left palm. This was stupid, stupid of him. He was internationally famous—revered, even—and he couldn't get past the fact that Elena King had thrown him over for Crane. He smiled self-derisively. He'd sent them the finest, most exotic and most appropriate wedding present he could find: a Chang Heng earthquake weathercock from the second century A.D. It was a large vase, the outside affixed with eight golden dragons, their bodies pointing downward. Below each dragon sat an openmouthed frog. A bronze ball rested in the mouth of each dragon and, should a tremor occur, the affected dragon would drop his ball into the mouth of his frog, setting off an alarm. The positioning of the dragon would determine the direction of the quake. In 138 A.D. that very urn had measured a quake four hundred miles away. Messengers, riding pell-mell to the capital city of Loyang to deliver the news, had discovered that their information already had been announced by the vase.

It was a delicate instrument, a beautiful gift. And it was all he could give them. He certainly could not give the gift of his presence at their wedding which, he suspected, both Lanie and Crane wanted for the closure, the reconciliation, the continuity of the relationship between all three that it would signify. But, Talib knew, watching them marry would tear him to emotional shreds, unman him. No, the ceremony would have to proceed without him.

Talib shivered with emotion. Was it love, race, ego, or competitiveness that drove his engine of jealousy and self-pity? He didn't know. He did know, however, that he did not want to spend his life alone and childless. There was Khadijah. . . .

Chapter 15

ENDINGS/ BEGINNINGS

THE HIMALAYAS—NEPAL, INDIA
23 JULY 2026, 2:00 P.M.

Alone, wearing a full-length cream-colored satin slip, Lanie stood at the teak-framed window of the old British lodge and gazed out in wonder at the twin peaks of Everest and Kanchenjunga. She hugged herself. In less than an hour she would become Lewis Crane's wife, in less than seven months she would bear their child. Her cup runneth over.

Crane had brought her to the roof of the world for their wedding, a place as high as the happiness they shared in each other, in their work, in their life together. The setting perfectly mirrored the way she felt, as Crane had promised it would. She was dazzled and amazed. The peaks she was staring at were nearly thirty thousand feet high, almost six miles up, and the range from which they soared, the Himalayan range, was nearly two hundred miles wide at certain points and stretched over fifteen hundred miles in length. All, of course, had originated in earthquakes. And today, this very afternoon, there would be the first quake since 1255 in this region.

Another boom shook the lodge, and Lanie felt plaster dust sprinkle her bare shoulders. She laughed aloud. Only Crane would choose this day, this place for their wedding. It was perfect.

She felt as if she hadn't been truly alive until she knew Crane had realized they loved each other. And she knew it was the same for him. Lord, he told her often enough. Perhaps even more importantly, he showed her . . . in every conceivable way. He treated her as an equal partner in their work and day-to-day lives; he treated her as the other half of his self in all things emotional, sexual. . . . She'd never dreamed she could feel so understanding of and understood by another human being.

Below, guests gathered in the front lawn under the politically correct Liang Int sunshield. A small but distinguished group of scientists and heads of state were gathering for the wedding, as well as their colleagues from the Foundation, supporters, and friends. The lawn turned into forest that rolled up the hillsides. They were at twelve thousand feet, the highest altitude where trees can grow. Farther up the mountains only grasses, lichens, and moss survived the cold, dry air. And higher than that, snow. Everyone, Lanie knew, was as affected as she by the awesome grandeur of the setting.

Turning away from the window, she caught sight of her gown, newly pressed and hanging in the open closet. She smiled and sat in one of the two leather chairs, separated by a small, delicately carved table, that was ideally placed to take advantage of the view through the window. Splendid Everest rose majestically into the clouds. Another foreshock hit. An incredible sensation, Lanie thought, so different from Sado, from Memphis. She had to laugh at herself. Being a thoroughly happy bride and mother-to-be must make her giddy.

Feeling awkward in his tuxedo, Crane stood in a tiny bathroom just off the kitchen on the main floor of the lodge.

Three other men were crowded in with him, and blue jamming lights arced all around them. They were passing the keypad, finalizing their arrangement. President Gideon sat on the closed commode; Vice President Sumi Chan was wedged into the corner in front of Gideon's legs. Crane and Mr. Mui were face-to-face, Mui leaning against the washstand.

"Will you begin the project soon?" the Liang boss asked, pressing his thumb to the keypad. The light registered green, indicating that his print had been identified.

"Right after the wedding," Crane said.

"No honeymoon?" Gideon asked. "That's a pretty little woman you got yourself there."

The concept had never occurred to Crane. "There's too much to do," he said. "We have only five years before it will be too late to make the weld. No time to waste."

Mui handed him the key pad. "Security around the site will have to be intense."

"We'll be operating as a deep drilling operation called Northwest Gemstone. Our avowed business purpose will be exploration primarily for focus crystals." Crane placed his thumb on the black metallic plate. It registered within a second. "We'll put up a security building called Gem Processing and work the nuclear materials in there. We'll assemble the devices on site. I've already contacted my weapons researchers to do the job."

"What about deliveries of the nuclear material?" Gideon asked.

"I've purchased several trucks, sir," Crane said, handing the man the pad, "which we are now retrofitting in order to haul atomic contraband. They'll have Northwest Gemstone logos painted on both sides and appear to be equipment haulers."

Sumi took the pad from the President, affixing her own thumbprint to complete the circle. An agreement had just been forged.

"Done," Sumi said, smiling as the machine registered a bindable contract, albeit a private one. "Your dream is online, Crane. How long before delivery?"

"Two years," Crane said, taking back the keypad and

interfacing with his wristpad to get his copy. The two machines sang together, then bleeped their satisfaction.

"Crane!" came a voice from the hallway. "Dammit, Crane! There's a party going on without you. Where are you?"

"It's Stoney." Crane smiled, disconnecting and giving the keypad back to Mui, who pocketed it.

"Does *he* know?" Mui asked.

Crane shook his head. "Outside of this room, only Lanie knows. Even the people I've hired to dig the tunnels don't know. They think we're making an underground vault to store records. The pyro guys who'll build the bomb think it's a secret U.S. mission leading to the renewal of underground testing, and were chosen for their security clearances."

"Crane!"

"In here, Stoney," Crane called, opening the door.

Twenty feet down the hall, Stoney smiled when he saw four of them coming out. "When I was a kid," he said, hobbling over to them, his cane the only reminder of his near brush with death in Memphis, "four men coming out of a bathroom together usually would have been followed by a cloud of smoke."

"Where's Lanie?" Crane asked.

"With the rest of the guests," Stoney said, waving to the other men as they hurried on. "She's attempting to keep from going crazy looking for you."

"Be a good guy," Crane said, clapping him on the shoulder. "Go back and tell Lanie I'll be right there."

"Your show," Whetstone said and shook hands with him. "Congratulations, old man. You know, I looked my entire life and never found a woman like Lanie."

"Thank you, Stoney," Crane said, hugging him. The man hobbled off then, leaning heavily on his cane made from Tennessee poplar.

Lanie. Crane had no idea of what he'd done to deserve her. He had orchestrated every other aspect of his life, but suddenly she had shown up and changed it all. It was the most wonderful thing that ever had happened. As far as he was concerned Lanie was the only woman in the entire world. And she loved to work as much as he did! His entire life had come together, all the pieces falling into place. Dreams, and dreams beyond dreams.

He savored the moment. He'd known too few of its kind.

His bad arm throbbed painfully, the quake nearly upon them. He supposed some would think him odd for celebrating his wedding amidst the devastation of an EQ, but he looked at it as a tragedy averted, a cause for celebration. There'd be homelessness and suffering, but nothing like what would have happened had no one been alerted.

He walked out onto the wide wooden porch. A hundred chattering guests silenced immediately. All eyes had turned toward him. A canopy hung above the wide lawn. Lanie, in white taffeta and sheer veil, stood fifty feet away, smiling calmly. She held a bouquet of white orchids. A red-cloaked Cosmie minister stood at her left; Kate Masters, also carrying flowers, was at her right. Stoney awaited Crane at the porch steps.

"Ready?" he asked.

Lightning crackled overhead, leaping between the mountains and the sky. The celebrants looked somewhat nervous.

"Ladies and gentlemen," Crane said loudly, opening his arms. "Trust me!"

They laughed then, relieving the tension. Crane looked at Stoney. "Now, I'm ready. Got the ring?"

"What ring?" Stoney laughed. "Bad joke. Sorry. Of course I have the ring."

To Wagner's traditional wedding march from *Lohengrin*, they walked down the red carpet toward Lanie. Crane surprised himself by being more nervous now than when he'd been affixing the agreement with Liang.

He reached Lanie's side and was trapped immediately in her luminescent hazel gaze. Her eyes were wide with love and inquisitiveness. "God, you're beautiful," he whispered to a loud rumble. He grasped her hands.

"Never mind that," she whispered. "How did it go?"

"It's done," he whispered in return. Lanie threw her arms around his neck.

"Perhaps we'd better get on with it," the minister said, looking around suspiciously at the quivering lawn furniture, the trembling ornamental plants and flowers.

Crane padded the time—2:36:30. He smiled at the man. "Your show, Padre."

"The name's Al," the minister said. "Just Al."

"Quickly, Al," Crane said, the ground shaking laterally beneath their feet.

"Brothers in Oneness!" the minister began. "As all life is made from the same molecules, so, too, do these beings who stand before us wish to become One through the pair bonding institution of—"

The rest of his speech was mercifully drowned out by the rumbling quakes, originating from a twenty-five-mile-deep hypocenter near Dhangarhi as the Indian Plate finally relieved its slippage. It was a monster quake, its likes not seen for almost sixty years, since the big Alaska quake in 1967.

As the minister pronounced them "co-beings in Oneness," the ground had begun rolling like waves on the sea, the shelf creaking above them. Crane kissed the bride and hoped the dams would stand despite his predictions, but he knew they wouldn't.

The sky had darkened now, lightning a continual fireworks show halfway up the peaks that towered over everything. Everyone walked out from under the canopy to watch the display as a section of Everest, large as a city, sheared off the side of the mountain and fell to the valleys far below.

"What a wonderful wedding present," Lanie said, her arms around Crane as they watched the spectacle. "It's amazing."

"Our child's first EQ," Crane said.

"What do you do, Crane," Lanie asked, "when you've finally achieved your dream and ended all this?"

"I don't know." He grinned. "Take up accounting?"

The valleys screamed all around them, whined—the sound like fingernails on a chalk board amplified billions of times. Crane almost could hear voices in it. Wailing. Forlorn and frightened.

The guests were bending over, hands covering their ears to shut out the din as the wind picked up, blowing wildly into their faces, whipping dresses and hair in swirling frenzy. The inferior Liang sunscreen collapsed in on itself, but fortunately no one was beneath the thing.

And then it happened, right before their eyes. Everest, amidst the howling wind and the cries of dying rock, shook like the old man it was, large bits of it cracking loudly just as the trees breaking in the forest and falling off were creaking loudly. And then it grew. As if rising to walk away, the six-mile mountain abruptly jutted upward, rising higher into the clouds, eating the slippage and growing—young again, a new mountain.

The whole process took three minutes to accomplish. Three minutes to change the topography of the planet. Three minutes to grow the world's tallest mountain fifty feet taller. The next man to climb it would be climbing higher than Sir Edmund Hillary did in the same spot.

Out of destruction, birth.

Sumi Chan stood with Burt Hill, who was wearing a too-small tuxedo. He looked like a monkey without an organ grinder as he watched the reception tangle all around them. The lodge's main hall was filled to bursting, wedding presents lining the walls and filling the small conference room next door. Professional talkers talked all around them, drinking synth before a fireplace so large it consumed whole treetrunks as its logs.

"Nine on the Richter," Hill said. "Higher than they could really measure precisely." He shook his head and took another sip of the dorphed booze in his glass. "Folks are calling it a miracle. The death toll's still under five hundred. It should have been hundreds of thousands. The four busted dams flooded out fifty cities."

She shook her head. "A massive cleanup."

"Yeah. But Liang'll spend the money here. They're busy fighting with the Moslems for control of all this. That's a lot of consumers."

Sumi sipped her own dorph blend, the only thing that

got her through social occasions these days. "Does Crane know about the results of the quake?"

"Naw," Hill said, pointing to Crane, who was dancing with his new wife. "For once in his life, the man is thinkin' about something other than quakes. A wonderful sight, ain't it?"

"I don't think I've ever seen him happy before."

"Buddy," Hill said, "that's 'cause he ain't ever been happy before. It's a scary idea."

"Scary . . . how?"

Hill got thoughtful. "When you get happy," he said, lowering his voice, "you forget to look behind you. You start trusting people. You make mistakes."

"Then, I guess," Sumi said, "I'll not make any more mistakes."

The man stared hard at her. "I'm talkin' about Crane," Hill said, finishing his drink. He looked at the glass. "I'm going for more refreshments."

She watched him leave, realizing he didn't trust *her*. Of course not, why should he? It didn't matter anyway. Soon, she would be exposed for more of a fraud than any of them thought. She hoped it wouldn't interfere in any way with Crane's dream. She'd wanted to give that to him, to make up for everything she'd done.

"I hate to drink alone," Kate Masters said from beside her. "How about you?"

Sumi smiled wanly. "I enjoy your company very much."

"Good. How about your dorph recipe?"

"My secret."

A group of Nepalese Sherpas had come out from their hidey-hole and were doing a vigorous display of acrobatics, tumbling and diving in syncopation over one another to the delight of the crowd.

"You have a lot of secrets, I think."

Sumi's body jerked involuntarily. "How so?"

"You really want to talk about this?"

"Yes."

"Well, first off, you're not who you say you are."

Sumi's heart was pounding. She could feel it in her throat as her face flushed. "You are mistaken, I—"

"I knew your mother," Masters said. "The Women's Political Association was in a limited partnership with your parents in a business deal. We all took a beating on that deal, your folks most of all. Your mother spoke of you constantly. It always bothered me that you dishonored her name by remaking your past."

"It would have been a greater dishonor had I not," Sumi replied, eyes cast down. "You knew, yet you said nothing?"

"I'd hoped we were friends. Are we?"

"Outside of Crane, I never had a friend."

"And look what you did to him."

Sumi was surprised again. "How—"

"I figured it out. I'm a smart girl."

"Yeah," Sumi said. "Me, too."

Masters just stared at her, but her eyes were different. They were studying, dissecting. "You mean that literally?"

Sumi nodded. "Mr. Li knew and forced me to change my ancestry. To keep the world from discovering my parents' deception I went along with him."

"Does anyone else—"

"Only you."

"Why are you telling me?"

Sumi took a deep breath. "I'm in trouble. I-I'm not sure what to do. I need . . . help."

Masters fell forward, as if she'd tripped, her hand swinging out, touching Sumi's crotch, pulling back immediately as she straightened. "Sorry, hon," she said. "I'm from Missouri, still the 'Show Me' state. What sort of trouble?"

"By law," Sumi said, "the President and Vice President must take a physical once a year. I've managed to avoid it far too long. The White House physicians are getting contentious about it. People are wondering why I'm avoiding it. Believe me, that kind of wondering will lead to terrible trouble for me."

"Why trust me?"

"Somehow I've always felt you were trustworthy. I don't know if I completely trust you, but I *do not* trust the White House physicians."

"Do you have to use them?"

Sumi shook her head. "I could demand my own doctor."

"Okay," Masters said. "We'll start there."

"You'll help me?"

"Hey, I represent the Women's Political Association, remember. Welcome to the club, sister." She hugged Sumi.

"Thank you," Sumi said, tears welling.

Kate Masters' eyes twinkled. "Thank me when you're President," she replied.

Chapter 16

COMPRES- SIONAL STRAINS

LA WAR ZONE
29 JULY 2026, 2:10 A.M.

"The proposal has some merit, and I'll certainly consider it," Mohammed Ishmael said.

Abu Talib sank farther down in his chair. "Brother Ishmael," he said. "I gave Mr. Tang my word on this."

"Tang," he said scornfully. "A flunky. Mui Tsao's harpy who is nothing but a double-ported chippy. And who were you speaking for, Talib?" Ishmael's expression was serious as he stared across the table at Talib.

They were in a bunker that was small, claustrophobic, the long, glowing table taking up most of it. Somewhere under the Zone, it was a redoubt that Talib hadn't seen before. The walls were lead, the door heavy and airtight like ones found in submarines.

Metal bunks folded out from the walls. Storage lockers and shelving covered every available space and were crammed with bottled water, canned food, and staples in sealed jars. A classically designed and supplied bomb shelter and bunker.

Ishmael walked around the table and leaned low, his face only inches from Talib's. "I asked you who you were speaking for," he said loudly. "Because it sure wasn't for me—and it sure wasn't for my people!"

Talib bristled and jumped up, his chair overturning and clattering to the floor. Martin Aziz darted around the table and placed himself between the two men.

"My brother," Aziz said to Ishmael, "Talib's agreement with Tang gets us almost everything we want, and in return all we have to do is to agree to stop the violence. Do you understand?"

"What I understand," Ishmael said, pushing his brother aside to face Abu Talib, the two men eye to eye, "is that my methods have brought us this far—a foothold in our Homeland, the whites sucking up to *us*, asking for favors. If these methods have brought us this far, why should we abandon them now?"

"Have you forgotten the focus buildings?" Talib asked. "Liang Int knows, and threatens to shut them all down."

Ishmael raised his hands in exasperation. "The focus buildings," he said. "Always the focus buildings." He arched an eyebrow. "You weren't around then, Brother, but we survived just fine before we had focus buildings to give us power. Damn!"

He walked away from Talib, squeezing past Martin Aziz to stand at the head of the table, fifteen feet distant. He slammed his hands, palm down, on the tabletop and stared fire at Talib. "And has it ever occurred to your rock head that if they were to shut down the focus buildings, we'd probably respond with a massive exodus to New Cairo? Imagine that, if you will. Imagine the Memphis exodus multiplied by fifty with no earthquake to cover it. Imagine the fights. Imagine the bloodshed. Imagine the public relations."

Talib felt suddenly stupid. "I never thought of that."

"Well, your white friend Mr. Tang certainly did! And so, for an end to the violence that's got us this far, what do we *really* get in return? Only a promise that they would keep doing what they're doing now—nothing. If they'd figured an advantage to be gained by shutting down the focus buildings, believe me, they wouldn't have consulted us about doing it.

"The reason they haven't fought it out with us is simple: We are a part of this . . . this landscape, part of the fabric of this country. If everybody else sees them going after us, it'll get them thinking about themselves. Case in point. The G was called off the Zone fighting in Memphis almost immediately for PR reasons, and Liang made sure the teev was full of pictures of the quake, not the exodus."

"Leonard," Aziz said softly. "Can't we use this as an opening, though? Can't we try and follow through? If they're willing to let us coexist now, why fight them? Already over a thousand of us, mostly children, have died in clashes with the G."

"Martyrs," Ishmael said. "And I *know* how many have died."

Talib drew himself up to his full height. He'd resigned from the Foundation and now he was about to resign from NOI. What was he to become: a man without a job, without even a place to call home? "Brother Ishmael," he said officiously, "given the nature of your lack of trust in me and the worthlessness which will attach to my work from now on, I respectfully submit my resignation as spokesman for Nation of Islam."

"Would you sit down, Abu?" Ishmael sighed. "I respect your opinion and the job you do. You're irreplaceable. We'll work something out with this Tang thing, all right? I told—asked—you to sit down."

Talib sat. "I've been working in New Cairo," he said. "A mass exodus isn't feasible. There's not enough housing. The people we displace will destroy much in order to keep it from us. People, especially city people, have to be taught how to farm, to work with their hands. Drop twenty million people into that situation and you'll have food and water and sewage problems you never even dreamed of."

"I know," Ishmael said. "We're not ready yet. That's why I'm considering the deal you're negotiating with

Tang." Ishmael looked over at Aziz. "Would you sit down, too? You make me nervous."

"I simply ask," Ishmael said, "that no one presume on my authority. May I have general agreement on that?"

Nods around the table.

"Good. I agree that movement to New Cairo will be slow. Let us get the first settlement entirely on its feet and we'll expand from there. Meanwhile, Brother Talib has done us the greatest service in bringing the news of Crane's ultimate goal: to use nuclear weapons to fuse the Continental Plates. Crane will be our focus."

"Why?" Talib asked. "He will not be able to get the nuclear material or the authority to do such a thing."

Ishmael looked at Talib as if he were a child. He smiled beatifically, sitting back in his chair, fingers steepled. "I continually wonder how it is possible," he asked softly, "for you to have worked so closely with this man and not recognized his power?"

"His power is in his madness," Talib said.

"His power resides in the clarity of his vision," Ishmael returned. "The same place my power resides."

"He's dead in the water," Talib said.

"He will find a way," Ishmael said. "And it will be up to us to stop him. Crane is my Satan, Abu. I want no misunderstanding. He is the greatest battle I will ever fight. Like Mohammed with the Meccans, 'Though they gave me the sun in my right hand and the moon in my left to bring me back from my undertaking, yet will I not pause till the Lord carry this cause to victory, or till I die for it.' Promise me that if I do not live to see this through, the rest of you will continue after me."

"I swear," Talib said, "that I will not stop dogging Crane if there is breath in my body."

"And I," Martin Aziz said.

"Good. It is Crane who will ultimately provide the key to our Homeland. I don't know how yet, but I can see it just as surely as I can see my own death calling out to me. Is there any other business from the outside world?"

Talib looked at the tabletop, then cleared his throat. "With all due respect and humility," he said, voice choked,

"I would like to ask your permission for your sister's hand in marriage."

"An alliance," Ishmael said. "You don't want Crane's woman any longer?"

"I was a fool," Talib said.

"Yes, you were," Brother Ishmael responded. He stood and walked around to Talib. "But you are a fool no longer." Talib got up; the two men embraced. "Welcome to our family. We will be real brothers now." He kissed Talib on each cheek. Smiling, he said, "Let me go to find Khadijah and bring her to you. We must celebrate."

In truth, Mohammed Ishmael could have sent someone to fetch his sister, but he needed time alone. He knew that Talib was a good man who was becoming a good Muslim, but the convert hadn't yet begun to grasp the proper attitude when dealing with the Infidel. Ishmael knew he'd have to watch his new brother carefully—especially since Crane was drawing Talib and him into the web that would ensnare the three of them and shape their fate. Ishmael could feel it drawing around him now. Tears formed in the corners of his eyes. Like Moses, he'd see the promised land, but not live long enough to enter it.

Out in the hallway, facing the wall so none could see, he cried for himself, then cursed his weakness. Only the words of the Prophet brought him any solace. "Be in the world like a traveler, or like a passerby and reckon yourself as of the dead."

So be it.

SILVER SPRING, MARYLAND
13 AUGUST 2026, 4:23 P.M.

Sumi Chan watched her security monitor as Kate Masters' helo glided gently onto the pad, disgorging the woman and an older man carrying a medical case. Lights around the pad blazed, catching the sequins of Masters' bright red body suit, lighting her up like the Chinese opera on festival nights.

Sumi saw the figures approach the house elevator. She

felt great trepidation, for she'd never trusted anyone with her secrets, not even Crane, and now she'd see what price she would pay for indulging in trusting Kate Masters.

The visitors disappeared from the screen and she switched to a shot inside the elevator. The doors opened and Masters and the doctor stepped in. Finding the camera immediately, Kate used its lens as a mirror and fixed her hair. "Hope these pictures look good in the archives," she said, pulling her low neckline down a touch and winking.

The Vice President's quarters were located in Silver Spring, Maryland, minutes from the Capital. The entire house was underground and electronically secured, leaving her protected without the expense of bodyguards. Sumi already had figured out a dozen ways in which the security could be breached here, but it didn't matter. No one in the history of the United States had ever gone after a Vice President. They were too powerless and easy to replace.

Sumi hit the door activation button and hurried through the small but elegant traditional Chinese house whose windows looked out at holo projections of the Henan Province where she'd grown up—rolling farmland, workers tilling the fields, the Huang He River flowing gently from west to east in the distance. Over the course of a year, she'd watched the planting, growing, and harvesting of two crops, complete with typhoons in the spring and killing frost in the winter.

The elevator doors opened into her living room. Masters bounced into the room and gave Sumi a hug. "All this secrecy is very exciting."

"I'm getting cold feet," Sumi whispered into Masters' ear. "This doctor, how do you know we can trust him?"

Masters smiled and straightened. "Vice President Chan, I'd like you to meet my father, Dr. Ben Masters."

"Pleased to know you," the man said, shaking a relieved Sumi's hand. She should have known Masters would handle things impeccably. "Katie tells me you've got yourself something of a gender problem here."

Sumi nodded. "I don't want them to know I'm a woman," she said, and the words sounded odd coming out of her mouth.

"I'll just give my report on your health," the man returned, his wrinkled face relaxed. "I'm not a census taker. How long since you've had a physical?"

"Not since I left China ten years ago."

"Okay, then," the doctor returned. "Where can I set up?"

"There's a guest room at the end of the hallway," Sumi replied. "Will that do?"

"Fine. Give me a few minutes to prepare." The man walked off, Sumi turning to Masters.

Reaching out, Kate tousled Sumi's severely combed-back hair, bringing it down on the sides and making bangs. She smiled with satisfaction when she was done as if, only now, could she truly accept Sumi as a woman.

"I'm ready back here!" Masters called from the guest room.

"Coming!" Sumi said.

Kate stopped her. "Sit for a second. I want to ask you something personal."

"About sex, right?" Sumi said, feeling herself tighten up involuntarily. "I'll tell you what I told Mr. Li. I have had to suppress those urges in order to maintain my charade."

"Are you asexual?"

"No."

"Do you like girls or boys?"

"I'm not attracted to women. Why are you asking me these things?"

"Okay. What kind of man do you find attractive?"

"Kate," Sumi said, nervous, "what are you getting at here?"

"Just answer my question. What kind of man attracts you—young stud? Muscleman?"

"No." Chan laughed. "This is silly. A game."

"Play. What kind of man?"

"I don't know . . . intelligent. Someone who'll give me a mental challenge. Middle-aged . . . past all that young man's nonsense. Strong but vulnerable. Sure of himself but open to interpretation. . . ."

"You're describing Crane."

"What?"

"This is Crane you're talking about."

Sumi flinched, a hand coming to her mouth.

"You're in love with him, aren't you?"

Sumi gasped and turned away. Now Masters knew all her secrets. The woman hugged her from behind, resting her head on Sumi's shoulder.

"I'm so sorry, honey," she said, then gently turned Sumi to face her.

"I've got something for you," Kate said and held up a small metal slot with double sets of three-inch-long sensors sticking out the end.

"A chip port?"

"My Dad can have one of these in your skull in five minutes. Trust me. It will help you with your sexual problems."

"Who said I had a problem?" Sumi asked sharply. "I'm not a chippie, Kate."

"Neither am I." Kate flipped up her red hair directly above her left ear, revealing her own port. "I'm a simple gal. If it's bad, I do it. If it's fun, I do it. Usually they're the same thing. Trust me, honey. I can fix you up so that you can lead a full sexual life without ever knowing a man. Five minutes of your time. Under the hair, where no one will see it unless you want them to."

Sumi Chan stared at her with wide eyes.

The holorain fell hard on Henan through Sumi's bedroom window, a cool, damp, fragrant breeze blowing in with it. Her lights were turned out. Occasional flashes of lightning brightened the room.

A slight ache in her head reminded her of the chip sitting in its little case beside her on the night table. The checkup had gone well and the surgery had, indeed, taken only five minutes, most of that spent shaving the inch-long spot on her head where the port was to be buried. An anesthetic had been administered, then a small incision made, the sensors put right into the cut. The sensors were very sharp. Ben Masters used a small hammer to tap them through muscles and bone. Once he was through the skull, one shove jammed the sensors deeply into her brain.

It had been painless.

Lightning flashed again, and Sumi turned to look at the chip box and the small tweezers attached to it on a chain. There was no reason for her not to use it right away, Kate had said.

She sat up, her silk pajamas slithering along the covers as she swung her feet to the floor and picked up the box. She opened it and tweezed out the chip. She felt for her new port with her little finger, then homed in with the chip. It slid effortlessly into the driver and engaged with a whirring sound only she could hear.

She waited for a moment, then looked around the room. Nothing was happening, no hallucinations, no bright colors, no altered states. She lay back down, disappointed, drew the covers over herself, and watched the shadows on the ceiling.

Then, a sound. Tapping. Someone was knocking lightly on her door. She pulled the covers up around her chin. "Who's there?" she called.

The door opened, and a man walked in carrying a candle. "I brought some light," he said in Chinese. "I thought the storm might frighten you."

Her heart was pounding as he walked closer, her hand edging toward the security alarm, though it would be too late to save her. How had he gotten in?

"I've been here all the time," he said in answer to her unasked question.

"Who are you?"

"Who or what?" He set the candle beside them on the nighttable, then sat beside her on the bed. She could feel their thighs touching as he stared innocently down at her. She reached out to the candle, could feel its heat.

"Start with who."

"I don't have a name. You name me."

"What, then. What are you?"

"I am your ideal man, I guess," he said. "I've been living in your brain ever since old Doc Ben put the driver in. It appears to me that I am a combination of Lewis Crane, your father, and a secondary school teacher you had a crush on named Mr. Weng."

"Mr. Weng," she said, burying her face in her hands, her face reddening in embarrassment. "I haven't thought of him in—"

"You thought of him today, when Kate asked you about the kind of man you liked."

"Why are you here?"

"I'm here to be your lover, Sumi, if you want. Your friend if you don't want a lover—though I must say, you'd be missing some incredible stimuli. This is a very good chip. I feel very much alive."

"But you're not . . . really here. I mean not physically."

"Your brain thinks I am. That's good enough for me."

He put out a hand to lightly stroke her thigh. Her tension began to ease. Somehow, knowing *she* was creating her lover made it much easier. No fears. No need for fears.

"I'm going to call you Paul," she said.

"Okay." His hand moved up to her face, his touch setting off electric jolts all through her body. "But, why Paul?"

She looked at him with wide eyes. "Because I don't know anyone named Paul," she said. Both of them laughed.

His arms went around her and pulled her close. She could smell his aftershave, feel the coarse texture of his curly hair.

"I love you, Sumi," he whispered into her ear.

"I know," she replied, tears running down her cheeks. "I know."

LA WAR ZONE
17 DECEMBER 2026, 7:03 P.M.

Abu Talib sat in the back of the large briefing room with Khadijah, his feet out in front of him, his head flung back. He was tired, bone weary. Five months ago he had completed negotiations with Tang for a deal that made him proud—and nervous as hell. In return for NOI's agreement to cease violent protests, Liang Int had prom-

ised a national referendum on giving NOI a homeland.
And tonight was the night, election night.

About thirty people filled the room, lining the walls,
watching large teevs. They were monitoring the voting in
cities that had War Zones. At the front of the room, the
one Talib had been brought to his first night underground
a million years ago, both Mohammed Ishmael and Martin
Aziz stood, black robe and white robe, day and night, two
men absolutely united in cause and diametrically opposed
in method. They were looking at a huge screen that filled
the front of the room. Khadijah sat with Talib, her head
on his shoulder, cuddling tiredly. Talib kissed her fore-
head.

He wondered what Brother Ishmael was going to do if
the vote didn't go their way. For these last five months
Martin Aziz had confronted Ishmael on a daily basis about
the issue of violence in the occupied territories. For five
months, day after weary day, his brother had convinced
Ishmael anew not to restart the riots and content himself,
instead, with the "public education" phase that Aziz mas-
terminded and Talib led. Talib's job consisted of making
speeches and Net appearances on anybody's show who'd
ask him, selling the fact that Nation of Islam was a peaceful organization simply dedicated to the formation of an
Islamic state and common brotherhood among all people.

He'd gone nonstop for the full five months, casting science aside completely, his dance card full. Even his dip-
lomatic duties in New Cairo were getting too little
attention. It had become disorienting, never knowing what
city he was in, always saying the same things. It had worn
him out completely, and was a damn poor way to start a
marriage.

Aziz had concurrently begun peaceful demonstrations
from the Zone, "informative riots" he'd called them.
Aziz's thinking throughout was that Ishmael had gotten
everyone's attention with the real riots, now it was time
to get their sympathy and, hopefully, their vote on the
homeland issue with education and PR.

"Why are you and my brother so worried?" Khadijah
asked. "Aren't we winning?"

"For the moment," Talib said. "You're not used to the voting process, but what happens is that very few people vote during the day of an election. Most everyone waits until they get home from work and get on the teev to see the pols' last-minute speeches and promises. They look at voting as another entertainment medium."

He felt rather than heard Khadijah take a shuddering breath. She pointed to a teev at the side of the room, and he turned to look. Crane and a hugely pregnant Lanie filled the screen, the bottom of which indicated audio on fiber M. He padded on and got the tail end of what Crane was saying.

"—and that is just one of the reasons why my wife and I support the cause of the Nation of Islam. We have voted for a homeland. We hope you will, too."

Surprised almost to the point of shock, Talib sat rigid, then quickly padded off. Beyond e-mailing a thank you for the support to Lanie and Crane, how was he supposed to react? Crane was a triumphal hero these days, and his slightest move was on the teev. The wedding in the Himalayas had garnered hours of coverage. Beyond those gossipy sorts of features, though, there'd been little on Crane and Lanie—their work, their new projects. Even the scientific community had been fairly quiet, although Talib had heard there was something afoot, some new area Crane was developing, but he'd been too busy to follow up . . . not that he was worried. It couldn't be the plate fusion scheme. Crane was rich enough since the wager to put such an effort together, but he'd never be able to get the approvals for digging that he'd need, much less the nuclear material. Still—

Khadijah was vigorously shaking his arm. "What's the matter with you?" she asked sharply. "You're upset. Does it bother you to see the white woman so large with Crane's child?"

"No," he lied. "That's all in the past."

"But you would like to have children . . . sons, right?"

He tilted her head from his shoulder and looked into her eyes. "Yes," he answered, "very much so."

"Good," she replied, matter-of-factly. "Because you're

going to have one. I've made you a son to rule New Cairo."

"What?"

Her eyes were playful. "You heard me," she said. "You shouldn't be surprised. We've been trying hard enough."

He hugged her, flooded with a feeling of bittersweet euphoria. "That's wonderful. When?"

"June," she said. "Next June."

"You know it's a boy? You've tested?"

"I don't have to test," she said. "I have made a male for Islam. We are very strong-willed in my family."

"Talib!" Ishmael shouted. "Turn on your damned aural!"

Abu kissed Khadijah, his stomach fluttery, and padded on the V fiber.

"Khadijah is pregnant!" he announced to anyone on the fiber.

A cheer went up from the assembled.

"We pray for a manchild," Ishmael said. "Now will you please look at the screen?"

Talib looked and wasn't surprised. On one side of the screen was a shot outside the walls of the War Zone in LA. Zoners, adults and children, stood in a large group, each holding a candle. They were singing. On the other side were the running tallies of the vote. NOI was losing.

"We are losing and my brother has our people singing *negro spirituals*!" Ishmael said, raising his arms to heaven. "A minstrel show!"

"Remember," Talib said. "We knew there would be setbacks and regions we'd lose."

"We're down one percentage point in Seattle," interrupted one of the poll watchers. "Down two points in Phoenix."

"We're losing our lead in New York!"

"That's it," Ishmael said low.

Talib looked at the overview board. The votes were swinging against the cause.

"Who's running the Detroit screen?" Ishmael called into the confusion.

"I am, sir!" answered a man standing near Talib, who was on his feet now, Khadijah rising, too.

"No!" Aziz said, grabbing Ishmael's arm. "You cannot do this."

Ishmael jerked his arm away and spat on the floor. "This is the result of my listening to you," he said. Then he asked the poll watcher, "Is Brother Elijah running the action in Detroit?"

"Yes, sir."

"Tell him to turn on the heat, Brother."

"Yes, sir."

Aziz had already moved the Detroit War Zone to the big screen, Talib watching as Ishmael's order reached the crowd. They broke from their singing immediately, throwing their candles at the FPF guard lined up fifty yards distant.

They charged the edge of the Zone screaming, "God is great!" They threw rocks, but when the nausea gas hit the blacktop, the real artillery came out.

"Guns!" Aziz yelled. "What are you doing?"

"What I should have done all along!" Ishmael returned. "At this point, this is the only way. Perhaps we can draw enough viewers to keep them away from their voting buttons. Maybe we can hold our lead. Get Miami on the horn!"

"The bottom's dropping out of Detroit!" the poll watcher called. "We're down five percent now."

"Tell them to hold," Ishmael said, pacing furiously. He pointed to a man working a small monitor. "What's the screen comparison breakdown?"

"We're still winning in cities where we have no presence," the man returned over the aural.

"Brother," Aziz said, intruding softly in the aural. "About Detroit. . . ."

"Abort Detroit immediately," Ishmael said. Frowning deeply, he strode into the midst of the action. People were furiously working their screens and downloading stats. "Cease all operations!" Ishmael commanded. The room suddenly quieted, all eyes on him.

The word went out quickly, the Zones breaking their

candlelight vigils, the Detroit rioters already escaping back behind their walls.

"Now what?" Aziz said.

"You have the nerve to ask me that?" Ishmael put a finger right in his brother's face. "We are going to lose, and I blame you." He then pointed to Talib. "And I blame you."

"Violence is not the answer. I'm begging you to keep peace," Aziz said.

"No!" Ishmael shouted. He whirled away from his brother and shoved through the crowd, exiting through the side door without a backward glance.

Chapter 17

THE SALTON TROUGH

**IMPERIAL VALLEY PROJECT
BOMBAY BEACH, CALIFORNIA
15 JUNE 2028, 11:00 A.M.**

Lewis Crane took the eggbeater up into the puffy clouds, bright white against a hard blue sky, then dipped quickly down. Charlie, two days shy of eighteen months of age, clapped his hands and giggled. He was sitting on his mother's lap, a huge, yellow plush elephant in his own little lap.

"You know what clouds are, Charlie?" Crane asked as he banked south, headed for the Project. "They're water."

Charlie made a gurgling noise. He seemed to adore his parents, and delighted them by listening intently to every word they spoke to him, responding often with a profound string of gibberish.

"And how much does a cloud weigh?"

The child's eyes, hazel like his mother's, opened wide.

As if he could understand everything his father said, he looked out at the sky. He was just learning to speak. He pointed a pudgy finger and said, "Coud . . . coud."

"That's right, pal. Cloud," Crane said. "Bet you think those clouds don't weigh a thing . . . like spiderwebs. But a really big cloud weighs a lot. Ten million pounds maybe. Big. Big, huh?"

"Big," Charlie repeated, opening his arms wide. He held up his stuffed animal. "Elly-pant."

"Yeah," Crane said, excited. "Maybe two elephants." Beaming, he looked over at Lanie. "Did you hear that? Two new words—cloud and elephant—and he got the point about size!"

Lanie chuckled, smoothing Charlie's hair while resisting the temptation to tease Crane. What the heck, though, Charlie *was* bright, probably not ready to make an acceptance speech in Stockholm, but Crane was justified in the pride he took in their son. How he loved Charlie. And what a terrific father he was. Most important of all, though, Lanie thought, was that Charlie was sweet-tempered, curious, and affectionate. Almost as if he could read her thoughts, Charlie twisted around and planted a wet kiss on her jaw. She was laughing as they spotted the Project hundreds of feet below.

As usual, there were protesters around the outer gates of the Project compound. They'd been there since groundbreaking, which had occurred just a few days after Charlie's birth. Mohammed Ishmael had enlarged the scope of NOI protests while escalating their violence. Their avowed purpose in picketing Northwest Gemstone was to stop Crane from pursuing what they called "his mad schemes to wreak nuclear havoc to stop earthquakes." That, Lanie and Crane knew, had come from only one source—Dan Newcombe. Well, Abu Talib, as he called himself now.

They'd feared when Dan had resigned from the Foundation that he'd go public with what he knew about Crane's dream; they were only surprised he'd waited so long . . . or that it had taken him such a time to learn about Northwest Gemstone and put two and two together. So far, they hadn't lied to the public. In fact, they hadn't

made any public statements at all. But they didn't have to
lie, because the public was disinclined to believe NOI. After the loss of the referendum on an NOI homeland, Mohammed Ishmael had become much more prominent, often
eclipsing Dan in the number and apparent importance of
speeches, appearances on teev, and before their people.
And it was no doubt that it was Mohammed Ishmael who
had returned the NOI to a warlike regimen of terrorist
attacks.

The War Zones had rioted all at once, then moved farther out into the cities themselves—suicide bombers, cars
full of gunmen shooting anyone unfortunate enough to be
on the streets, full-scale urban warfare.

And every time another shooting, another bombing occurred, Mohammed Ishmael immediately claimed credit
and said that the terror would stop the moment that NOI
got a homeland—and Crane was stopped.

Liang Int continued to back the project, mainly because
they couldn't afford to lose face to Yo-Yu, whose new
logo, the letters YOU done in blood red seemed to speak
directly to the common man. Yo-Yu had been a phenom-
enon. Their chips had become remarkably sophisticated,
able to create effects in which the brain couldn't differ-
entiate between reality and illusion. They'd gotten so
good, in fact, that Mr. Tang's attempts at competing with
a similar product were failing miserably due to inferior
quality. There was simply too large a technological gap,
and Yo-Yu guarded its secrets very carefully.

Then there was the Mississippi Valley. Yo-Yu, flush
with chip capital, for chips were indeed superseding dorph
in the marketplace, had made an offer for the entire area
which Liang had accepted. It had made Mr. Mui happy,
since it enabled Liang America to show a profit for calendar '27. Yo-Yu then had pumped money into the entire
midwest, which had energized the area. It had become a
frontier boomtown, the disenfranchised moving in from all
over, taking the places of those who'd left after the quake
and its persistent aftershocks.

Boisterous and beyond the law, the people of the Mississippi Valley had turned it into the hot spot for fast

money and easy deals—and that had given Yo-Yu the foothold it needed in basic areas—land ownership, timber, chemical plants, agriculture—so it could make a real run at breaking Liang America.

And they'd gotten the people. The best public relations project the world had seen was the ozone regeneration project, an idea they'd stolen from Liang. Yo-Yu's project had replenished twenty-seven percent of the atmosphere's ozone supply, helping everyone without cost. People were once again going out in the sun with no fear of skin cancer. Trees thought long dead were regenerating. In the off-year elections in '26, Yo-Yu had taken eighty-nine seats in the House of Representatives, so many that a kind of political balance had been established, and actual debate on real issues was heard once more in Congress.

Crane buzzed the protesters, padding to his outside loudspeaker as a small sea of faces cursed and shook fists up at him. "You are trespassing on private property," he said, Charlie laughing and clapping again when he heard his father's booming voice. "Leave the area immediately. We are going to begin riot exercises with a deadly chemical spray. Leave immediately."

He banked up, watching them scatter below him. He padded onto Project Control. "Turn on the sprinklers," he said, all of them laughing as the plain water hoses came on, spraying the people. The protesters ran, stumbling and choking, gasping for breath—brought to their knees by the power of suggestion. Crane changed the joke every few days so that word wouldn't get around.

They cleared the ten-foot fence, their small FPF contingent waving as they passed. For all his bluster, Brother Ishmael had never attacked the compound directly, perhaps afraid to wander too far from a core War Zone. Or he might have been afraid he was right about unstable nuclear material being worked in the compound.

"He said the machines won't dig?" Lanie asked as they cleared the fence to take the last five miles to the compound.

"Mr. Panatopolous is very upset and wants to change the finish date."

"So, what's new? He bellyaches more than any ten people."

"That's Mr. Panatopolous' forte, my love. Our Pany's creative contribution to the world. I'd kind of miss it if he changed."

"What did you tell him?"

"I told him I'd have my wife look into it," he answered, wiggling his eyebrows. "You will look into it, won't you?"

She nodded. "It sounds like a calibration problem again. The diggers go off line after awhile and nobody notices until they stop working."

They bullseyed the two-story containment building, its windowless, domelike construction a concrete wart on the flat desert of Bombay Beach. The site was on the eastern shore of the Salton Sea, several miles from a large retirement community. Farther east were the San Bernardino Mountains. Salton gleamed like diamonds under the bright morning sun. Thirty miles long and ten miles wide, it had sprung into being in 1905 when the Colorado River broke through irrigation headgates and flooded the area. Though called a sea, Salton was actually a shallow saline lake. The Project pulled water from it for its reactors.

But that wasn't why they'd built here. Salton was 232 feet below sea level, so they could dig from a low point. More importantly, the Salton Trough sat squarely atop California's most important fault convergence. Just beneath the Sea, the San Andreas and Imperial Faults became one, the Imperial Fault the final tear all the way to the Gulf of California. The joined faults then moved north, interconnecting with other faults and inactive volcanoes. Not only was the Salton Sea the place to bottle up San Andreas, but also to coldcock at least three other faults at the same time. The globe showed how important it was to get at these other faults, because it demonstrated that by 2070, thirteen years after Southern California would become the island of Baja, the rest of the state would crack right up through the Salton from the Mexican border to Oregon, turning California into a jutting peninsula, the shores of the Pacific lapping against Arizona and Nevada.

Crane was planning to stop all of that in one bold action two weeks hence.

He landed on the blacktop next to the containment building, where workers were hosing it down after a Masada pass-over the night before. Masada was finally beginning to dissipate and would be gone in the next few years. Endings and beginnings. Three months earlier a group of forty Jewish scientists had braved the still intense radiation of Israel to set up a closed-environment settlement in the leveled city of Jerusalem. Their dome abutted the remnants of the Western Wall, all that was left from Solomon's temple built three millennia previously. The Islamic world complained mightily and made threats. The Jews stayed in Jerusalem. Two babies already had been born in the land of their forefathers.

Turn of the wheel, Crane had thought at the time. *Take that, Brother Ishmael.*

They set down next to Containment, climbing out and walking toward the profusion of small buildings scattered across the flat plain. There were barracks for the permanent troops, a cafeteria and amusements building, equipment sheds, and the motor pool area where all of Mr. Panatopolous' bizarre anthropomorphic digging machines lived. In the distance on the salt flats, a two-hundred-foot hill of excavated rock and dirt stood as the highest point in the immediate area.

The elevator to the cavern looked just like another building. Three stories tall, it also had no windows. Yellow dust blew through the camp on the hot desert air. They hurried to the entryway, Lanie carrying Charlie. She pulled his brimmed cap down over his face to keep the dust out of his mouth, he pushed it back up. Charlie took naturally to the desert.

They voiceprinted into the entry, then walked the fifteen feet in darkness to the inner door, equally large to get heavy equipment in and out. Here all three went through optical scan and fingerprint.

The elevator doors came open with a hydraulic whoosh, and they stepped into a plain metal cylinder twenty feet high with a thirty-foot radius. It could carry a hundred people or sixty tons of equipment. The elevator was a giant electromagnet that used the earth's own magnetic field as propulsion. The elevator hovered at the top of a twenty-mile abyss with no external apparatus to hold it in place and with no brakes. There were two buttons just inside the door—an up arrow and a down arrow.

The center of the cylinder was carpeted, comfortable seating and amusements awaiting guests for the twenty-minute ride down. Lanie plopped heavily onto a couch. Charlie went right for the holobuilder, a handheld projection machine that created blocks that could be stacked and arranged to construct almost anything. Charles Crane enjoyed stacking them up to the top of the room, then knocking out the bottom one to see them tumble.

Crane watched his son, doting only the way an older father could. At forty-one, he didn't feel especially old, but he'd led an eventful life, enough for any ten people, and his recent mellowing had made him glad he was seeing his dream through now. He feared losing the manic energy that had driven him before. This was too important to the world to take off the pressure. He was becoming damned civilized; and soon, he suspected, would come acceptance . . . then complacency . . . then the death of creativity.

"Are you going to have to put back the date?" Lanie asked as Charlie's tower of blocks toppled into their midst, much to the boy's glee.

"We'll be fine," Crane answered from an easy chair, Charlie zapping his blocks and beginning again, this time with pyramids. "I'm just glad we're getting this done before the next elections."

"Maybe all that horrid violence will stop then, too." She stretched out on the sofa. The elevator moved soundlessly except for a small contact point clack every ten seconds.

"Are you all right?" Crane asked.

"It's nothing . . . I'm a little tired. I didn't sleep well last night."

"Bad dreams?"

"It's nothing, I said."

"Lanie. . . ."

She sat up, on the edge of the couch, tensed. "Do you remember that dream I used to have?"

"The Martinique dream? Sure. It went away after your memory returned."

"It's back," she said. "I had it last night." She shook her head. "So . . . real. I could feel the fire burning my legs, and the screaming and—"

"It's just a dream, Lanie," he said, moving to the sofa to sit next to her. He put his arms around her and held her tight.

She melted against him. "The crazy part is . . . the place, the place where it happens in the dream looks a lot like where we are right now."

He kissed her on the cheek. "Your brain is simply putting what you know into the dream, that's all."

"No," she said, stiffening in his grasp. "It hasn't changed. It's always looked like that in the dream."

He turned her face to his. "What are dreams?" he asked.

"Random electrical impulses in the cerebral cortex. The brain interprets them as it chooses." She held his gaze. "So how come I saw this place in a dream four years ago?"

"Coincidence," he said. "One cavern's pretty much like another." The Project had been a strain on everyone, and he'd be glad when this was done. When he sold the package to the world, it would be with someone else as coordinator. He was ready to rest, to spend some time enjoying his family.

"Maybe."

They were getting closer. Crane could feel the deceleration in his stomach. The elevator disgorged them in a large lobby of concrete walls and steel supports, well lit. Several hallways ran off the lobby, going to different parts of the Project. They took the administrative hallway past visitor reception/processing and down to the computer room.

They stopped at the doorway, Lanie handing Charlie to Crane. "Here, go with your daddy to visit Mr. Panatopolous while Mommy puts the big project back on stream."

"Come on, pal," Crane said. "We'll go watch the diggers."

"Dig-gers!" Charlie said, excited.

The hallway ended at a set of metal stairs, an Authorized Personnel Only sign tacked beside it. They took the stairs and entered the cavern.

It was huge, over fifteen hundred feet across. The natural cave's ceiling was one hundred feet overhead. Branching out on either side of the main cavern were Mr. Panatopolous' caverns. Wide enough for trucks and equipment, they stretched for three miles in either direction. Brilliant lighting made the place glow, though it stayed cool at the natural sixty-nine degrees of the earth's underground.

The computer room, large and glassed-in, overlooked the cavern. "Wave to your mother, pal. She expects it."

Crane and Charlie waved up to the window, Lanie smiling warmly and returning the wave. They were symbiotic, Crane and Lanie, meshing perfectly in every aspect of their lives. They shared the duties of caring for Charlie, worked when they wanted to or needed to. More than anything, they understood and respected what drove the other. Neither was subservient. For the first time in his life, Crane understood the saying, "Man was not meant to be alone."

He put Charlie on the floor. The boy made a beeline for the three-wheeled carts used in the caverns. Crane hurried after him and they climbed in. "Call Mommy," he said, holding his wristpad out to Charlie, who immediately reached over and hit the P fiber. Lanie came over Crane's aural. "Hey, we're working up here."

"Yeah, yeah. Would you tell me where Panatopolous is?"

"Corridor A," she replied. "All the way down."

"Thanks, love. Bye."

He padded off and keyed the focus, the vehicle jerking off to purr along the poured concrete floor. As they made their way through the cavern toward corridor A, the power came into view. Holes the size of swimming pools and spaced every thirty feet were cut straight down into the rock. They were surrounded by rails. Each hole went down four miles, and running up its center was a tube with a one-foot diameter, packed with nuclear material. There were one hundred tubes.

The cart veered to the left, taking A corridor, which twisted and turned by the holes with their packed tubes meant to weld the widely divergent faults that crisscrossed the area. They were so far beneath Salton now, the lake so shallow the explosions below would barely ripple the water.

Large readouts posted every half mile kept track of the radiation in the chamber. There were occasional small leaks, easily plugged in a system not meant to last beyond the week after next. With the amazing amounts of radioactive material they'd been using the last eighteen months, it was remarkable they'd never had a real problem. It was what enabled them to finish ahead of schedule and before the elections, which, it was universally expected, would result in a Yo-Yu sweep victory and, since word about the Project was spreading and gaining credence with the public, it might mean the cancellation of the Project.

The corridor kept twisting, fault stress, shearing, and compression fractures evident everywhere on the rock walls, a geological treasure trove of Nature's possibilities. This entire landscape would become molten rock when the devices were triggered.

They hit a straight stretch of corridor, and spotted Mr. Panatopolous' rockeater about one hundred feet ahead at the end of the line. The little man paced back and forth angrily, as always. True to his word, Crane had thought of the man who'd helped them dig through the alluvial mud in Reelfoot when it came time to award the digging subcontract, hiring Panatopolous for the entire job and offering him a fifty percent incentive if he brought it in by the end of March.

"It's about time you got here," Pany said as they drove up, relaxing into a smile the moment he saw Charlie.

"Hey, there's my big boy," Panatopolous said, pulling him out of the cart to hold him in the air. Charlie laughed but his eyes were fixed on the ten-foot digger that looked like a praying mantis. "You're growing every day."

Charlie was the unofficial mascot of the Project, having literally grown from a sprout to a toddler under the watchful eyes of sixty employees.

Crane walked to the machine, its snout dipped down into the half-dug hole, the hole's terminus too far below to see. A man-size cage hung just inside the lip of the hole. These cages were designed to carry a worker down to check for leakage in the core, and eventually to trigger the thousands of pounds of plastique built into the tube that would begin the nuclear reaction.

The digger had a powerful drill bit on the end that literally chopped up the rock below. The rubble was then sucked back up the tube and into the machine's innards, a long, cylindrical chamber that powdered the rock to dust with ultrasound, then spewed it into the back of a waiting dump truck for transport to the man-made mountain aboveground.

Panatopolous carried Charlie over to his father. "I could'a been finished with this if I wasn't tied in to your damned computers. A hole's a hole. Why do you have to check my holes?"

"You know a great deal about holes," Crane said. "I know about what's in them."

"There's nothing in a hole. It's empty."

Crane smiled at him. "How much does a cloud weigh?" he asked.

"What?"

Crane's pad bleeped on Lanie's fiber. He tapped on. "I'm looking at a non-op digger," he said. "Talk to me."

"Don't you dare let Charlie down on the floor near that open hole," she returned in his aural.

"Roger."

"Tell our unhappy friend that he has to recalibrate his digger point oh nine five centimeters at twenty-three degrees. . . ."

"Point oh nine five centimeters at twenty-three degrees," Crane said, Panatopolous cursing, then excusing himself to Charlie.

". . . he's making the fault part of his tunnel. The computers won't deal with the inherent incongruity of a moving tunnel."

"Got it. Anything else?"

She was silent for several seconds.

"Lanie?"

"There are two groups here for a scheduled tour."

"So?"

"One of them is a small group from the Nation of Islam."

"What? I never authoriz—"

"I'm sorry, Crane," she said softly. "Sumi called me yesterday and asked if we could do this as a personal favor, a way, perhaps, of curtailing the violence. You weren't available; I was up to my ears . . . I said yes, then forgot to tell you."

"Don't let anybody past reception. I'm on my way," Crane said, already moving to take Charlie from Panatopolous. Crane was so famous that he commanded great attention. At the onset of digging, people had clamored to come to the site to meet Crane. The best public relations, they'd decided, was to accept a few groups for limited tours focusing on the geology of the cavern. All part of the cover, too, to keep the project secret.

"Crane," Lanie said. "Dan's part of the team."

Anger burst inside him. "I can't believe he'd have the nerve to come here."

"I'm looking right at him," Lanie said.

Abu Talib stood uneasily in the locker-filled visitors' lounge with Khadijah, who was pregnant with their second child, and Martin Aziz. He could feel the hatred for Crane that he knew now he had felt from the first, but had suppressed totally in the early days.

Here, in the caverns of Crane's insanity, he knew the structure of Evil. A gaggle of fifth graders from Niland Elementary charged around the room, chased by their teacher trying to calm them down. Talib noticed none of it. He listened to the sounds: mechanical sounds, workers' voices, the drone of the circulation systems. They were the sounds of an online operating system, the reality of Crane's exercise in playing God. If he'd had the slightest doubt about his suspicions before, it was gone now. He didn't even have to look around. He knew there would be shafts below, many of them, and all packed with nuclear explosives.

Though godless himself, Talib was very sensitive to the notions of natural law. The Earth was good, a product of all that had gone before. Its processes were sacrosanct. Study them, certainly, try to live in harmony with them, absolutely. Control them? Blasphemy. He thought about Newton's laws of motion—every action causing an equal and opposite reaction. How would the Earth react to Crane's assault?

Abu Talib felt rage rise in him. He carried the weight of righteousness on his shoulders. He had to do what no one else could: stop the madman before he destroyed the planet.

"I can't believe you'd actually come here."

Talib's head snapped in the direction from which Crane's voice had come. Crane was flanked by two G, Lanie hung back somewhat, holding her child, her white child. "And I can't believe you're actually going to do this," he said.

Lanie shoved through the G to enter the room. "Hello, children," she said to the fifth graders, who had stopped playing when they'd heard the exchange between the two men. "I'd like to ask all of you to choose a locker and remove any communication equipment you may be wearing. Turn off your aurals. Remove your pads and put them in the lockers."

They did as they were told. "Thank you," Lanie said. "Now please go with the policeman, who will give you a tour of the rocks and gems room."

The children filed out behind one of the blank-faced security guards. Crane and the other G moved into the processing room to circle the three people.

"So how many people have you killed today, Dan?" Crane asked. "Have we topped the three-thousand mark yet?"

"Leave him alone," Khadijah said. "We fight a war of liberation. People die in wars."

"You must be the wife," Crane said, moving close to her.

"I will ignore all that, Crane, as NOI is not the issue," Talib said. "I'm here to give you one last chance to come to your senses. Please stop this insanity now. Walk away from it."

"You know me one hell of a lot better than that," Crane returned.

"But I do not know you at all, Dr. Crane," Martin said.

Crane stared at the man's white robes. "And who might you be?"

"Someone who abhors violence as much as you," Aziz returned.

"Then you're associating with a bad crowd."

Lanie stepped forward with the baby, Talib's insides tightening up. "Hello, Dan," she said softly, and he folded his arms to keep his hands from shaking.

"So you're Lanie," Khadijah said, stepping between the woman and Abu. "I am Khadijah, the wife of Abu Talib. You have a beautiful son."

"Thank you," Lanie said, her eyes still fixed on Talib. "I hear you have a daughter?"

"And a son on the way," Khadijah said, patting her stomach. "Did your son inherit his father's insanity?"

"I hope so," Lanie said coldly, still looking at Talib. "Why can't you leave us alone, Dan? What have we done to you?"

He broke the eye contact as he felt his resolve crack. "You don't understand," he said. "Lanie, this may destroy the planet!"

"Okay," Crane said. "I want you out."

Talib had never known Crane to hate anyone, but he could feel it now, pulsing from the man in agonizing waves. The enemy. Talib did not protest Crane's order.

They returned to processing from the computer room, where a janitor was sweeping just outside. As Talib passed beside the man, a disk was slipped into his jacket pocket.

They reached Processing, and Talib slipped the disk

from his pocket, fed it into the slot in his pad and copied it. He coughed to cover the copy completion bleep, then palmed the disk, slipping it into the trash can by the door as the janitor moved into Processing to sweep.

Crane and the FPF led them back to the elevators, the fifth graders charging down the hall to join them within minutes. As they walked into the massive lift, Crane grabbed Talib by the arm to stare furiously at him. "I don't know what you're doing here after all this time," he said, "but make it the last time. I don't ever want, or intend, to see your face again."

"Take your hand off of me," Talib said, jerking free as the door closed between them.

Crane's last view of the man was his eyes, bright as lava with hatred. The pipeline of negative emotion worked both ways.

"Crane!" Lanie called, charging down the hall, Charlie happily riding on her back. "Crane!"

She reached him, out of breath, frowning at the closed doors of the elevator. "They've gone," she said.

"Immediately. Of course. Did something happen?"

"We're missing a disk."

"Which one?"

"Basic design schematics, blueprints, structural analysis."

"Show me," he said, already heading down the hallway. "If they took something, we've got time to stop them aboveground."

They rushed to the computer room, dark and cool, hewn out of bare rock.

"I'd pulled it," she said, "to check Pany's alignment problems, then set it right—"

"Here?" Crane said, picking up a small disk from the other side of the keyboard and holding it up for her.

"That's it!" she said, taking it from him to stick in the disk lockbox. Then she turned and looked hard at him. "I didn't put it there."

"Are you sure?"

She nodded, Crane staring straight up at the ceiling as if he could see Talib right through solid rock.

Chapter 18

HIDDEN FAULTS

**IMPERIAL VALLEY PROJECT
30 JUNE 2028, 9:18 P.M.**

Harry Whetstone's voice echoed down the cavern as he spoke from the small podium set up in the main cavern to the cadre of associates who'd worked the Project. Crane watched him with a strange sense of calm, of demons conquered.

"We stand this evening at a crossroads of history," Stoney said, looking frail, looking old. "I never thought that I'd stand inside of a bomb, much less the biggest bomb in the history of the world. I never thought I'd *want* to see a bomb explode, but in this case I can't wait. We stand on the brink of mankind's next step—the taming of our own environment for the good of not only everyone alive, but of everyone yet to be born. And I'm proud to have played a small part in its realization.

"I say a small part because only one person is primary in the achievement of this great goal, a man whose insight and tireless devotion alone has made this gargantuan leap possible—Lewis Crane!"

Cheers and applause broke out from the seventy people present, sounding louder because of the echo. The attendees included the Project laborers, plus the power brokers and supporters who'd given themselves to Crane's dream—Sumi Chan, Kate Masters, Stoney, Messrs. Tsao and Tang, Burt Hill, and the key personnel from the Foundation.

Crane waved to the crowd, and Whetstone raised a glass of champagne. "To you, Crane!" he called. "You have challenged impossible odds with indomitable courage!"

Everyone drank, Lanie moving up beside him to hug his good arm tightly. "You did it," she said and kissed him on the cheek. "You really did it."

"We all did it," Crane said. "Everyone here has helped make it happen . . . especially you."

"You're the fulcrum, Crane."

"Are you okay?" he asked. He'd been wondering about her all day. She was there physically, but seemed to be deep in thought, thoughts she wasn't expressing in words.

"I'm feeling strange," she said. "This has been a hell of a haul."

"Yeah," he returned, hugging her close, drinking in her feel, her smell. "I love you so much."

"Oh, Crane," she said, kissing him deeply on the mouth, then smiling up into his eyes, "you'll never know . . . never understand the magic you've made in my life."

"Can I ever understand," he whispered. "I never had a life until I met you. A wife . . . a family—I never thought these things were possible for me, I—"

She silenced him with a kiss, then said something quite odd. "Never forget the moments we've had," she said in deadly earnest. "They'll keep me with you always."

There was something about how she said those words that chilled him to the bone. The hairs on the back of his neck stood on end.

"Congratulations, Crane," said Mr. Mui, bowing formally. "You've delivered early, within budget, no labor problems, no scientific problems. You paid for it yourself and have pledged to return the area to its natural state when you leave. You are a man of your word, sir. I appreciate that."

"And I appreciate Liang Int's commitment to our goal." Crane also bowed. "You didn't buckle, even under pressure."

Again Mr. Mui bowed. Smiling, Lanie said, "Well, in just about twelve hours we will have the culmination of the project—and my husband's dream. You gentlemen will have to excuse me. I seem to have misplaced my son."

She left them then, though Charlie had been merely an excuse. She knew exactly where her son was. She was doing everything she could to hold herself together tonight. While everyone else was celebrating, she'd drawn inward, fearful. The nightly dreams of death were more intense than ever and all day today she'd felt a cloud of doom floating about her. She'd been unable to shake it and spent most of her time trying to hide her apprehension from others.

Kate was lugging Charlie around. He was a boy whose feet very rarely touched the ground. Kate and Sumi were talking by the buffet table, Charlie leaning out to sneak canapés, which he promptly threw at anyone walking past.

Lanie made her way through the excited crowd to join them, grabbing Charlie's arm just as he was about to launch a food missile on a low trajectory right at Whetstone's head.

"So who's handling whom?" she asked, taking the boy, who was beginning to look tired and irritable. It was way past his bedtime.

"I'll take aunt duty anytime to motherhood," Kate said, realigning her sequins. "Play with 'em, wear 'em out, then give 'em back to mama."

"You have a very wonderful child," Sumi said, turning to her left and speaking to empty air. "Don't you think, Paul?"

"Paul?"

"I'm sorry," Sumi said, shaking her head. "Let me introduce you. Paul, this is Elena King Crane."

"C-call me Lanie," she said, narrowing her eyes and looking at Kate.

"Paul is Sumi's chipmate," Kate said. "A friend from Sumi's own mind. Someone to talk with, share with."

"You mean like an imaginary friend?" Lanie asked.

Sumi laughed with Paul, her gaze on thin air. "Imaginary to you," she said. She looked at Lanie. "To me he's my better half. He's intelligent, wise . . . loves to do things: to travel, go to parties, hiking. In fact, we were wondering if it would be all right if Paul and I did a little exploring down here?"

"Well, sure," Lanie said. "Take one of those carts parked beneath the computer room overlook. Go wherever you want, but watch out for the nuke ports. Fall down one and it's four miles nonstop to the bottom."

"Thanks." Sumi smiled, then turned to Paul. "Let's go."

They wandered off, Lanie looking at Masters. "Is Sumi all right?'

"Yeah." Kate smiled. "It's a Yo-Yu thing. The chip draws directly from the subconscious, but it also stores previous load, like an extra brain, enabling each experience with your 'friend' to be recalled and built upon. You've been locked up underground too long or you'd have seen this with many people. The chip is a way for basically lonely people to have companionship. Better than that, older people who are not only lonely, but alone, find a whole new world of attachment and happiness in a relationship that doesn't tax them or judge them."

"But Sumi's Vice President of the United States," Lanie returned. "Does he always go out in public that way?"

"Not always," Kate said, "but a lot. I think that Paul is relatively aggressive in not wanting to miss anything."

"You better be sure to warn me when Paul's around. I don't want to step on his toes or anything."

"The chip is very agile. It avoids contact with others."

"You act as if we're talking about a real person."

"As real as Sumi, I suppose," Kate said. "What about you? You don't look as excited as I would have expected you to be on the most important night of your life."

"It's that obvious?"

"In fact you look scared, honey. What's wrong?"

"I don't know," Lanie said, holding Charlie close to her breast, nuzzling him with her cheek. "This cavern has begun to feel like a . . . a crypt, or something. When this is over, I never want to go in another cave as long as I live."

"You're the second person I've heard say that tonight."

"Who's the other?"

"Burt Hill."

Burt Hill was at the bottom of Tube #33, systematically searching for conspirators. He had climbed out of the cage and was walking around the nuclear core, a journey of ten seconds' duration. He'd felt danger all over him, the way he used to before Doc Crane had taken him out of the hospital and given him a job. Like a sudden chill descending and enfolding him, he could feel the icy grip of betrayal strangling his heart.

He looked up to see faint light, a glowing spot four miles above, a giant eye looking down at him. He climbed back in the cage and hit the lever. The cage zipped silently upward, markers on the wall indicating how far he'd risen. The wall was paved with explosives. He could never check all hundred tubes tonight. He'd have to think of something else. Then an idea hit him.

Crane sat with Whetstone in the computer room. For once, Stoney was more drunk than Crane. Although, Crane thought, that wasn't quite true. Since Lanie had stepped into his soul, he scarcely drank. They watched the party through the window, its sound muffled.

"Do you find it like a dream sometimes?" Whetstone asked, his skin pale, nearly translucent, his lips tinged purple.

"All this?" Crane asked. "Not a dream, actually. Hell, I was here for every shovelful of dirt that came out of that stinking desert ground. It's too real to me. But . . . there *is* something . . . I don't know how to put it."

"Let me help you." Stoney smiled. "You've devoted your entire life to one thought, one goal. Now that you're on the verge of achieving it, you feel disconnected somehow, maybe even useless."

"You've been there, haven't you?"

"That's where I was when I met you, dear boy. A man can make only so much money before its pursuit loses its fire. You and your wild notions put the fire back in my life. And, with this, I feel like my life has been worthwhile."

"So, what do we do now?"

"I die now, Crane."

"Oh, come on, Stoney. This isn't the night to—"

"No," Whetstone said. "It's true. My life of drive and dissipation has finally caught up with me."

"Isn't there anything to be done?"

Whetstone shrugged. "They have all these extraordinary machines for keeping rich folk alive for decades after we should have died. That's not for me. Too ghoulish. I lived as a man. I'll not die as Suction Valve A-57 of some damned machine."

"How long have you got?"

The man looked wistful. "How long does it take a leaf to detach itself from a tree in the fall and float to the ground? It's fall, Crane."

Crane looked him in the eye without pity or anguish. They were both men who knew what death was and weren't afraid of it. "I'm going to miss you," he said.

"You and my ex-wives." Stoney laughed feebly. "They'll have to find a way to support themselves now. I'm leaving everything to the Foundation."

"The Foundation doesn't need your money."

"I know you, Crane. I know how you think, how you live. Your life will have to go on beyond tomorrow morning. You'll have to think of what to do next. The Foundation, at this point, pretty well runs itself. You'll be at a loss."

"I've thought about that."

The man set his drink on the floor and reached out for Crane's good hand. "You're a wise man, Crane," he said, "but age also brings its own wisdom. Listen to me: Dedicate your life to something new, something positive.

You're a special human being and have dreams to contribute that no one else has. Don't lose sight of yourself. Work as hard on the last day of your life as the first. You taught me the value of dedication. I'm giving it back to you now. Remember our three-billion-dollar bet?"

"Remember it? It made all this possible."

"Well, sometime you're going to want to take another three-billion-dollar gamble and my old bones will dance with joy in my grave if I am the one who can make it happen."

"Thank you, Stoney. For everything. You've been like a father to me."

"It's been my most extreme pleasure to have known you, to have shared your dreams," the man said, standing, leaning heavily on his Tennessee poplar cane. He started for the door, then stopped and turned back. "Except for that plane you gave away that time." He shook his head. "Lost a wife over that one. It had been a birthday present."

"Are you talking about Yvette . . . the wife who was playing hide-the-stick with every delivery boy who walked in the front door?"

"Yeah. I guess there was that about her. I find as I get older, I only remember the good things." He stared at Crane for a long moment, then raised his cane, pointing it. "I'll see you in hell, boy."

Crane watched him go, and knew he'd never see Stoney again. Man's bodily functions moved only toward death, but the mind could continue to enrich itself even as everything else embraced entropy. It was dignity that Stoney exemplified tonight, and Crane hoped he was half the man Harry Whetstone was.

Suddenly, Burt Hill replaced Whetstone in the doorway. "Boss, we gotta talk."

"All right," Crane said. He moved over to the radiation monitoring station, a hundred green lights blinking there. "What do you want to talk about?"

"How long would it take to blow this thing?" Hill was pacing, wringing his hands.

"I don't know . . . an hour or so to get everything set,

then the time to get out, get some distance. Remote trigger, you know."

"Let's get everybody out of here and do it now."

"May I ask why?"

Hill walked closer. His eyes peered wildly at Crane. "Because they're watching us, is why. They're just hangin' back, waiting. Waiting. Waiting for us to let our guard down."

"Who is?"

"Them!" Hill said loudly. "Can't you feel them? Their eyes crawling over us?"

"You're off your medication, aren't you, Burt?"

"I been off my medication for three years, Doc," he said loudly. "I'm telling you that if we're going to blow this thing, let's get everybody out of here and blow it now!"

Hill had been a strong right arm for ten years, but the strain down here was getting to all of them, Crane decided. He'd hired Burt for his paranoia. Maybe it was time to listen to it. "Okay, let's do it," Crane said. "I'll start moving the party out of here, while you take the service shaft up to ground level. Check around up there. Search the barracks and the other buildings. Tell the G to do a security sweep. When you're satisfied, get back down here. You and I will set up. We'll trigger when we get the urge. Fair enough?"

"Now you're talkin'," Hill said. "I'm on my way."

The second Burt left, one of the panel lights went to red with a quiet buzz, Crane bringing up the status report on the screen. Tube #61 in B Corridor was leaking a small amount of radiation, nothing serious, but a good enough excuse to clear the place out.

He found himself liking the idea, anxious now to get on with it, excited, in fact.

Abu Talib stood next to a Joshua tree. Through infrared binocs strapped to his head he watched the G moving around the outer perimeter fence of Crane's project three miles away. There were forty men with him, tucked in the San Bernadino foothills unseen, waiting for the right moment.

An avalanche of thoughts tumbled through his head. Lanie, her child, Crane, the Foundation—all producing a jumble of conflicting emotions. God, if only it could have been otherwise. Right. Wrong. Love. Hate. Loyalty. Abu Talib had no idea of what these words even meant anymore. The thrust of his life had become simple forward momentum, a ball rolling down an inclined plane.

He pulled off the binoculars and hung them on a Joshua branch. Strange how this desert tree, small and skeletal with clumps of leaves on the ends of the branches, reminded him of immature cotton plants. Or was the comparison farfetched, and he thought of the cotton because he'd much rather be in New Cairo preparing for harvest than here preparing a military action?

They were protected in a small gully, their three trucks, affixed with cattlecatchers, nearly invisible beneath desert camouflage.

Brother Ishmael walked up, handing him a cup of coffee. "Anything?" he asked.

"No," Talib said. "The guests are still there; the protesters have gone home; the G isn't alert."

"Good. Let's check the aerial view, then do the last briefing."

They moved back to their men, who were dressed in black and had on pulldown masks peeled up now to rest on their foreheads. The desert night was clear and cold with a brilliant full moon; the men, sitting on the ground, huddled together for warmth. A small screen that leaned against one of the Joshuas received its feed from Ishmael's condor, sweeping lazy circles in the sky over the Imperial Valley Project.

They saw a quiet compound with a parking lot full of cars and helos. Most of the permanent workers lived a few miles away in Niland. When they left tonight, all the cars would go with them. A lone man seemed to be methodically going through the outbuildings and speaking with the guards.

"Who is that?" Ishmael asked.

"His name's Burt Hill. He's Crane's ramrod and security chief. Only doing his job."

"Good. Allah guides our path tonight." Ishmael turned to the others. "As soon as the guests leave the party, we move in," he announced. "Put on your goggles and turn to the C fiber."

There was a groan from a platoon of men who'd gone through these steps many, many times in the last two weeks. They dutifully put on their goggles, Talib juicing the disk he had copied the day he'd inspected the underground abomination.

A virtual layout of the cavern appeared on the screen. The view moved past the computer room and down the stairs to the main room.

"Remember, there are carts at the bottom of the stairs," Talib said. "You are to use them. Red Team will take the corridor to the left . . . see it? That's A corridor. This was not a structure meant to stand for long, so it's unstable. Red Team will plant the satchel bombs on all the pillars in that corridor. Blue team will do the same in B corridor. The rest of you will carry three satchels each, everything set to blow in an hour. You'll drop your satchels down the tubes containing the bombs."

"And you're sure that throwing the satchels won't set off the nukes?" Ishmael asked.

Talib sighed. "You've asked that question a dozen times, and I have told you a dozen times that it takes a huge effort to set off a nuclear bomb, Brother. Our little bombs won't accomplish that. What they will accomplish is radiation leaks. Once we bring the place down, we want it to be so hot in there that no one would or could go back—ever. I'll get us in and handle the computer room. The truck bomb will take care of the shaft once we're done. Remember, if we handle this right, nobody gets hurt."

"The guests should leave very soon." Ishmael walked over to the tan-and-pale green camouflage cover and lifted it from one of the trucks. He got into the back and emerged with two heavy suitcases. He set them down and opened them. Weapons. Weapons he began to distribute to the Fruit of Islam.

"What is this?" Talib asked, following Ishmael to the back of the truck where a crate of ammo sat on the edge.

"You told me there'd be no violence," Talib whispered harshly.

Ishmael went back to the suitcase and pulled out a small submachine gun which he slung over his shoulder. "Brother Abu," he said. "We're getting ready to blow up an entire underground complex, and *you* set it up. That's violence in my dictionary."

"But the guns," Talib said. "We made a deal that no one would get hurt, that we'd only do this when the place was cleared."

"Do you hear that, my friends?" Ishmael said loudly. "Our brother wants us to fight a war with no casualties."

"Me, too!" someone shouted. "At least no casualties for us!"

Everyone laughed as they filled the ditty-bags hanging on their belts with extra clips of ammunition.

"Wait!" Talib said, grabbing Ishmael's arm. "This wasn't the deal we made."

Ishmael jerked his arm out of Talib's grasp. "You're a dreamer, Abu, without the guts to see your dreams through. How the hell do you expect us even to get on the grounds, eh? Ask the nice G if they'll invite us in for tea?"

"I just thought, I . . . don't know what I thought."

"Right," Ishmael said, donning a bandolier full of shotgun shells to go with the sawed-off weapon he carried in his free hand. "Remember, Brother Talib: Thinkers prepare the revolution; bandits carry it out."

He addressed his men. "Once we've committed, there's no turning back. We either succeed or die trying. We fight the Great Satan himself tonight and if we have to, we fight to the last man. Shoot to kill anyone or anything that gets in your way. We probably won't all make it back. If I get to Paradise first, I'll prepare the way for you by trying out the houris!"

The men cheered, holding their weapons in the air. Confusion paralyzed Talib. The event was suddenly upon him, happening fast. It wasn't talk anymore.

Ishmael jammed a pistol into his hand. "Here," he said. "You'll probably need this."

Talib looked morosely at the gun, then stuck it into the waistband of his black drawstring trousers.

Crane and Charlie waved good-bye to partygoers as they climbed onto the elevator, calling out their final congratulations. The radiation alert bleated gently in the background. As the doors closed, Lanie walked down the hall from computer control. She took Charlie from Crane. The boy immediately rested his head on his mother's shoulder and closed his eyes, thumb in his mouth.

"Sure you don't want to go with them?" Crane asked. "I may be a couple of hours here."

She shook her head. "Charlie can sleep in the computer room," she said. "I've got plenty of work there to prepare for tomorrow."

He nodded. "We're thinking along the same wavelengths. Burt and I decided to go ahead and rig the detonation now, no reason to wait. I'll get to it as soon as I check that leak in #63."

"It's a good-sized bleed-off," she returned. "Enough to be dangerous in a few hours' time. Did you tell anyone to send the elevator back down once they reached the top?"

"Burt's up there," Crane said, shaking his head. "He'll ride it down."

"You're going to trigger it tonight?" she asked, slowly rocking back and forth with Charlie.

He smiled. "Yeah."

"What made you decide to do it now?"

"Burt's antsy . . . I trust that," he said, raising an eyebrow. "*You're* turning claustrophobic. And the thing's as ready as it's ever going to be. Why wait?"

They started walking back down the hallway toward the computer room. "It's fine with me," she said, "but I've got a feeling there's a ton of inspectors and officials—"

"And demonstrators, and terrorists. If anyone's unhappy with this, they can sue me."

Both of them laughed, Lanie giving him a lingering kiss

when they reached the computer room door. "You seem happier already," he said.

"Are you kidding? You can't imagine how happy I'll be to get out of this place. I'm going to walk in that room, pack up my personal items, shut down the systems, arm the plastique, and kiss this place's ass goodbye. Where do you want to trigger it?"

He pressed her up against the door. "At home . . . while we're making love. We'll make the earth move."

"You already know how to do that, honey," she said, kissing him again. "Let's fly back to the Foundation tonight. Do we, uh . . . have *another* house somewhere?"

"Not that I know of."

"Maybe we should think about buying one. Charlie's going to need to know at some point soon that he's not the only child in the world."

"Noted," he said. "In fact, there's a lot of things we can do now that we're finished here. Let's take a vacation. We can go tomorrow. What's to stop us? We'll toss our wristpads and return to nature."

"How long has it been since you've been on a vacation?"

"I've never been on one," he said. "Thought it might be fun to try."

"I'll believe it when I see it."

"You will see it. I promise."

Chapter 19

DANSE MACABRE

**IMPERIAL VALLEY PROJECT
30 JUNE 2028, TWO MINUTES BEFORE MIDNIGHT**

Abu Talib's insides were in knots as he watched the guests emerge from the elevator tunnel and head toward their vehicles. He felt even worse than when he'd learned about Northwest Gemstone, understood it for the ruse it was, and forced himself to go public with scathing attacks on Crane.

Several helos belonging to guests leapt into the night sky, flying northward; cars lined up to move down the strip from the parking lot to the front gates.

"This is it," Ishmael said. "They'll hit us with nausea gas and disorienting soundwaves." Years of rioting had taught him and his Fruit of Islam well. "The rebreathers in your masks will protect you. If any of you have aurals, turn them off. They'll broadcast the sound right into your head if you don't. Know your assignments and keep the deafeners in your ears. They've got electric water cannons, but we'll be grinding them under our tires before they have the chance to turn them on. You know your jobs. Get to your vehicles!"

Yelling and cheering, getting themselves up for battle, the men hustled to their trucks. Frozen in place, Talib could only watch.

"If you don't have the strength of your convictions, stay here," Ishmael sneered at him.

"Crane's helo is still sitting in the yard," Talib said, pointing at the screen.

"Really?" Ishmael looked at the helo on the teev. "Allah blesses us. We can take care of the blasphemy and the blasphemer at the same time. Are you coming?"

His paralysis suddenly broken, he shouted, "Damn right I am." He hurried after Brother Ishmael to the deuce and a half. "We agreed: no killing."

Talib climbed into the passenger side of the heavy vehicle; Ishmael slid behind the wheel. In the distance, the line of headlights had snaked away from the gates of Crane's compound and was moving southward.

Brother Ishmael's mask still sat atop his head; his eyes glinted hard in the starlight. He opened the focus, and the truck shot forward, its cowcatcher zeroed on the gates three miles distant. Ishmael's jaw was set, his teeth bared. "They won't even see us until we're on top of them," he said low.

"Please," Talib whispered. "Promise me you won't hurt Crane if you find him."

"I won't hurt him," Ishmael said. "I will kill him."

"Ishmael—"

"Savor it," Ishmael said. "You are about to see justice in its purest form."

Ishmael reached up and hit a switch that activated all the cams they'd brought with them, including one in the truck. Both Ishmael and Talib, their faces exposed, were already flashing through the Net.

The three speeding trucks were abreast now, separated by thirty yards, bouncing on the uneven ground as the perimeter warning lights flared brilliantly white, lighting them to daylight. Added to this visual excitement was a prerecorded, carefully crafted speech by Ishmael explaining the objective and purpose of the holy mission they were undertaking.

"Here we go!" Ishmael yelled. He activated the sound blockers in his ears, pulled down his mask, and jerked up the hood of his burnoose.

Talib fumbled with his gear, his mind numb, heart racing, sweat pouring off him.

Gas!

They were driving blind, through roiling clouds of noxious gas, both men pulling down their goggles and going to infrared. Talib was shaking uncontrollably, his mouth dry. What was he doing here? What madness had put him in this truck?

They hit the razored fence with a loud clang, chain link hooking on the catcher, then whipping back to smash their windshield, turning it into a kaleidoscope of spiderwebs in the thick smoke.

He turned to Ishmael, who'd picked up his shotgun and set it against the windshield, then pulled the trigger and blew out the vestiges of the windshield. Suddenly a man stood before them. The catcher hit him at knee level, cutting him in two. His torso bounced onto the hood; his head punched through Talib's side of the windshield. The still-living man bled through the eye and mouth holes of his smiling FPF mask as his arms flailed wildly on the other side of the shattered glass.

Talib was screaming inside his own skull.

Burt Hill had just gone into the equipment shed to return a shovel he'd found on the grounds, when he heard gunfire popping like fireworks. He cautiously looked through a small window in the door to see three trucks in the compound.

The perimeter guards went down within seconds, their defensive systems useless against such a savage, surprise attack. One truck veered toward the barracks; the other two headed straight for the elevator building.

Explosions wracked the barracks. The first truck to reach the elevator plowed through the concrete-covered walkway leading to it. Chunks of concrete flew in all directions; screams mixed with the sounds of gunfire at the barracks.

Burt's finger went to his pad to hit Crane's emergency fiber, then froze. They'd be scanning for transmissions. If he communicated with Crane, they'd know Crane and his family were down there. They'd know where *he* was. There was nowhere to hide below except in the tubes themselves. Silence was his ally right now. He'd take the shaft service elevator down and make his stand in the tubes.

Shovel still in hand, he moved to the back of the equipment room and voiceprinted into the small elevator that serviced the shaft coils for the main lift. He climbed in, grimly determined, and hit the down button. This elevator wasn't as fast as the main lift, but it would get him there soon enough.

Abu Talib jumped out of the truck, yanked up his mask, and vomited. The G who'd come through the window had finally died, but not before pumping most of his blood through the carotid artery onto Talib. The dead man still lay on the hood of the truck. Talib shimmered with blood, dark heart blood, his clothes heavy with it.

Smoke drifted through the compound, and alarm horns blared. Automatic weapons fire finished off the rest of the G in the barracks. Talib was in shock.

The masked men, loaded down with satchels and weapons, poured out of the back of the truck into the thick of the rubble in the elevator entryway. At Ishmael's signal, everyone with an aural deactivated his sound blocker.

"God is great!" Ishmael shouted. "And we are His instruments!"

Ishmael grabbed Talib by the arm and pulled him to the entry security controls. "What does it take?" he asked. "Quickly!"

"Eye scan," Talib said. "Uh . . . uh . . . fingerprints. Sorry, I'm—"

"Bring the prisoner!" Ishmael called. The third truck

screeched to a halt and a G was dragged to the big sliding door.

Ishmael ripped off the smiling mask on the G to reveal a woman, her lips moving soundlessly, her eyes listless. Blood bubbled out from under her slick white uniform. Ishmael slammed her face against the scan screen as Talib stuck her right thumb on the plate. The controls went green; the big door popped open to cheers from the Fruit of Islam.

Ishmael heaved the woman aside. She slid down the wall to a sitting position, and he kicked her body into the doorway to keep it from closing.

"Bring in the bomb truck!" Ishmael yelled. The truck eased forward, men walking next to it through the wide doorway. Talib entered slowly, moving as if in the grip of a dream.

The bomb truck drove into the center of the elevator, knocking furniture aside, the rest of the men rushing in. It was meant to take out the elevator shaft, to seal the works below into a sarcophagus.

Ishmael shoved the G's body out of the way, the door closing immediately. He walked over to Talib.

"Pull yourself together, Brother," he said. "Be a man."

"If Crane's down there," Talib said, "it's possible that his wife and son are down there, too."

Ishmael smiled in satisfaction. "We could clean out the whole nest of vipers," he said, then turned to the man sitting in the driver's seat of the truck. "Hit the timer on the truck charge. Brothers, we have exactly one hour until the shaft blows."

Talib felt the elevator jerk to a start, then begin its slow descent into the precinct of Hell.

Lanie Crane heard the elevator's arrival bell from the computer room, followed by a lot of voices. For a moment she thought the guests had returned for some reason. Then Mohammed Ishmael's booming voice told her it was the end of the world.

She grabbed Charlie from where he slept on a blanket on the floor and raced into the hallway to the stairs.

Charlie awoke and began to cry. She covered his mouth with her hand and turned right at the bottom of the stairs, darted past the line of carts there and ran to the shaft maintenance elevator. She hit the button.

"I'm sorry," the pleasant computer voice said, "but the shaft maintenance elevator is in use."

She could hear them now in the computer room, hear their gunfire and the crashing of blasted items onto the concrete floor. Large shards of glass exploded out of the observation glass, showering her and Charlie, who screamed in terror.

She charged back to the carts and grabbed one, tearing off down B Corridor, her child held tightly in her right arm. She fled because she had to . . . knowing there was nowhere to go.

Three and a half miles down Tube #63, Crane stood in his sealed elevator cage inspecting the leak. Minimal. It wouldn't interfere with the blast. He shouldn't have worn his burn suit. It made maneuvering too difficult. The suit was large and hot, its hard-shelled exterior designed to protect the wearer from falling debris. Even a pebble dropped four miles could be deadly.

Above he thought he heard a small clicking sound, like the rat-a-tat-tat of a stylus being tapped on a table. He looked around and saw nothing close to him that could produce it.

He looked upward into an infinity of tubing. If the sound was coming from the cavern, it would have to be damned loud to reach him at this depth. A chill went through him.

He turned up his bulky helmet's aural apparatus, amplifying the sounds. Hollow, echoing booms. Explosive booms. They *were* coming from the cavern.

His pad was beeping in his ears. He tapped to hear Lanie's anguished voice. "Crane! Please answer!"

"What's happening? Lanie!"

"Men . . . with guns! They're destroying the place, they've already shot at me, I—"

"They're scanning!" Crane said. "Get off the fiber! Hide!"

"But wh—"

He cut her off and levered up, the cage swiftly starting to glide along its track. "Hurry," he whispered, holding the lever down, trying futilely for more speed. "Hurry." The cage's top speed was about thirty miles per hour, over six minutes to the top. Anything could happen.

He knew it was NOI. He knew it was Newcombe, come to finish their *danse macabre*. His only hope lay in reaching the cavern and offering his life in exchange for Lanie and Charlie.

He hit "open signal" on his pad. "Whoever's listening," he said, the helmet's mike transmitting through the pad, "this is Crane. I will surrender myself to you, do whatever you ask. Please, let my wife and son live. They are innocents."

"Everyone is innocent," came Ishmael's voice in return, "and no one. Life is cruel. God is great."

He could hear explosions as he passed the two-mile marker. They were bringing down the whole cavern! Something came falling down his tube, passing him in a blur.

Ten seconds later, the bottom of Tube #63 exploded, the light flashing, followed seconds later by the sound. The tube rumbled, his cage strained against its rail. Fire burned below, thrown everywhere, phosphorous eating through the lining of lead shielding that covered the hot material.

His cage kept creaking upward, threatening to jump its rail in the last mile. He finally reached cavern level to see carts retreating around the snaky bend in the distance, back toward the main cavern. At that moment, an explosion went up at the far end of his corridor. Supports tore, hunks of the ceiling fell as a rush of dust and stone fragments blew down the corridor.

His cart was still parked against the corridor wall. He stumbled to it, feeling his way, protected by his helmet. He jumped in and opened the focus as the next explosion went, shaking the chamber, rock powdering down on him from above, bouncing off his helmet as more dust obscured his vision.

He raced forward by memory, bumping the right wall to avoid running into the tubes as another explosion went, the entire chamber behind him collapsing as he made an S turn into another corridor.

Focus open full, he raced through the weaving corridor even as tubes exploded to his left. Crane's world and his life were disintegrating all around him. None of it mattered except Lanie and Charlie. He had to get to them.

He hit the main cavern at full throttle, men in black charging toward the stairs, fire pluming out of the computer room, main room tubes rumbling, belching smoke and fire. The whole cavern was shaking, rock shearing from the ceiling to explode on the concrete floor.

It was perdition, hand-delivered by Brother Ishmael. He drew gunfire as he sped toward B Corridor, slamming his cart into a man running out, hearing distant explosions as that corridor collapsed in on itself from the far end.

The radiation warning horns were blowing loudly, the wall monitors flashing at the top end of the red zone. His cart popped into a clear space and he saw a full picture of destruction in an instant. A man in a cart was laughing, aiming a weapon down Tube #21. The rail had been knocked away; a cart had fallen in the tube and blocked the descent of the service cage.

He had only one shot and took it instantly. Foot to the floor, he broadsided the gunman's cart. The blow knocked man and machine into the tube as Crane turned hard to keep from going in with the enemy.

And the man exploded.

Crane jumped out of the cart and ran to the tube. Burning phosphorous was strewn over the cavern floor. Two burning carts were jammed between the tube side and the middle post; fire everywhere threatened to set off the plastique. A cage had torn loose from the track and was balanced precariously atop the wreckage of the two carts five feet down, all of it threatening to lose its fragile wedge and fall the tube's length. Lanie and a hysterical Charlie were in the cage, fire all around them. Lanie had a death grip on the boy as she crouched fetally within the cage, staring up through its torn back.

"Climb up!" he called, reaching down. "Grab my hand."

"I-I can't!" she called back. "I'm dizzy . . . my knees won't . . . God, help me, Crane."

The word hit him. Vertigo. She was frozen, out of the game. He went to his stomach, leaning into the hole, reaching. Her eyes widened in horror. And Crane realized she was living her dream.

She reached up with her left hand, Charlie in the crook of her right arm. She couldn't stand and was shaking uncontrollably. The mass of wreckage creaked loudly, then jerked, Lanie screaming as everything moved.

He leaned way out and grabbed her wrist with his good hand. The wreckage screeched loudly on the inner tube, then broke free and fell. Crane's arm jerked hard and nearly dislocated at the shoulder. Lanie was dangling above the abyss. Fire clung to the surface of the tube and flared out to burn her.

"Hang on!" he yelled, but she couldn't hear him through the helmet. He tried to pull her up, but the weight was too great and he had no leverage. Sweat was pouring from him, dripping on his faceplate, fogging it.

He had nothing to anchor to. He tried to rise enough to get to his knees, but he couldn't. She screamed as flames bit her leg.

"Take Charlie!" she yelled, trying to raise the boy within the embrace of her right arm.

The sound was loud in the suit, rumbling round and round Crane's head. He brought his bad arm around, dangled it in the tube. "I can't!" he shouted in response to the question in her eyes. "My arm! My bad arm!"

"Take him!' she screamed. "Please, take him!"

"I can't!" An explosion farther down the corridor rocked them, and she started to slide from his grasp, his hand cramping as he tried to hold on. Lanie squirmed, trying the impossible—to hand her screaming child up.

"Oh, God, Lanie . . . Lanie!"

She slipped.

Just like that. He watched her fall, clutching Charlie. In his mind's eye, she froze in that position, forever hanging in midair like the imprint on the event horizon of a black hole. Forever pristine. Forever alive. He had a single goal: to follow Lanie and his son into the well of death.

"So," came a voice behind him, and Crane turned. Mohammed Ishmael kicked him down and stood over him with a shotgun. "The seed is gone. Now we must uproot the weed from which it sprang."

"Thank you," Crane said, for he understood that, finally, this man would give him lasting peace.

Then Ishmael half turned. Crane saw Burt Hill running toward them, his eyes crazed, his shovel already half through its slashing arc.

He caught Ishmael on the back with the sharp edge of the shovel, the man going down hard, his body vibrating wildly.

Hill raised the shovel again, high over his head.

"No!" Talib shouted from behind. Hill swung around to go after him. "Don't, Burt!"

Burt charged. The gun in Talib's hand coughed twice, scored twice. Hill stumbled, collapsed face forward as another explosion, very close by, rocked the chamber, a support beam crashing down between Crane and Newcombe.

"Are you satisfied?" Crane screamed, rising to his knees, thick dust blowing through the chamber, Newcombe trying to cover his face with his free hand. "You've killed her! You've killed the baby. . . ." Crane broke down, bending at the waist, crying, his face buried in his hands.

"Crane," Talib said, moving closer. "I never meant . . . for this . . . I never—"

"Kill me!" Crane screamed, looking up at him. "Would you have the human decency to spare me this pain?"

"Crane," Talib whispered.

"For God's sake, kill me! Kill me!"

Talib raised the gun, his lips sputtering. His hand began to shake uncontrollably and his breath came in sobbing gasps. He dropped the gun. Tears running down his face, he grabbed Ishmael by the collar and dragged him into the thick dust clouds blowing through the corridor.

Crane quavered on his knees, crying. As he turned to jump into the tube he heard the moans.

A dust-and-blood-covered Burt Hill grabbed his shoulders. "C-Crane," Hill said in a rasp. "We've got to . . . got to. . . ." He stumbled, fell to one knee.

Crane stared down the tube, then turned reluctantly from it. "Damn you for being alive," he muttered. Tearing himself from the lip, not selfish enough to force Burt to die with him, he cursed before he climbed over the fallen beam, got to Burt, and levered him to his feet.

"C-can't hardly breathe," Hill said.

"Dust," Crane said, knowing the man couldn't hear him. "You've probably got a punctured lung."

Somehow he got Hill in his cart, negotiated the cross-beam in their path. He took off, the area of Tube #21 collapsing behind them, burying his entire life for all time.

He got them back to the shaft service elevator, large chunks of cavern wall and ceiling crashing to the ground. He clumsily unbolted his helmet and carried Hill to the elevator, stumbling inside with him.

The door closed. He hit the Up arrow as the cavern ceiling gave way completely. They were moving.

Crane didn't remember the trip up. Hill had a sucking chest wound and a superficial wound in the forearm. The sucking sound meant the wound had to be closed quickly.

He removed the burn suit's plasteel gloves, using one to cover the wound. A container of lead putty was in his utility bag. He used it around the edges of the glove to seal it to Hill's skin and create a vacuum. Then he rolled Burt onto his injured side to ease the breathing in his good lung. If he were to survive, he'd need help quickly.

He sat with the groaning man, cradling his head, crying. It was over. Everything. Over. What kind of a fool had he been to think he could change the course of history? What arrogance. Life was pain and nothing else. His mind held one image only—Lanie and Charlie frozen on their event horizon, his wife's eyes filled with a kind of celestial disappointment.

He heard a bell and realized they'd reached topside. The door slid open into the equipment shed. As he rose, dragging Burt with him, a massive explosion blew them both out of the elevator, collapsing the shaft completely, the equipment shed shaking to rubble all around them.

He stared into the night. The sound of distant sirens provided music. Helos overhead danced spotlights all around him. Beauty in the midst of horror. He stared up at a starfield that was startlingly brilliant and cold . . . and wondrous through the haze of his tears. The Moon was round, full, the letters YOU printed on its surface in blood red. You. YOU.

FOREST LAWN CEMETERY—LOS ANGELES
5 JULY 2028, MID-MORNING

The mausoleum was very old. It was marble with pillars like the Parthenon and decorated with cherubs whose faces were dark from years of exposure to the elements. There was some lateral fracturing near its base, and a couple of large jagged cracks on the vault itself indicated some seismic meandering in the area. Crane had chosen this mausoleum because it was directly across from the memorial graves of Lanie and Charlie, and he could sit scrunched up on its steps below ground level without being seen. He sat perfectly still, like one of the cherubs, wearing sunglasses and a mild sunblock.

The funeral for Lanie and Charlie had been large and ostentatious. Crane saw to that. Their bodies were lost, of course, so empty coffins had been ceremoniously paraded through town and brought here for burial before a large gathering. People felt as if they knew the Cranes, so public had been their lives. Thousands had turned out. All camheads, of course. Even a Yo-Yu representative had given a eulogy that had rivaled Liang's for sheer triteness and empty condolence.

Lanie would have hated every minute of it just as Crane did, but he was putting on a show for one, and if it worked, the sham funeral and all the agony it had caused him would have been worthwhile.

NOI had gotten away. Talib and his ilk apparently rat-holed in their maze of underground passageways, sitting out the furor. And quite an amazing furor there was. Brother Ishmael had miscalculated public reaction to his savage attack on the compound; the viddy of the G being cut in half and going through the windshield of Ishmael's truck was replayed over and over around the world. But worse, a cam attached to Brother Ishmael showed him standing happily by as Lanie and Charlie died. Everyone's heart, regardless of their position on the Imperial Valley Project issue, went out to the baby. The public was clam-oring for Liang to mete out the most severe justice to the "holy" man and his henchman, Abu Talib, the only two faces the public had seen.

Crane crept slowly up the stone stairs and looked at Lanie's and the baby's memorial graves fifty feet away on the gently rolling hills of Forest Lawn. In the far distance, he could see a figure moving slowly in his direction, con-stantly checking over his shoulder.

The dead, hollow shell that had once been Lewis Crane felt a spark ignite within. Hatred, pure and simple. He was surprised that he still could feel any emotion.

He padded the P fiber and wished the answering voice a belated happy Independence Day. Then he padded off and climbed the stairs.

The figure reached the graves and stood, head bowed. He was dressed in the green coveralls of the cemetery's groundskeepers. A wide-brimmed hat was pulled down over his face, but Crane would recognize Abu Talib/Daniel Newcombe if the man were covered with fur and barking like a dog.

Talib looked up, his eyes betraying no emotion as Crane stopped in front of him.

"I've never in my whole life wished anyone dead be-fore," Crane said. "But you I could kill with my own hands."

"I loved her, Crane," Talib said, tears filling his eyes.

"I wouldn't have hurt her . . . or your child for the world. I'm so sorry."

"I've been waiting for you, you know."

"I knew the risk when I came here. I-I just couldn't stay away. Maybe I'm weak . . . I don't know."

"If it was me you wanted, you could have killed me any time. Why did you have to do it the way you did?"

The man looked at the ground. "We felt it was important to stop your work, not just you."

"To stop science, Dan, is that what you were trying to do?"

"What difference does it make?"

"It makes a difference to me!" Crane screamed. "You've taken my life from me." He grabbed the man's coveralls with his good hand. "You've got to tell me why . . . you've got to!"

Talib's lips moved, but no sound emerged. Finally, he said, "I don't have any answers for you. I don't know anything anymore. I've got this b-blood on my hands and I . . . I don't know what to do to make it go away. You ask me how it all came to this? I don't know. I keep trying to put it together, to . . . figure out . . . why. But it's like I can't think anymore, can't g-grasp hold of a concept without it slipping away. I shot Burt. I-I shot him. Me! Is he . . . is he. . . ."

"He'll live," Crane said, noticing helos overhead, white-clad G making their way through rows of headstones to reach them. "Where's Ishmael?"

Newcombe grimaced. "Burt's shovel did major damage to his spinal cord, paralyzed him. Martin Aziz decided it was time to step into Ishmael's shoes. I presume that means our leader is now expendable. . . ."

"That makes you expendable, too."

"You warned me about politics. I should have listened."

The G were on top of them, surrounding Talib, who looked up at each smiling facemask one at a time as if he could tell differences between them. They had stunners in their hands.

"I'm not going to resist," he said.

"That's a most mature decision," one of them replied, friendly. The G reached out a hand to take his arm. "You'll come with us now."

Crane watched them lead Newcombe away.

"Why?" Crane screamed to the receding figure. "Why?"

He'd wanted to say something to Talib, to somehow confront the madness of it all. But when the time had come, there'd been no words, no deeds that could possibly matter or help assuage his terrible sense of loss. For a fleeting time he'd had everything and now it was gone forever. There was no why.

He looked at the ground, at the phony headstones over the phony coffins. There certainly was no comfort here.

A helo dipped down at the edge of the cemetery. Talib was put aboard and whisked away.

And just like that it was over, wrapped in a neat package to be filed away and quickly forgotten as the world went on with its business.

Lewis Crane was alone again.

Chapter 20

SHIMANI-GASHI

SOMEWHERE IN AMERICA
SPRING 2038, MID-MORNING

Abu Talib began what would be the most extraordinary day of his life the way he had begun every day for the last decade—by deciding not to kill himself.

He'd stared at the rope they'd left him, the hangman's noose already formed. He felt its contours. The smooth nylon fibers slid easily through his palm. It was compelling, that notion of suicide, that control over his life, but it was not the option he would entertain today.

Every day for ten years he'd taken the noose out of the small drawer in his room—he hesitated calling it a cell since it had no bars—and held the rope, feeling the pull toward death. Every day for ten years he'd denied the pull, though sometimes it was stronger than other times.

At his trial—or the sham they'd called a trial—he'd been sentenced to an indefinite time in *Shimanigashi*. Isolation. The prisons and the FPF and the courts were run by private enterprise. There'd been no witnesses at his trial, no jury, no spectators, no lawyers. There'd only been an unidentified man in a business suit, the viddies of the attack on the Imperial Valley Project, and, of course, himself. He remembered signing some papers in triplicate.

The man in the business suit had been the last human being he had seen for ten years.

He'd been knocked out with some sort of gas and had awakened here, in this room with beige metal walls but no windows, a bed, a table and chair, a single light. And the rope, of course. There was also a very nice shower stall that ran for exactly sixty seconds a day, and a toilet that flushed by pushing a button on the wall. There were no mirrors.

He had no books, no teev, no music, no paper—except in the toilet—or pencils. His prison uniform consisted of a black jumpsuit made of a flimsy plastic material. At the end of the day he'd throw it in a disposal hole in his wall, and a new one would appear during the night. If he didn't toss it at night, he didn't get a new one.

As far as he knew, he was the only prisoner in this place. No guards ever walked by to check on him, no other sounds except his own kept him company. His food showed up twice a day through a slot in his door. The meals did not vary. Rice and broth. In the last few years, though, there had been an occasional meal of beans and pita bread, which made him think changes were occurring in the outside world . . . or in the management of his prison.

His hair and beard had grown for ten years. He'd discovered he had gone gray when his beard got long enough for him to pull it up and look at it. His hair hung almost to his elbows.

He'd been expected, of course, to go crazy, and had accommodated his captors by losing his mind more than once. Each time he went crazy he hoped that it would lead to human contact, an exchange of some kind. But it never had, and he was always left to confront his own mind again. Even the time he'd gotten extremely ill, sick to his stomach, there had been no contact. The room had filled with gas. When he awoke, he was on his bed with a scar where his appendix had been.

But it had been a start. It meant someone was watching him. If he talked, it meant someone was listening. It was reassuring in a strange kind of way.

Getting a fix on time and keeping track of it had been his first and most difficult challenge, especially during the time he'd been "out" with the appendectomy. Not knowing day or night, he'd had nothing to relate to; but it had occurred to him during the initial days of his imprisonment that if he lost all awareness of time, he'd only have the rope. That was when Abu Talib, born Daniel Akers Newcombe, began exercising his mind.

He'd counted out the seconds—one Mississippi, two Mississippi—for days on end until he had the internal rhythm of a day. He'd considered trying to lengthen his nails, instead of biting them as he'd always done, to scratch a mark for each day somewhere into the metal of the room. Then he decided against it, reasoning that they'd repaint the walls to thwart him. If he was going to be a human clock, he'd have to go all the way.

And, so, having nothing else to do, he'd become a human clock. He chose to believe that in the ten years he had counted, he wasn't more than a week or two off. Once he'd gotten comfortable with his clockhood, he'd found that he could sublimate it and think about other things.

He'd remembered reading once—why hadn't he *read* more?—about a man isolated in a prisoner-of-war camp who'd survived by playing chess in his head, visualizing the board and the movement of the pieces. Talib found that after several weeks of futile effort, he was able to play chess in his mind and passed many hours that way.

He'd dealt with sleep-time by simply calculating how many hours of sleep he usually needed each night to feel rested, how many his body would take on its own. Seven seemed to have been his ideal number when he'd lived in the real world, so seven it became. He never took naps and made sure he was awake seventeen out of every twenty-four hours.

Having nothing else except physical exercise to keep

him occupied, he would explore his mind—sometimes happily, sometimes not so happily. He had good powers of concentration and was able to re-create people and events vividly in his mind's eye, to relive his past. Much of it was embarrassing to him, though what bothered him the most was the realization that he'd wasted an immense amount of time in his life that could never be recovered.

Of course, he dwelled a great deal on why he'd chosen every morning to live under such a ludicrous regimen rather than simply use the rope. He never had come up with a real answer except an ingrained competitiveness with those who sought to break him. It was not a satisfying answer.

What he had discovered in himself, though, was a core notion that redefined his thinking processes. He used his isolation metaphorically by isolating his mind, separating his thoughts from each other and from their emotional/ egotistical components. He dealt with his thoughts and feelings indifferently, the way people do to relieve anxiety, examining them as he would earthquake data.

He didn't much like the skull he'd seen beneath the skin. It seemed to him that too much of his time had been spent following the commands of his gonads and his emotions. Too little time had been spent thinking reasonably. It was difficult to be angry with those who'd imprisoned him, since he felt he deserved the sentence. Without sustaining anger, he'd managed to get beyond the human barrier of rationalization and see himself for what he was—an animal, acting out animal passions. Once that particular pathway was traversed, it became impossible to go back to blissful ignorance. He'd learned to accept responsibility as a human being. People had learned less in ten years, he figured.

Then there'd been the "episodes," the bouts with insanity. Each time he'd gone nuts, it had been after a particularly dark journey within himself, when he'd let a slow psychosis creep in that could overcome his reasoning processes.

One time he'd decided that he had been killed during the raid on the Project and was living in a hellish afterlife, that he would batter around in this room for an eternity of loneliness and silence. He went hysterical and starved himself for three days until they'd gassed and force-fed him. He'd awakened feeling much better, after an unknown number of days unconscious. He could conclude only that his jailers would not permit him death by such a passive method as not eating. Was his sole option the active one of using the hangman's noose?

In another episode of insanity he'd fantasized that he was free and could come and go at will from his cell. He chose to stay because, as he'd loudly told himself over and over, "It was all for the best." They'd ultimately had to gas him that time, too.

Now he feared it was happening again.

After he'd finished his morning ritual with the rope, he'd retrieved his rice and broth from the slot in the door and sat down to eat. He hadn't taken three bites before he'd heard an unfamiliar clicking sound from within the door, followed, seconds later, by the door creaking open halfway. It had never done that before.

He'd stared at it for a long time. There was a hallway on the other side of the door, he could see that much. Painted blue, the hallway had a pale yellowish light spilling down its length.

That had been quite an extraordinary amount of data to receive all at once. He'd gone back to eating his breakfast and dwelled on it for a while. Between every bite, no utensils, only hands, he'd look up at the door to see it still open, to see that marvelous blue running to washed-out green under the fuzzy yellow light. The colors seemed alive, organic, breathing, interacting.

He finished the meal and took the tray back to the door slot, the door opening even farther when he touched it. He looked down the hallway, which traveled on for a hundred yards in either direction, the yellow ceiling bulbs spaced twenty feet apart. Doors filled the hallway on both sides and there were numbers on the doors.

As he stood there with the tray in his hands, he realized he was supposed to walk through that open door. It was the worst moment of his incarceration. He didn't want to go. The fear flashed so strong that he physically recoiled from the door, the tray flying out of his hands and clattering onto the floor.

He wanted to think about that open door, to reason out its existence for several days, but the fact that it hung wide made its immediate use impossible to avoid. He took a deep breath and strode out into the hall.

He felt the fear for only a second, then pride welled within him. He'd done it, walked into the outside world.

There was a door on each end of the hallway. Which to choose? Suddenly the notion of a choice other than suicide excited him. Being right-handed, he decided that his natural inclination was to go to the right. He went that way.

As he passed other doors, he wondered who, if anyone, was on the other side of each. He'd never heard any sounds from outside his room save the mechanical sounds of the foodcart grinding down the hallway.

It was strange to walk so far in a straight line. When he finally reached the door at hall's end, he once again overcame his inner fears and pulled it open. He stepped through.

He was standing in a room that was about twenty feet square. The room was beige and bare except for a metal chair bolted to the floor on one side and a metal bench bolted to the floor on the other. The door he'd come in was near the chair. There was another door by the bench. He sat in the chair and waited.

In due course it opened, and an attractive woman and two children walked in. The woman's eyes opened in horror when she saw him and the children stepped back a pace. "Abu?" she said.

It was then he recognized her. "Kh . . . Khadijah," he said, his voice hoarse. He hadn't used it in a long time. "Is that really you?"

He stood and moved toward her. She put up her hands to keep him back. "No physical contact," she said. "It's one of the terms of the visit."

"What are the . . . other terms?" he asked quietly, reseating himself.

"I can't give you anything," she said. "I can't tell you where you are. I must leave when they say."

He nodded. "I see."

"You look ... like a wild man," she said. "Your hair ... your beard. Haven't they cut your hair at all?"

"No," he answered. "Are these the children?"

She nodded, taking the bench, a boy sitting on one side of her, a girl on the other. "Najan?" he asked the girl, bright-eyed above her veil. "Do you remember me?"

"No, sir," Najan answered quickly. "But I know you're my father."

"And what's your name?" he asked the boy, about nine by his calculations.

"Abu ibn Abu Talib," the boy said, standing. "I was named after you."

"And I'm very proud. You look like a fine young man. And that shirt you're wearing ... does that change colors?"

"Yes, sir," his son said. "Everybody wears them."

"Do you get any news here at all?" Khadijah asked.

He shook his head slowly. "Nothing," he said, then pointed at her. "March 13, 2038."

"It's April 24th," she replied, narrowing her eyes.

"Close," he said triumphantly.

"You must have a million questions," she said, leaning forward as if to study him better.

"Not so many. I gave up asking questions. You're looking wonderful, though. You've rounded out."

"Childbirth had its advantages." She smiled, and he smiled in return, but his cheek muscles tired immediately.

"Are they going to release me?"

He'd been afraid to ask the question, tears coming to his eyes as he said the words. He choked them back.

"No," she said. "They're too afraid of you."

"Afraid ... of me?"

She nodded. "Once Ishmael joined the long and distinguished list of assassinated—"

"Assassinated? No! When ... how?"

Her brows rose. "Of course. You wouldn't know. A few years back. Assassin unknown, never caught."

She took a breath. "You, then, were the only visible symbol of the movement. Martin took over. He's a good administrator, but no one knew him. To keep the flame of rebellion alive we made you our cause. We began demanding your release as a political prisoner. You became the glue that held the Islamic State together in the War Zones, a worldwide symbol of an imprisoned people. You got the Nobel Peace Prize last year. Your influence is global."

"Well, imagine that," he said without enthusiasm. "It sure sounds like I've been having a good time."

"I want to show you something," she said excitedly, sliding a disk into her wristpad. It was half the size of the pads he remembered and was smooth without symbols.

A viddy came up on the beige wall. It showed the War Zone emptying of people, huge groups migrating southward as the Islamic State was opened.

"When?" he asked.

"Last year," Khadijah said. "President Masters signed the Partition Order on Thanksgiving Day of 2037."

"President Masters?"

"Kate Masters? I think you know her."

"I thought I did," he said enigmatically. "How did they work it?"

"The government and the YOU-LI Corporation have been quietly buying people out for years in those states. The earthquake in Memphis helped a lot. Most of the whites wanted to go anyway." She pointed to the screen, house-to-house fighting in a small southern town, race against race. "Those who didn't want to leave held out for a time, but we eventually got rid of them all."

"Got rid of them? There's an Africk army?"

The kids giggled, Talib cocking his head.

"That term isn't used much anymore," Khadijah said, smiling.

"Why not?"

"Our African Islamic brothers didn't think many of us were black enough to call ourselves African." She smiled. "They started calling us 'mestizos.' The name stuck."

"It's not a complimentary title," he said.

"We've made it one." She sat up straighter, regal all of a sudden. "So the country is now called the United States of America and Islam. New Cairo encompasses Florida, North and South Carolina, Georgia, Alabama, Louisiana, and Mississippi."

"Why did they give in after all this time?" he asked. "It must have been damned expensive to buy out that many people."

"They had no choice," she said. "The world is seventy percent Islamic. The Chinese Syndicates are dying fast because they no longer control trade. Africa is the seat of economic power right now. Ultimately, the Chinese cut a deal with us to funnel trade to the rest of America through our back doors at preferred prices. It keeps both countries alive."

The wall now showed Martin Aziz waving to crowds and making speeches. "He is in charge," Khadijah said. "But *you* are the heart of the people. We wouldn't accept a settlement with the whites until they agreed to either let us see you or see your body. Nobody knew if you were alive or dead. Now that we know, I promise you, Abu, we won't rest until you are free."

"Why do I have the feeling this has very little to do with me?"

"You're a symbol. You're Abu Talib, larger than life. The people of New Cairo need a figure to look up to in these difficult days. When the whites left after partition, they burned everything behind them. We've been building from scratch. Your example is their strength."

"My example," he said, smiling again, the muscles hurting again. "I have set no example. I've been surviving like an animal here. I want you to know it hasn't been easy. I've . . . changed quite a lot. To be even more honest, I haven't thought much about the movement since I've been in here. Instead, I've thought about smelling real air again, or seeing the sky." He held his hand out, slowly forming it into a fist. "I've thought about grabbing rocks out of the ground and knowing everything about an area there is to know through its rocks . . . a whole history through rocks to the beginning of time! I've thought about sex. . . ."

She looked down instinctively, every gesture reading like a roadmap to him. "It's all right," he said. "Ten years is a long time. You didn't know if I was alive, I—"

A loud buzzer went off; Khadijah immediately stood up. "It's time to leave," she said. "Is there anything you want to say to the people?"

He laughed. "Today's the first day I've heard a voice other than my own in years. I don't even live in the same world you live in."

She shrugged. "I'll make up something."

Her door clicked and popped open. The children moved toward it. So soon. How could it be over so soon? This was worse than the isolation. "Crane," he said as she hustled the children out the door. "What's Crane doing?"

Her brittle laugh startled him so much that his body twitched.

"How the mighty do fall. A pariah, that's what Crane is. An outcast. Reviled . . . for planning to set off nuclear bombs. The tide turned against him when his insane plan was fully revealed. Then for years he was ranting and raving all over the teevs about some terrible disaster coming in California. Nobody listened to him. And I haven't heard anything about him in a long time." Halfway out the door, she turned back and said, "We're going to get you out of here."

"Come back for more visits," he said, but she was gone. The door closed quickly, he heard the lock snap. "Tell them I must have access to information!" he shouted. "For God's sake, do something!"

He slouched in the chair. His door clicked and popped open. Slowly, he got up, then trudged back to his cell. He'd live from visit to visit now, in the hinterlands of hope. He had lost the ability to track time . . . and he never would get it back.

Lewis Crane sat in the back seat of the Moonskimmer with Burt Hill. The all-terrain vehicle's bulbous helium-filled underbelly made it feel as if they were floating over the stark lunar landscape. The stars were brilliant pinpoints above, the crown of Earth just passing over the horizon behind them. The real estate man talked nonstop, continually forcing internal adjustment of the cabin's carbon-dioxide monitors. A pale trail of light from the Earth's corona illuminated the landscape, this band of surface getting ready to enter a two-week period of "night."

"We don't get a lot of Darksiders up here," the real estate man, named Ali, said. "People want the good property lightside, where you get the view of Earth."

"That's exactly what I don't want," Crane said, turning to the windows. They were skimming the Southern Sea, Galileo's *Mare Australe,* on their way to YOU-LI's defunct titanium mining operation in the Sea of Ingenuity. The Jules Verne Crater rose majestically on their left. The *mare* was dust, though, not water as Galileo had surmised, powdered rock and glass and asteroid scum.

"I don't know why you want to look at places on the darkside," Burt said, wheezing. "A man likes a little sunshine from time to time."

"They get as much light over here as on the other side," Crane said. "You just don't have to look at the Earth, that's all."

"I got's lots good property over there," the salesman said. "Prime Earthrise."

Crane ignored the comment. "Now, anything I buy here is mine, right?"

Ali turned to him, black moustache arching over a wide smile. He formed his fingers into a circle with his thumb. "Absolute sovereignty," he said, snapping his fingers open. "Many groups buy lands for their religious freedom, you know? Or for their politics. No Earth governments involved, see? It's good system if you like 'a take care of yourself."

"How about access to water?" Hill asked.

"How about it?" Ali returned. "You make whatever deals you can make to get what water you can. The consortium up here charge a lot, you know? Most people, if they can afford it, truck it up from Earth."

Crane grunted. Earth wasn't the place to find water

nowadays. Oh, it was better in a number of respects. The atmosphere was ozone-regenerated, people living in the sun again the way he'd remembered from his childhood, and Masada had disappeared completely five years ago with barely any notice. Everyone was too busy worrying about the amount of radioactivity in their water supplies to care about too much else. The fallout from Masada had contaminated more than water. Waste products had leaked through their safety containments all over the world because nobody was willing to look at the problem until it had become a catastrophe. Tainted water was everywhere.

He'd begun working it out on the globe at the Foundation, simply inputting rate of leakage data and the presence and speed of movement of underground water supplies. The hope was for a prediction, well ahead of time, as to where and how the disease would spread itself to the body of the planet, so that mankind would know where to entrench to fight the invader. But to some, the poisoning of the Earth's water supply seemed like a reasonable perdition. Every age has its optimists.

The globe was a wonder, his wife's living legacy. Many issues like the radioactivity project had been run through its cogitative senses and resulted in real conclusions. But it had broken down in some ways, which he knew would not have happened had Lanie lived. The result was disappointments, unpredicted quakes, for example, including one in California. Until now, the globe had seemed infallible.

It always made him think about Lanie's theories of swimming pools dug in Rome starting quakes in Alaska. In fact, two of the unpredicted quakes had finally been attributed to lakes being dug, one as far as five hundred miles away, water filling the lake, filtering down into the cracks in the rocks and lubricating hidden faults. He wondered if one day, though, it would be possible to know enough to tell people where *not* to dig lakes . . . or swimming pools.

"Here we go, Misters," Ali said, pointing through the windshield at a glowing area several miles distant. "I had them turn the lights on for you."

Crane wondered what Lanie would think of this—him buying a piece of the Moon with Stoney's three-billion-dollar endowment. Stoney had told him to use it to buy another dream; now, ten years later, he was taking the man at his word.

Ali reversed the thrust fans to slow them, the skimmer bumping rudely into the middle of a small ghost town of interconnected domes and square, metal prefab buildings stacked like the holoblocks Charlie had used to play with on the elevator ride in the Imperial Project.

"Are the mine shafts still open?" Crane asked as he looked at a series of abandoned restaurants with familiar names.

Ali hesitated. "We can discuss the shafts. I'm not sure how much happiness it will bring YOU-LI to come in and fill—"

"I *want* the shafts," Crane said. "I'm going to tap the core for heat and power."

"You want shafts," Ali said happily, twirling his hand in the air. "You got shafts. They're everywhere . . . all over this damn place. The man wants shafts. He wants them!"

Ali eased them to the lock, bumping up, magnetic clamps catching and sealing tight. "You've got to put on the helmet," he said. "I can't afford to turn on the life support in here just to show the place."

"How much space does the entire operation cover?" Crane asked, as Ali put on his helmet, then pointed to Crane's.

Crane let Burt help him into the helmet. "Think of these constructions as the center point," Ali said. "The operation extends for a thousand square miles all around us. You'll own the Van de Graaff Crater, the Leibnitz Crater, and the Von Karman Crater. The Sea of Ingeniuty is yours, all of it."

"The price?"

"Three point two billion," Ali said. "Now, I know that's a whole lot'a money. I got smaller plots on the light-side that—"

"Make it three billion even and you've got a deal," Crane said.

"You've got that kinda collateral?" Ali asked. "Not to be blunt, sir."

"We'll be paying cash."

"My friend!" Ali said. "You have made an old camel trader very happy. Nobody wants the darkside."

"I insist on it. Shall we tour the facility?"

The tour lasted less than an hour, Ali anxious to get back to the lightside and Crane not all that interested in the accommodations. The YOU-LI camp had been a typical mining operation, spartan and barely supported from corporate. Crane would be tearing down the buildings in due time, constructing his own. But the existing construction would house the initial planners and engineers whose task it would be to turn a darkside mining camp into a new civilization. It would be a long and difficult project, but Crane had undertaken many such projects before.

Later, back at the Moonbase Marriott, Crane and Hill sat at a table in the bar, Crane's back to the magnificent Earthrise shining through the huge, thick windows. The hotel was full, the area around the hotel beginning to look like a small city of domes and skydecks. The Moon was new territory, optioned for quick sale by YOU-LI, the previous owners. The Chinese were consolidating their holdings and the Moon didn't figure in their future. So, a piece at a time, it was being developed by the people who always open new territories and settlement—rogues and heroes. Crane wasn't sure which category he fit into.

Hill, frail and quiet since being wounded years before, raised a beer. "I guess this is to you," he said. "I'm not sure what you did, but congratulations."

"We're taking advantage of an opportunity while we can," Crane said, touching his glass of Scotch to the beer bottle, then sipping. "I always wanted to run my own government."

"Bullshit," Hill said. "All you ever wanted to do was kill EQs. All of a sudden we're buying up the Moon."

"It's not sudden. I've been thinking about it for a long time . . . years. It was never feasible until now. I don't tell you everything on my mind, Burt."

"That's a fact. You never told me Sumi was a woman."

"I figured that if you were dumb enough not to know," Crane said, "I wasn't going to be the one to tell you."

It was an old joke between them. Truth to tell, neither of them had had the vaguest idea about Sumi. Her story had been fascinating and most nearly tragic. So much had happened over the years.

Barely a month after the attack on the Imperial Project, President Gideon had slipped on a bar of soap in the bathtub and promptly died—at least that was the story released by the White House. Sumi had become President, immediately appointing Kate Masters as her VP. Because Liang Int and Yo-Yu had split the electorate, Sumi was able to beat both companies' tickets and get elected President without affiliation in the November '28 elections.

It was Sumi who'd laid the groundwork for what had ultimately resulted in the Islamic State. Because of what she termed "health reasons" she chose not to run again in '32, even though she'd been a balanced and respected Chief Executive during her term in office. Then, at the same news conference, she'd revealed her true gender, saying she could "no longer pretend" to be a male.

Kate Masters had run and won big, leapfrogging from her already huge power base and cashing in on anti-Chinese sentiment. The economy continued to falter because of a barrage of sanctions imposed upon Chinese business interests by a worldwide Islamic movement whose global view was ethnocentric, to say the least.

The reasons for Sumi Chan's declining to run again then became immediately apparent when she was checked into a mental institution. Paul, the lover devolved from her chip, had managed to take over her life completely, making all her decisions, choosing her advisors, and drawing her into an ever-downward spiral of xenophobia and closed-mindedness. She'd become the entire loop of humanity all within herself. No one else was allowed in by Paul.

Crane had maintained a loose contact with her through this period, buying from YOU-LI, at Kate's insistence, Sumi's ancestral lands, which he then leased back to her at the price of one dollar per year in perpetuity. Sumi needed—and was granted—a legal divorce from Paul. So strong was his presence that he was even there when the chip was removed. She wasn't the only one with a problem. Millions had become addicted to Yo-Yu's chips, and an entire branch of medicine called Personality Replacement had sprung into existence to deal with the fallout.

Sumi Chan spent four years locked away, Yo-Yu doling out billions in hospital and damage payments for addicted chippies, taking enough of a hit that it was forced into a worldwide merger with its struggling rival, the YOU-LI Corp. The Companion Chip went the way of the dinosaur, even as educational chip implants were increasing in popularity. Crane himself was ported in '35 and found the device invaluable for research.

Kate Masters, meanwhile, had been re-elected in '36 and was now serving out the last two years of her second term. Sumi lived quietly on her ancestral lands in China.

Stoney had died within a year of the Imperial catastrophe.

For Crane, though, the last ten years had been a waking nightmare. Shortly after Talib's arrest and imprisonment, when the story was out about the Imperial Valley Project, public sympathy turned sharply. Quickly, he, Crane, became the villain for daring even to think of detonating nuclear devices . . . for daring even to believe he could change the very substructure of the Earth or had any right to do so.

His became the voice crying in the wilderness. Over and over again through the long years he tried to warn his countrymen of the terrible catastrophe to come in California. Worse than the insults, worse than the laughter greeting his recorded, written, and live messages, was the deafening silence with which his warnings were met. And, finally, he had given up hope.

And he had become more hollow . . . and more hollow still.

Then the Moon had gone up for sale and he'd felt something down in the pit of his stomach, a spark. He'd pounced on it.

"You're really going to put in . . . buildings and stuff up here, huh?" Hill asked.

"Plan to," Crane said, "I want to build a whole city up here, Burt. A place where people would *want* to live."

"You gonna be livin' up here, too?"

Crane smiled. "No, friend. I think we're both a little too long in the tooth and cantankerous for this kind of pioneering."

Hill sat back and sighed heavily. "That's a relief. I just couldn't imagine myself in one of those damned helmets all the time. What happens if you gotta sneeze, or blow your nose?"

"We will visit sometimes, though. There's a lot of work to be done, decisions to be made." Crane took a sip of the Scotch, watching a crew of construction workers in their muscle exo's walking into the bar and sitting at a back table. "I don't like the idea of being dependent upon Earth for my water supply," he said. "Wonder if we could dredge permafrost on Mars and ship it here ourselves? Whoever controls the water, controls the environment."

"How many people you want to put out there?"

"A few thousand at least, I'd say."

"You've been all fired up about this project for months. It seems crazy to me. Why do it? What's the point?"

Crane grimaced, finished his drink. He held up the glass and got the bartender's attention, the man nodding and going for the Scotch bottle. "It's all that money Stoney left me," he said. "I couldn't find anything worthwhile enough . . . lasting enough, to spend it on. Then this opened up."

"Why this?"

"I had an aquarium once . . . well, twice, actually, but the one I'm thinking about I had when I was a kid living with my aunt," Crane said. "I'd saved up for it myself. I had a lot of different kinds of fish in it over the years, but once I put a shrimp in, a delicate, beautiful little thing. I couldn't find anything to feed it that it wanted to eat. After a while it began eating itself, day after day, a piece at a time just to stay alive. Eventually it hit a vital organ."

He turned then and looked at the Earth, huge and blue and cloud-shrouded through the viewports. He pointed to it. "That's what I think they're doing, eating themselves alive. They murder in the name of God and blindly destroy the very ecosystem that sustains them."

"People are people." Burt shrugged.

"What you're really saying is that people are animals," Crane replied. "And I say to you, it doesn't have to be that way. We can make a civilization, a real civilization, built on real understanding of ourselves and our universe. I bought property on the darkside because I don't want my people seeing the Earth die before their eyes. My . . . city may be the last best hope for the human race, Burt. That's why I'm doing it. Is that dream enough for you?"

"You couldn't save the Earth, so you want to make a new world?"

"I'll accept that interpretation."

"What're you gonna call this place?"

"Charlestown. I'm going to call it Charlestown."

Burt nodded, his eyes misting. "I think that's real nice, Doc. Real nice."

FIRESTORM

**SHIRAHEGA FIREBREAK—TOKYO, JAPAN
1 SEPTEMBER 2045, NOON**

From the air, the Shirahega firebreak was impossible to miss, even in the world's largest city. It was an apartment building, or rather a length of apartments, designed to cut off the firestorm resulting from a major quake, designed to protect the northernmost districts from the poorer southernmost ones. It was the Great Wall of Tokyo.

Crane and Burt Hill were riding in the passenger section of a Red Cross relief helo, a dozen or so white-garbed medtechs, young people mostly, filling the benches beside and across from them. They didn't know who Crane was, had no connection to the aging countenance that had once held a world in thrall with his exploits and his tragedies.

The techs were gaping as they looked out the large ship's bubble ports. The sight of Tokyo spread out beneath them would take anyone's breath away. The buildings of a major city dominated the landscape, yet it was the surrounding city, the ramshackle dwellings of thirty-three million people, that commanded the attention. Wooden houses jammed together along narrow streets made it look like a patchwork quilt. Millions of wooden houses. More houses than the human mind could truly imagine. Only seeing was believing.

But what was worse were the huge propane tanks sitting beside the dwellings, sometimes dwarfing them. They still used gas here. When the quake started—and it would start soon—the fires would ignite quickly. Within fifteen minutes a third of Tokyo would burn to the ground, a half million buildings destroyed. Crane's arm hurt.

"You're a damned fool to come out here," Hill said, "chasin' after EQs like you ain't done since '28. Somebody ought to get you to a psychiatrist."

"You are the most disagreeable man I've ever known," Crane said. "Why I put up with you is a mystery to me."

"You need me, because you're too much of a baby to look out for yourself. Hell, you'd'a been dead twenty times over if it wasn't for me. And I'm here to tell you now, that this may be the twenty-first time. I'll bet you Doc Bowman didn't give you the okay for this."

"Didn't tell him," Crane said. He hadn't been able to shake Bowman since his brush with colon cancer the year before. It had been caused by radiation exposure during the fight at Imperial Valley. The cancer was why he was here, wanting to experience a massive earthquake once more. It had been seventeen years since he'd allowed himself to visit a quake site—he was flagellating himself; Burt was right about that—yet as great as his pain and loathing for the Beast, so too was the exultation and excitement. The Beast provoked an exquisite enmity.

He'd been at Moonbase Charlestown, supervising the unending small details of a project so massive and in such unlivable conditions as to overpower anyone, when he'd gotten sick. He'd never really been sick before. The cancer was advanced when they discovered it. They'd treated him chemically, then told him his body would do the rest. What they didn't tell him was the terrible price he'd pay physically. The war his body waged had gone on for eight excruciating months. When it was finally over he was cancer-free, in fact, immune to most forms of the disease, but he was weak; he tired easily. He couldn't drink anymore and felt like an old man at fifty-eight. And this day he was going to witness a quake the likes of which he'd never seen.

Tokyo sat at the juncture of four plates: the Philippine, the Pacific, the Eurasian, and the trailing edge of the North American, by way of the Japan and Isu Trenches. A major subduction quake was getting ready to occur at the Japan/Izu Trench conjunction, and it would destroy most of Tokyo.

An eerie scenario had developed around the Crane Report in recent years. Discredited by many, respected by others, the Report was used by a few to plan their adventures and their deaths. Whenever a major EQ was predicted, hundreds, sometimes thousands, of people showed up to test themselves against its power. Like running with the bulls, men used it as a proof of manhood. Others planned it as a dramatic suicide.

The firebreak loomed below, a jagged gash of buildings butted together, cutting the city in half. Their steel shutters were already locked down tight, huge water cannons at the ready. Ironically, it was September 1, traditionally Earthquake Day in Japan since September 1st, 1923, when forty thousand people burned to death in the firestorm that leveled Edo, as Tokyo had been known then. All told, one hundred and fifty thousand people died that day.

The helo stalked Shirahega. There was a crowded observation station built atop one of the central buildings, a helopad right alongside. The pilot banked them in and bullseyed the pad, the young techs jumping out of the machine no sooner than it had set down. They were there to help with the survivors—for besides the gatecrashers, there were always people who refused to evacuate.

Crane and Hill climbed out last, Crane waving Hill off when he tried to help him. "I may be a cripple," he said, grunting as he took the long step down, "but I'm not a *damned* cripple."

He had only been on the roof for a number of seconds when he experienced the first tremor. "Do you feel it, Burt?"

"Sir?" Hill mumbled.

Crane was feeling the temblors up his leg, shaking his whole body, vibrating it like a tuning fork. "I think you'd better position yourself. It will only be moments now."

Sway belts were connected to the metal front wall of the firebreak. Hill helped him belt in. He picked up a pair of binoculars hanging beside the belt. Below, groups of people on the surrounding streets were still partying, many dressed alike. There was a group in black shiny suits with bright red stripes shoulder to ankle. There was another group of young men, and a few women, who were naked except for shoes, their clothes tied in bundles they carried on their shoulders. Another group dressed in clown outfits. All young, foolish people. They were called Rockers because they challenged geology on its own terms.

The suicides he could see farther back in the city, all ages, all looking for a shaky building to scale, for some large structure beneath which they could wait. The Rockers stayed close enough to the firebreak to run. The suicides wandered aimlessly, but far enough away from Shirahega that they couldn't reach it in a firestorm. Those who simply refused to believe in the quake were, he presumed, in their homes or offices, doing whatever they normally did.

"Got a moment for an old friend?" came a voice from behind. He turned to see Sumi Chan. Her hair was shoulder length, her eyes made up with pale blue shadow.

"Oh, my," Crane said. He reached out as Sumi hurried to hug him. "Let me look at you."

She stepped back from their brief embrace. She wore a black jumpsuit and hiking boots and looked sexy. She had aged well: A lifetime of controlling her emotions had left her with a remarkably unlined face. In fact, Crane realized, Sumi was beautiful—all the more so because her eyes were friendlier than he'd ever seen them, more intimate in their gaze. He nodded, once he was able to discern that she was healthy and quite comfortable with herself.

"What are you doing here?" he asked, as she moved to hug an already-strapped-in Burt Hill.

"I heard you were coming, so I popped over," she said. "We're practically neighbors."

A loud rumble bellowed out of the earth. The building began shaking, and Crane grabbed Sumi. He pulled her to the wall to help her strap in.

"Hang on!" he yelled. "It's going to be a rough one!"

The building shook violently from side to side, S waves, big ones shivering the mantle. It didn't stop, it intensified, P waves joining the assault, up-and-down waves making the earth heave.

Crane grabbed the facade before him with a still-strong right hand, his gaze locked on the city twenty stories below. People were scattering, everyone forgetting mock heroic plans in the face of catastrophe. They ran, falling, back toward the firebreak. Huge rumbling fissures opened in the streets and the whole group of naked Rockers disappeared into the bowels of the Beast.

The shaking intensified, entire blocks of buildings simply falling over where the ground turned liquid. The smashing of glass and concrete as buildings fell mixed with the rumble of the EQ in an overpowering wall of noise. A cloud of dust rose from demolished structures and spread across the city.

The explosions started, the temblor only thirty seconds old. Bridges and overpasses fell, dumping cars full of last-minute evacs into empty space, spilling people and automobiles across the crumbling cityscape.

And then the fires began.

Ninety seconds passed and still the ground rolled and pitched, the firebreak creaking beneath them. Thirty feet away, the helo that had brought them bounced itself to the side of the building, then pitched over the edge.

"I told you, Crane," Hill said. "We're right in the damned middle of it again."

"And it's great," Crane said low, his insides burning, alive! He could feel himself surge with the Beast's power, his enemy putting life back into him. He hadn't felt this good in years.

"Look at Tokyo Bay," Sumi said, taking his bad arm, grasping hard.

The Bay was drained, empty, the ugly jagged scar of the trench evident several miles out in the mudhole.

"That wind," Hill said.

"The firestorm's creating a vacuum, consuming all the oxygen around it," Crane said loudly, above the noise. "That wind is just the air rushing back in to fill the space."

The shaking had slowed. But the firestorm was moving closer to them, eating Tokyo a block at a time.

"Feel the heat?" Sumi said, her hands in front of her face, the fire now an unbroken line ten miles long and two miles wide. It roared toward them, a mile and closing, as an aftershock jerked them sideways.

The smoke was thick, Crane's blood hotter than the inferno he faced. The fire, huge and unrelenting, rolled like an ocean in shimmering waves that crashed and broke, leaping up like bright orange surfspray.

They were sweating, all of them, as the water cannons came on, pumping sea water under pressure, a wall of water to match the wall of fire. A thick spray of water refracted the bright orange, producing countless minirainbows in the midst of conflagration. One of the cannons was pointed straight up, the water spraying over the top of the building, cooling them, drenching their legs before hitting drainholes and arcing back out toward the fire. The same drama was being enacted along the entire firebreak. Shirahega was the city's only hope.

The temperature was up, way up. Burt ripped off his mask and coughed. "Are you okay?" Crane called into the man's ear.

Burt hacked and spit. "Hell, I told you I could never go around in a space helmet . . . didn't I? But I can take it as long as you can!"

Sumi was giddy with it, laughing. "You're high octane one hundred percent!" she screamed, water streaming out of her hair, eye makeup running down her face.

"I didn't invent it . . . I just predicted it," he called in return, feeling the heat on his clothes. Everyone's face was blood red.

There were exclamations farther down the line. People looked up. Crane followed suit. The sky was orange above him, the fire attempting to leapfrog completely over the break to pick its targets on the other side.

"The trees'll go like candles!" Crane said, unbuckling and sloshing away from the southern view to watch the building's north side, Sumi and Burt right behind him.

He looked north, half the city already rubble there, many small fires burning off into the smoke-shrouded horizon. Below, the evacuation park was jammed with people who'd somehow survived the temblor and the firestorm. Two trees were already blazing from airborne embers, and people lay huddled on the ground to escape the smoke. It was the same way everyone had died on Edo a hundred and twenty years earlier.

He looked back at the firebreak. Most of the water cannons jutted from the edifice of the building itself, but three large ones, the size of howitzers, were buttressed on the roof. He looked at Hill. "Think you can handle one of those things?" he asked.

"If it's mechanical, I'm its daddy," Hill responded, ripping off his mask to spit again.

"Take the southeast cannon," Crane said. "Turn it around, onto the park. Go! Now!"

Sumi followed him dutifully to the southwest cannon, the one pointed straight up. It was massive and heavy enough to not buckle under the intense water pressure. Two large handles jutted from the back of the machine. Crane and Sumi each took a handle and jerked, slowly bringing the cannon down and around, arcing the water over the facade to spray the park.

The Japanese on the roof ran to the north wall and gazed over. Then they turned around and politely applauded.

A tired Crane and Sumi Chan leaned over the wall and stared down into the park at medtechs smoothly working triage and giving emergency care. Hill was off somewhere, trying to arrange transport out of the damage zone since they'd lost their helo.

"How long since we've seen each other?" Crane asked. It was fascinating to him, but he had no problem accepting Sumi as a woman.

"I don't know . . . fifteen years, or so. I was still living as a man then."

"With Paul." Crane smiled. "We all assumed you were homosexual. You see Kate anymore?"

"She came out to visit a few months ago. Stayed a week. Same old Kate. She was in the process of divorcing her fourth husband and acquiring her fifth."

"The one fixed point in an everchanging universe," Crane said, wondering why Sumi really had come to see him.

"How is the worldwide water situation?" she asked. "I assume the Foundation is still involved in the radiation cleanup projects."

"We provide daily updates after receiving word of what's being done, then counterbalance with suggestions for the next day. Some of it is quite remarkable. There's a fellow in Colorado, America, and one in Argentina who are diverting underground rivers, bringing them to the surface and controlling their flow to avoid hot areas. Things are still bad, obviously, and rationing is still necessary, but I think we may hit turnaround in a half dozen or so years."

"How about the Mideast?"

"Still hot as lava," he returned. She was good, professional. "Now tell me why the hell you're really here."

"Sure," she said, smiling. She patted his hand. "I have two propositions for you."

"Kate Masters' visit wasn't just a vacation, was it?" he said. "She was lobbying you, wasn't she? Successfully, I guess."

"Correct on all counts," Sumi answered, the smile leaving her face. "Crane, right now America is on the verge of a race war. There's fighting all along the border with New Cairo. The issue of Abu Talib has dwarfed everything— logic, life itself."

"I don't want to hear this," Crane said. "And when Burt walks back over here, he's not going to want to hear it, either."

"Burt will hear exactly what you want him to hear," she said.

"Was that supposed to be offensive?"

"No, truthful. He idolizes you. You know that. He'd listen to me if you'd tell him to. Let me make my pitch before you throw me out. For old times' sake, huh?"

"I find this entire discussion unsettling," Crane said. "Make it fast."

"Okay. The remnants of leadership in Washington have no idea of what they've got in their jail. Kate should have pardoned Talib years ago, but she didn't because of her respect for your feelings. Now she regrets it. The people in charge think he's some sort of monster who'll lead New Cairo on an Islamic bloodbath across America. The Muslims think America is holding Talib as an affront to them, an attack on *their* religious leader."

"Newcombe . . . religious?"

"His wife is the only one who talks to him. She keeps bringing all these messages, the NOI religious protocol, back from her visits. She's very powerful and persuasive. People believe her."

"And Kate wants to force it into the open?"

"She's got a lot of pull still, even though she's retired from politics."

"Yeah, I see how she's retired."

"Just listen. She wants both you and Burt to testify. People who really knew Talib. Your voice would be the loudest in the country raised in favor of his release. We both know that Dan wouldn't lead any revolts or anything."

"I watched him shoot Burt. He fronted the raid that killed my family. I believe he's capable of anything."

"I've gone through all the disks, all the history of the event," Sumi said. "From everything I've seen, he went on that raid to try to stop you, but also to prevent bloodshed. His shooting Burt was pure self-defense. He'd have gotten his head bashed in if he hadn't."

"Don't you understand," he said slowly, sounding out each word, "that however many people died in this mess today, however much damage was done, it wouldn't have happened if Newcombe hadn't led those people into the Project? By this point in time, the planet would have been earthquake-free."

"You're only speculating," she said. "You have no idea

if the rest of the world would have gone along with your scheme."

"I hate him," Crane said.

"This is bigger than you and him. People's lives—"

"I'm not in the lifesaving business anymore," he interrupted.

"Then what were we doing with that water cannon?" she asked.

He looked at her, wishing he could share with her, somehow let her feel the pain that still ate him alive every time he saw a toddler, every time he saw a husband and wife holding hands. The tears came unbidden. "He ruined my life, S-Sumi," he choked out. "I don't want to s-stir it up. I don't want to th-think about it. Can't it just be left alone to work itself out without me?"

"No. It can't be worked out without you. And you're the one who doesn't understand. Facing this won't just release Abu Talib. It will release Lewis Crane also."

"Release me to what?"

"Maybe peace . . . finally."

He looked at her for a long moment. "You said you had two propositions."

She held his gaze. "I want you to marry me," she said without inflection.

"What?"

"Paul was a substitute for you," she said, "the years I spent living with, then trying to get rid of, him were hard, destructive. I'm fifty-two years old and have no understanding of how to meet or approach men."

"Are you saying you're in love with me?" Crane asked.

"I always have been . . . for almost twenty-five years now."

Crane sighed and slid down the wall to a sitting position, sloshing right into the water still pooled there. "It's been so long since I even thought that way," he said. "Since Lanie, there's been . . . there's been nobody."

"Are you ready for the grave, then?" she asked. "Are you already dead? Because if there's the least spark of life in you, you'll think seriously about my offer. I understand your work and I understand you. I know this is difficult.

You've always thought of me as a man. But I'm not. I never was. I was an actress playing a role. I love you, Crane. And I'm so damned scared of getting old and dying without sharing my life with you that I'm willing to sit here in the water and make a fool out of myself to be near you. I'm not ashamed of it."

Crane leaned his head back against the wall, the wail of sirens a ubiquitous reminder of their location. Yesterday he would have been horrified by Sumi's suggestion, but that was yesterday. Before today. Before he'd discovered there was still something inside of him that wasn't hollowed out.

"So, when would we set all this up?" he asked.

"Kate's hearing?"

"No," he said, smiling at her. "Our wedding."

FPF DETENTION BUILDING #73—DENVER, COLORADO
13 MARCH 2046, 10:45 A.M.

Crane sat with Sumi on a hard bench outside the hearing room in the drab, colorless jailhouse, listening to Joey Panatopolous, Mr. Panatopolous' grown son, getting excited in his aural.

"Crane . . . it's working. Do you hear me? It's working!"

"The generators are up?"

"Up and running! We are running entirely on thermal power as of right now. The turbines are singing, the heat is channeling through the domes. We no longer need solid fuels *or* focus. Charlestown is now energy self-sufficient."

"The moon is feeding us," Crane said. "It's working with us, not against. You've done a great job, Joey. Your Dad would have been proud."

"I wish he could have been up here to see it."

"Yeah . . . me, too. He's the only other man besides you who I would have trusted with tapping the core."

"He was my teacher."

"I know. My regards to everyone in Charlestown." He

began to sign off, then added, "Make this a citywide holiday. We have attained our independence today. Let's celebrate it every year."

"Done," Joey said. "Talk to you tomorrow."

"Tomorrow it is." Crane looked at his pad, then said, "Off," the line clearing, the comlink shutting down.

Sumi wrapped her arms around him. "Good news?"

He smiled at the love in her eyes. "We have successfully tapped the core and are using its power."

"I never doubted you'd succeed."

"You've never doubted anything I've said," he returned, leaning down and kissing her on the end of her nose. "That's why I always wanted you to work for me."

"That's because you haven't been wrong yet," she said.

"Just once," he returned, feeling even the happiness of Charlestown's good news drain out of him. "And now maybe twice."

"Don't torture yourself," she said, pointing a finger in his face. "You'll get yourself all upset. And you do *know* that you're doing the right thing."

He frowned. "Am I, Sumi? I trusted him and he abused my trust on all levels."

She shrugged. "You took his girlfriend away and he got jealous."

"Don't make it sound that crass and petty. It's not—"

"You're the one who's reduced it to the level of who hurt whom." She hugged him quickly, then cradled his face between her palms. "Crane, I love you, but you're bullheaded and blind when you want to be. You preach tolerance, politeness, but you do the same thing everyone else does—you try and build some cumulative tally of pain and loss, then compete to see who got hurt more. You can't base your relationship with the world on that."

"Sumi, I—"

She put her finger over his lips. "Listen to me: No one is asking you to forgive Newcombe. Your pain scorecard is your own business. But, my God, Crane, that man's been in solitary confinement for seventeen and a half years. What I'm asking you to do is realize that justice has been done and say so, then talk about the Dan Newcombe you knew before."

"He was a hell of a scientist."

She smiled at him. "Then tell them that. That's all. Be bigger than your feelings. Tell the truth."

Crane nodded, enjoying her hug. He wondered how it was going inside right now. Burt was giving testimony. Others, mestizos, were walking up and down the hallway, waiting. From time to time they'd glance nervously at Crane, then look away when he'd catch them watching.

It was so odd to see them, supporters, he supposed. They all desperately wanted Newcombe freed—but why? They were too young to know the man or care about him as a person. It was something else they wanted from him, something more fundamental.

He realized it was unity they were after, a closed nurturing circle of beliefs and ideas, a well from which to drink. It's what everyone wanted, really. It was what Charlestown was all about. And Newcombe was their elder statesman, just as Crane was Charlestown's. The faucet through which the ideas poured.

"Please tell me you haven't testified yet," came Kate Masters' voice from down the hall. "Tell me I haven't missed it."

Masters never so much walked as swept into a room. She was even able to make the drab hallway hers as she glided up to them, wearing diaphanous chiffon, not looking a day older than she had twenty years ago.

"Hello, hello," she said, kissing Crane on the cheek. "How's the happy couple?"

Sumi jumped up and hugged her. "We go next," she said. "I'm glad you made it."

"Made it? This is the biggest thing I've ever put together." Masters sat beside them, leaning out so she could speak with both. "Believe me, if this doesn't go today, you may as well pack up your stuff and move to another country, cause things are getting rough out there. We're looking at military and militia buildup on both sides of the border with New Cairo. This whole country could go."

"I've heard worse notions," Crane said.

"What's with you?" Masters asked him.

"He's just grumpy, that's all," Sumi said. "He's still having a problem with T-A-L-I-B."

"I can spell, dammit," Crane said. "And we're calling him Newcombe, remember?"

Masters put her hand on his arm. "You're not going to turn into a headjob on me, are you?"

"Leave me alone, Kate."

"I will not. You have a responsibility to go in there and settle this issue before things get out of hand."

"Why? Why is it my responsibility?"

"You already know the answer to that," Masters said coldly, standing. "I'll see you inside." She stalked toward the hearing room.

"Now you've got *her* all upset." Sumi made a clucking noise of disapproval.

"Do you ever do anything but negotiate?"

"No. It's my best skill."

"Oh, I don't know," Crane said, smiling. "Last night you showed me a few tricks."

"Stop," she whispered, slapping his shoulder. "Someone might hear you."

The hearing room door swung open again, Burt Hill walking out, shoulders slumped, head down. Hill had agreed to testify from the start, and Crane, for his part, had refused to influence him in any way. The two had never discussed what they felt, what they would say.

"Are you all right?" Crane asked as Sumi said, "What happened?"

"I'm a damned fool, that's what."

Crane grabbed his arm. "Burt. . . ."

"I was gonna burn him," Hill said. "I was gonna burn him to the ground. Hell, I ain't been half a man since he shot me. But . . . but I walked in that door. . . ." Burt looked confused, hurt even.

"What happened?" Sumi said loudly. "Burt, if—"

Crane stopped her with a raised hand. He turned and nodded. It was coming.

"I walked in there," Hill said again, "and I . . . I saw him. Oh, God, it tore my heart out. It was Doc Dan, but it was ... it was—oh, my." He put a hand to his chest. "I've got to sit down."

The man collapsed onto the bench, staring at nothing, shaking his head. He took deep breaths.

The door swung open and a veiled woman stuck her head into the hallway. "Lewis Crane," she said, then motioned him in when he waved to her.

"Will you be all right out here?" Sumi asked.

Burt mumbled a "yes," and Sumi and Crane entered the hearing room hand in hand.

As many as fifty people stood in one end of the room. There was no seating. The crowd was a mixture of aging camheads and citizens of New Cairo. Camming was rapidly turning into a pastime for the middle-aged, chip technology far enough advanced that the younger generation found a *raison d'etre* within the confines of their own skulls. The tech kids who'd been raised on nothing but the pad were at the forefront of the giant Plug-in.

Crane recognized Khadijah in the crowd of people wearing colorful robes, her stance straight and tall, fire in her eyes. On either side of her stood two young adults, Newcombe's children, he supposed. Little Charlie flashed unbidden through his mind. He didn't see Martin Aziz in the gallery. Intriguing.

At the other end, the room was bisected by a yellow line over which no one crossed. There was a desk there, a simple gunmetal-gray plastic desk. A man in a dark suit sat behind it. He wore a red-and-white-checked ghutra on his head, the fashion of the clerical class. Behind him stood a Chinese, probably a representative of YOU-LI Corp. Beside the desk was a chair bolted to the floor.

And then he saw Newcombe. Shackled to the wall. The man's hair was bright white, his long beard also snow white. He was wan and emaciated, his eyes dark, empty. Four G surrounded him, as if he could possibly escape, their new black exos and menacing faceplates making them look like storybook monsters, trolls from under the bridge. Crane realized then that the G had lost a lot of personnel at the Imperial Valley Massacre, as it was now called, and probably felt as if they, too, had a personal stake in the hearing.

"Dr. . . . Crane?" the man at the desk said, using a stylus as a pointer as he read directly from a screen on his desk.

"I'm Crane."

"Step forward."

Crane complied, moving to stand before the desk, ready to be sworn in.

"Are you a consumer?" the man asked.

Crane nearly laughed. "Well, of course I am. Everyone is."

"Excellent," the man said, nodding judiciously. "Please take a seat."

Crane sat. The man slid a pressure pad toward him on the desk. "This is the standard agreement," he said, "stating that you came here of your own free will and that LOK-M-TITE Security Service, Inc., owns all intellectual property rights connected with this hearing and that you will not be reimbursed for this appearance. If you accept the agreement, press your thumb to the pad."

Crane did, then sat back. He turned to look at Newcombe again. It was hard to hate the pitiful, all-but-broken, man who was chained like an animal. Their gazes met. Held. He saw sorrow in those sunken eyes, but he saw something else, too. Despite the horror Newcombe's life had become, his eyes still held pride.

Crane looked at Sumi. She was nodding to him, but seemed worried, nervous.

"The floor is yours, Dr. Crane," the nameless man behind the desk said.

Crane cleared his throat, having no idea of what he was going to say. His feelings were in turmoil. He opened his mouth and just let it out. "My wife . . . er, excuse me, Madame President Emeritus, reminded me before I came in here that all I had to do was tell the truth," he said. "The question is: Whose truth? My truth? Or is there a greater truth beyond mine? I'm a man of science, like Dr. Newcombe was. We became men of science because we hate the burden of subjectivity. I've always tried to gear myself to the higher truth of science, the knowledge; but I fail. If you want to know my truth, I will tell you that I hate that man over there. I still can't believe he violated me in so many ways. He took my dreams."

He shook his head. "That's my subjective truth. But what's my analytic truth? My analytic truth is that this is a man I once loved very much who made a mistake that led to tragic consequences. His mistake was that he traded gods, science for Allah, and hence, traded goals without knowing it. He is as much a manufactured product of his religion as I am of mine, and as much a victim of it. But this is not about victims. Everybody's a victim. That's what Kate Masters prompted me to remember. Before it's done, we all lose everyone and everything that was ever important to us, and then we lose ourselves. We've got to get beyond our own victimhood and take the long view, the view to what we leave behind and what follows us."

He felt his voice rising on its own, realizing that this wasn't about Newcombe, and Sumi already understood it. This was about Charlestown and the true art of community. "It's so easy to justify committing violence and inflicting pain. It's always the first, and most natural reaction. I must ask myself, what is the *right* thing to do?" Crane looked squarely at the man behind the desk. "May I ask the prisoner some questions?"

The bureaucrat nodded.

Crane stood and walked to Newcombe, the man's face wrinkling into a posture of near amusement. "Have you paid society's debt for the crimes you committed?"

"The bill plus change," Newcombe said immediately, imperious. Crane smiled when he realized the man's body was broken but not his mind. He sounded sharp.

"Did you intend to kill anyone when you went to the Imperial Valley Project that night?"

"No."

"Are you remorseful for what occurred?"

"I am remorseful for the loss of life. I always have been. That's not the way."

"I agree. Are you a violent man by nature?"

"I'm a scientist."

"Yes," Crane said. "And a very good one, sir," he added for the benefit of Mr. No Name.

"Thank you," Newcombe said. "You're not bad yourself."

"Do you consider yourself civilized, Dr. Newcombe?"

"The name is Talib, and yes, I consider myself civilized."

"Even after spending nearly a third of your life in jail?"

"I've already answered your question."

Crane moved within inches of his face. "Do you accept responsibility for the death of my wife and my son?"

"No," Newcombe said, and his voice caught slightly. "The death of your wife and son was my punishment for everything else I'd done."

Crane backed away from him, a hand to his mouth. He'd been so caught up in his own pain and loss he'd never considered that Dan's love for Lanie could have been as great as his own.

He looked at the man, really looked at him, and saw a mirror of his own soul, his own feelings. They saw it in each other, Newcombe nodding acknowledgment of a great truth. Crane reeled, staggering back several paces.

There was a commotion in the gallery. Khadijah was pushing her way through the spectators to get out of the room. She was followed quickly by his children.

Crane swallowed hard and faced Newcombe again, the feelings charging through him, pulsing like pressure waves. "I think," he said quietly, "that I can be man enough to set you free without forgiving you, and that you can achieve freedom without asking my forgiveness. And I think that's what's called civilization."

He turned and looked at Sumi. Tears were running down her cheeks.

He looked at the bureaucrat at the desk. "Sir," he said, in almost a whisper, "I believe we have come to a crossroads in society. Two great nations are grinding against each other, tearing at each other like the strike-slip fault that is ripping California apart. Mr. N . . . Talib is the pressure point on the plate, the bumper, that is keeping both societies from moving forward. Everything compresses on this point and if the pressure isn't relieved, the fault will rupture completely, destroying much for no reason."

Crane looked down at the floor. "I've hated earthquakes all my life because of what they took from me and I've hated Mr. Talib for the same reason. What a stupid . . . stupid fool I've been." He stared out at the gallery. "Hatred, I've realized, accomplishes nothing positive. It is only destructive. It is the active agency of fear. What does it get us? What good does it do us? I implore you to set this man free, no matter how much you may hate or fear him. Ease the pressure on the fault for the good of all. Talib is no danger to anyone, surely you can see that. He's merely a man who made a mistake, and that is all. Let him go home, and we'll all put this behind us."

He walked immediately out the door without looking at Newcombe. The pain was still there, but more than anyone, he had always known that life was pain.

In the hallway he shared a look with Newcombe's wife, the woman hating him despite his positive testimony. Khadijah seemed a person of deep and abiding anger. Too bad. She turned abruptly and moved into the protective circle of the mestizos in the hall.

He sat down beside Burt, the man taking one look at him and nodding. "You didn't burn him either, did you?" Crane shook his head. "We're both a couple of old fools, that's what."

"Ah, what the hell," Crane said, letting his head fall back against the beige metal wall. "Life goes on. You can't live for hatred, not really live."

The door swung open, and Sumi came out, a huge smile on her face. "You did it!" she said, hurrying to him to throw her arms around him.

Within a second, people exploded through the doorway, cheering, a confused Newcombe being swept along on a tide of love and support. Neither man looked directly at the other. Crane's gut clenched when he saw the royal treatment Newcombe was getting, but it didn't clench as much as it would have yesterday.

And that was called progress.

Chapter 22

RICHTER TEN

THE FOUNDATION
3 JUNE 2058, AROUND NOON

Crane could pinpoint the time when he had known his life was over: the spring of 2055. One day he'd started going through storage cubes, dragging out all the testimonials and awards and service medals he'd received in over half a century of trying to slay the beast within. He'd framed the most significant honors and hung them on the walls of his office at the Foundation until there wasn't any more wall space. And he'd looked at them, reflecting. It was then he knew he was living in the past, not the future. It was then that he began planning for today.

He sat with a young man named Tennery in his office, embarrassed that the display on the wall seemed gaudy, ostentatious. He spoke simply to hold Tennery's attention and keep him from looking around. "Why do you want to join our little colony?" he asked.

"I've heard that it's . . . different," Tennery said, curly

red hair falling to his shoulders. He was twenty-four years old. "I heard that you're trying to build a world where logic speaks loudly, where people think before they act." He laughed. "I've always wanted to live in a world like that, because it seems to me I'm surrounded by maniacs."

"True enough," Crane said, his gaze drifting to the view of the globe in the main room. It was turning slowly, lights and whistles signifying geologic movement on San Andreas. "You're a botanist?"

"No," the man said. "A farmer. Just a plain, simple farmer. I do have my agricultural degree, but—"

"But it's useless as far as real farming goes?"

The man nodded. "Getting up at 5:30 in the morning takes something more than a degree. Besides, I'm interested in Moondust."

"Yes. I know. Sterile soil, totally devoid of any organic compounds. Yet, when mixed with regular dirt. . . ."

"The Sea of Ingenuity dust I've been receiving from Charlestown has increased my corn production by nearly fifteen percent. I also hear you have a mix."

Crane smiled again. He liked this one a lot. "Yes. Delta dirt, Ganges dirt, Amazon dirt, Himalayan dirt. We're mixing up to fifty different soils, looking for the best pH and natural nutrient balance. Interested?"

"Am I?" The man looked at his hands, then back at Crane. "My wife wanted me to ask you something. We've been hearing there's a lot of problems with water supply on the Moon—"

"Not at Charlestown," Crane said. "When the Islamic consortiums got control of all the shipping of water Moonside, they started using it as a blackmail device, rationing, threatening to cut it off if the Moon didn't become an Islamic State. We had already anticipated such an eventuality and had been secretly mining Mars for permafrost. We now have a permanent, dependable shipping system from Mars, new water arriving every six weeks. We're hoping we'll have enough to sell to the other colonies to make some money and keep the region autonomous."

"Good luck."

"I should wish it to you. You're the one who is going to live in Charlestown."

"You're not going to be there?"

"Not like you think." Crane smiled. "Welcome aboard."

"So I'm accepted?"

"You and your wife, Mona, and your two children." He thought for a minute. "Lana and Sandy. We need people like you in the colony. I think eventually it will be the last refuge for humanity. As such, it should be represented by people who are decent, honest."

"We know very little about Charlestown."

"Intentional," Crane said. "We're not advertising. The right people tend to seek us out. In that way we're kind of like a lighthouse."

"What are the rules?"

"Be polite," Crane said, "and live your life. We have no police, no jails, no courts. It's been set up as a large family unit. Whatever earnings we generate go to the maintenance of the city itself. Whatever's left is divided up. People seem satisfied with it. I don't know, to tell you the truth. The city seems to be self-perpetuating, evolving its own way of life. I learned a long time ago that I don't have all the answers. I meet the applicants. If I like them, they go up. If I don't, they don't. You're the last."

"The last applicant?"

Crane nodded. "The last that I'll screen. You will bring the total to five thousand citizens. I've thrown the stew together. It's up to you to cook it."

"You've got schools?"

"All the comforts of home, though our schooling tends to be very old-fashioned. We teach kids to work their brains, not their pads. And I don't know that religion plays a very large part in Charlestown life."

"My religion's always been self-reliance," Tennery said, standing. "When do we leave?"

"Tomorrow," Crane said, "from my complex in Colorado Springs. Pack as much as you carry."

Burt Hill filled the doorspace. "Dammit, Crane. You haven't packed a blinking thing yet."

"All in good time, Burt. Meet our newest citizen of Charlestown, Jackson Tennery."

"It's on the darkside, you know," Hill said, shaking hands with the man.

"I know."

Hill cocked his head. "You're as crazy as the rest of them up there," he said, then looked again at Crane. "If you want to do that stupid teev show, we have to leave now."

"Good," Crane said, standing also. "We'll accompany Mr. Tennery to his helo."

They walked out of the office. The Foundation was a beehive of activity as scientists and workmen hurried around carrying boxed equipment and personal belongings. Mendenhall was evacuating. Within several hours, the debris of the Foundation would be part of Baja Island, a new addition to the map of the Pacific.

They moved through the globe room, Crane stopping for one last look at the machine that encompassed all his dreams and all his frustrations. It had been Lanie's. It had belonged to many others since then, including Sumi, who'd died two years ago of a genetically created cancer virus. The virus had been unleashed by the Brotherhood, the terrorist arm of the Religion of Cosmic Oneness—the Cosmies—who were seeking their own State free of the religious persecution of the world's Moslems. The plague had killed nearly forty million people worldwide before mutating into a common cold germ, to which Crane had been immune because of his earlier experiences with the disease. Brother Ishmael inadvertently had saved his life.

Sumi. . . . It was Sumi, ultimately, who'd made today possible with her work on the globe. It was Sumi who'd made him understand he didn't have all the answers and that the pain of life wasn't his alone to command. It was Sumi who'd come up with the idea that synthesized his entire life, that made today—3 June '58—the culmination of all his dreams and hopes and expectations. If Lanie had been his great love, then Sumi Chan Crane had been his great teacher. She'd made his life, and his death, worthwhile.

He'd completely rethought Charlestown because of Sumi's forcing him to testify. He'd realized he was no smarter than anyone else when it came to telling people what to do. It had made all the difference.

Their years together had been the best, the happiest of his life, and he felt doubly blessed for having known two women of remarkable character and insight, two women he'd loved dearly and had to let go of reluctantly.

It was difficult to imagine sometimes that he had known Sumi for nearly fifty years and Lanie for less than five. Years compress like fault lines in the mind. While everything else changes, the mind remembers exactly what it wants to remember. A decade can be lost and a year seem like forever. When love is abruptly taken, love remains active.

He'd learned, finally, how to relax under Sumi's tutelage. He'd learned to sail and they'd taken up oceanography together. He'd seen Charlestown to completion, happily turning the running of it over to its citizens. He'd seen the radioactive cleanup of the water systems finally complete itself when Crane freighters hauled all the waste into a Moon orbit, then slingshot it toward the Sun. The things he'd seen, the things his mind had held, filled him up. No man could have asked for more and no longer did he feel plagued by the failure at the Salton Sea—only one of many things that had happened to him. One of many dreams.

The years had passed quickly, but had left a million memories behind, enough for a king's lifetime. What more could anyone ask?

The globe was still operating and would continue to operate until the forces of Nature pulled it apart. The Foundation itself was being split between his Cheyenne Mountain headquarters and the Isle of Wight globe station, good, trained people left behind to carry on.

They moved out of the mosque to stand on the flat plain of the Mendenhall Ledge, a continual surge of helos filling airspace around the Foundation. One thing he'd learned in life in seventy-one years was that no matter how far in advance a person knew about something, he would still wait until the last minute to take care of it.

"Is all this really going to be gone later today?" Tennery asked, as they walked him to his rented helo.

"Yes, it is," Crane said, and a lifetime swept through

him like a wave. "Gone but not forgotten. Life changes whether we want it to or not."

The man, excited, not giving a damn about California, climbed into the helo. "I can't wait to talk to Mona. She's really going to sky out. Is there anything you want me to tell them when I get up there? Any messages?"

"Yeah," Crane said. "Tell them to do the right thing." He shut the man's door and smiled at him. Then he turned and walked away, Hill hacking beside him.

"You know you didn't leave yourself enough time to pack," the man said, leading Crane toward a passenger helo in the midst of the swarm.

"That's all right," Crane said casually. "There's nothing I need to hold on to."

"You're in a hell of a good mood today. I figured today would be a bitch for you, was wonderin' how I'd keep you glued together when you knew your dream was really over."

Crane put his arm around the big man's shoulder. "Nothing's ever over, Burt. The circles just spin smaller. Besides, I did everything I could to avert this catastrophe— everything."

"You're crazy, you know that?"

"Yes!" Crane answered emphatically. "Gloriously crazy. Today is just the beginning, Burt."

"The beginning of what?"

"Stage two." Crane winked.

Hill shook his head. "I'll get somebody to pack your stuff up while we're gone," he said, reaching the sleek, bulbous ship, climbing in to help Crane up.

"Whatever."

The seats were plush, and Crane sank back into his, eyes still fixed on the Foundation compound, the chalets on the hills, the covered walkway from Lanie's level to his. He'd never see these places again, yet felt no remorse. They'd live on in their own way.

The ship rose smoothly into the air, its props silent as they angled toward Los Angeles. The sky was full of ships, hundreds of thousands of people getting out, heading to refugee camps in Oregon and Arizona. No matter how many times it was explained to the population that every-

thing from the Imperial Valley north to San Francisco
would be gone, most people still thought in terms of a
quake they'd bounce back from, in terms of returning to
their homes after the temblors were done.

He wasn't sure what the fate of Baja was to be. Cosmies
in huge numbers were pouring into the area even as so
many others left. They intended to declare Baja a free nation the moment it broke from the continent, an island
republic belonging to them. It was even possible they could
pull it off. There was no power structure in America that
would try and stop them and the Islamic world was already crumbling under its own puffed-up weight as the
remaining non-Islamic world forged defensive and economic alliances against them. New, streamlined power
brokers were emerging from such places as Stockholm and
Toronto. Islam had always been as much an emotional
issue as an economic one. Once it had reached the limits
of its fierce domination of the world, its members immediately began to squabble among themselves and wither as
a group. He loved to watch the wheel turn.

New Cairo was feeling the burn, too. Its relationship
with the rest of America had soured as soon as America
was able to forge non-Islamic alliances, and they'd had the
expense of two costly wars with Central American Islamic
States over trade issues.

Abu Talib had taken religious and political control over
New Cairo within a year of his release, following the assassination of Martin Aziz. As in the case of Ishmael Mohammed, Aziz's murderer was never found. Talib's path
hadn't crossed Crane's since the hearing in which he'd
been freed. The times Crane had seen the man on the teev,
Talib had been quiet and soft-spoken, talking of unity and
brotherhood. His wife seemed to do the lion's share of the
political work, Talib content to stay in the background.
Crane thought about Newcombe—not Talib—a lot these
days. And he regretted that he hadn't contacted the man
and made peace with him. His next project was one that
would probably appeal a great deal to Dan.

The helo passed above the old War Zone, a regular part of
the city again, and moved toward Sunset Boulevard and the

KABC studios where he was supposed to give his interview, direct from the heart of the conflagration. Cars and helium floaters clogged the roadways both in and out of town, Crane wondering if those escaping had enough time at this point, for even as the helo set down in the parking lot, he knew the compression on the fault near Mt. Pinos was straining on the edge of rupture, the Imperial Fault also rupturing, beginning the process of rending California in twain from the Gulf of California through the Salton Sea and the San Jacinto Fault all the way to San Francisco. Meanwhile, the Emerson Fault near Landers would tear under the Salton Sea and begin a rupturing process that would stretch six hundred miles to Mt. Shasta, beginning the clockworks that would put Nevada and Arizona on the shores of the Pacific in the next few years. He wouldn't be around for those. He'd had his shot and was more than ready to leave the world to—what had been Tennery's word?—maniacs. He liked that. The maniacs.

They stepped out of the helo and into the madness of an open city. All around them, looters smashed store windows. Those too poor or stupid to get out were having a party to celebrate their inheritance of the city. Sirens were sounding, but no authority figures could be seen. The city was sitting on the cusp of its own eternity.

"You really wanted to come here," Hill said, "to see this?"

"I want to wallow in it," Crane said, walking toward the building. A car out of control careened past them to smash against a brick wall, throwing the driver into the windshield. "My whole life has been tied to this day."

"You don't have nothin' nuts in mind, do you?" Hill asked as Crane moved through the doors.

"Depends on your definition of nuts."

They entered into the cool darkness of the small, one-story building. Crane was pumped up, excited. Ever since the day Sumi had died, he'd been counting down until today. She'd have been proud of him.

A man with a cam-eye where a real one should have been hurried up to them in the empty lobby. He wore a shiny, lime-green plastic suit with ruffled shirt and gold ascot.

"You're Crane, right?"

"That's correct."

"My name's Abidan. Quite a show you've cooked up here." He was sweating and seemed nervous, shaky.

"I don't make them," Crane said. "Are you staying behind?"

"That's what journalists do, sir. They stay behind."

"That's what geologists do, too, son. Let's get on with it."

"We're going to broadcast from back here," Abidan said, leading them through a ghost studio, devoid of people, full of bleeping equipment. "This is a main news webset. We have uplink capabilities here to forty-seven hundred news distribution points worldwide and I'm going to be juicing to all of them."

He opened the door for them into a small studio, a living room setup surrounded by black curtains. The lighting was somber.

Hill gasped when they walked into the room. "Son of a bitch," he said. Seated at one of the chairs in the living-room set was an ancient-looking Abu Talib, dressed in his usual black suit, minus the fez. Talib stood up.

"Just because we're old, boy, don't mean we can't whip you," Hill said, Crane putting out a hand to silence him.

"It's all right, Burt. In fact, it's perfect. Like old times." His excitement grew. It was coming together—and without him even having to work at it. Dreams really did come true.

He moved across the empty floor to the set. Hand extended, Abu Talib, seeming hundreds of years old, stood and smiled warmly. "It is good to see you, old friend," he said, shaking Crane's hand.

"It's good to see you, too. . . . What do I call you? Your Eminence or Mr. Talib or—"

"Call me Dan." He smiled. "I think it's the most comfortable thing for both of us."

"Here it is, ladies and gentlemen," Abidan said, his cam-eye glaring at them, "the meeting between two great enemies. One man who wanted to save California. One who was willing to kill to stop him."

"Not very cordial," Talib said, shaking his head at Abidan as if he were a naughty child. "We've been had,

Crane." He nodded in acknowledgment at the figure several feet away. "Burt."

"Dr. Crane," Abidan said, goading, "how does it feel to be standing here on the eve of the cataclysm with the man who destroyed your life?"

"If Mr. Abidan wants a fight, I think he's going to be very disappointed." Crane laughed; smiling, Hill applauded softly.

Newcombe's brows knit deeply. "Mr. Abidan has already been less than gracious," he said quietly. "I would think that if he wanted any kind of interview at all, he'd shut up and let us talk. Don't worry." He grinned at Abidan, the wrinkles in his weathered face folding upon one another like accordion pleats. "We'll be through soon enough."

"Why did you come here?" Crane asked Talib. "You have a country to run."

"*That* we'll talk about after the camera's off. May we sit, please?" he asked, motioning to a chair on the set. "My back's not what it used to be."

"My everything's not what it used to be," Crane said, sitting down. "And I'm dying to talk to you. I have a proposition for you."

Newcombe sat back, his deep, sunken eyes lighting up. "A proposition," he said. "I'm intrigued."

Abidan started for the third seat, Newcombe waving him off. "Burt, come up here and sit with us. Let that young man stand . . . though I bet he won't be standing when the EQ hits."

The three of them laughed. Crane pointed at Abidan. "Know how to save yourself, boy?" he asked, then glanced at Burt and Dan. "Look at him, he's already sweating. He's shaking so much, the picture's probably wobbly. I can already hear it, down in the Imperial Valley, the fault howling like a wounded animal as it rips apart, pushing farther west, yanking that kink right out of Mount Pinos. Do you understand the immensity of what you have so blithely undertaken, young man? Those people on the streets . . . they're ignorant, or out of control, or crazy, or ready to die. The men who sit before you have no fear of death. Do you?"

Mute, Abidan shook his head.

"You're going to get to witness *firsthand*," Crane continued, "a monster tsunami *east* of LA as the Pacific rushes in to fill the mammoth tearing gouge in the body of the Earth. Do you know you'll see your streets explode before your eyes? Afterward, when the quake is over, you have to live with the consequences. Fresh water runs out first. Then, as you return to a prehistoric environment, diseases are rampant. Are you prepared to bury a couple million bodies? That's what you'll have to do to keep the diseases and the smell away as your own sweat makes *you* smell like death, and your house and your friends and everything else are gone."

"Do you think," Newcombe said to Abidan, "that this cataclysm will be like a gentle push of a raft away from a riverbank? Try to imagine the strength of forces that can level and raise mountains as easily as you turn your eye on. Do you realize that Los Angeles stands zero chance of surviving as the Elysian Park Fault fissures up the whole city, dropping entire blocks miles down into the ground, never to be seen again? California is going to be ripped asunder. There will be a conflagration the likes of which hasn't been seen on this planet in millions of years. Is it really important that you die in California, at this time?"

Abidan gulped and shook his head, the cam-eye not moving with his head. "Good," Newcombe said. " 'Cause I want you to let us finish our say, then I want you to get on your horse and get the hell out of here. You've got some good years ahead of you. Try and stay alive for them. Don't be like those idiots on the streets."

"T-thank you," Abidan whispered.

"I'm surprised," Crane said to Newcombe. "You've learned how to use power."

"And you've learned to keep your mouth shut occasionally," Newcombe replied. "We've both changed."

"Oh, boy," Hill said, rolling his eyes. "Here we go."

Crane leaned toward the cam, pointing to Newcombe. "This man dogged me from the day I hired him in '23. This man never went along willingly with me on anything in his damned life."

"It's because you were a dictator." Newcombe laughed. "And you had a hidden agenda."

Crane threw his hands in the air. "I guess today we can see why I kept it hidden."

"Neither one of you would have done anything without me to keep you off each other's throats," Hill said. "It's me you ought to be thankin'."

"Thanks, Burt," they said in unison.

"You're welcome. I didn't have nothin' else to do anyway."

Crane turned back to the cam. Abidan was shaking visibly, his real eye opened wide in near panic as a small foreshock rumbled through, shaking the set and causing a bank of lights to crash to the floor. The three of them laughed as Abidan hit the deck.

"Not going to be safe here for long," Hill said.

"Let me do this." Crane got out of his chair and walked over to Abidan, who was lying in a fetal position on the floor, covering his head.

"Roll over and look at me, son," Crane said.

Abidan unwrapped himself slowly and rolled onto his back. The red light on his cam-eye stared up at Crane. "I want to get out of here," Abidan said.

"I've got a helo waiting in the parking lot," Crane said. "I've saved a seat for you. Just let me say my piece first." He looked straight at Abidan's cam-eye. "Ladies and gentlemen, the things we are saying are not exaggerations. If you live west of the San Andreas Faultline, you are in deadly peril. Don't take for granted that you will be safe anywhere."

Crane took a deep breath, preparing to launch into the familiar litany and hoping against hope that there were people out there listening to him who would heed his advice.

"If you can't get east of the line in the next hour or so, do not go into your homes. They are deathtraps. Avoid large trees. Get to as much open ground as you can find. This advice will save some of you, some it won't. I've personally witnessed five dozen quakes in my lifetime and been on site at hundreds more. Believe me. Los Angeles: gone. San Francisco: gone. Santa Barbara, San Bernardino, San Diego, Tijuana, any large city from Baja to San Francisco is probably going to die today. If you don't want to die with it, listen to me. You can't control this with your mind or your rationalizations. It's going to happen and it's going to happen to *you* unless you do something now! *Now!*"

Crane stood back. "That's it. Cut it off. Let those people go."

He helped Abidan to his feet. "The helo's in the parking lot," he said. "Get in it."

Abidan ran.

"We need to talk," Newcombe said, joining Crane in the front of the set.

"You have a helo waiting?"

The man shook his head. "Interesting," Crane said. "You're welcome to mine."

"Thank you."

"Come on," Hill said. "Let's put some miles between us and this damned place."

He led them out into the parking lot, Abidan already strapped in and holding tight in one of the ten passenger seats. Hill climbed in and reached for Crane.

"You go ahead," Crane said, shaking his head.

"You ain't comin'," Hill said in sad resignation. "I knew something was up." He looked at Newcombe.

"Me either." He smiled.

Hill's face went slack, and he searched for words.

"You've helped me say the final farewells to two wives, Burt," Crane said, moving to the loading bay to embrace him, without tears, without remorse. They had both done as well as they could have and there was no sadness in that. "You helped me through the death of a son. You helped me when I was so down I thought I'd never laugh again. You've saved my life a thousand times in a thousand ways. Thank you."

"I-I can't come with you on this trip." Hill sniffed. Pulling away, he hacked, then spit. He looked from Crane to Newcombe and back. "I'm not ready for it yet."

"I didn't expect you to be," Crane said. "Besides, I've

got to learn to do something for myself. Sit down, Burt. You understand I have to close the circle?"

Hill nodded, then sat. "I'm gonna miss you, Doc."

Crane nodded, smiling, then slapped the side of the machine, pointing up with his thumb for the pilot, who took to the air immediately.

They had about an hour.

"Care to take a walk?" Crane asked Newcombe.

"Sounds good." He leaned close to Crane and whispered, "You know, what I'd really like is a drink."

"It's not Islamic."

Newcombe smiled wide. "I think Allah will understand, given the circumstances."

"Good. Let's find a rooftop restaurant somewhere, a really tall one where we can feel the whiplash."

They walked into the guts of the city, destruction and anarchy reigning all around them. So much had changed in Crane's time on Earth; so much had stayed the same. There were the looters, the Rockers, who were now called Seismos, the suicides, and the Cosmies dressed in white robes with the Third Eye emblazoned in red on their chests. Today Crane was one of them and maybe he'd always been. Part of the city was burning. Looters helping the EQ. Thoughtful.

They moved along unmolested. The suicides always had the *look* about them, and people automatically granted them privacy for their demise.

After several blocks of brilliant sunshine and a warm wind in the city of angels, they found a shaky-looking tower of steel and lots of glass on Wilshire that had a working elevator up to its rooftop restaurant. It was whiplash material if Crane had ever seen it.

The restaurant had a marvelous view of the city in all directions. They smashed through the glass door to get inside, then chose a table with a view to the west. Crane went behind the bar to grab a bottle of good Scotch. The sky was full of hovering helos, thick, like swarming flies—curiosity-seekers there to watch one world die and another come painfully into being.

"Why are you doing this?" Crane asked as he found a

couple of clean glasses. He hadn't had a drink in nearly fifteen years.

"It completes my circle, too. I spent years thinking about this moment in prison . . . my own punishment, I suppose."

"You've served your time, Dan." Crane came back with the bottle and glasses and poured them each a highball glass full. "Let it go."

"If you were me, could you let it go?"

Crane raised his glass. "I don't know. Pick up your drink. To you, old friend."

"To both of us," Newcombe said, toasting, then grimacing at his first taste of alcohol in decades. "You seem awfully happy, considering this is the last day of your life."

"Endings and beginnings," Crane said. "You seem pretty happy yourself."

"Are you kidding? I'm ecstatic. This is the first real decision I've made on my own in nearly thirty years. For seventeen years, I woke up with a hangman's noose every morning. Death certainly holds no fear for me."

"I died years ago," Crane said, watching his glass of Scotch shake and shimmer, reacting to the vibrations running through the ground. "Then I came back. I realize now that life and death are only words. I don't hate EQs anymore, either. Funny how everything changes." He took a long drink, his stomach already burning. "I'm going to get snookered."

"Me, too," Newcombe said. "And it'll take about five minutes."

Crane nodded. "I still don't get you. My business here is long finished. I can't wait to move on. But you . . . you've got a wife, a family, social and political responsibilities."

"Let's set the record straight about my responsibilities," he said, opening his eyes wide and grinning. "It's a funny story, but this is what I discovered after getting out of prison. My wife, who was sleeping with every man whose pants she could get off, personally killed her brother Ishmael, to get him out of the way. She had his murder passed off as an assassination and used it for propaganda purposes. Then she worked behind the scenes against her other brother, Martin, until I was set free. At that time she had her loyalists kill Martin Aziz so I could assume the position of public demigod and private servant."

"I . . . I would never have guessed, never."

"I'm not finished," Newcombe said, taking another drink. "Prison changed me. I had no desire for power or fame on any level. I would have given anything to go back to geology, but there I was, stuck, the symbol of Islamic unity for millions of people. My wife said, 'make the speeches.' So I made the speeches she wrote. I was just her mouthpiece. I put my time in for the good of the people. Boy, there's a loaded term. But Khadijah's ambitions know no boundaries. There have been three attempts on my life. I was able to trace all three back to my loving wife, the last time aided by my loving son, who is apparently what this is all about. Trust me. Khadijah will rule New Cairo through Abu ibn Abu. She's been ruling through *me* long enough. I'm happy to get the hell out."

"That's a damned poor way to live, Dan."

Newcombe shook his head. "I didn't want any of that. In the sixty-seven years of my life, my happiest—my best— years were spent with you, working on EQ-eco and running around the world chasing your damned demons. My work with you was the single best human gesture of my entire life."

"My testimony at your hearing was mine," Crane said. "It finally made me question myself. It humanized me. Lewis Crane was able to stop playing God. I thank Sumi for that. She was a hell of a woman."

"To Sumi," Newcombe said, raising his glass again.

Both men drank.

"You said something at that hearing I've never forgotten," Newcombe said, both of them watching the ocean in the distance, slight smoke from a dozen different fires making the view hazy. "You said that you could free me without forgiving me and that I could go on with life without asking for forgiveness." He shook his head. "I can't. I want your forgiveness now, Crane. I don't want to . . . move on without it."

"I forgave you years ago, Dan," Crane said. "I had to in order to go on with Charlestown, in order to put it behind me."

"But you never told me."

"No . . . I never did. And for that, I apologize. Seeing you today has been my chance to rectify that error in what I hope will be a profound way."

They both drank, then refilled their glasses.

"Is Charlestown that Moon colony you're tied up with?"

"Yeah," Crane said, leaning close to Newcombe. "Do you have any money?"

"In my pocket, you mean?"

"No. Money money."

"I'm filthy with it," Newcombe said. "Rulers of countries do quite nicely. I've managed to sock away several hundred million."

"I want you to give it to me," Crane said, "and I think we need to hurry." He nodded out the window, buildings were swaying. The ground vibrations from the Imperial Valley quake were being felt this far north.

"What do you want it for? You're getting ready to die, too."

"Are you ported?" Crane asked, his voice slurring just a touch.

Newcombe nodded quickly.

Crane took a small chip out of his pad with tweezers from his pocket. He passed the tweezers to Newcombe, who was weaving, a touch high, missing the port at first, then hitting the slot and sitting back.

Crane smiled as Newcombe closed his eyes. The chip was a distillation of Charlestown, an optical/vid tour of the place overlaid with Crane's emotions concerning it. And then there was The Plan.

The experience was designed to hit the brain like a thought stored lifelong, everything Crane knew and felt and believed about Charlestown soaking through osmosis into Newcombe's mind in an instant—Crane's feelings, his feelings. The speed of thought.

"Oh, yes . . ." Newcombe said, smiling, nodding. "This is nice. I understand."

He tweezed the chip out. "This is amazing," he said, passing it back to Crane, who slotted it into his pad, transmitting it for the first time to the Moon's systems. "You can really do this?"

"Sumi thought it up," he said. "Spent her last years working on it. We're all a part of that globe, Dan."

"Are you. . . ."

"Asking you to join us? Yes! Will you?"

"Crane, you son of a bitch!" He laughed. "You've beat the system after all. Better believe I'll join you. It's the offer of a lifetime."

"Good. Let's get all your money first," Crane replied. "I don't think your wife and children need it."

The rumble began then, loud, louder than Tokyo, the buildings outside shaking violently. They shook violently. Newcombe pointed to the floor, at rats charging out of the walls.

"You can't escape it even in the nice places!" he called over the clatter of breaking glass and crockery. Crane grabbed the bottle just as their table fell over.

"Bank accounts," Newcombe said, his pad automatically entering his accounts.

"Charlestown account," Crane said to his pad. "Accept ID funds transfer."

The building swayed, the glass of their windows popping out to plummet thirty stories to the ground. Huge structures collapsed all around outside. The ocean was throbbing and churning in the distance. It was beautiful, exciting.

"Transfer all funds," Newcombe said, both men reaching out to place their thumbprint on the other's pad.

"Transactions complete," the pad returned in both aurals.

"Good man," Crane said, pulling out another chip. "Now, hurry, put this in your port."

"What is it?"

"I'm going to copy your mind and put it into the computers. That chip is blank."

"Give it to me!" Newcombe yelled. A chair hurtled past. Newcombe went down hard, but protected the Scotch in his hand. The EQ roared all around them.

"Here!" Crane shouted.

Newcombe reached up to grab the chip and port it.

"Do it . . . hurry!" Crane said.

The chairs and tables were bouncing across the floor even as the entire structure moaned and danced. Crane reveled in experiencing whiplash firsthand. Another violent jolt or two and the restaurant was going to be first-floor property.

Newcombe ported, his head twisted as the chip sucked his mind into an inch-square sheet of clear plastic. The building was bellowing as it swayed dangerously. Crane, on his knees now, took a quick drink.

Newcombe pulled the chip out of his port. "I'm ready to go," he said, handing it to Crane, who quickly fed it into his pad and transmitted. "God, am I ready to go."

A wild spasm caught them, both men tossed across the room, slamming into the bar which was bouncing in their direction. And, then, the Beast began to scream in earnest as the rending agony built.

"It's the craziest thing," Crane shouted over the roaring, "but my arm . . . it doesn't hurt!"

The building began to crumble, bits of ceiling falling in on them. And the world tumbled then. Lewis Crane jerked a chip out of his own head and jammed it into his pad, even as he felt himself falling . . . falling . . .

. . . the image pulling away. Distant. A city collapsing, a house of cards built in a wind tunnel, swept away in an instant.

EPILOGUE

The geography helo vanished, replaced by Moonscape. Geodesic domes, reflecting brilliant sunlight and stretching to the horizon, were connected by skyways and tunnels and catwalks. A central plaza sat just within view; a working King Projection globe of the Moon dominated it.

"And that, children," said a virtual Lewis Crane as he walked through the fourth grade classroom, "is how Moonbase Charlestown came to be."

His good arm holding his bad behind his back, he reached the front of the room. The virtual Lewis Crane was a globe projection that held its namesake's soul within its electrical charges. It wasn't real, but it *was* Lewis Crane. And, with pride, he drank in its surroundings, the product of his imagination.

"This . . . city," he said, "is yours to create, you know. What will you do with it? I ask only that you use your minds before you make your choices, and that you feel the pain of others as intensely as you feel your own." The Virtual smiled. "I want to introduce a couple of people you might recognize."

He reached his good arm out toward the door, and Burt Hill, Dan Newcombe, Sumi Chan, and Lanie King walked in. Crane's virtual self felt a flush of joy as the children gasped in happiness, then applauded the other minds that Crane had stored in the machine.

Lanie, Dan, and Sumi stood with him in the front of the room. "Believe," Crane said, moving to embrace the people who'd made his life worthwhile. "Believe in dreams. They never die."

He looked toward the classroom door, Lanie already staring that way, Hill, Newcombe, and Sumi smiling broadly.

"Well, don't just stand there," Crane said. "Come on out and let the kids see you."

"Yes, please do," Lanie said.

And, much to the delight of his father and his mother and his other adult friends, little Charlie Crane, eighteen months old, toddled through the doorway, arms outstretched.

Author's Note

Many years ago I was standing in a Delhi hotel, when I became aware of a faint vibration underfoot. "I had no idea," I said to my hosts, "that Delhi had a subway system." "It doesn't," they answered.

That was my one and only encounter with earthquakes—so how did I get involved with *Richter 10*? Well, the initial inspiration was undoubtedly the January 1994 Northridge earthquake, the aftermath of which I had witnessed on local TV. Between the first and the third of February, while this was still fresh on my mind, I wrote an 850-word movie outline, which I immediately faxed to my agent, Russell Galen. I did not have the necessary background to take the matter further, as my knowledge of California was restricted to the MGM backlot and the foyer of the Beverly Wilshire Hotel. So Mike McQuay was commissioned to do all the hard work, and he succeeded magnificently.

Another very important input was the program California Earthquakes, created by John Hinkley, the computer genius whose Vistapro virtual reality program[1] made possible the "before and after terraforming" Mars illustrations in my own *The Snows of Olympus.* This plots over 20,000—that's right, *20,000*—earthquakes during the period 1992–94. When turned on, it shows a map of California, and one can select by color-coding all the earthquakes between the magnitudes of 1 and 6. They can then be shown at rates from one second equals one minute, to one second equals one year. A zoom function also allows examination in detail.

When switched on, the display is amazing—and terrifying. Little circles of various colors and sizes explode all over California, and after a short time the outline of the San Andreas fault becomes clearly visible, as does a second fault line along the eastern border of the state. The central region is completely free from quakes, and one can see at once where any sensible person would wish to purchase real estate. The Northridge event is truly spectacular, particularly if one zooms in for a close-up. When it is displayed at the slowest rate, literally hundreds of aftershocks are visible, continuing for over a week. It's a very scary program indeed, and I'm surprised that the California Chamber of Commerce hasn't banned its export—or declared John (who's still living there!) *persona non gratissima.*

During the year after the *Richter 10* contract was signed, I never received any communication from Mike or sent him any further ideas of my own. So when the manuscript arrived, I had no idea what to expect. He had done such an amazing job of fleshing out the bare bones of my synopsis that I read the manuscript with mounting excitement, turning the pages more and more feverishly in my anxiety to know what happened next. . . .

[1] It comes on a single diskette from Progressive Products, P.O. Box 1575, Pablo Robles, CA 93447.

Although I have actively collaborated with other authors on a few occasions—notably, with Gentry Lee on the *Rama* series—this is the first time that I have given an idea to another author to develop entirely as he wished. But it may not be the last: I've discovered that this gives me all the fun of creation—but none of the lonely hours slaving away at the keyboard.

I hope that you have enjoyed the resulting novel as much as I did.

Arthur C. Clarke
26 April 1995

Postscript
Barely a month after I had written the above note, I received the tragic news that Mike had just died of a heart attack at the age of forty-six. Apparently there had been no prior warning.

I am indeed glad that I had written to him at once after receiving the manuscript, expressing my admiration for the skill with which he had developed my synopsis. And I was delighted to receive his very friendly and heartfelt reply—doubtless one of the last letters he wrote.

Though we never met, I feel sure that with his untimely passing the science fiction field has lost one of its most able, and promising, contributors.

Arthur C. Clarke
27 July 1995

About the Authors

ARTHUR C. CLARKE is one of the most celebrated science fiction authors of our time, named Grand Master by the Science Fiction Writers of America in 1986. He is the author of more than fifty books with more than 50 million copies in print. His bestsellers include *Childhood's End, 2001: A Space Odyssey, The Hammer of God,* and, most recently, *Rama Revealed* (with Gentry Lee). He co-broadcast the Apollo 11, 12, and 15 missions with Walter Cronkite and Wally Schirra and shared an Oscar nomination with Stanley Kubrick for the film version of *2001: A Space Odyssey.*

MIKE McQUAY is the author of thirty-five novels, including *Puppetmaster* and *State of Siege.* In 1988 he won the Philip K. Dick Award for his novel *Memories.* He died shortly after completing *Richter 10.*